Dragon's Bane

Book 1

Sunset Red

Azriel Johnson

Azriel Johnson

Sunset Red
Writing Knights Press — Cleveland, Ohio

http://writingknights.com
http://facebook.com/writingknights
http://facebook.com/DragonsBaneSeriesOfficial
http://dragons-bane.blogspot.com
http://facebook.com/azrieljohnsonauthor
http://azrieljohnson.com

Cover Art by Lauren Haynes
Author Photo by Winston Wylie

ISBN 978-1-51536-913-4

This book is dedicated to everyone who helped it come into being, from the smallest piece of inspiration to those who endured my ramblings when I get excited talking about it.

This isn't just a story, this is a prophecy. Prophecy is hard to keep inside my mouth and off of my fingers. I just need to share it and when I find someone who will listen you better believe I'll talk your mind off about it.

More specifically, I dedicate this book to: Jess, Jessie, Jessica, Kara, And(y)i, Anita, Melissa, Liss, Bonnie, Donovan, Ryan, James, Odd (and Dean), Aaron, Lestat (and Anne), Komodo Dragons, MSN TV role players, anyone else who has in some way inspired a character, anyone brave enough to have purchased and/or read "A Warrior's Destiny: Red", Lauren, Zack, Dora and last, but never least, Skylark

Other Books by Azriel Johnson

Poetry:
Poemaholic (The Poet's Haven, 2014)
Hellfire, Heavensent (Writing Knights Press, 2011)

Future releases include:
The Gravity of Chainsaws" (Crisis Chronicles, 2015)
"Hack" (Sybaritic Press)

Upcoming Titles in the Dragon's Bane Series:
"Rust & Blood" (Writing Knights Press, 2016)
"The Black God" (Writing Knights Press, 2017)

Contents

Contents

Sneak Preview: Book 2: Rust & Blood

Dragon Dictionary

1 — Freedom

April 28, 1998

"Lying is not always wrong, John Ross. It's only wrong when someone stands to get hurt."

I was finally free.

My Dragon's bane katana banged rhythmically against my bow and quiver of arrows as I walked. I left the life I knew behind me and I headed towards a new life in a new city with new possibilities. The life I lived in Meton faded in the distance as I walked towards a life of glory in the Supremacy War.

My mother told me pain is inevitable, but suffering is optional. I'm not sure where she got that idea, but I agree with her. Looking back, I haven't lived what some might call an entirely blessed life, but my blessings and curses tend to balance each other out.

My curses consisted of with constant torment from bullies in Meton. My blessings consisted of the love of my mother, my uncles and my cousins. My first love, Diana betrayed me, but there was a nameless, ever present guardian who would be there when I fell. Nightmares made my sleep restless, but in the waking world I felt no fear.

I walked half the day and I reaching halfway between Meton and Bellato, where my uncles lived. I intended to rendezvous with them. They would show me around the city and I would to begin my training to join the Human army at Fort Kingsley. Bellato hosted one of the most highly fortified settlements in the New World. Every house concealed a door leading to the underground caverns for citizens to escape Dragon attacks. However, by my birth Dragons knew which cities to stay away from if they valued their scales.

Times were different in the year 1998 than in the 1950s and 60s. Dragon's Bane alloy was developed in the 1970s and Humans learned to use it effectively. The early genocidal attacks of New York City, London, Tokyo, Washington DC and Los Angeles left the Human race beaten, but not defeated. Cries of *"Remember Marcinelle!"* elicited forth from Human lips as often as the Dragons breathed fire, rained boiling water, spewed ice, or blew smoke with molten rocks.

August 8, 1956 in Marcinelle, Belgium. The day the Dragons returned to this world. Any Dragon bones found were attributed to dinosaurs. Hundreds of years passed. The Dragon became an animal of myth. There were 262 casualties in Marcinelle that day.

Reports said, coal mine fire.

"Lying is not always wrong, John Ross."

Reports of flying creatures laying waste to small towns grew and exactly two months later New York City was destroyed.

My grandfather, John Ross Gerstung, was one of the first Humans to witness the aftermath of New York. Most of the Human leaders of the time perished. He'd heard the stories of Dragons, but hadn't believed it until he saw for himself what they could do.

My grandfather became the first Human to kill a Dragon. He did so before Dragon's Bane was developed, even before the 27 Guild came into being. He waged legendary battles with Jonathan the Tyrant. My mother named me after him, to honor the sacrifices he made for the Human race.

My grandfather trained many great warriors and put together the Hell Bringers, the Elite of the Human army. My grandfather trained arguably the most famous fighter of the Human army, Lieutenant Plato Kingsley and the current General William Braggs. My uncles Oliver, Maxwell and Zachary were among Kingsley's students. I wanted to do my grandfather's memory proud and do my part to free the Human race from the terror of the Dragons.

But first I had to deal with one last problem of my own.

"Strike!"

My constant tormentors: Todd Bollin and his brothers, Don, Mike and Craig. I guess they saw fit to see me on my way. I'm surprised they followed me so far out of Meton, they must have really wanted to wish me well.

I turned to face them. They all rode horses. I smiled grimly as they surrounded me and rode around me. They smiled back and their eyes gleamed in a way I did not recognize.

"We're here to make sure you *never* come back to Meton, Bastard," Todd said.

Bastard. The name the villagers called me for as long as I could remember. Seventeen years ago, a drunken lout raped my mother and I was conceived. I guess I technically *was* a bastard, but that shouldn't have been *my* fault or the fault of *my mother*.

"It's only wrong when someone stands to get hurt."

"I hadn't planned on coming back right away, Todd," I replied.

Todd and his brothers dismounted and pulled their horses to a tree and tied them up.

"I guess there's no reasoning with you. You are bent on running me off but good huh?" I said as I removed my sword, my bag, my bow and quiver.

Craig Bollin was the oldest. He trained in the Human army and was four years older than Todd. He came back on leave from training before being deployed for service. The twins, Don and Mike were two years older than Todd and about to leave for war themselves. Todd was a few months older than me. To the average onlooker, this fight was not in my favor.

"We are here to make sure you never bother the village again," Todd said.

All four boys were built like strong, working villagers. Fortunately for me, Todd, Don and Mike were also mostly untrained. Craig was my primary worry.

The boys circled me pounding their fists into their hands. I stood with my feet shoulder width apart and my hands at my sides open, but ready. My uncles trained me every summer since age five. My muscles relaxed ready to act and react. The 20 mile walk had not fatigued me. Spring heat dripped sweat down my face.

I thought of my grandfather and the stories I heard of his battles with Jonathan the Tyrant. I wondered if his heart raced like mine when he fought his nemesis.

Craig attacked with a punch from behind. I twisted my body down and to the left firing a straight right punch into Don's gut. I shifted my weight back to my right leg and pushed off with my left hitting Mike with a straight left in his gut to match. Todd came down with a right hammer fist. I blocked with my left forearm and shot up with a right uppercut to his chin. I swung a right roundhouse kick and clobbered Craig in the left side of his face.

Don came at me clumsily with a haymaker that I blocked then fired off another right to his nose. Mike received a similar send off. Both collapsed holding their bleeding noses.

Craig staggered back towards me grabbing my brown leather tunic in both of his hands. I reached up under his arms to clinch his head with my hands. I yanked him around by his head and threw a couple knees to his stomach. I pushed him back and kicked him hard in the chest. He flew backwards into the nervous hooves of the horses. They whinnied in fright, but didn't stomp on him.

Todd came at me from the back. His right arm wrapped under my chin and he locked the hold with his left arm at the back of my head. I grunted and turned inward to free my airway. I hit him with my left elbow hard enough to make him loosen his hold, and then wrapped my left arm around his body. I lifted Todd up and put his shoulders down hard to the ground with a Gerstung Slam that my uncles would have been proud of.

All four boys lay in various states of pain and defeat.

I looked at them each and shook my head.

"No one is going to keep me from coming back. As long as my mother lives in Meton I will return. Make sure everyone in the village knows that if my mother is harmed in any way, there is no power in the world that will stop me in getting my revenge. Is that clear?"

I waited and all four boys said a quiet, "Yes."

I put my bag over my shoulder, then my quiver and bow. I strapped my katana back around my waist and walked towards the horses. Craig scuttled out of my way on the ground. I untied the horses one by one and drew my katana. I slapped the horses all hard on the rears and they took off into the forest.

My last words to the Bollin brothers, "You'd better get home fast. I heard there are packs of ferals roaming around the area. They won't hesitate in taking down four unarmed boys. Good luck."

I turned my back to the Bollin brothers and Meton. I turned towards Bellato and my impending future.

I was finally free.

2 — Ferals

March 30, 1995

After the first Humans were killed in the 1950s, the orphaned dogs banded together. Ferals were the descendents of these orphaned dogs. The dogs formed packs and roamed the land. They weeded out the weaker, smaller dogs and morphed into large, strong, intelligent dogs that were no longer afraid of Humans. This made them dangerous. Unlike wolves, the strongest feral dogs bred, but there were no alphas to speak of. This meant the population grew much faster. Feral dogs inherited all of the best qualities of their ancestors. Ferals in warmer climates grew short hair. Ferals in colder climates tended toward longer coats. Few creatures, Dragon, Human or otherwise were safe if caught unaware.

Ferals posed a problem for anyone who raised livestock or walk outside on their own. When I was 13, I tended my mother's sheep a mile outside of the village. Romulus and Remus, our two rams, helped guard the sheep so I wasn't worried. I lay on my back in the field looking up at the sky, noticing all the different cloud shapes that floated.

I must have dozed off because I didn't hear the first bleating of the sheep. I felt a kick in my side, and I jolted awake. I thought I caught a glimpse of someone in white, and then I saw a pack of dogs worrying the sheep. The rams stood their ground, but the number of dogs coming into the field grew. I rose and carried my staff to meet the dogs. I had to simultaneously shepherd the sheep away and somehow scare the dogs into leaving. I didn't like my chances.

With a ram on either side of me, I started poking at the dogs hard, catching a few in the face. The hungrily salivating beasts didn't give up so easily. I screamed and ran at them swinging wildly, whacking a couple in the nose. They came back with their teeth bared and snapping. I narrowly evaded their teeth.

I heard growling from behind me. I saw more dogs on the other side of the gathered sheep harassing them. I cursed and ran to the other end of the flock. When I reached the other end I swung my staff down hard onto a dog that tried to hamstring one of the sheep. It fell and scooted back into the pack.

More and more dogs came out of the trees to the field. Feral packs in the hundreds were not uncommon.

I considered yelling for help, but the village was a mile away. Even if someone heard me they weren't likely to come to my aid.

I ran around the edge of the flock, beating on any dog that got in my striking range. I knew this couldn't last; there were more dogs than my stamina could handle. I felt trapped. The only thing I could do was make myself more annoying than the dogs were hungry and that didn't seem possible.

I heard a pained bleat coming from the rams. I looked and saw a few of the dogs had grabbed Remus and brought him down. I ran as fast as I could through the flock of sheep. I screamed and swung my staff at the attacking dogs knocking a few of them off of the ram, but more just jumped into the fray.

Behind me I heard a loud roar. I turned to look and saw a Red Dragon beating its, his, above me.

Stupid boy.

One of the dogs bit into my left knee, drawing blood and I cried out. I turned and dug my thumbs into the dog's eyes and it released its hold. I limped back a few steps leaning on my staff.

I turned to look at the Dragon. He spit small bits of fire at the dogs and they dispersed. The dogs trying to kill Remus hung on so I swung my staff down and cracked them in the head rendering them motionless. More dogs scampered away. The rest of the dogs gave up and I stood alone again with the sheep and the Dragon flying above me.

Stupid boy.

I shook my head. I felt funny. I looked at my knee and it was mangled. I couldn't put weight on it. The dog wrenched it when he bit. I looked at the ground and it was spinning. I don't remember falling.

Snapping fangs. Growling. Roars. Blood. Cries of pain. Then something else, more protective and closer to me. My mother. Another figure. A man.

I woke up in my bed. A bandage wrapped around my left knee. I touched it gingerly and felt some pain, but nothing unbearable. My mother dozed in a chair next to my bed. Her black hair tied back in a leather string. Her face creased with worry, but still wore the serenity of sleep. She stood about five feet four inches tall and couldn't have weighed more than 120 pounds. When she carried huge sacks of corn meal from the market or when she hugged me I could feel her sinewy strength.

I touched her hand and she instantly awoke. She smiled at me. "My son. How are you feeling?"

"My knee hurts. How did I get back home?"

"One of the villagers saw you and carried you home."

"Really?"

Mother didn't respond. She stood and left my room. I heard her fiddling in the main room. I looked around my wooden walls. My uncles built this house for my mother when she came to Meton the year before I was born. She told me it wasn't that she wanted to be away from my uncles. Her brothers all had families and my mother wanted to be on her own and make her own way in the world. I could see trees swaying in the breeze from my open window.

My room was fairly unadorned. There were some books and blank notebooks for when the occasional poem struck me, but mother and I didn't have a lot of time or desire for special trinkets.

I sat up. My bed had a wooden frame supporting a wool stuffed mattress. It wasn't too comfortable, but better than sleeping on the wooden floor. My blanket was the most expensive piece of cloth in the house, cotton. Cotton by this time was a rare commodity, but both my mother and I had cotton blankets.

Mother came back into the room with a bowl of steaming soup and some milk in a wooden cup. I swung my legs off of the left side of the bed and drank the soup and milk eagerly.

"Did the sheep make it back safe?" I asked.

"Yes," she answered.

"And Remus?"

"He was too hurt I had to put him down." Mother wiped a tear away.

"I need to start carrying my bow and arrow with me for cases like these. I bet if I had started taking dogs down they would have backed off."

Mother didn't respond. She didn't like when I talked about killing the ferals that roamed. I made a mental note for the next time I was out.

"Your uncles will be here in a couple days to take you for the summer," Mother said.

"I know. I'm excited," I replied.

As far back as I can remember, my uncles would take me to their homes in Bellato for the summer. Mother never came with us sadly. I always begged her to come. She always declined and never said why.

That night I looked at the sky outside of my window. The full moon shone in. I studied the clouds as they went past the moon and I wondered how many clouds there could be. My window suddenly darkened and a familiar shadow covered my face.

"I heard you were attacked today," the shadow remarked.

"From whom would you have heard something like that?" I queried.

"Oh you know how the village does with rumors especially with you and your family."

"Yeah, don't remind me. What are you doing here?"

"I was checking on you, of course."

"Won't your parents be mad?"

"My parents are asleep. What are you so worried about," the shadow teased.

"I'm not worried. I just don't want to be blamed for corrupting the Chief's daughter, again, when it's obvious she is corrupting me."

"Very funny."

Silence passed for a moment. I looked up at her shaded face and I assumed she could see me looking up at her. This was the person who inspired more nightmares and wet dreams than anyone previous to her or since her. She was the source of a few of my blessings, but more of my curses in the village.

I said, "Have I ever told you the name of the Roman Goddess of the moon was named Diana?"

3 — Bellato

April 29, 1998

I woke up in a tree about a mile from where I left the Bollin brothers. The reports of ferals were true. I was not in the mood to fight, and my knee had never really healed correctly after the attack three years before, so I couldn't run far or fast. I wasn't a cripple, but I lacked stamina.

I climbed down from the tree and combed my hands through my shoulder length brown hair. A few twigs were released and I started on my way towards Bellato again. I wanted to make it by the end of the day.

My destination was Bellato, more specifically my uncle's compound. They inherited it from their father, my grandfather and namesake. After his death, my uncles split from one another to explore the continent, grieve and find themselves. They eventually reunited and joined the Human army in quick succession. I hadn't really discussed with them or my mother what the exacts of their trips were, but they came back powerful and passed it onto their children.

My uncles' wives were no typical helpmeets. They taught in the Bellato school and weighed in on city politics just as fervently as my uncles did. They raised nine children of varying ages, and during the summer raised me to inherit their intelligence, will power and empathy.

My cousins ranged in age of Alana who was two years older than me and Ajax who was a year older to as young as

Lexie who was ten years younger. Each of my uncles had three children, just like their father.

My uncles had a wide range of training and learned from their father the dreaded Gerstung Slam. This translated to locking their hands around an opponent and lifting the opponent up to put them down on either their shoulders or their neck depending on if they were fighting or sparring.

My uncle's property took up an entire city block in Bellato. They had a total of four buildings, three for living and one for storage. The storage building also doubled as a guest house and this is where I stayed when I visited.

The area between the buildings was open and with the multitudes of random grazing animals that wandered around Bellato the grass stayed more or less trimmed. This was where my uncles taught their children and me to fight.

It was my uncles' philosophy that we all should be ready for a fight because the Dragons could attack at any time. The variety in combat skills possessed by my uncles made all of us well rounded fighters. Every day there was a wooden training weapon in our hands or we were learning combat maneuvers. My uncles developed a game similar to tag where at any time a younger member of the family could surprise grapple an older member of the family. If the younger member of the family could take down their elder, the elder had to do a chore of the younger's choice that day. If the elder won, the younger had to do the chore for two days.

The only restriction was no attacking at dinner time. Dinner was chaotic enough. Most of the time, we ate in the field between the buildings at three large tables that accommodated us all. I rotated between tables. I would have breakfast at one table, lunch at another and dinner at the third.

There was never a shortage of love in those houses. I was finally returning to them, albeit for a short time since Fort Kingsley was a mile outside of the city limits. When I was near my family in Bellato I felt free, I felt safe, I felt loved. I loved my mother dearly, but living in Meton had never brought me that kind of security.

The stone walls around Bellato were 20 feet high with pointed tops. The walls were assembled with bits of old buildings that were cemented together to make them stronger. There were four main gates at compass points North, South, East and West. The city itself spanned about a mile in each direction from the main gates.

Between the main gates, there were a number of minor exit gates that only opened from the inside in case of a Dragon attack and a necessary evacuation. Outside of the gates there were people living in small houses, but never too far from the gates in case they needed protection.

Bellato was next to a large river that had cleaned itself after the elimination of heavy industry. The river fed into the expansive Lake Erie. One could not see the other side of even on a clear day. The occasional transport boat braved the lake, but mostly the lake was free of travel since a Blue Dragon could be lurking at any time.

In almost the exact middle of Bellato was the Arena. The Arena was known all over the New World for hosting the most skillful and powerful warriors.

When the Dragons arose, other formerly mythical beings also started making their presence known. Vampires, were-creatures, and any other beings imaginable stopped hiding and started interacting with the Humans and Dragons.

Jonathan the Tyrant, the Dragon King of Meton, employed a clan of vampires called the Seven Deadly Sins. They were his terror squad and personal body guards.

The Tyrant once claimed Bellato for his own, but my grandfather and the Hell Bringers fought him off. The city guard with my uncles now stands vigil against Jonathan's return.

I walk through the East Gate without being accosted by the city guards. They knew me if not by name, by sight. In Bellato, the name Gerstung meant a lot.

The city was busy. The marketplace was open and the citizens were browsing others' wares. I wandered around, but I had everything I needed. I had my pouch of shuriken throwing stars dangling around my neck. I hardly ever used them anymore, but I kept them for sentimental value. I was more of a bow and arrow man when it came to hitting things at long range, but they were still good Dragon's Bane weapons for when I needed them.

I was baffled why someone would want to steal a pouch

from me considering if they needed something to eat all they needed to do was go to the marketplace to grab something.

I growled and gave chase. I saw the pouch being passed from boy to boy. I was able to follow the action but the crowd was thick enough I couldn't properly chase them. The pouch passed to a fifth boy who ran smack into a young man about a head taller than me. The man grabbed the boy by the hair and grabbed the pouch back from him.

The boy kicked at the man yelling various obscenities, but the man held strong. I walked as quickly as I could to the two and said, "Thank you so much for retrieving my purse. I had no idea Bellato had become so corrupt."

The man said, "Well, people have to eat. Right you little scamp?"

The boy struggled. "Go to hell."

I leaned down to the boy. "What would your mother think if she saw you doing this?"

"My mother's dead you asshole. Let me go!" The boy kicked the man in the shin, but he held on and ruffled the boy enough to cause dust to fly off of him.

I sighed and straightened up. "Let him go. I think he's learned his lesson."

The man ruffled the boy again. "I doubt that. He'll probably go back to it once we are out of sight."

I looked at the boy. "What's your name?"

The boy struggled. "Let me go goddammit!"

The man said, "That's a horrible name! No wonder you can't get an honest day's work."

I laughed despite myself. "Alright, alright. Let him go he's suffered enough. But I have to ask, why would you steal from me?"

The man released the boy, knocking him roughly to the ground. The boy stood quickly and looked at me. "My name is Nicky. We snatch things we think are valuable and people will come after. I gotta boss who... well... he ain't a good guy."

"Does he hurt you, Nicky?"

"Not if I bring him what he wants."

"Why does he want me?"

"It ain't you, it might be just the pouch that looks like it's worth something."

Before I could respond Nicky was gone.

"Well that's troubling. I don't really have time to deal with that right now though." I sighed. I turned to the man. "I'm John Ross Gerstung, JR. You are?"

The man extended his hand. "Walt Gelh."

4 — Clan Gerstung

April 29, 1998

"Gerstung, like the Courageous Gerstung brothers? Like John Ross Gerstung, first leader of the Hell Bringers?" Walt asked as we walked.

"My uncles and grandfather," I replied.

"That's awesome," Walt said. "I used to pretend to be your grandfather for Halloween. Unfortunately people are less likely to give you candy when you scream, 'Bring them Hell!' instead of politely saying, 'Trick or treat.'"

I laughed. "At least you could trick or treat. My village hated me so much if I would have gone door to door I would have had my ass handed to me instead of candy."

"That's rough," Walt said. "How old are you?"

"Sixteen, you?"

"I just turned 18 a couple months ago. I'm here to join up with Fort Kingsley. My father and older brothers were in the war, so I'm a high priority to get in. Nepotism and all that."

"I'm here to join up too."

"Isn't the minimum age to get in 18?"

"I'm not sure, but I figure since there is a two year training period they might make an exception."

"Yeah, pfft, speaking of nepotism right?" Walt laughed.

"If that's what you want to call it. Would you like to come to my uncles' house for dinner? I'm sure they'd love to meet the man who saved my shuriken pouch from evil child thieves."

"Sure that sounds great," Walt answered.

Just then I felt a powerful presence walking by us. I perked up and looked around. I zeroed in on a man walking with a much younger woman. The thickly built man wore a short cropped grey hair cut. He stood about my height and moved gracefully. I pointed at them.

"Walt, do you know who those two are?"

Walt looked. "Oh! That's Plato Kingsley and that must be his daughter Rebecca. I've never seen her before, but I heard she was gorgeous. Those reports were not exaggerated."

"You're telling me," I said. I continued to stare at them. Everything she wore fit her form starting at her leather peasant blouse that tied in the front. Her leather trousers didn't look too tight. Her lightly freckled face matched her reddish brown hair, more red than brown in the right light. I couldn't see her eyes at this distance, but I desperately wanted to.

"JR, you're staring," Walt said with a smile on his face.

"I'm enamored," I replied.

"Go talk to her then," Walt said.

"No, I can't, she's too perfect. I don't want to ruin it."

"What are you talking about?"

"The last girl I fell in love at first sight with got me kicked out of my village."

"I can see why you'd be gun shy, but you can't live your life in fear. Go talk to her, you won't regret it."

"My uncles are waiting for me. I have to get going." I tore my gaze away from Rebecca and turned back to Walt. "Are you coming?"

"Not yet, but it's a definite possibility tonight," Walt said. He stared in a different direction at three milk maids who walked by us. He smiled and waved. They smiled back and giggled. "You know JR, I think I might have to get a rain check for that dinner. I'll see you around tomorrow, yeah?"

Before I could respond, Walt caught up to the milk maids and wrapped his large arms around two of them. They disappeared into the crowd. I turned back to see if I could catch a glimpse of Rebecca, but she was gone.

I turned back towards my uncles' home and ran smack into a burly chest of a man wider than me and taller than Walt.

"Oh, excuse me," I said as I tried to step around him.

He stepped into my way. His burly voice said, "Excuse you pipsqueak."

"I, uh, just did," I replied.

"No one runs into Crush and gets away with it."

"Sorry, really I am, but I have an elsewhere to be, so...."
I tried to step around him again, but he put his huge hand on my chest.

"The only place you're going is the medic," Crush threatened.

"Look, I don't want any trouble."

"Too bad, looks like you found it anyway."

"You really don't want to do this."

"I really do."

Crush pulled back a huge fist and swung it at me. I dodged the fist and pushed him as hard as I could. I took off running as fast as I could with my knee and the crowd. Luckily, Crush ran even slower than me.

I lost sight of his huge body in the crowd. I slowed down and I caught a glimpse of Walt entering the house across from my uncle's. I walked up the steps to the door of Uncle Oli's place and knocked three times.

The door opened and a man of six feet, short salt and pepper hair and blue eyes answered. He considered me momentarily and clapped his hands on my shoulders. "John Ross, good to see you made it."

"Thank you Uncle Oli," I hugged him.

"Come in, the family has been waiting."

Uncle Max greeted me next. He wore his hair a little longer than Oli's. Other than his brown eyes they were spitting images. Uncle Zack trailed in behind Max. Uncle Zack's black hair flowed past his shoulders and his black eyes resembled the night sky.

My uncles took me out to the field between their houses. Dinner laid ready and the whole family sat except for my eldest cousin, Alana. She enlisted at Fort Kingsley about a month before. I would see her if I got in. I took Alana's place at Oli's table.

We discussed my trip from Meton to Bellato. I told the

family about the painful parting from my mother, but I expressed my eagerness to start my own life now. We discussed the circumstances of my leaving without getting into too many graphic details for the kids. My uncles empathized with me and told me that Diana's father, Jorge Gomez had been an idiot and a jackass when they knew him in the Hell Bringers.

The kids, Lexie, Jack and Buck twitched with anticipation for a new playmate, but their mothers' herded them off before they could torture me so soon after my arrival. My uncles really picked the pinnacle of beauty in their wives. All three were elegant, intelligent and perceptive.

The Jessica, Jennifer and Jane Gerstung founded and helped run the Bellato School. Unlike the one room, Meton School, Bellato actually lauded advancement by merit and provided multiple subjects to explore. The school house had many different sections. For example, the building provided a section of the school dedicated for each facet of the Greek philosophic learning. Rather than being taught what to think, children learned how to think. Well rounded, intelligent Humans graduated from Bellato school.

My uncles and I cleared up the plates after dinner and moved the wooden tables out of the center of the field. Ajax, Junior and Toby did a quick scan of the field for animal droppings and found none. Arthur and Anita grabbed wooden weapons from the storage building. Soon, my uncles, myself, Ajax, Junior, Toby, Arthur and Anita all held wooden swords.

Oli said, "Now kids, your cousin is going to the fort tomorrow to begin his training. We have to give him a send off befitting a Gerstung. You remember how we sent off Alana correct?"

Junior whacked me in the back with the flat side of his sword. "Like that?"

I winced.

Oli chuckled. "Yes, basically we are going to see if JR is ready for the rigors of training."

My cousins left my side and joined my uncles facing me. I groaned and swung my sword around once loosening up.

"Remember, if you're hit, you're dead and you back off. Got it kids?"

My cousins nodded and attacked without warning.

I parried Junior's frontal attack and ducked a shot from Arthur. I brought my sword up to Anita's midsection that she blocked, but she didn't block the strike to her shoulder. I blocked Toby's attack at my back with my sword behind me. I tagged Arthur in the chest with the same movement. Junior's downward chop missed and I kicked him. I swung my sword at Toby's midsection, but he blocked it. Ajax came out of nowhere with a thrust that barely missed my stomach. I jumped backward and toppled over Junior. I hit the ground, but rolled back into a crouch position. Ajax swung hard at my head. I ducked and chopped his legs. I rose and grabbed Junior's sword hand as I thrust my sword into Toby's chest. I lifted Junior's hand and brought my sword back at Junior's ribs.

I stood breathing heavily as my cousins all backed off from me. I turned to see my uncles approaching quickly. Individually, their skills were unmatched, but I was most worried about Zack.

I parried Max's first attack. Oli came at me with a thrust which I dodged. Zack attacked my legs. I jumped over it. The attacks came too fast to anticipate. There was no time to attack and barely enough time to defend. It was apparent, the years of training with my uncles was half speed for them.

Zack lashed out with exactness and technicality. He alternated between low and high shots. Max used fast and repetitive thrusts. Oli's blows were powerful and rung through my arms when I blocked. I needed to be strong, fast, and skillful if I wanted to win.

I grunted and swung my sword hard at Zack's next attack. The force rang through my hands as well, but it shot Zack's sword off its course. Max's next thrust I parried off to the side. As Oli came down hard with an overhead chop, I dodged out of the way and quickly brought my sword up to his midsection. Before I could make contact, Zack's sword blocked the strike and as I turned to attack Max he was not where I left him. Instead he was behind Oli.

In the next instance, I was defeated with three swords touching my back.

5 — Recruiting Day

April 30, 1998

I awoke nervous the next morning. I wasn't sure what to expect from recruitment. I was lucky to have made a friend already, but that didn't allay my concerns.

I went into the field. Breakfast had already started. I sat down. Except for the sounds of eating, everyone was unusually quiet. This made me more nervous.

"Why isn't anyone talking!" I said at last.

"We are worried about you, JR," Oli replied. "We know you'll be fine, but family worries."

"At least I'll have Alana there," I said.

Oli didn't respond. I finished my breakfast and went back to the guest room. I gathered my bag and my weapons. When I exited the house the tables were moved. My cousins, aunts and uncles stood in the field waiting for me. One by one we hugged or shook hands. Everyone wished me good luck.

When I reached my uncles they smiled and patted me on the back. Max said, "When you finish you'll be able to beat all three of us with swords."

I smiled. "I just let you win last night you know."

"Care for a rematch?" Zack responded.

I shook my head and laughed. "No time. I have to get going. The recruiters are waiting at the North Gate."

I hugged all three of my uncles and walked out into the dirt street. I looked at the door Walt had gone into with the milk maids and he came out with tousled hair and a big grin. The milk maids followed him out hitching up loosened cotton garments with equally bedded head. All three glowed.

"Hey! JR!" Walt said. "Ready for the big day?"

I nodded as I watched the milk maids giggle their way back into their house.

"Jealous? I'm sure I could put in a good word for you when we have a break in training," Walt said. "The blonde was a real tigress."

"They were all blonde," I replied.

"I know!" Walt laughed and slapped me hard on the back. "Let's get to the North Gate."

As we headed towards the gate, I noticed quite a few young people going our way. Crush walked among them. Rebecca Kingsley strode gracefully in the same direction. Raspberry scent clung to her. Walt jostled me for not having the courage to talk to her despite getting within five feet of her.

A line formed at North Gate. Three recruiters sat at a table. Each recruit had a brief interview and the recruiter wrote down their information. When the recruit finished the recruits joined the others outside the gate. I stood behind Walt. Rebecca stood in the line next to ours.

I heard Walt's interview:

"Name?" "Walt Gelh."

"Age?" "Eighteen."

"Date of Birth?" "March 1, 1980."

"Training?" "Boxing and Claymore sword."

"Why are you here?" "To carry on the legacy of the Gelh family and to defend the Human race."

"Who should we notify in the case of your demise?" "Well there were these three milk maids I met last night, but no, my father Thom Gelh of Bellato."

I heard Rebecca's interview as well:

"Name?" "Rebecca Kingsley."

"Age?" "Seventeen. Here is my permission slip."

"Date of Birth?" "November 13, 1980."

"Training?" "Kingsley style Dragon slaying."

"Why are you here?" "To acquire the skills necessary to

defend the Human race."

"Who should we notify in case of your demise?" "My father Plato Kingsley."

My interview went a little differently.

"Name?" "John Ross Gerstung."

"I'm sorry, say that again."

"John Ross Gerstung."

"John Ross Gerstung is dead son."

"He's my grandfather. His sons are my uncles Oliver, Maxwell and Zachary Gerstung of Bellato. Their sister is my mother is Aurora Gerstung."

The recruiter looked at me skeptically then continued: "Age?"

"Sixteen."

"You do realize the minimum age for recruitment is 18, 17 with permission slip."

"Well, here is my permission slip, signed by my mother and I figure since training lasts two years I'll be 18 by the time it's done anyway."

"We'll have a talk with Lieutenant Kingsley later. Date of birth?" "January 18, 1982."

"Training?" "Gerstung style hand to hand combat, katana, staff and bow and arrow."

"Why are you here?" "I have nowhere else to go. I want to somehow contribute to the Gerstung legacy as well as defend the Human race."

"Who should we notify in case of your demise?" "Aurora Gerstung of Meton and Oliver, Maxwell and Zachary Gerstung of Bellato."

The recruiter grabbed a dog tag from the bag and stamped my name and basic information into it. After handing it to me he said, "Gather with the others."

I walked out of the North Gate and saw Walt as he spoke with Rebecca. My palm hit my forehead as I approached.

"There's JR now, Rebecca," Walt said. "What was the word you used? Enamored."

I blushed. "You're a jerk and I'm going to kill you in your sleep."

Rebecca took a step towards me. "So you think I'm

pretty?" Her green eyes flashed in the sunlight.

Her eyes hypnotized me. "Uh, yes."

"That doesn't sound convincing," she said.

"Sorry," I mumbled.

"Oh, give JR a break, he's only 16 and he's shy around new people. Give him time to warm up." Walt certainly enjoyed himself at my expense.

Rebecca took another step towards me. Her raspberry scent filled my nostrils, but it wasn't overpowering. I could feel my neck vein rushing blood to my head. "Sixteen, huh? That's a little young to be in the army."

"I am not unskilled," I said.

"I suppose with a name like Gerstung you couldn't be unskilled. I guess we'll find out how good you are when the time comes."

Rebecca touched my left cheek with her right hand then turned away. I watched her walk towards the Fort as the recruiters lead us away from the gate. Her body moved like a muscled jungle cat. She shifted her hips as she walked and her ass mesmerized me almost as deeply as her eyes.

Walt slapped me in the back of the head. "Let's go Romeo."

I hiked up my possessions and started walking the trail to Fort Kingsley. Some people ran. Some walked slower. I tried to keep pace with Walt, but my knee was feeling weak. I kept him in sight, but barely. As I walked, I felt a tap on my shoulder. A man about five feet six inches tall walked next to me.

I looked at him as I walked. He spoke, "You Gerstung?"

"Yes. John Ross. You are?"

"Cole Chen. Dragons near. You feel them?"

I didn't, but I looked around as I walked.

"You no see them. White Dragons blend with clouds. They close. They attack soon. You fight and I fight them."

"Why don't you tell the recruiters?"

"Glory. We know they coming. We first to fight. We heroes."

"I don't want to be a hero."

"I want your reputation."

"What?"

"Today, we fight Dragons. Later, I challenge you. Your reputation comes to me."

"Whatever man." I put my hand on my bow ready to draw it at a seconds notice. Chen walked next to me unspeaking. He was scanning the sky.

Ready. Steady. Now!

Behind us ripped a loud screech. I turned and drew my bow and an arrow. The White Dragon swooped down from the sky. I took aim and fired, but I missed. I drew another arrow quickly and aimed again. I held my breath and fired and the arrow struck the Dragon in the neck. It screamed in pain and pulled the arrow out.

Three more recruits and the three recruiters pulled their bows and started firing at the Dragon. The Dragon rained down a sheet of ice at our column. Most of the recruits got out of the way. A shard of ice caught one recruit in his shoulder. He looked like he might survive if he got attention. I ran to grab him by the uninjured arm and drag him under a tree. Chen pulled him by the injured arm. The recruit screamed in pain until we released him.

I stood and fired another arrow at the Dragon. I hit it in the hind leg. Another volley of arrows struck the Dragon as it screeched and delivered another sheet of ice down at the now hidden column. This time no one was hurt and anyone without a bow and arrow ran the way of the fort beneath the trees.

With the next volley of arrows I managed to strike the Dragon in the throat. The recruiters each put an arrow into the Dragon's head and it crashed down to the forest floor. We all rushed to it and watched it claw at the ground in its death throes.

Nest. Nest. Must protect nest.

I was hearing voices again. "Shouldn't we finish it off?" I asked.

"Why bother? It's just a stupid scale head." One of the other recruits responded.

"Because you shouldn't leave one injured and not dead," said one of the recruiters. He walked toward the Dragon and pulled another arrow. He shot the Dragon in the eye and it stopped moving.

6 — Good Impressions

April 30, 1998

"Recruits! Form up!"

Close to one hundred new recruits entered Fort Kingsley that day. Once a month recruitment set up at the North Gate of Bellato. Some months were richer than others. Fifty recruits at a turn were about average. One hundred recruits at a turn was either a gold mine or a bit of cannon fodder.

To say we were a bunch of rag tag misfits would give rag tag misfits a bad name. We came from all different backgrounds and most of us had never seen the inside of a fort before. However, we all had a guiding desire: To Defend the Human Race from the Dragons.

The recruits formed two half lines. We all faced the sergeant bawling at us expectations of a Soldier and expectations of the leaders of the Fort who stood behind him.

"Fighting Dragons is about awareness. Dragons are huge creatures, but they also can sneak up on you without a moment's notice as you saw today. Dragons are capable magical creatures as well. Some Dragons can shift into Human form. Dragons have infiltrated forts before. No Dragon has successfully infiltrated this fort and we will keep it that way.

"The leaders of this fort are responsible for your training. Your training will teach you how to survive in multiple situations, both in combat and out of combat. Among other things you will be taught what wild plants you should eat, which you shouldn't and which can help to heal you if needed. Your combat training will help open up your awareness of your surroundings. This will encourage your five senses to work together. This will encourage your sixth sense to develop and expand. By the time your two years are up, you will be sufficiently able to defend the Human race from Dragons.

"Some of you will show high aptitude in combat and awareness. You will be chosen to train with Lieutenant Kingsley. Lieutenant, would you care to share any thoughts?"

The sergeant stepped back with the other officers and Plato Kingsley stepped forward. He did not yell. Unless you were listening you wouldn't hear him at all, but the power with which he spoke stirred my heart as I didn't know possible.

"You all are brave men and women. You will make fine soldiers, but a Hell Bringer is a special kind of warrior. A Hell Bringer has the zeal, determination and skill necessary to wage war on their terms instead of as a reaction to the Dragons.

"Becoming a Hell Bringer is not easy. There are no set requirements. It is not something you achieve. Becoming a Hell Bringer is something you are chosen for. Throughout the course of your training, some of you will be chosen. Don't expect to be chosen. Don't even think about being chosen. Don't try to impress anyone, just be in the present moment wherever you are and you may surprise us."

And yourself.

Kingsley stepped back to his place at the center of the line. I watched him intently, I felt fire rise in my eyes.

The sergeant stepped forward and addressed us again. "You lot will be divided into four groups. The other sergeants and I will be responsible for your training in these groups. Training at this fort lasts for two years. By the end of this time, these trainees in your group will be like your family treat them as such now, and it will pay off later.

"Recruits! Pair up. Find yourself a partner for your first sparring session."

I looked at Walt and nodded. We squared off against one another until Crush pushed his way in front of Walt.

I said, "Hey, uh, Crush. I was going to spar with Walt."

Walt said, "Don't worry about it JR." He smiled and

found another partner.

I looked up at Crush and he cracked his knuckles. "Time to die, pipsqueak."

"Die?" I said. "This is just sparring. We're supposed to be family, remember?"

"Yeah, you're going to be my dead dog." Crush's deep laugh rumbled in my chest.

I brought up my hands in readiness. Crush stood with his arms at his sides and a smirk on his face.

"Begin!" the sergeant yelled.

Crush swung his huge left hand at me and cracked me in the right side of my face. I hit the ground hard. Crush laughed again. "What a warrior."

I growled and came up to a crouching position. The blow didn't hurt as much as my pride did at that second. As I rose from the crouch, Crush swung at me with a straight right, but I moved faster. My left blocked his right and at the same time my right hand caught him on the point of the jaw. Crush crumpled to the ground.

The sergeant walked to me. "This was supposed to be sparring son."

"I'm sorry sir, but he started it."

The sergeant looked down at Crush then back at me. "That was a helluva punch though. You're only about half his size."

"I've had some good training," I replied.

"Gerstung, right?"

"Yes, sir."

"Thought so. Lieutenant Kingsley would like to speak with you."

"Now sir?"

"Yes, now. Get going."

I walked towards what I thought were the offices of the fort. They weren't the offices. I spent the next half hour looking for Lieutenant Kingsley's office. During one of my wrong turns I found the medic and saw Crush lying on a cot with an ice pack on his chin. I got a little satisfaction from that.

Eventually I made my way to Lieutenant Kingsley's office. I knocked on the door and heard him call me in. I entered and shut the door behind me.

"Gerstung, John Ross, I presume," he said.

"Yes, sir."

"I fought with your uncles and your grandfather."

"Yes, sir."

"They sent their share of recruits to the medic in their early days too, so I can't hold that against you."

"Thank you, sir."

"It was brought to my attention that you are only 16 is this correct?"

"Yes, sir."

"You do know the earliest recruits are allowed to train is 17, correct?"

"Yes, sir."

"So why are you here?"

"I was sent away from my village and I had nowhere else to go, sir."

"Meton, correct."

"Yes, sir."

"Why were you sent away?"

"The villagers hated me, sir."

"Why is that?"

"I honestly don't know, sir."

"I received word from Sergeant Jorge Gomez. Are you familiar with this man?"

My heart dropped. My throat stung. I swallowed. "Yes, sir."

"He told me you were sent to the Fort because you were spying on his daughter is this true?"

I paused and remembered. I remember Diana teasing me with her words. I remember being discovered.

"Yes, sir."

"Why were you doing this?"

"She asked me to, sir."

"And if I were to ask her side of the story."

"I'm guessing she would lie and say it was all my doing. It's kind of the way of the village. No one liked me as far as I can remember."

"Have you always been a pervert?"

"I'm not a pervert, sir. I never would have done

something like that without her asking me to watch, I swear."

"I am not sure I believe you, Gerstung. But I'll give you the benefit of the doubt. However, if you are found even once spying on or violating any of the females in this fort, you will be expelled and probably killed by the other males of the fort. Is that clear?"

"Yes, sir."

"This goes double for my daughter. If I find you paying her any unwanted attention, they won't find your body and you will bring a lot of disgrace to your family by going AWOL. Am I clear?"

I shivered. "Yes, sir."

"I'm taking a chance approving your presence here, Gerstung. You know this right?"

"Yes, sir."

"You have a lot of potential. You could be a Hell Bringer. Even your uncles didn't send anyone to the medic on the first day."

"Thank you, sir."

"Dismissed."

I high-tailed it out of the office and found my bunk. Walt and I were assigned the same unit and the same bunk since our last names came so close together alphabetically. This I was thankful for. It's good to have a friend in an unfamiliar environment.

"So what did Kingsley want to see you about?" Walt asked.

"Oh, nothing. Just my age and such."

"You know, we're probably going to be best friends after this is all said and done. You shouldn't keep things from your best friend."

I laughed. I told him the quick and dirty version of what went on with Diana and by the end of it Walt was definitely on my side.

"That girl is a bitch. I'm surprised you put up with her that long," Walt said.

"Stupid things you do when you think you're in love," I said.

7 — Alana's Issues

May 15, 1998

Physical training for the first month consisted of calisthenics, a lot of calisthenics. We did push ups, sit ups, pull ups, chin ups, squats and squat thrusts, running. We did not fight at all. After the first day when we sparred against each other none of the recruits were permitted to hold a weapon or train in any kind of combat with any other recruit. The only physical contact we were allowed was fireman's carry running. This is was when you put a member of your squad over your shoulder and run with them through an obstacle course. I always felt sorry for those of us who had to carry Crush, but we all had to do it at some point or another. This was both to foster good physical stamina as well as a bond between recruits. It's hard to be angry with someone who has carried you a quarter of a mile over small rocky crags without dropping you.

Crush, however, held hard to his grudge for some reason. He wriggled when I carried him and held me too tight when he carried me. I didn't complain because that's what training is about, accepting what you are given without complaint. His staple verbal taunt was "pipsqueak." While annoying, I didn't find that nearly as offensive as "bastard."

His taunts annoyed others as well.

Crush pushed past me in the chow line without saying so much as "excuse me." I sighed at his standard fare. He ignored me and I thought that was it. I looked away for a moment and when I looked back I saw Crush's head bent sharply to the right and his tray on the floor. Someone's claws clutched one of his monstrous ears.

"I've had about enough of you," the heavy, but feminine voice said. "You've been nothing, but rude and discourteous to JR and he knocked you out with one punch on his first day. I think you should show him a little respect."

I turned to see my cousin Alana yanking on Crush's ear. I chuckled.

"Lucky—punch," Crush grunted as Alana pulled him out of line.

She returned a moment later and took his place, turning back to me, "Hi cuz!"

Alana and I sat together. She did not have much on her tray except a shaker of salt and a slab of meat. She would slather salt over the meat then she would cut and chew pieces, but not swallow them. She also kept getting up to get water during our conversation.

She asked, "How's the army been treating you?"

I replied, "Not badly, other than Crush and he is only a minor annoyance. We haven't started fighting yet, which is fine I guess, but I feel grossly unprepared to battle Dragons thus far."

Alana said, "Fight training doesn't start until six months in or so I've been told. The physical training gets harder as the months go on, first month is pretty easy compared to what I've been doing and I'm only a month ahead of you, but it gets you into fine shape by the time you start to fight and train to kill. You've seen the officers, they are at peak physical and mental condition. They start with the mental training at six months too."

I nodded, but I had nothing else to say.

Alana leaned in close to me and whispered, "To tell you the truth JR. I need to leave. I can't stand it here."

"Why not?"

"I feel so, out of place. I feel like I'm stronger than everyone…. I have these dreams."

Being no stranger to strange dreams I asked, "What kinds of dreams?"

Alana said, "I'm having the kinds of dreams where I'm attacking and killing Humans…. And I'm drinking their blood."

"Wow that is strange. Most of my strange dreams have to do with being chased by Dragons," I said.

"And these feelings don't just hit me at night. Sometimes I look at people and I just want to attack them."

"Have you ever actually attacked anyone?"

Each breath was a silent confession.

"Alana?"

"I can't talk about this right now." Alana stood with her tray and threw away her chewed bits of meat.

The rest of the day was filled with musings about my cousin. I had to find out the truth. I found her bunk which was close to mine and I waited. Her bunk mate came to rest, but she didn't know where Alana's whereabouts. I asked about the various things Alana did when not training, but the bunk mate didn't talk to Alana.

Lieutenant Kingsley walked by as I continued to sit outside Alana's bunk room. I didn't want to miss her when she came back, but Kingsley gave me a cross look as he passed. He probably thought I was up to no good since I was sitting in front of a female's bunk room.

The bunk houses themselves were no more than sleeping pods for recruits. They slept two recruits and no more. The bunk houses had enough room for the recruits to store their personal belongings in lockers and climb up or into the bed. That was it. The bunks had no windows, but the wooden walls were breathable. When it rained recruits would put up plastic sheets to keep the water from coming in. The sides at the stone walls leaked less. The wood was adhered to the stone by mortar. It sealed the bunks tightly on that end. Overall the bunk houses served their purpose without being too uncomfortable after a hard day of training.

Night fell and Alana still hadn't returned to her bunk house. I wondered if she watched me and waited for me to leave before she came back. Just then Kingsley circled back by.

"What in the Three Hells are you doing, Gerstung?"

"I'm waiting for my cousin, sir. She's supposed to bring me something."

"I'm going to bring you some bruises if you don't get to your bunk."

"Yes, sir." I trudged off to my own bunk dejectedly. I kept watching back to see if she came out of hiding, but by the last turn to my own bunk I could no longer see hers.

May 16, 1998

The next day I avoided Alana directly, but I watched her covertly. I trained in the different exercises and kept an eye on my cousin as she trained with her unit. Male and female recruits had the same expectations. No one received slack due to their gender. The army expected females to do equivalent work as males. As training progressed, males and females fought without holding back on one another. The officers knew that the Dragons would not discriminate between male and female Humans and we couldn't either.

Physical training ended for the day and I caught a glimpse of Alana departing the fort. I quickly ran to the gate she exited and tried to follow, but the gate guard stopped me.

"Where do you think you're going, Recruit?"

"I was going to go for a stroll outside the fort, sir."

The gate guard shook his head, "Only recruits with special permissions are allowed to go out at night."

"What kinds of special permissions can I get?"

"Talk to one of the administrative officers for that kind of information. I'm just here to stop unauthorized recruits from going down and raising hell in the village."

"Yes, sir."

May 17, 1998

The next morning I went to the administrative office and asked for the information. The permissions granted based mostly on supply. Recruits purchased most of the supplies in Bellato and it was mandatory those recruits returned before a nine o'clock curfew. Recruits performed supply runs every day on a set schedule. I happily volunteered. The administrator informed me that due to my special probationary status it would be six months of training before I could do supply runs.

Frustrated, I returned to my bunk. Walt already lay in his

bed, but was not asleep. I climbed up to the top bunk. I stripped down to my loin cloth and stretched.

Walt said, "Hey buddy, what's on your mind?"

I honestly didn't know what I could share with Walt. Sure, he and I got along famously, he certainly was the most interesting male recruit in the fort as far as I knew, but this thing I dealt with didn't feel like something normal one shares with a new acquaintance.

Screw it. I needed someone to talk to about this. "I think my cousin's a vampire."

"Alana? How could she be? She trains in the sun just like everyone else."

"I don't know.... Maybe she's an evolved vampire that can stand the sun. All I know... I think she has attacked people when she goes to Bellato on her supply runs. I feel like I am responsible to stop her."

"Well she is your cousin."

"What would you do?"

"I would make sure I had cloves of garlic around my neck and a stake handy."

I laughed, more out of necessity than his humor.

"I really hope I'm overreacting and there is a perfectly logical explanation for her attacking people and drinking their blood."

8 — Remembering Diana

June 14, 1998

In the second month of training, our group of recruits filled assignments of weaponless, overnight guard duty. We received orders to ring the alarm bell until those more capable arrived to defend against any attacks.

Rebecca was not in my unit. That being said, I only caught glimpses of her from far away as she trained with her own unit. However, guard duty put Rebecca and I together frequently.

Historically a surprising amount of attacks befell the fort. Dragon Sympathizers attacked forts and harassed soldiers. They must have missed the part where Dragons were trying to destroy Humanity.

I didn't see Alana during these times. She must have been scheduled differently to go on her supply runs. I still waited worriedly and hoped I would be able to talk to her again, but she avoided me during training hours as well. It was as if she didn't exist.

Rebecca noticed my worried look one night. "Hey kid, what's bugging you."

"My cousin. She's avoiding me."

"Why would she do that?"

I didn't want to tell Rebecca a lot of details, lest she think me insane. "Oh, we had a fight about something and I'm trying to apologize, but she won't see me."

"Have you tried her bunk?"

"Yeah, but as long as I wait, she just isn't there."

"Are you sure she's still at the fort?"

"I catch a glimpse of her every once in a while so I know she's still here. She's a month ahead of us and she got supply detail, so I keep hoping she'll go on a supply run while I work the gate. But so far, no luck."

"That's tough."

I had nothing else to say.

Rebecca spoke again, "So tell me about where you come from. I heard some rumor about you and some girl from your village and how you were some kind of secret pervert."

I scoffed. "Hardly."

Rebecca stepped closer to me. "So tell me the truth of it. What happened exactly?"

September 9, 1987

The story of Diana began when I was five. It was a school day like any other. I was the primary target of schoolmate abuse and largely ignored by the teacher. I sat in the back corner of the school room, the place where I sat the rest of my school career. There was at least one seat between me and everyone else in the school.

The teacher spoke, "Class, I'd like to introduce you to our new student, Diana Gomez."

I expected to be unimpressed, but I looked up and saw an angel. Her perfect brown hair was not too wavy and not too straight. Her skin was the color of leather and looked soft.

"Diana, tell the class about yourself."

Diana waved to all of us. "Well, my daddy and mommy brought me here from Bellato. My daddy was in the war and was a very brave soldier. My mommy put together Bellato's school system all by herself. She wants to help the Meton School be just as good. I like fairies, they are so great."

The older students laughed good-naturedly.

Diana took the seat directly in front of me. She immediately turned around to look at me. Her eyes were so brown they would make a crayon jealous. Diana whispered, "Hi, what's your name?"

"John Ross," I whispered back.

Diana asked, "Do you want to be my friend?"

I smiled. "I would like to have a friend."

"Do you want to come see my new house?"

"Okay."

The teacher yelled, "Gerstung, stop distracting Diana!"

Diana and I walked from the schoolhouse hand in hand that afternoon. I showed her a short cut back to the village. I used this way when I tried to avoid the Bollin Brothers.

"Strike!" Speak of the devils.

The four brothers surrounded me and pushed me. Craig led the charge. Todd had always been a part of the taunting, but he took a more physical role by pushing me down.

Diana immediately jumped to my defense and pushed Todd. "Leave him alone, you big bullies!"

Diana grabbed my hand as I got up and we walked quickly away. We reached the town and we walked to the largest house in the town. I had seen workers building the house, but I didn't know who it was for before I saw it with Diana.

No one was home when we reached the house. Diana led me to her room and the wooden walls were covered with fairy pictures. There was wallpaper, which was basically unheard of, and the windows actually sealed.

Diana said, "I just love fairies. They are so pretty and cute. Don't you?"

"Yeah," I said. I would have agreed to anything she said at that point.

I heard thumping sounds coming in the door to the house and down the hallway toward her room. A giant head poked into the room. Diana turned.

"Diana," the man said. "Who is this?"

"Hi Daddy!" Diana jumped up and hugged him. "This is my new friend, John Ross."

"John Ross... Gerstung?"

"Yes sir, Diana's Daddy."

His deep voice rumbled and scared me. "Get out of my house now."

Diana said, "Daddy? Why? This is my friend!"

"Out! Now!"

Gomez stepped aside. I scurried out of the house. I listened below her window as he yelled at her. I only caught the words, "Bastard" and "Never see him again."

When I reached my home my tears were mostly dried. When my mother saw my mottled red face her voice was full of a frustrated bite. "Did those boys beat you up again?"

"No Mommy. I made a friend. Then I lost her."

"A friend? Tell me about her."

So I went over the whole story with my mother and I cried a little again at the end when I thought about how the huge man had been mean to me.

September 10, 1987

By the morning I was back to my general state of mind. I was still a happy kid more or less. I just had to deal with mean people.

I walked past Diana's house and stared wistfully, but I kept walking without even a pause. About 50 feet past her house I heard someone running towards me. I didn't know if it was the Bollin Brothers or if I was being chased by another set of kids. I felt two small hands grab my shoulders and I turned, ready to fight.

It was Diana!

I smiled, but then I frowned. "Your daddy said you can't see me anymore."

"I know, but we go to the same school he can't stop me from seeing you all the time. Maybe around other people we can't be friends, but maybe when it's just you and me we can. Like a secret."

"A secret?"

"Yeah, we can be secret friends. Can you keep a secret?"

I said, "That don't sound fun."

"I know, I don't like it either, but I want to be your friend and I don't want to get in trouble for it."

"Ummm…?"

"Please JR?"

I grimaced as a smile and we walked toward the school house. We walked separately in sight of other people. If people taunted me, Diana joined in for appearances. When we were alone she apologized, sometimes more sincerely than others. She called me her best friend and how she could never want me to go away and how she always wanted me around. I loved her in every way a young boy can love a girl.

October 13, 1996

The good times with Diana felt really good. The moments grew fewer and further between than I would have liked. As I matured, my frustration grew with her especially since her taunting became more and more mean spirited. One of the biggest blows to my self confidence was when she informed me that Todd Bollin was her boyfriend and their parents were lobbying hard for them to marry.

I said, "You're only 14, how is that even right?"

Diana replied, "I guess they wanted to get a good start on things. Our parents don't want us to get married right away, they want us to wait until we're 18 and we're legal adults. Apparently it's important for the Human race that we start having sex and making babies."

Diana mimicked Todd Bollin's father. "You two kids are fine specimens, you'll make strong, warrior children and when they grow up they'll join the Human army and take down the Dragons with ease."

I sighed. "I always kind of hoped I'd be the father of your children."

"Me too."

April 27, 1998

I started writing poetry because of Diana. I never showed her the poems I wrote until the day before 'the incident.' We met up after school in a place only we knew about. After greeting and sitting I pulled the folded piece of paper out of my leather trouser pocket and handed it to her.

My love for your is blatant
Our friendship is a secret
I wish I could have you
Where others could see it

I'll suffer the silence
As long as there's a chance
That someday you'll love me
And someday we'll dance.

"Strike!"

We stood quickly and saw the Bollin Brothers headed towards us. Diana put on an angry face. "You stupid idiot! How dare you write garbage like this to me? Get out of my face right now."

Diana crumbled the paper and pushed it into my chest. "Get out of here before I have my boyfriend Todd and his brothers beat you up. Bastard!"

I didn't cry this time as I ran away, but I did run. Who knew what the Bollin Brothers would do if left long enough trying to defend their little brother's honor, but I had no tears for the situation. I kept telling myself that Diana was doing this as a way to not get me beat up. I had to keep telling myself that or I would have cracked.

June 14, 1998

I stopped speaking and looked at Rebecca. She looked back at me without words. I smiled after a moment. "It's over now. With all of the shit I went through with her.... She's in the past now. The future looks pretty bright."

Rebecca said, "While this does explain the kind of bitch you had to deal with, it doesn't explain why you were kicked out of your village."

I started, "Well, that's another story."

Our guard duty relief came and we stepped down from our post. As we parted ways in the court yard of the fort, Rebecca touched my hand. "You're going to have to tell me the rest of this story some night, kid."

"I'm looking forward to it."

9 — Kingsley's Story

July 20, 1998

"Man, my shit was green today," Walt said, as if I had asked.

I hadn't.

During Month Three a stomach bug circulated Fort Kingsley. As it so happened, I was one of the only people completely unaffected by the bug even though I had constant contact with Walt who was one of the most affected.

Being one of the healthy ones in the fort, lead me to being assigned more guard duty. I still held no weapon even though the armed guards suffered some degree of discontent due to the stomach malady.

Lieutenant Kingsley himself acted as my guard duty partner. Needless to say I was less than enthused when I discovered this.

We spent most of the nights in light conversation keeping watch over the sleeping and shitting fort. All night there was a line leading into the latrine and a staggering wave of perpetually tired warriors coming out. I was glad to be on guard duty.

Our conversations seemed like Kingsley was dancing around a subject. It felt like he used these times of small talk to put me at ease. Or maybe, they were to put him at ease for what we eventually discussed.

One night, Kingsley brought up my family. "How are your uncles? I don't get down to Bellato much to see them."

I replied, "Oh, they were alright when I stayed at their house before recruitment, but I haven't seen them since then. I assume they would have sent word if something was wrong."

"I suppose so," Kingsley said. "I always heard interesting things about your mother. What is she like?"

"Uh, sir?" I think the term here is, 'out of left field.'

"I was only able to meet Aurora Gerstung when your uncles were training. She was a teenager and I was one of their instructors. We had a good time getting to know one another. This was before I married my wife Annie."

"My mother, she is alright. Strict, stubborn, loving. You know how mothers are."

Kingsley paused, "I don't really remember my mother. It was so long ago."

I eyed Kingsley. He didn't look that old to me. He presented about the same age as my uncles.

Kingsley said, "You know, maybe if I had been able to get to know your mother a bit better, I may have courted her instead. I had intended to court her when she turned 18, but things got in the way. Had I not met Annie around that time, I might have considered it a lost opportunity, but Annie was the love of my life."

I asked, "What was she like?"

Kingsley sighed. "She was everything a strong man needs in a strong woman. She was intelligent, stable, and beautiful. I had to fight off some real competition to win her. It was the only fight I ever thought I might lose.

"I had to fight for her. I couldn't leave the fort to be exclusive with her, but she understood my commitment. She was a trainee as well. Her other suitor was named Hunt. Looking back I can't blame Annie for being attracted to him. He was handsome, strong, a slick talker. He had every woman he met at his fingertips, but he had his sights set on Annie, even when he knew I wanted her. You see, Hunt and I were friends for a long time before I met Annie. I made the mistake of introducing the two of them, and then our friendship went out the window.

"When I found out Hunt had been courting Annie behind my back I was furious. When I accused him, he denied it, but I saw the lying glint in his eyes. When I caught them in bed together I almost left them both behind, but Annie came to me that night and apologized she said being with Hunt was a mistake and she had told Hunt it was over and she wanted to be with me.

"We made love that night and the next day I saw Hunt. He was angry and tried to duel with me, but I took care of him."

I asked, "You killed him?"

Kingsley shook his head. "No, no, I could never kill my former best friend. But I made sure that he would never go for Annie again."

"How?"

Kingsley replied, "Some things are better left unspoken.

"Anyway, Annie and I were soon married and we soon found out she was with child. The pregnancy was hard, but I stayed with her throughout helping her however I could. The midwives said she had to remain in bed, which she hated. I tried to keep her entertained and calm.

"The delivery... was...." Kingsley trailed off.

Pain. Blood. Agony. Death.

Kingsley said, "Rebecca was born and she became the light of my life. I didn't know how to be a father and I had no mother to help me, so I raised her the best I could. I went on a hiatus from the Hell Bringers as long as I could, then finally they offered me a chance to stay active in the Human army and still raise Rebecca. While she was a baby, she had a wet nurse in Bellato and I would try to make it down to see her three times a week at least.

"When she was old enough to walk she started coming up to the fort to stay with me for a week at a time, but she would spend most of her time in Bellato playing with other kids her age. She grew up fast and I started training her to fight as she became more mature. She is my greatest student. Every time I see her flashing green eyes I think of her mother."

Kingsley didn't speak for a few minutes so I felt it prudent to ask....

Kingsley interrupted my thought process, "I'm telling you all of this because I know you and Rebecca have been spending time together and I want you to know why I am so protective of her. I know you like her and she is starting to like you and I want to make it perfectly clear that if you hurt her, it will not end well."

"I had no intentions of hurting Rebecca sir."

"Intentions and potential are two very different things Gerstung."

"I know this sir. Also, I don't think Rebecca is actually that interested in me," I said.

"Well, you don't know her as well as I do. She has told me how you and she have been sharing stories from your childhoods. She said you were getting around to telling her about the incident that got you expelled from your village. I know the story already. I can't really hold it against you, but there is a lot of stigma associated with that kind of accusation."

I sighed. "Don't I know it."

"I would appreciate if you were not so candid with her in the future. She has to focus on her combat training. She cannot be distracted by you or anything else. In a few short months you recruits will be training with weapons and that is when things get deadly serious. Distractions in a life or death game can only lead to injury and pain. If you don't want to cause her pain, you will respect this process."

I reply, "Sir, I don't intend to become a distraction for Rebecca. Yes, I admit, I think she's pretty and the only interactions I've had with her have been pleasurable, but the last thing I would want to do is cause her any harm or be a hindrance to her training. I only want to honor my uncles' and my grandfather's name. I want to keep the family name positive on the tongues of the Human race."

"That's good to know." Kingsley sounded satisfied. Our conversation returned to the small talk, probably as a recovery stage for revealing so much to me and making himself vulnerable to me like this. Nothing particularly untoward happened for that night, or for many nights following.

I still hadn't seen my cousin in many weeks. I figured she was still avoiding me. I didn't want to ask the Lieutenant about it lest I make him angry. I wanted to be able to take care of this myself, but I was growing more and more frustrated at my inability to do so.

The guard came to relieve us. I took my leave of Kingsley and he patted my arm as we parted. I walked toward the latrine, but the smell didn't allow me to get closer than 50 feet. I was about to turn away when Walt came out. He stumbled toward me and I helped him the rest of the way to our bunk. He told me about how this time his shit was brownish green so he knew he was getting better.

I still hadn't asked.

Walt stumbled with weakness and possible dehydration. I stumbled from the weight of Walt leaning on me. Eventually we made it back to the bunk and I tossed him onto his bed. He didn't mind the roughness. I heard him snoring seconds later.

I took off my shirt and trousers then climbed up into my bunk. I saw an envelope waiting for me on my blanket. I read my name was on the outside. I opened the envelope. I scanned the letter. The name at the bottom was "Alana."

10 — Alana's Note

July 27, 1998

Dear John Ross,

By the time you read this, I should be gone.

I'm sorry I've been avoiding you these past few weeks, but I've been undergoing some changes. I wasn't sure how you'd take being around the new me. If you haven't heard already, I've gone AWOL from the fort, it wasn't something I originally intended to do, but now it seems like the right thing.

I know this letter will come as a shock to you. I'm not a quitter. Well, I'm still not, but I cannot take it at the fort anymore. It's too hard to stay there and not feel like I want to eat the rest of the recruits. I want to be able to do my dad proud, but this feeling inside me is driving me crazy.

I've finally found out who I am. Or what I am. I met someone in Bellato who was able to level with me on the feelings I've been feeling. I don't know how much I can tell you without you thinking I'm crazy, but John Ross... I'm evolving.

Every time I drink the blood of someone, I feel myself changing. Food was always making me sick because there were always unnecessary components in the food that my body didn't need. My new friend has shown me, that all I need is the minerals in the water to subsist and drinking blood is a special act which can make me stronger.

I know what you're thinking, I'm a vampire and someone will end up staking me. But I'm something more than a vampire.

I don't have a need to drink blood. I can go out in the sunlight without fear. My new friend calls us Hemathropes.

I want to ask you not to show this letter to my dad, but I know you are going to anyway. So I have to put this proscription into the letter: "Don't try to find me." My new friend is very strong and does not take kindly to Humans. I think he's strong enough to kill my dad and his brothers. There is something otherworldly about him. It's scary and exciting.

This will be the last time you hear from me John Ross. I wish you a happy life and I hope you get everything you desire. I love you cousin!

Sincerely,
Alana

I folded the letter and sighed. The tenth time reading the letter did not make me any less perplexed than the first. A week passed since I'd discovered it on my bunk. I kept trying to figure out a way to ask to go to Bellato, but the supply run group had no openings. I either had to sneak out, or try to exploit Lieutenant Kingsley's newfound over-sharing to get his permission.

I don't like exploiting people, so I chose to sneak out. It proved to be more difficult than it might sound.

I watched as the supply run recruits were readying themselves to leave. Recruits stocked the freezer wagon. Four huge horses stood ready to tow the wagon. I made my way nonchalantly towards the group of them carrying my katana. When they armed themselves, I slung my katana over my shoulder. I casually ingratiated myself into the group of 20 or so recruits as they walked towards the gates. The sunset glowed red. I made sure I did not make eye contact with either of the ground guards as we walked. I kept my eyes front staring into the horizon.

I heard one of the guards say, "I don't recognize him."

I turned slightly so I could see out of the corner of my eye, they were pointing at me. The leader of the supply group said sharply, "Well neither do I, but the supply teams change every day. He's probably just new."

The guard said, "What's your name recruit?"

I thought for a moment. "Gerstung, Alan A." I held up

my dog tag and carefully covered the "John Ross" portion of my name.

The guard looked at the dog tag, then back to his list. "It says here 'Alana' you don't look like any Alana I've ever seen."

"Well, they obviously misspelled my name."

The guard paused, looking me over. "Alright, get out of here." I heard him whisper to his partner, "We're going to have to see that this list is updated."

As the group of us walked to Bellato, the leader of the group took me aside. We walked behind the rest of the group. "Hi. I'm Lance Robbins. And your ass is not nearly nice enough to be Alana Gerstung. You must be John Ross."

I saw no point in continuing to lie. "Yeah, that's me. I'm sorry I had to lie to the guards like that."

"Not a problem kid. I know Alana pretty well, or I thought I did, until she went AWOL. Do you know what happened?"

I sighed. "No, that's why I had to sneak out. I have to show the letter she gave me to her parents. Maybe they'll have some answers. Do you know anything that might be of use?"

Lance said, "Well, she would always get her supply order filled, but she was always a minute or two late and always seem a bit out of breath. I didn't understand it and she never gave any reason, but she got the job done and that's all that mattered."

I asked, "When was the last time you were on a supply run with her?"

Lance said, "About a week before she was reported missing. It was strange, as she was coming back to the group, she had her supplies, but there was this guy with super long black hair staring at her. It was dark so I couldn't see his face, but I could feel this power behind him. I lead supply runs every night so I would have noticed her if she had come out again."

I scratched my chin as we walked.

Lance asked, "Do you know who the guy might have been?"

I shook my head, "No clue. But I think he might have been the guy who coerced her away."

"Coerced?"

I said, "In her letter, she said she had a new friend

who...."

Lance pressed the question, "A new friend who, what?"

"I can't say. Not yet."

Lance walked next to me for most of the journey. An over excited recruit let out a whoop as we drew closer to Bellato.

As we entered Bellato, Lance handed me a list of supplies. "You're here, so you may as well do something useful."

"Lance, I need to get to my uncle's house," I said.

"Then get the supplies quickly and do that. You have two hours. And if you don't do it, people are going to find out you snuck out and that will be disastrous for your military career."

"You're a jerk, Lance."

"Yeah, I know. Now hop to, Recruit."

I ran as fast as my knees would allow to my Uncle's house. I knocked on my uncle Oli's door. His wife Jessica answered. "John Ross! What are you doing here? This is such a surprise!"

I smiled. "Is Uncle Oli here?"

From behind her, "Jess, who is it?"

I spoke louder, "Uncle Oli, I have news about Alana."

A moment later, Oli came to the door. He and Jessica read Alana's letter. A tear crested Jessica's eye, but she didn't sob. They closed the letter together and looked at me. I looked back, but I had no words.

At last Oli spoke, "Okay. Well, I guess Max, Zack and I will try to find her."

I asked, "What about this guy she mentioned. Do you think there is a threat?"

Oli said, "Maybe, but I can't just do nothing. This is my daughter."

Jessica said, "I can't believe she is drinking blood. This is insane."

We stood in silence for a few minutes. Finally I said, "I am out on a supply run, I have to gather what's on my list and be back to the gate in about an hour and a half. I don't know how long this is going to take. I love you both, but I need to get to it."

"Be careful, JR," Jessica said. She hugged me.

Oli shook my hand. "I'm glad you brought us this information. Don't worry. We will take the right course of action."

I turned away and started walking back into Bellato market district. Even after dark the city was still booming with people buying and selling. My list was simple: five dozen eggs; 50 pounds of beef; 50 pounds of chicken. I found the items quickly enough, but I had to take the meat products before I grabbed the eggs otherwise I might have dropped and broken them.

I gathered the supplies and took them to the freezer wagon. I felt eyes on me. I looked around, but saw no one. I loaded the eggs carefully into the wagon and shut the door. I turned and stood face to face with a man with long black hair.

11 — The Man with Long Black Hair

July 27, 1998

"She asked you not to meddle."

The man with long black hair grabbed me with both hands under my arms. My feet left the ground and I flew. Before I knew it I hit a stone pillar hard and cracked my forehead on the ground as I ricocheted off.

I slid my hands under my shoulders and pushed up. Before I could get further, the man grabbed me by the hair and pulled me standing. I swung my right hand at his ribs, but he blocked my strike and backhanded me into the pillar again. I shot a forward kick at the man, but he caught my foot and flipped me backwards onto the ground.

I looked up from my position on my stomach. Lance and three other recruits came at the man, but in four successive punches they dropped and groaned on the ground.

The man with long black hair stepped forward and crouched down as low as he could. I groaned as I tried to get up. He put his powerful left index finger under my chin and lifted me higher.

"If anyone comes after Alana, they will die. She is your cousin no longer. She is more."

I started to speak, but his right fist cocked. Things went black.

I awoke in the bottom bunk. My head throbbed. Walt sat next to me, he snored, but I couldn't blame him for that. Watching your unconscious friend can't be that interesting.

My chest hurt as I coughed. Walt nearly fell out of his chair in surprise. After he recovered, he said, "Hey man. You alright?"

"Head. Hurts."

"Yeah, you and the rest of the supply team. Kingsley is pissed at you by the way."

"Don't. Care."

"You were only out a few minutes. You came to long enough to tell the medic what happened. Then you went back out the rest of the night. You had me worried for a bit. But Kingsley wasn't worried at all. I've heard him fuming a couple of times. He's already reprimanded Lance, which is completely unheard of since Lance is king of the goody-two-shoes. Here's some aspirin."

I took the aspirin and closed my eyes. "What time is it?"

Walt said, "Just after sunrise. I was told to monitor you until you were coherent, and then march you to Kingsley's office."

I sighed. "I don't feel coherent."

Walt replied, "I didn't figure you would. Relax a bit longer and we will get to Kingsley's office when you're ready. You don't want to have to withstand a bitch fest while under the influence of a fist to the face."

I rubbed my head. "This guy was so... powerful. He wasn't just fast. He wasn't just strong…. It was scary."

Walt said, "Yeah, you're no slouch in your own right, but the way you put it last night he just took you apart."

"He lifted me up like a baby and tossed me like a piece of garbage. It was not a good feeling. I want that kind of power."

Walt said, "You mean you want to fight him again."

I scoffed. "Not today. I mean, I want that power so when I do fight him again he actually feels like he was in a fight."

"Well, we are coming up on six months pretty soon. We're finally going to be able to fight. That should help."

I considered being able to fight at the fort. My heart beat a little harder and the pain in my head lessened. "I think I'm more coherent now, but I'm not marching."

Walt accompanied me to Kingsley's office. He kept time with the traditional: "One, two three four, keep it up two three four."

I did not walk in time, but he smiled as he called out the marching time so I didn't stop him.

"Company halt!" Walt giggled like a school girl. He knocked on the door.

"Come in."

We walked in slowly. I was cautious, Walt was just clumsy.

"Gelh, dismissed," Kingsley said.

"Yes, sir." Walt left the office.

I looked around the room. I saw only a few pictures of Kingsley and Rebecca. A javelin hung on the back wall behind Kingsley's chair. He also had a collection of swords on either side wall. Water sealant stained the walls red.

Kingsley said, "Gerstung, you remember that you are on probation right? Being only 16, I shouldn't even have let you into this fort."

"Yes, sir."

"Add to that, you snuck out of the fort under the guise of being on a supply run. You colluded one of the top recruits, Robbins, into your little plot. Then you end up getting the shit beat out of the entire supply team. Does that about cover it?"

"Yes, sir."

"Give me one good reason I shouldn't kick you out of the fort right now."

I opened my mouth to speak. I wanted to tell him about Alana. I wanted to tell him my devotion to my cousin drove me to do these asinine things. I closed my mouth.

"I'm waiting."

"I have no good reason, sir."

Kingsley said, "You know what I hate even more than irresponsibility, Gerstung? I hate liars. I hate to sound like anything except a hard ass, but when I look at you, I don't get the feeling that you would do something like this without a just cause. You come across to me as a young man who believes in honor. Am I wrong in this?"

A long minute floated in the air between us. "No, sir. At least I hope I can be a man of honor."

"Then tell me what is going on. We are more than just warriors here. We need to know that every single member of this fort is family that we will support one another. It's come to my attention that your cousin, Alana Gerstung, has gone AWOL, is that true?"

"Yes, sir."

"Robbins told me you were looking for her in Bellato. Did you find her?"

"No, sir."

"But you found the person who you believe took her?"

"Yes, sir. But I don't think she was unwilling. I just wanted to talk to her before she went, to try to convince her to come back to the fort. But I didn't get the chance."

"Because of the attacker."

"Yes, sir."

"You informed your uncles while you were in Bellato?"

"Yes, sir."

Kingsley paused. "I hope you enjoyed your time in the city because I'm continuing your probationary period until the end of your first twelve months. You will not be permitted to leave the fort for anything less than a life or death emergency. If you leave for any other reason than an emergency or a superior officer leads you out, you will be expelled from the fort and you can kiss your family's reputation good bye. Do I make myself clear?"

"Yes, sir."

I left the office. My head hurt even worse. I wanted to lie back down in my bunk, but my orders were to join up with my unit. Walt stood on the outside of the group so I formed up next to him.

He asked, "So were you booted?"

I replied, "No, this is pretty much my last chance. I'm on probation until the end of twelve months. I have to walk the straight and narrow now."

"Good. I would have missed having you around, buddy.

It would have been a shame to have you gone after only three months."

We continued our exercises until lunch. In the lunch room I sat quietly as I ate. I contemplated things with Alana as Walt blathered on about some girl he saw after hours. Rebecca joined us.

She said, "So, kid, I heard you almost got expelled."

I replied, "Yeah, I was pretty close to gone today."

Rebecca smiled. "I'm glad you're not."

I smiled back. "Me too."

The rest of the conversation was less than important. What was important was that Rebecca was sitting two feet away from me. I could have touched her if I had reached out. She would have probably slapped me, but I could have done it. I could smell her faint scent, a mix of raspberry and physical exertion. When something she talked about excited her, her green eyes flashed. Her reddish brown hair was tied in a pony tail and it bobbed cutely back and forth.

I didn't speak much. I just watched her. I tried really hard not to be enamored with her.

"There's that word again," I said softly.

Rebecca looked at me. "What word?"

I said, "Oh, nothing. Continue with what you were saying."

Rebecca resumed her speech and I listened, sort of. I focused on the shape of her mouth and the movement of her tongue and lips. Despite the admonitions from her father, I felt myself falling in love with Rebecca.

12 — Sparring with Walt

November 13, 1998

I ran as hard as I could from the man with long black hair. I couldn't run fast at all with my knee in the condition it was. I burst through door after door after door. Each time I met him face to face and was just barely able to avoid him. I kept turned and twisted and each time he was there. Finally he caught me, cornered me. He grabbed me and held me fast. I struggled, but I could not release myself. Suddenly I dangled over the edge of a cliff. "No, no," I screamed. I looked down and saw the rocks in the water. The man with long black hair released me. I watched myself fall and a Red Dragon swoop up towards me with its mouth wide open, its teeth gleamed.

I sprang up from my resting position in the bunk. I almost knocked my head on the ceiling of the bunk room. My nightmares continued and lately they happened more and more since my encounter with the man with long black hair. Funny thing is, the usual occurrences of my dreams: the Red Dragon; flying (or more often falling); and fire all continued to arise as well.

The birds chirped outside the bunk. The faint glimmers of dawn leaked through the wooden walls of the bunk. I figured now was as good a time as any to get up and take care of my morning routine.

After being chewed out by Kingsley for sneaking out of the fort, I purposefully made the four months that followed uneventful. Aside from the random run-ins with Crush I succeeded. Chen become more present as he reminded me without reminding me of our impending fight.

We were in the middle of month seven and we were (finally) allowed to spar and carry wooden versions of our weapons. Of course we still worked out in the morning, but the afternoon was full of combat training, both armed and unarmed. This was where I shined. Every lesson my uncles had taught me about combat applied here.

The morning passed quickly. We were encouraged to push ourselves every morning to make us better warriors. The afternoon came and we were tired, but stronger.

Our drill sergeant was obsessed with Arena fighting. This being said, he patterned our sparring after Arena battles. He would have us spar with a different person every day. He would take notes of how we sparred. If we did well we would "advance" to the next round. If we did not do as well as our partner we would be shuffled down to the bottom of the list and have to fight our way up.

By the middle of the month, Walt and I had advanced to the top of our recruit group. As we stood facing each other and smiled, the drill sergeant called out to the group, "The better fighter between these two will be the recruit to beat from your group. You should aspire to be better than this recruit. You should aspire to be better than you ever thought possible.

"You all have your partners for today. Begin!"

Walt and I smiled at each other and bowed respectfully. I saw Rebecca out of the corner of my eye. She watched Walt and I circle each other. As my back faced her I lunged. Walt dodged my punch and tried to hit me in the stomach, my left hand brushed his out of the way and my right hand changed directions to hit him with a back fist. He moved his head as he spun with a right back fist of his own. I ducked his attack and pushed him off balance. He caught himself and growled at me. "Don't mess around JR."

I jumped towards him with a flying knee. Walt blocked the attack and shoved me out of the air with both hands to my chest. I toppled down and rolled over my back into a crouched position. Walt came at me with a punt kick, but I rolled out of the way and sprang into his left side. My left arm locked around his body and I lifted him up for a Gerstung Slam. Walt didn't let go when I slammed him and instead we both went down. He rolled us until he ended on top of me. "I'm a wrestler too, JR, did you forget?"

I grunted. "I must have. I won't forget again."

I rolled us over. My left arm still wrapped around his body. I punched him a couple times in the ribs from the back then pushed him off. I thought we would square up again. Instead he held fast to my left arm and pulled me with him into a clothesline. I hit the ground hard, but I was up just as quickly. Walt came at me with a flurry of punches, all of which I dodged. His mention of boxing came back to my head after his precision attacks.

We circled each other again. We both breathed heavily. He stood too close to kick, so I had to match his punches. He threw a right. I slipped under and threw a right of my own to his chest. He blocked and threw a left to my head. I blocked and responded with a left of my own to his ribs. He grunted as I struck, but at the same moment his right hand connected with the left side of my head.

I stumbled back and swung a left roundhouse kick at his head. He got his right hand up in time, but I still clobbered him with it. As Walt caught his balance he caught the full force of my right front kick to his chest. Walt dodged my follow up right sidekick and cracked me in the face with a left hook.

Walt and I both circled cautiously. We breathed heavily as we watched each other's eyes, shoulders, and feet. We feinted, but made no attacks. Neither of us would give up.

"You ready," Walt asked.

I nodded.

It felt like slow motion as we fired right fists at each other. Our knuckles cracked against one another as hard as we hit. The force of contact instantly doubled the pain. I didn't feel any bones break, but the stinging shot through my right arm into my shoulder. Walt showed a similar reaction.

Time returned to normal as we both yelled in pain and surprise. The drill sergeant walked quickly towards us with his hands upraised. We had not realized, but everyone had stopped sparring and watched us.

"These recruits BOTH have the fire in their eyes," he said to us all. "Aspire to be better than these recruits."

The recruits who had watched applauded us briefly then dispersed back into their pairs to spar with each other. The drill sergeant told us to head to the medic to get our hands checked out. I noticed Rebecca had watched the whole fight.

Walt, Rebecca and I ate lunch together more often than not over the past few months. We grew into a friendship that felt deeper than any that I had before the fort. Walt knew that I liked Rebecca and he waved as he passed her, but continued to walk to the medic, even though I stopped.

Rebecca sported a fur lined, leather jacket. She smiled. "Great fight, kid."

I said, "Thanks a lot. Walt's really tough."

Rebecca said, "Don't I know it. You guys are some of the better fighters in the fort right now."

"You think so?"

"Surely. Dad, I mean Lieutenant Kingsley doesn't choose anyone for his personal training until they have been at the fort for a year, but you never know. Keep fighting hard."

"Oh, I will. You know it. So I have to go to the medic to get my hand checked out." I cracked my knuckles for effect. "Do you want to…."

I trailed off. Rebecca looked over my shoulder.

"Christofer? Is that you?"

"Happy Birthday baby!"

I turned and saw him. I saw a wiry blonde, about as tall as me, but not nearly as muscular. His short cropped hair emphasized his severe, angled, comely features. Rebecca practically flew to him. He gathered her up as he clutched the roses in his left hand and supported her hugging body with his right. I kept my reactions in check well enough so she wouldn't see my dismay at this new arrival.

Rebecca turned. "John Ross, come meet my, uh, friend from school, Christofer."

I walked slowly towards them. I extended my left hand. "Hi, I'm John Ross Gerstung."

Christofer shook my hand awkwardly after switching the

roses to his right hand. "Christofer Osborne. Gerstung? Like the Courageous Gerstung brothers of the battle of Yorktown?"

I nodded. "Yes, they are my uncles."

"Well it is certainly an honor. I hear you've been taking care of my little Rebecca in my absence."

Rebecca twitched hearing 'my little' before her name.

"Well, Rebecca can certainly take care of herself," I replied.

Christofer said, "Of course she can. Say, let's get something to eat."

I motioned to my hand, "I'd love to, but I have to get to the medics. Maybe later huh?"

"Definitely, later."

13 — Rebecca's Birthday

November 13, 1998

After the Dragons began waging war on Humanity, Humans appreciated life much more. Birthdays were like holidays. The person celebrating was treated like royalty for that day. Depending on the status of the person, there might be a parade or a huge bash to commemorate their life. Even in an environment as unforgiving as Fort Kingsley, birthdays granted a day's reprieve from training or duties of any sort. A recruit in their second year could obtain permission to go to Bellato and cut loose as long as they were back by midnight.

Rebecca looked like she had a good birthday this year. It felt less than good for me. Of course, I wanted to see her happy, but my feelings stood in the way of this benevolence. My blood bordered on boiling in my veins as I watched some other man touch her so familiarly. Christofer was touching her hands. He touched her face. I watched them kiss when they thought no one else saw.

Friend from school, huh?

I didn't mean to be so: attentive, stalker-like, or weird, but I couldn't help it. Walt even tried to distract me by poking my injured hand, but the hand had never felt better after the medic had cleared me. There were no bruises or any marks, while Walt's hand was purple.

I grabbed my katana to practice. I had to focus my mind elsewhere. I couldn't let Rebecca see me reacting this way on her birthday. Each swing of the katana I mentally repeated: *She's happy. Be happy for her.*

I worked up a sweat as I practiced. I remembered back to training with my uncle and how he taught me to be of no-mind when I fought.

June 9, 1995

Uncle Zack said, "Now John Ross, when you swing, you are thinking of too many things. When your mind is distracted, your sword will be distracted. Anger can be useful, but only as a focusing tool, not as the power behind your swing."

"I'm sorry Uncle. Todd Bollin and his brothers...."

"They don't matter here. Now focus."

I closed my eyes and held my wooden katana. My head flashed with Todd Bollin and his brothers as they chased me. Craig held me back as Todd punched me. I tried to fight them off, but I wasn't strong enough. I went home bruised as usual. I'd been training for eight years and I still couldn't defend myself.

I yelled and attacked my uncle. I immediately felt the wooden smack in my stomach.

"You want to defend yourself. You cannot let yourself be overcome by your opponent. More importantly, you cannot be overcome by yourself."

I nodded. I closed my eyes and took in a deep breath. I tried to focus on the sword. Whenever my mind wandered to something else, I brought it back to the present moment and focused on my sword. With each breath I took I drew my focus. I felt the world fall away.

My eyes snapped open and they focused on Uncle Zack. He stood ready. Without thinking I swung the katana forward. I heard the clack of our wooden swords. Then I felt a thick whack on my stomach again.

"Good," Uncle Zack said. "You have the focus. Now you just have to acquire the skill."

November 13, 1998

I sat across the table from Rebecca and Christofer. Walt noticed I wasn't watching them. This was rare since I almost always had my eye on Rebecca in some fashion. But now I averted my discomforted gaze because I didn't want to see them in love.

"So, John Ross, what brought you to Fort Kingsley at such a young age?" Christofer asked. "Was it the beautiful, Dragon filled Lake Erie?"

I looked at him. I sensed no haughtiness or superiority from him. I replied, "I had to get away from my village, Meton. It was time for me to move on. You know how that goes."

"Yes, but Rebecca tells me you're only 16. Didn't you feel like you could have stuck around for a couple more years to advance yourself towards maturity?"

Walt chimed in, "I think JR is pretty mature for his age, or for anyone's age really. He's more mature than me, that's for sure."

I smiled. "Yeah, there was nothing left for me to learn in the village. I wanted to experience the world." I paused. "So Christofer, tell Walt and me about yourself. What do you do?"

Rebecca looked on with a small smile. Christofer responded, "Well, I am a political activist. After my time with Rebecca in Bellato, I went to Omaha to try to improve the standard of living for people there. The energy barrier that protects our dear capital city does nothing to make life inside cleaner or safer from internal threats. There is a high rate of crime perpetrated by Humans on Humans. It's like the people inside forget that the war is going on out there and we need to collaborate with one another against the Dragons."

"Dragon Sympathizers," I said.

Christofer responded, "Not just the Dragon Sympathizers, there are people who are literally just in this for themselves. They don't realize that if we act as a community we can overcome and survive and live. Everyone is too worried about their own skin. That's what caused the fall of Los Angeles in the 1970's.

"You know how the energy barriers work right? It's science. A barrier is created when nonphysical energy is gathered to such a degree and focused by a strong conduit into a shield. So far the conduits have been members of the 27 Guild. For the strongest conduits, their abilities are most focused in the 27th year of life. It's related to the idea of trinity where three of something is powerful, then a trinity of trinities is more powerful, then a trinity of trinitied trinities is much more powerful and with the right contribution from everyone under the shield it can resist any Dragon attack. Theories are, it could resist a nuclear bomb, but no one is brave enough to test.

"The shield allows anyone to leave at any time, but to enter the shield one has to concentrate for long enough to have a piece of their energy incorporated into the shield. The shield grows ever so slightly when a new energy is incorporated. This is also how the guards know who is truly committed to the perpetuation of the shield, if they can't get in, they aren't to be trusted.

"Anyway, when the Dragons started attacking people panicked and stopped contributing to the protective energy barrier and eventually the city fell. The ghost of the shaman Jim Morrison still inhabits the area, but without a group of people willing to donate a piece of themselves to the rebuilding of the barrier it will never come back up and Los Angeles will remain lost.

"Unfortunately there is no way to force people to give part of their energy for community. We can't exactly enforce an energy Gestapo to monitor the energy donation people give during the day. Instead, there needs to be political activists like me to remind people to concentrate and send energy up to the shield and what happens when they forget to contribute to the greater good and attack one another. Hopefully we can get through to them and keep the tide of Dragons away."

"That's pretty noble of you, Christofer," Walt said. "What brings you to Fort Kingsley?"

"Well, I'm here for Rebecca's birthday, of course, and I had something I wanted to ask her. I suppose now is as good of a time as ever."

Christofer knelt next to Rebecca. He pulled a box out of his pocket and opened it. The box revealed a ring with a shiny diamond. Rebecca did not look pleased.

"Rebecca, would you marry me?"

Rebecca looked at Christofer, then looked at me, then looked back at Christofer. "I can't answer this question now. I'm sorry."

Rebecca stood and walked out of the cafeteria. Christofer

followed her. I stood to follow them, but Walt put his hand on my shoulder. "Maybe you'd better not."

"I have to see what is going on."

I shrugged off Walt's hand and left the cafeteria after them. I scanned the courtyard of the fort and saw Christofer go around a corner. I ran as fast as I could and when I reached the corner I heard them speaking so stayed put to listen.

Christofer asked, "What is the matter? I thought we had something good."

"We do Chris, we really do, but I don't think it is something that will last."

"Don't you love me?"

Rebecca responded, "Yes, I do, but love just isn't enough. There are other factors at work."

Christofer said, "Is it that punk kid, Gerstung? Are you in love with him?"

"No, this has nothing to do with him. It has to do with me and you. I know that if you and I got married, you would try to make me move to Omaha. That is just not where my destiny wants me. I am supposed to learn to fight Dragons and defend Humanity in whatever way I can."

Christofer replied, "I would never want you to not be who you are."

Rebecca retorted, "But Christofer, that's exactly what you would do. You tried to do it when we were in school. When we started talking about the future, you were making all of these plans for us and I didn't fit anywhere except by your side as your submissive little wife. That's not who I am. I might be your wife one day, but I'll never be submissive and I'll never be just your wife. I am my own person. I am a warrior. You need to understand this."

Silence.

Finally, Christofer said, "I just can't believe this Rebecca. You would rather fight than be with the person you love."

Rebecca replied, "The person who truly loves me back would understand this desire without being so caught up in their own heart. They would be willing to heed my wishes even if it meant they had to sacrifice something of themselves. You will never sacrifice anything for me Christofer. That's why we broke up before."

"Argh!" I heard a thump. Christofer spoke, "I need to get out of here. It was a mistake coming here."

Rebecca said, "I'm sorry Chris. I really am."

Christofer turned the corner and was face to face with me. He gasped sharply, then his face focused its anger at me. "So you heard all of that did you? I bet you're having a laugh now. You know, your uncles weren't all that they were cracked up to be. I heard what really happened at Yorktown and how they weren't the Courageous Gerstung Brothers at all. Rather the Cowardly Gerstung Brothers."

I slammed my fist into Christofer's face repeatedly until it was nothing, but a mass of red. Rebecca jumped into my arms and we lived happily ever after.

I shook my head. "You need to leave now before I end you."

Christofer pushed past me and out of the fort gate towards Bellato.

Rebecca came around the corner and looked at me with tears in her eyes. Her green eyes still flashed. "I can't believe you'd eavesdrop like that."

"I-I didn't mean to. I was just coming to make sure you were okay."

Rebecca stalked off to her bunk. "Yeah right, JR."

14 — Remembering Yorktown

November 27, 1998

Except for New Year's Day, religious or any other, holidays were forgotten after the Dragons attacked Humanity. I heard buzz about older people complaining how no one celebrated Thanksgiving anymore, but when I researched the subject and found out what actually happened I was not impressed. With all the barbaric things Dragons did to Humans we didn't need a holiday to remember the barbaric things Humans did to one another a long time ago. That would have been like having a holiday for the Holocaust.

Nevertheless, the fort had managed to procure an extensive amount of turkey for this particular Thursday. I wasn't going to complain about turkey since it is delicious, but the irony was not lost on me since in my research I saw that was a common meal for Humans on this day before the Dragons came.

There didn't seem to be anything for me to be thankful about. Rebecca hadn't spoken one word to me since Christofer left. I don't know if she blamed me for his leaving or if she was just mad because I eavesdropped on the conversation, but Walt suggested it was best I give her some space.

This was fine because Chen had been hinting that he and I would fight soon. I had to stay sharp for that. I sparred with Chen in a few training sessions. While his strikes lacked power he was as quick as a rabbit.

Chen eyed me as Walt and I entered the cafeteria and

walked towards the food line. I inhaled the stuffing and it smelled divine. Unfortunately, I heard a grunt behind me. I turned to meet a fist in my face. The punch knocked me into a group of standing recruits. "Come on Chen. I thought you had more honor than to hit a guy from behind."

But it wasn't Chen. Crush had decided to take another shot at me. His lumbering gait shook the ground as he stalked towards me. Walt tried to stop him, but Crush threw Walt away with his right hand into a table of suddenly unhappy recruits.

I rose to a crouching position. Crush reached down to me. I jumped up with a right knee to his nose. With my left leg I threw a kick to his right knee which buckled at impact. I grabbed Crush's hair with my left hand and slugged him once in the stomach then once in the face. My right hand joined my left hand in holding Crush's hair as I pulled his head down and slammed my knee up into his nose again. Walt was standing beside me, so I let Crush fall back onto the unhappy recruits' table.

Officers rushed in and saw the carnage. I raised my hands in innocence and pointed to Crush, but we were both taken to Kingsley's office. Walt tagged along as a witness.

In Kingsley's office, we three stood silently as Kingsley considered us from his seated position at his desk. He focused his gaze on myself and Crush.

Why in the world does he keep jeopardizing his training here?

I shook my head at the voices again.

"What is wrong with you Gerstung? Why do I see you in my office under these kinds of circumstances more often than I would like? Are you trying to get kicked out? I know what would happen if you were kicked out. You'd have to leave the fort and your mother would be put into danger by the people of her village."

"Sir," I said. "I did not start this fight. I was standing in the chow line, smelling the stuffing and I was hit from behind, by Recruit Crusher."

Kingsley said, "Recruit Crusher is that true?"

Crush looked away. "Yes sir."

I was surprised he admitted it.

Kingsley responded, "Why in the hell would you start a

fight with someone out of nowhere? You two are supposed to be fighting together, not against each other. We have much bigger problems to face than each other. There should be no reason why you should want to start a fight with Gerstung."

Crush was silent. Both Walt and I looked over at him. He bit his lips as if to stop himself from speaking.

Kingsley spoke again, "Recruit Crusher."

Crush inhaled sharply and then slowly exhaled. "My father was killed in the battle of Yorktown. And it was the Cowardly Gerstung Brothers who had him killed."

Immediately my anger erupted, if Walt hadn't been standing between us I would have torn Crush's head clean off.

Kingsley held up a staying hand in my direction and looked at Crush. "Recruit Crusher, what do you think happened at the battle of Yorktown?"

Crush said, "The Gerstungs sold their unit out so they wouldn't be killed."

Kingsley replied, "That isn't what happened at all."

November 27, 1980

The battle of Yorktown was important, not only due to the historical significance of Yorktown for the Humans of America, but also because of the Dragon's Bane factory. The leader of the Hell Bringer force was a man of Germanic origin named General Werda. Werda was a confident man having been the top general in the Human army since the death of John Ross Gerstung the Elder. Some could mistake his confidence for arrogance.

Zack Gerstung just completed his training a month earlier and had been chosen to become a Hell Bringer like his brothers and father before him. The three Gerstungs served under Werda happily since he had a great respect for their father.

Everyone thought the battle of Yorktown would be another step toward wiping the Dragons out of the Eastern part of the former United States. Being that close to Washington D.C. would give the Humans a tactical and morale advantage for later battles.

The battle plan should have been simple. Oliver Gerstung had orders to lead an attack force of about 50 warriors straight ahead at the Dragons to draw them away from their roost. Simultaneously, Werda would lead the other force of about 50 to destroy the roosting area. Werda's force was intended to destroy any eggs they found and kill any straggling Dragons that stayed behind to guard them. After this, Werda's force would flank the Dragons and the Hell Bringers would meet in the middle with only dead Dragons between them.

Werda's force came too late. Gerstung's force fought, but they were outnumbered two to one. For Hell Bringers this isn't usually a problem, but the terrain made the attack difficult. The force was down to its last three men, the Gerstung brothers. Before the final killing stroke was struck, Werda's force finally attacked. But by this time the Dragons were completely in the thrall of blood lust and decimated the Hell Bringers.

One Dragon blood lusting is a rampaging beast. Nearly 100 Dragons blood lusting is a problem no Human, Hell Bringer or not, should tackle.

The Gerstung brothers avoided being killed by sheer wits and will. They followed the battle, but by the time they reached where Werda's men had launched their attack their nostrils were met by the smell of burning flesh and the sight of dead Humans and Dragons.

The Gerstung brothers walked back to where the roost was supposed to have been and they found nothing. Their scout was mistaken or lying. Either way the scout was not found among the dead.

After piling together the bodies and collecting the name tags, the Gerstungs walked over 100 miles to the closest Fort. The brothers reached the fort hungry and exhausted from carrying the weight of defeat.

The brothers told their story, but there was a lot of gossip that perpetuated the rumor that the Gerstungs were cowards and sold their unit out. An investigation brought no evidence contrary to their story and they were restored to active duty as Hell Bringers. They all served as trainers for the next decade, but there were always those who spoke against them behind their backs. Only people who really knew the Gerstung brothers knew what happened and what could have never happened.

"My father was in that unit," Crush spoke softly with one tear rolling down his cheek. "I never knew him because those cowards ran from the fight. I was born just before that battle and he wasn't able to come home to see my birth."

I turned to Crush. "Look, Michael. I'm sorry that you had to go through your life without a father. But I know my uncles would never have abandoned your father or anyone for that matter. I hope you can find a way to let that anger towards me go and direct it at the beings really responsible, the Dragons. And if it makes any difference, any difference at all, I never knew my father either."

Crush didn't speak.

Kingsley said, "Okay, Recruits. I'm going to let you off with a warning. This will NEVER happen again, do you hear me? If it does, you BOTH will be expelled from this unit, no ifs, ands or buts. Am I understood?"

Crush and I spoke simultaneously, "Yes sir."

15 — Kingsley's Birthday

November 28, 1998

Chaos reigned in the fort over Lieutenant Kingsley's birthday. Kingsley stayed out of the great deal of hustle and bustle the day before, especially when having to deal with the trouble Crush and I caused. This was his special day and he didn't intend to waste it. Recruits continued their training for the day. Sundown brought the birthday banquet and the after party gave the recruits and the officers a much needed rest.

My sparring partner that day was Chen. We didn't speak at first. Crush's leering and snarling distracted me. My mind felt divided between defending myself from Chen and hoping that Crush wouldn't jump me from behind again.

Chen came at me with a snake style attack to the face which I narrowly avoided. I tried to throw a jab with my right hand, but he batted it away and his snake hand closed into a crane hand and tagged me in the left temple. My left hand reached up to grab his offending hand, but it was gone, so my right hand reached down to grab his left ankle, which also moved. Chen laid into me with a kick that knocked me backwards, but not down.

I steadied myself as Chen came at me again. I blocked his back fist, but missed with my counter punch. Chen's leg kick struck me in the knee and I cringed. I tried to return the favor, but Chen was out of the way before my kick landed.

Chen jabbed me in the face. I shook my head as he jabbed me again. I readied myself to grab the third jab. Instead he slugged me in the stomach knocking the wind out of me. I doubled over. Chen threw a knee at my head that I clinched with my left arm and I wrapped my right arm around his body.

Chen immediately started wriggling and striking me with elbows and off center punches. I lifted him awkwardly and he continued to struggle, but if I could get him down in with a Gerstung Slam I would have the advantage. Unfortunately, Chen threw off my center of balance and instead of slamming him, we both fell to the ground, I was on my back and he was on my chest with my left arm trapped.

Immediately, Chen rained punches down on my face. My right arm worked its way around to Chen's face and pushed him up and away from me. This wasn't productive. I used my right hand to deliver kite strikes repeatedly to the back of Chen's head. I got my feet flat on the ground with my knees bent and I bridged up as I hit Chen. Chen rolled off of my chest as I was able to get back up to a standing position.

Chen immediately sprang at me with tiger claw hands. I grabbed his wrists with hands and rolled backwards landing on top of him. I forced his hands together and worked his wrists into my right hand. From there, I punched him solidly in the face with my left hand.

"Do you yield?" I asked.

"No!" Chen called out.

I punched him again. "Do you yield?"

"No!" Chen yelled again.

Walt came up from behind me and grabbed me. "JR, this is just sparring, not blood sport. Lay off of him."

I released Chen and stood up over him. I looked down at Chen. "You started this."

Walt pulled me away. I watched Chen stand shakily. I felt bad, but not bad enough to apologize.

Walt said, "What did you mean by 'you started this'?"

"Chen. He's been telling me over the past few weeks that he wants to fight me for my reputation. His family doesn't have the same kind of reputation my family does and he wants to prove that his family is something too. He has made it more apparent lately that he was going to try something. That's part of why I went off on Crush yesterday, I was expecting it to be Chen. Damn, Walt. Why do people have to care about reputation? It's all bullshit."

Walt shook his head. "I have no answers for you. I'm sorry."

"Not your fault the world is messed up."

We walked back to the bunk to clean up. Kingsley's festivities cut training short that day. I dressed in my cleanest clothes, brushed my lengthening brown hair and tied it with a leather string.

I started making the rounds of the fort, smiling at people I was friendly with and ignoring those who ignored me first. I waved at Lance Robbins and he trotted over to me. I surveyed the makeshift stage and the recruits setting up lights.

"How's it looking, Recruit?"

"It looks pretty good. I hope Lieutenant Kingsley enjoys his birthday celebration."

"I think Kingsley is going to hate it honestly. He keeps telling the sergeants to put a stop to it, but they all love him a lot and want to celebrate his day."

"Hate it? That doesn't seem like him."

"Well, hate is too strong of a word, but he doesn't like a fuss to be made over his age."

"How old is he? He looks about 40 and still bad ass."

"Lieutenant Kingsley is 63 years old."

"What? You're shitting me."

"Not at all. Remember he was one of the first recruits of your grandfather Gerstung."

I paused. "You're right. Wow. Sixty three years old and he's still spry as ever and probably could kick the ass of anyone here."

"Easily, with a hand tied behind his back. Even the other Hell Bringers can't touch him."

"Yeah, I'm sure they would give him a fight though."

"No, I mean, literally, no one can touch him."

"Explain."

"Since the days of the early Hell Bringers, no one has been able to lay a hand on him in battle, Dragon or Human. This is a feat that still stands. If you remember, Plato Kingsley has also fought and killed four Dragons at once, another feat that has been matched, but never surpassed."

"I remember. Wow. He's 63 years old and still kicking ass like a young warrior. My respect for him has just grown."

"I hear you. Hey Gerstung, I have to get going, I'm part of the organizing committee, if you need something to do, come with me."

At that instant I saw Rebecca coming out of her bunk room. She turned her head and I caught her sight. At first, I thought I caught a glimpse of a smile. I imagined her green eyes flashing as she turned away angrily.

"Yeah, okay Lance. Lead the way."

I spent the rest of the afternoon hammering nails into the stage and rigging the lights. I smelled the kitchen hard at work preparing a feast like none other for the fort. According to some of the other recruits, the musical group for the night "Jeweled Ram" hailed from Bellato and was really good.

The sky slowly darkened and autumn chilled the air. I ran to my bunk to grab my leather jacket with the deer fur lining. As I exited my bunk, Rebecca stood just outside the doorway.

"Um, hi," I said, pleasantly surprised.

"Hi," she said, probably annoyed.

We didn't speak. I waited for her to say something, but she didn't.

"So, it's going to be a good party tonight, huh?" I asked.

"Yeah. Thanks for helping out. My dad is sure to appreciate it."

"And what about you?"

"Yeah. Me too."

"Does this mean we're friends again?"

"No. I just wanted to tell you I appreciated your help."

"Oh, okay. Well there is more work to be done."

"Right. Okay. Thanks again."

Rebecca turned and walked quickly away. I went in the opposite direction towards the stage. Black sky replaced red sunset. The recruits tested the lights and surprisingly, they worked.

That night, the band played, recruits and officers danced and schmoozed. I caught various glimpses of Walt perusing the female contingent of the fort. He shamelessly flirted with female officers and recruits alike sometimes at the same time, except, of course, Rebecca.

I saw Rebecca a few times. She spent some of her time near her father. She spent the rest of her time around recruits I didn't know.

Crush sat by himself partaking of the food on the buffet line. Chen sat by himself ignoring the food on the buffet line, ignoring the women, ignoring Kingsley and staring straight at me.

Kingsley stood surrounded for most of the night. He did eventually get a moment to himself. I ruined that moment to talk to him.

I began with a traditional greeting, "Lieutenant, congratulations on another lap around the sun."

"Thank you Gerstung. Did you know, it was your Grandfather that came up with that greeting?"

"Yes, sir I did. He came up with a lot of stuff, huh?"

"Yes. You're going to have big boots to fill, so to speak."

"I can fill them."

"I'm sure."

I paused, and then said, "I heard you have yet to be struck in battle since your training. That's remarkable."

Kingsley laughed. "Well, that's the rumor anyway."

"You mean it isn't true?"

"Well, I let everyone think it is true. But there have a couple lucky fighters."

"Who?"

"Well, that'd be telling, wouldn't it?"

"It's why I asked, sir."

Kingsley laughed again as he walked away. "Don't worry about it Gerstung. Enjoy the party."

"Yes, sir."

Walt stumbled up to me with two lightly muscled female recruits on his arms. One had long brown hair, the other had ear length blonde hair. Both wore black cotton, form fitting tank tops beneath fall leather jackets. I could smell the alcohol on Walt's breath. "You know, JR, you are going to just have to move on from Rebecca. So I've got the perfect solution. Meet Maria Ward."

Rebecca stared at me as intensely as Chen had all night. I enclosed the blonde's hand in mine and shook it.

16 — Maria's Dedication

December 15, 1998

Two things of significance happened the day after Kingsley's birthday party. First, a fog descended upon the area surrounding Bellato and Fort Kingsley. Second, it began to snow. Sometimes it snowed hard. Sometimes only a few flakes fell, but the snow did not cease for more than a few minutes as far as any of us knew for over two weeks.

Maria started eating meals with Walt and me in the cafeteria on a regular basis. Okay, so three things of significance.

Even before Maria joined us, I caught myself staring at her. I couldn't resist. She stood about five feet four inches tall. Her skin had a natural tan to it. I suspected some Italian ancestry. Maria's fluid form held her soft curves spread over toned muscles. When she walked or ran her curves she became a pleasant distraction to the other recruits and officers alike.

Maria became a recruit the month after Walt and me. She was a month younger than Walt, this still made her almost two years older than me. Unlike some of the other recruits and officers, she never acted like that was a negative against me. She portrayed a soft manner, except when she fought. In those cases she was as fierce as anyone else in the fort.

Maria dedicated herself to the Human cause full force. She left her little brother in Bellato because she felt so strongly about training to fight. She told Walt and me the reason she became a recruit was because of a Thomas Jefferson quote,

"Every citizen should be a soldier. This was the case with the Greeks and Romans, and must be that of every Free State."

She continued by saying, "I'm not the biggest person, nor am I very strong, but I need to be able to do my part when it comes to fighting the Dragons. It was situations like this that Jefferson was talking about."

"I'm sure Jefferson didn't count on Dragons," Walt said.

"Maybe not, but the idea of tyranny transcends species," Maria replied. "Maybe that's why we have ferals. Maybe we were so oppressive towards dogs for thousands of years that when the Dragons started attacking and the dogs started escaping their natural reaction was to rebel and be a problem for us to face so we would know what it was like."

Walt said, "That seems a little farfetched, even for a good dog."

Maria and I laughed. She called him a jerk and we moved on to less serious topics of conversation.

When we all sat at the table I would lean close enough to see her dark blue irises and the golden rings around her pupils. Maria fascinated me to no end with her unique mixture of beauty, intelligence, kind hearted nature and her commitment to the freedom of Humanity more than herself.

The yelling of guards woke us when a supply team did not return at their appointed time. Maria volunteered immediately as part of the search party to retrieve them. Of course, I also volunteered, but I my probation status denied me immediately. Walt volunteered and soon a team lead by Lance Robbins was dispatched with torches to find them. Lance had the night off for his 19th birthday, otherwise he would have been leading the lost team.

I waited at the East Gate outlook post fed from the road to the North Gate of Bellato. However, the fog and snow made it varying degrees of impossible to see more than 100 feet ahead. I waited for what seemed like forever, dividing my time between the ground inside the gate and the outlook post. I worried about the other recruits, but I worried more about Walt and Maria. I can't say I was in love with Maria, but she brought something positive to my life and I didn't want her to be hurt. Walt brought comic relief and perspective I needed in certain situations.

I wanted to get out onto the trail and help them search for the lost team, but if I broke protocol again I would be expelled from the fort. I beat my fist against the East Gate until the guards gave me sharp looks to stop. All the other recruits and officers were in their bunks. I stood alone with the guards waiting for the search party. I didn't know what else to do.

What is this boy doing?

To my surprise, I noticed Kingsley walking towards me. I tried to relax and to not wear my agitation on my sleeve. Kingsley spoke, "What are you doing up this late?"

"Recruits Gelh and Ward are in the search party to find the missing supply team."

"And you think staying up waiting will help them somehow?"

"Well, no."

"Then go to bed. Gelh and Ward will be fine. And if they're not, you can say 'I told you so, sir' okay?"

I sighed. "Yes, sir."

I walked in the direction of my bunk when I heard the gate open. I turned and saw twice as many torches coming in as had left and some recruits pulled along the broken wheeled freezer wagon. I saw none of the supply team horses.

I ran at the group happily. I saw Maria and I lifted her and twirled in a hug. We smiled at each other briefly. I said, "I was so worried about you! What happened?"

"Later, JR, help Walt," she replied.

Walt's muscles strained as he supported the heavy freezer wagon with four other recruits. Icy wind, snow and exertion reddened his face. I released Maria and grabbed the corner behind the broken wheel and lifted it up so Walt could let it go without the wagon falling. A group of recruits set up wooden blocks under the freezer wagon to stabilize it for repaired during the day. The supply team set to work unloading the freezer wagon.

Walt, Maria and I walked back towards Walt and my bunk. Without words, Maria took my left hand in both of hers and kissed my cheek. Then she scurried off to her bunk.

I turned to Walt and patted him on the back as he entered the bunk room first. Once we were settled in our beds I asked him to tell me what happened.

Walt explained: "Well the lost supply team wasn't really lost. They had been attacked by Dragon Sympathizers who had not only broken the wagon wheel, but had driven off the horses. The Symps weren't tough by any means, but they were chaotic enough in the fog and snow that the team had a difficult time driving them away. Finally the Symps backed off, but the damage was already done. The team was only about halfway back from Bellato when they were jumped so when we showed up there was still a long way to travel with the wagon. We had to switch off between the stronger recruits while others held the torches. We were lucky the Symps didn't come back, that would have taken even longer."

"Wow," I said. "I'm glad you are okay. Are your arms sore?"

Walt's sarcasm reared its ugly head, "No JR. I feel like I just carried some flowers a few hundred feet.

"Anyway, I saw how excited you were to see Maria. Does this mean your obsession with Rebecca is over with?"

"I don't know if I would call what I had with Rebecca was obsession, but I have definitely cooled off towards her. I mean, she doesn't want to be friends with me, I can't force it right?"

Walt said, "Yeah you're probably right. Maria is a better fit anyway. She actually likes you and she's a lot nicer."

"Yeah, but I'm not sure how I feel about Maria."

"I wouldn't worry about it honestly, we have too many other things going on in the fort right now."

"Like what?" I asked.

"Well, we have a traitor in the fort is the rumor. The Symps were better organized than usual and they attacked even in this overwhelming fog and snow. They must have known the supply team would be weaker."

"You make a valid point, Walt," I said. "Who do you think it is?"

"It's too early to make accusations, but we had better root out the rat soon. We only have so many replacement wagon wheels and horses," Walt said.

"At least they didn't kill any of the supply team."

"True," Walt agreed.

The horses made their way back to the fort by morning. Some of the recruits fixed the wagon wheel. An air of accusation wafted throughout the fort over the rocky emotional and political landscape. No formal inquisition of recruits or officers ensued, but eyes grew sharper on the look out for suspicious activity. No one knew who might be a traitor and who they could trust.

17 — Walt's Parents

December 22, 1998

The fog still hadn't dissipated seven days after the Sympathizer attack. That didn't bother me so much since I was still not allowed to leave the fort and the lights inside the fort usually took care of visibility. Everyone still worried about the supply teams that went out, but with Lance in charge of them. They always made it safely back.

Cold weather made training harder. Snow fell intermittently, but never reached blizzard-like proportions. With the virtual stopping of the industrialization of the world, weather started to go back to normal. This means it cold, but it never reached horrendous levels.

The cold made calisthenics in the morning. Our push ups and sit ups happened on the cold, wet ground. It wasn't pleasant, but war isn't either. Most of the recruits complained, but those who knew our purpose and who believed in our mission did not, at least not out loud.

In the afternoon, we fought with wooden weapons. We recruits slipped and slid so much that accidental strikes would have killed most of us before we reached combat. It became a game. If someone fell towards you with a weapon, you didn't catch them. Instead, you bat their weapon out of the way and let them fall.

The nature religions and astronomers called this day the Solstice. Night fell earlier and stayed later than the rest of the year. No one celebrated the Solstice. To Humanity it became just another day to train and get stronger to fight the Dragons. Some families of the recruits sent packages in association with their religion's holidays. This was an important celebration time for some. Others called it a time to reflect on the meaninglessness of religion in general and how it divided Humanity before the Dragons attacked.

My mother never celebrated any holidays during this time so I never got into the habit. My uncles felt much the same and they reportedly met some gods in their time. None of which claimed any day on the calendar. Gods want more than just a day to themselves.

When I returned to the bunk after training, however, I saw a big box with a card on top. It read "Walt Gelh" so I left it alone. I climbed up to the top bunk and reclined until Walt came in from the cold. He saw the box upon entering and sighed.

"What's wrong?" I asked. I'd never seen Walt in any mood less than jovial.

"My Dad, he and I used to celebrate the holiday around this time until mom passed."

I paused, and then asked, "How did it happen?"

"I don't really want to talk about it."

"Come on, Walt. We're best friends, we're supposed to be able to share stuff like this."

Walt sighed. "It's just really difficult for me."

"I can tell, look, take your time, it's not a big rush, but just know I'm here for you if you want to get it off of your chest."

I heard Walt move the box to the floor of the bunk room and crash onto the bottom bunk. I heard one thump, then a second thump of his boots. I heard him shuffling on the bed, probably taking off his shirt and trousers then getting under his blanket.

"The town shaman keeps saying that if I talk about the situation it'll make things easier to deal with. I'm not sure if I believe him, but you're right, we are best friends. I should be able to talk to you about something like this."

Walt paused.

"My mom and dad didn't get married until I was nine years old. When they finally did it was a joyous day in the Gelh house. My grandparents were all abuzz on both sides of the family. My mom looked as beautiful as I'd ever seen her. She was a large, Amazonian type of a woman, actually a little bigger than my father, but they loved each other fiercely. They just happened to be poor. Even with my father and mother's army pensions it wasn't enough to afford a marriage right away.

"Anyway, I was staying with my father's parents and those two were going out for a winter expedition by Lake Erie. I think they just wanted to get away from me for a week. I was a hyper kid.

"Two days later, dad comes back to the house and he's dragging mom on a stretcher made from pine tree branches and their tent. The rest of the blankets were wrapped around mom, but she was unresponsive. I ran as fast as I could to the town shaman, who was also doubling as the medic. He came, and treated mom, but she didn't wake up again.

"Later, dad told me what happened. He and mom were in their tent asleep… having their honeymoon… so to speak."

Walt paused again. I heard his voice starting to tear up.

"All of a sudden there was screaming and it wasn't either of them. Dad and mom sprang out of the tent after getting pants on, but dad was cracked in the head with a club right out of the tent. He told me, and he was proud of the fact, that he didn't go out when they hit him, but he was virtually useless at this point. He fell right out of the tent, so mom had time to grab her sword. She was the only woman dad knew who could wield a Claymore sword better than he could. It's actually her sword that I carry now. He let me have it the day I told him I wanted to be in the army.

"The way dad told it, mom was back in her old form. It was like she had never stopped fighting. The attackers just kept coming and she kept fighting. He said it was the most beautiful moment of his life watching mom defend herself. It's hard to be graceful with a Claymore, but she pulled it off. But there were too many of them."

I couldn't see his face, but I could hear the tears streaming through his memories.

"There was a kick. Then a punch. She drove her sword to the hilt through one of them, but the others ganged up on her.

Dad never went into details of what he saw them do to her. He only told me she fought to the end. She killed one with a kick to the balls as two others held her arms back. She killed another by tearing his throat out with her teeth as they held her down on the snowy ground. She didn't stop fighting until one of them pulled the sword out of his comrade and held it to my dad's neck. Dad looked deep into her eyes as they...."

He couldn't say the words. I didn't blame him.

"Finally the group left. Dad lost consciousness briefly, but when he came to he could move again. He checked mom's pulse and she was alive. He made the stretcher out of the branches and tent and wrapped her tight in blankets. He ran with her as fast and as carefully as he could. They were half a day's walk out if they were both mobile, but he crossed that distance in less time.

"When they reached home and the shaman came and went. Dad and I sat with her until the end. We barely slept. We barely ate while we waited to see if she would come around. I had dozed off before the end. When I woke, dad told me the news. He said she never woke up, but right before she died she squeezed his hand as tight as she had ever done."

A meditative silence followed. I let Walt relive his memories alone. I lay on my bunk reliving my own memories of my mother and how she told me she of her rape by a traveling stranger. After a considerable amount of time I asked, "Did your dad ever find out who did it?"

Walt replied, "Not specifically. Dad thinks it was a pack of Symps. He says they were all wearing green and growling, but they weren't tough individually so there is no way they were of supernatural origin. But he told me about the zealotry in their eyes.

"Eventually dad was able to move beyond the attack. But I know he spends an hour of every day thinking about mom. I know he looks at me and sees her sometimes. I know he trained me to be a fighter like they had been together so that if something like this happens and I can stop it, I will. He didn't tell me to hate the Symps, which would have been the natural reaction. I learned that on my own."

I didn't dismount my top bunk to hug him. It wasn't what

he needed me to do. He needed me to absorb this story and embrace him as a brother in the morning when we went back to training. He slept fitfully that night. We both did. When we woke in the morning, Walt returned to his regular smart ass self. I accepted that and I cherished it.

18 — Experience

December 31, 1998

The world changed when the Dragons attacked humanity. Fewer things mattered, but the things that survived the litmus test of importance began to matter more. Holidays were forgotten for the most part, but one holiday that remained was January 1st. New Year's Day.

When someone had a birthday, people said, "Congratulations on another lap around the sun." It was also a day where if someone knew your birthday, they would insist you did not work as hard or at all. Truthfully, birthdays were intended to celebrate the hyper vigilance a Human should keep the rest of the year when concerning the Dragons. Birthdays were meant to be an individual day off so to speak.

New Year's Day on the other hand intends that every Human take a day off, at least in part. The greeting for New Year's again is, "Congratulations to all on another lap around the sun."

The day before New Year's is often the hardest day of the year. For one, it is in the beginnings of winter and that can be singularly difficult. At the fort, the officers made sure the recruits would enjoy the day off the next day by working us extra hard. They assigned twice the calisthenics and twice the combat training. Walt and I still fought at the top of our group, but even we felt the effects of the training.

The snow hadn't ceased making movement difficult, but

we kept at it. Slowly, but surely, the recruits got a handle on snow movement, before long some of us would be ready to serve in the colder regions against Ice Dragons.

Another important aspect of our training involved the discovery of our strengths and the reduction of our weaknesses. For example, Maria knew she would probably not be as strong as her opponent, but there were few that could match her in dexterity and speed. Her focus then became honing her dexterity and speed while improving her strength. Walt's strength put him on the other end of the spectrum, but he lacked finesse. He continued to cultivate his power, but made a concerted effort to be more graceful. My power lay in my skill. My childhood training came from three renowned Hell Bringers who all had cadres of children having equal training. My weakness lay in my inexperience. Being the youngest recruit in the fort was a fact that no one let me forget. My intention was to improve my skill and experience as many things as I could.

Our sore muscles screamed at us as we ate lunch that day. Walt's head lay on his arm as he carefully spooned soup into his mouth. I stayed upright as I sat, even as Maria leaned her head against my left side. Through my exhaustion I felt a tingle somewhere not unfamiliar.

The well insulated mess hall cultivated the burning fires. This allowed for recruits to take off our winter coats. Maria's soft blonde hair lightly brushed my bare arm. The tingle increased. I spooned another mouthful of soup and looked down at her. She ate her own soup slowly, as worn out as the rest of the recruits. I only saw the top of her head and a brief outline of her cheek and nose.

The tingling sensation increased as Maria adjusted her hair on my arm. She turned her head to look up at me as I stared down at her. She said, "JR, your arm is tensing. What's wrong?"

"Nothing," I replied.

"Well cut it out, you're arm is too muscle-y, you're bouncing my head all around," she said with a smile.

"Sorry," I answered.

She turned her head back to her soup, but slid her right arm under my left and wrapped her right hand around my left elbow as if to steady me. The feeling of her touch was electric and the tingling sensation I felt below the table grew. I rarely touched Maria, or any girl for that matter, and it was not unpleasant.

I started to feel my pulse race as if I were still fighting. My pulse, however, manifested elsewhere than in my arms or legs. It became more difficult to sit comfortably. My mind raced, but I kept a mostly relaxed exterior as I ate my soup.

Certainly I thought about the soft touch of Maria's hair and her fingers wrapped lightly around my elbow, but I also considered Rebecca and our previous flirtation as well as the general disdain she felt for me now. Part of me even remembered Diana and the unrecognized, but requited attraction she claimed for me.

I shifted in my seat again and Maria looked up at me. "JR, are you sure there isn't something wrong? You're all antsy all of a sudden, that isn't like you."

Walt had taken notice and raised his head from the table. "JR, are you alright man?"

I looked at Walt and I felt my cheeks grow hotter. I didn't often blush, but if I wasn't blushing it was a miracle.

Walt looked down at Maria's hand curled around my elbow and he understood. He said, "Oh... JR is fine. He's just having a moment."

"Walt," I started.

"What kind of a moment?" Maria asked.

At that instant, I saw Rebecca approaching.

She stopped at our table. She said to Walt, "Lieutenant Kingsley wants to see you in his office after your meal." She turned to me, "You too."

"Th-thank you Rebecca," I said.

"Whatever, Gerstung." She turned angrily and left.

Maria asked, "What's her problem?"

I explained, "She's mad at me since I accidentally eavesdropped on a serious conversation she had with her ex-boyfriend. He proposed and she told him no and when they came around the corner they saw me. He threatened me. She shunned me and has pretty much avoided me since then."

"How do you accidentally eavesdrop?" Maria asked.

"I just wanted to make sure she was okay."

Walt chimed in, "He had a thing for Rebecca for a while and thought she might have had a thing back."

Maria smiled coyly. "Do you still have a thing for Rebecca?"

I groaned. "Not so much. I mean, I would still like to be her friend, but I can't really press the issue. I'm here to learn to fight. I can't let myself be distracted by... things."

"Love?" Maria asked.

"Yeah, I suppose," I replied.

Walt smiled. "Other things too."

Maria looked at him and then back at me. "What is he talking about?"

I glared at Walt. I could feel my cheeks heating up. I could also feel the tingle below the table. "Nothing."

Walt laughed. "Yeah, nothing."

Maria looked at me puzzled. "What is he talking about?"

"I..."

Walt grinned ear to ear, but had presence of mind to lean over the table and whisper in Maria's ear.

She looked down at the bulge in my trousers and then back up at me. She smiled. "That's nothing to be ashamed of."

My cheeks blazed with Dragon fire!

Maria's hand moved from my left elbow down over my left thigh to my left knee. "Don't worry, I consider it a compliment."

No woman had ever touched me like that before. I didn't know what to do, but my body definitely reacted without any guidance from me.

Maria's eyes met mine. She smiled deeply and removed her hand from my leg. She turned her attention to the last of her soup. Walt looked at me grinning like he had just stolen something then turned his attention to the remainder of his soup. I took one deep breath. Two deep breaths. Three deep breaths. Finally the tingling sensation went away and my reflex subsided. I, too, returned to my soup.

When I could stand up safely without fear of other recruits seeing my compromised state I got more soup and some bread to go with it. This certainly wasn't the first time I'd ever had an erection. I knew what was happening, but it was easily the first time anyone else had ever been in a position to notice. This is what I meant by having as many experiences as I could and this wasn't an entirely unpleasant one.

Walt and I walked in the cold to Kingsley's office after lunch. Even inside the fort the fog lingered, but we knew well the offices throughout the compound so we didn't get lost.

Our coats clung to our bodies. We noticed Chen walking towards the office. Walt and I looked at each other and then back to our destination. The three of us reached the office at the same time and entered. Rebecca was already in the office. Kingsley was not.

Walt spoke, "So where is the man?"

Rebecca replied sharply, "He'll be here soon. Quiet."

Moments later Kingsley entered. We stood at attention and waited. Kingsley said, "At ease" and we relaxed.

Kingsley sat in his chair and smiled at the four of us. "I always like this time. It gives me the chance to give select recruits the simultaneously best and worst news they have ever heard.

"While it isn't finalized yet, your instructors tell me you four recruits are doing an amazing job in your workouts and in your combat training."

Kingsley paused, for effect I'm sure. "Chen, Gelh, Kingsley and Gerstung, you four are on the trajectory to be trained as Hell Bringers."

19 — A Beautiful Night

December 31, 1998

Walt and I stood on the fast track to greatness.

After afternoon training, we changed into unsoiled, sweat-free clothes in our bunk. Every New Year, the fort held a banquet for the recruits and officers. The Hell Bringers were highly respected members of the warrior class. Walt and I already told Maria and a few other random recruits. By the time we reached the gathering the group was abuzz with talk of Hell Bringers.

Lance Robbins congratulated us. "Hey recruits! I just heard about your good news. It'll be good to have you at my side training to be the best."

"Thanks Lance," I replied.

Walt just nodded and half smiled.

Lance quickly turned his attention elsewhere and walked away. Walt remarked, "Is it me, or does there seem to be something off about Lance?"

"I don't know what you're talking about. He's never been anything, but nice to me," I said.

"Yeah, me too. That's what I'm saying. Everyone has bad days, except Lance. Everyone yells and bitches and is generally unpleasant at one time or another, but not Lance."

"Maybe he's an eternal optimist," I said.

"Maybe. I just get a bad feeling around Lance." Walt said.

"Well, don't let your bad feeling ruin our night. We have a lot to do before midnight."

"Like what?" Walt asked, thankful for the distraction.

I gestured to the crowd. "There must be at least one female recruit you haven't tried to sleep with eh?"

Walt considered carefully. "Well, there might be one."

We walked through the crowd. Recruits danced to the music by Jeweled Ram. I saw Crush out of the corner of my eye, but he was busy talking to a female recruit. Chen smiled leaning against a post, but not engaged with anyone. Rebecca stood near her father as per usual. I looked for Maria as I scanned the crowd. I lost Walt along the way, probably to lust. I didn't see Maria even with torches posted every 10 feet though out the fort congregation area.

I wandered away from the crowd. I've never been much for parties. I made my way to Maria's bunk and knocked on her door. "Maria, are you there?"

No answer. I tried to peek between wooden bars. The dark insulation prevented my sight. I shrugged and walked toward my own bunk. I felt tired. Everyone tended to gather around midnight to wish one another a Happy New Year, usually with a midnight kiss. I had no reason to stay awake.

I opened my bunk door and saw the back of Maria. I stopped. "Maria? What are you doing here?"

She turned. "I was waiting for you. I was beginning to think you weren't coming."

I closed the bunk door and stepped closer. "How long were you waiting?"

"Not long really. I was just tired of the party."

"Yeah. Me too." I didn't know what else to say.

"Which bunk is yours?" Maria asked.

"The top." I said.

Maria smiled and climbed up into my bunk. I just watched her. Correction. I intently watched her. The tingle I felt earlier returned.

"Are you coming?" Maria asked.

"Not yet," I said under my breath.

"What?"

"Umm yes I'll be right up." I said. I climbed carefully up

into the bunk.

I slid under the blankets with her. My legs shook. I lay awkwardly next to Maria. I felt her breath moving the air around me.

I said, "So not that I'm complaining, but what really brought you here."

"Well, the tradition is you spend the turn of midnight of New Years Eve with the person you want the most. Right?"

"You've never struck me as someone who adheres to traditions."

"Only the traditions I agree with," Maria said.

I smiled. "Lucky me."

Maria laughed. "I think you're a very handsome young man. But I'll let you know, I'm not seducing you tonight, not that I'm not interested, but you're too young."

I wasn't offended. "I'm almost 17."

Maria smiled. "It isn't really your age that is my concern, although that factors in." Maria paused. "Sex is difficult terrain to traverse if you do not know what you're getting into. You don't want to just jump in."

I chuckled. "Well, I didn't figure on any jumping."

Maria laughed. "It depends on what kind of sex you are having. Just don't be impatient about sex. When it happens for you I hope it is the most beautiful moment in your life."

I replied, "This is one of the most beautiful moments in my life."

Maria put a finger to my lips. "Thank you, now shush."

She curled her body against mine. She lay on her left side and I lay facing her on my right. Her left hand touched my heart. My left arm draped over her and my left hand drew her as close as we could get without suffocating one another.

I watched Maria's closed eyes. She snored softly. I couldn't sleep. I pondered her. She was one of the most beautiful women I had ever seen. I felt privileged to have her next to me. I closed my eyes in quasi-contentment.

My eyes snapped open as I heard people cheering. My eyes caught Maria's. She said, "We should go out and celebrate with the rest of them."

We exited my bunk room and joined the fringes of the

group. I caught a glimpse of Walt standing with two recruits, one I recognized from the day I met Maria and another brand new woman.

We watched the giant clock in the fort. The count down began.

"10!" I wrapped my left arm around Maria.

"9!" She wrapped her arm around my waist.

"8!" My right arm enveloped her.

"7!" My head turned down to her.

"6!" Maria's head turned up to me.

"5!" We seemed to look through each other.

"4!" Our faces drew closer to one another.

"3!" We smiled.

"2!" Out of the corner of my eye, about 10 feet away I saw Rebecca staring at us.

"1!" The momentum in my lips met Maria's.

My eyes didn't close. I saw Rebecca's face grow redder. She turned away and I lost sight of her.

"Happy New Year!"

January 1, 1999

I softly broke the kiss with Maria. We smiled at each other. The back of my mind churned thinking about Rebecca. Did she come to apologize and try to patch things up with me? Why did she wait until that moment when I was with Maria? I shook my head.

Maria asked, "What's the matter?"

I said, "Just amazed that I could bring a New Year in so well."

Maria smiled. "Me too."

The party started dying down slowly, but surely. I knew Walt probably wouldn't be back in until dawn which was fine with me.

I led Maria back to my bunk and we returned to snuggling beneath my blankets, this time with fewer clothes. I wore my usual sleeping attire, rabbit fur trousers and no shirt. Maria disrobed down to a cotton halter top and she borrowed a pair of my soft leather shorts.

Maria turned her back to me and I pressed my chest against her back. Under the guise of putting my hand on her heart I briefly caressed Maria's breasts. She didn't seem to mind, but I didn't go further than that. I was surprisingly tired and Maria felt comfortable in my arms.

I awoke a few hours later, but Maria was gone. She left a note for me.

JR,

Thank you for a beautiful night. I think it is better for the both of us if we cool off for a while. Please don't take it the wrong way. I cherish your friendship. I don't intend to stop hanging around with you and Walt unless you ask it of me. The way I feel about you and the way you feel about me will just distract us from the reason we are here, to fight the Dragons to make Humanity safe. You are almost a Hell Bringer now, this is what you should focus on and as your friend this is what I should support you in.

I'll see you at the table for meals or in the field for training. You are destined for greatness. I just know it.

Your friend,
Maria

I put down the letter and sighed. I knew she was right, but the letter felt so wrong. I closed my eyes and turned my head into the pillow to take in her scent again. I knew I wasn't in love with her, seeing Rebecca red faced and caring was my proof of that. However Maria and I spent a beautiful night together. I felt like Maria and I could have had something if we could cultivate it.

Sigh. I opened my eyes and lay on my back in the bunk looking at the ceiling not far above me. I was on my way to becoming a Hell Bringer and I couldn't let anything distract me.

20 — Birthday 1999

January 18, 1999

It was my 17th birthday. I wasn't a celebrity around the fort or anything, but a vast majority of the people knew who I was and congratulated me on another lap around the sun. Early that morning, my uncles showed up to the fort to a mixed welcome of recruits who knew them as the Courageous Gerstung Brothers and the ones who didn't know their asses from holes in the ground. I sent post to my uncles telling them of my inability to leave the fort due to my probation. Instead they brought their wives and children to the fort to visit me. Uncle Max said they tried to get my mother to come with them, but she could not get away.

Walt and Maria took a brief break in their training to see the commotion. Civilians rarely came to the fort. The families of most recruits did not make the trek even from Bellato for birthdays. Lieutenant Kingsley joined Walt, Maria and me waiting at the gates as soon as the guards noticed the group of Gerstungs approaching.

Uncle Oli led the way as usual. It wasn't a particularly treacherous mile between Bellato and Fort Kingsley so no one held their weapons, however Gerstungs exist with a sense of readiness. At last my family entered. Most of the recruits stopped and saw them walk into the double reinforced doors of the fort.

I smiled and strode quickly to my uncles. We shook hands and hugged strongly. I noticed Lexie and Jack were enamored with the amount of equipment and all of the people who were staring at them. I crouched down to the two girls playfully. "Now, you had better be careful. We have a lot of mean soldiers here who will beat you up if you get in their way."

Lexie responded, "Our daddies will kick their butts if they try."

Jack chimed in, "I'll kick their butts if they try."

"Good girls," I said and straightened up.

Ajax approached me. His broad shoulders brushed against mine. "So cousin, I'm going to be a recruit soon. I've got everything ready. I'm just waiting for 18."

"You'll be joining up just as I reach one year," I said. I clapped his shoulder. "It'll be good to have another Gerstung in the fort."

Maxwell Junior build was wirier than his cousin seemed less interested in the fighting and more about the architecture. I asked, "Max, are you coming in at 17 so you can have Ajax as a buddy?"

Max Junior replied, "I'm not sure if I'll be ready." It felt like he wanted to say something else, but he kept it to himself.

Ajax said derisively, "Max doesn't want to fight. He wants to be a builder."

I nodded. "Building is important. Without buildings we wouldn't have this kind of protection from the Dragons. But I think learning to fight isn't a bad idea either."

Max Junior responded, "I know how to fight."

Uncle Max said, "I'll support my son in whatever he wants to do with his life: soldier; builder; painter; or wizard. I only want him to contribute to Humanity in a positive way."

Max Junior replied, "Thanks dad."

Uncle Oli said, "So show us around. We haven't been at the fort in a while."

I turned to face Lieutenant Kingsley. "Well, here is my Lieutenant. You all know him."

Lieutenant Kingsley shook hands and embraced my uncles. When Ajax shook his hand he said, "It is an honor to meet you sir, I only hope I can become as great of a warrior as you are."

Kingsley replied with a smile, "I admire your passion, but

don't be in such a hurry to grow up."

I turned to Walt and Maria. "These are two of my friends, Walt and Maria."

Walt and Maria shook hands with my uncles. Maria smiled at the girls who gathered around her commenting on how pretty she was. I hadn't really looked at Maria since New Year Eve. I hadn't avoided her. I just kept my eyes to themselves.

Kingsley said, "Okay recruits. Get back to training. You can schmooze after you're done for the day. Hop to it." Kingsley paused. "And Oliver, Maxwell, Zachary, it is great to see you again. Have your nephew bring you to the office later today and we'll catch up."

"Sure thing," Oli replied.

Walt and Maria went back to the other trainees who had long since lost interest in us. Kingsley started back towards his office.

Lexie tugged on my left hand. I looked down at her. Her brown hair extended down her back. She pointed at Maria. "Is that girl your girlfriend?"

I shook my head. "Nope. She's just my friend."

Lexie said, "You should make her your girlfriend. She's pretty."

I said, "I don't have time for a girlfriend right now. I have to train hard so I can keep the world safe."

Lexie said with a smile in her blue eyes, "You should make time."

It's hard to argue with the logic of a seven year old.

I showed my family around the fort. They saw my bunk. They saw the various training areas. I took them around the offices. When we reached Kingsley's office, my uncles said they were going in to talk to him and the kids should go burn off some energy in the training areas. My aunts had no interested in burning off energy so I escorted them to the mess hall which was quiet since it wasn't a meal time.

We sat down where I usually sat with Walt and Maria. Jessica, Oli's wife, sat next to me. Jennifer, Max's wife, and Jane, Zack's wife, sat across from us.

"You know JR, it's a tradition for us Aunties to coddle you and whatnot for your birthday," Jessica said as she pulled back her graying blond hair.

I smiled. "Yes, I remember the story. You three were there with my mother from the beginning to the end of her labor. You brought me kicking and screaming into the world."

Jennifer's salt and pepper hair hung shoulder length. She said, "There wasn't really much screaming on your part. You were certainly surprised to be out in the cold world, but you weren't upset right away."

Jane's fire red hair was cropped short. "As a baby you were pretty well acclimated to life from day one. Of course, when you were hungry or wet you bitched and complained like any other baby would."

"I can only imagine," I said. "You know, this is my first birthday on my own and yet, I'm still not on my own. I still have you all, my family, here to support me. I just wish I could see my mother."

Jessica said, "We tried to get her to come. She responded to our letters, but she insisted she couldn't leave."

Jennifer offered, "You'll go to see her when your one year leave comes right?"

I said, "Yes, that's my intention."

Jane said, "You'll have to be careful, Aurora says the village is still talking about you and it isn't a good thing."

I said, "I'll just have to straighten them out."

The door to the mess hall opened and there stood Rebecca. She immediately looked embarrassed. My aunts all looked at her softly. I looked away briefly then back at her.

"Oh, um, hi… Gerstung. I didn't know you were going to be here."

I stuttered. "Uh, yeah. Reb-Kingsley, these are my aunts. It's my birthday so they are here with the rest of my family to celebrate with me."

"Yeah, I saw them come in. Happy Birthday."

"Thanks. What are you doing here?"

"I just was passing through the mess hall. Sorry to interrupt you. Have a good day ma'ams. Congratulations on another lap around the sun, Gerstung."

I could barely get a thank you before Rebecca crossed the mess hall to the other door exit. There was no strategic reason for her to come through the mess hall.

"She seems nice," Jennifer said.

"Yeah, she doesn't like me," I said.

"Oh, she likes you," Jane corrected.

Jessica chimed in, "Definitely. This was no accident. She was trying to catch you alone."

I asked, "How do you know?"

Jennifer replied, "The look on her face to see you not alone in the mess hall. She probably had something she wanted to say to you."

This wasn't a conversation I wanted to have.

Later in the day my family prepared to leave. It was getting dark and the winter had not let up. Everyone was bundled to go.

I embraced everyone from youngest to oldest. Lexie whispered in my ear about making Maria my girlfriend. Jack said she was going to beat my record at becoming the youngest recruit in Fort Kingsley. Buck hugged me and told me I was his role model. Anita took the stance of a disaffected youth and groaned when I hugged her. Arthur stopped me from hugging him and instead insisted on a handshake. Tobias clapped my shoulder as we shook hands. Max Junior shook my hand without words, but I could feel some hesitance in his grip. Ajax grabbed me and hugged me tight. His hug was overwhelming as he stood taller and wider than me. He expressed his jealousy of me for the umpteenth time this visit and said would see me in April.

My three aunts hugged me in tandem. They reminded me that Rebecca had something to talk to me about and they would give my mother my love.

My uncles congratulated me on being on the track to become a Hell Bringer. The only words of wisdom they imparted on me: "Grow eyes in the back of your head."

I walked my family out of the fort and the guards closed the doors behind them. I turned to head back to my bunk. Rebecca stood 10 feet away from me. She definitely had something to say.

21 — Another Experience

The day began just like any other day. The morning felt chilly, but the day promised to be a beautiful one. The sun already cleared the horizon. I saw no clouds in the sky.

My group of recruits prepared for our leave of absence in three days. I planned to walk to Bellato, stay an hour or so with my uncles, then walk to my mother's. I would stay two days with her and then I would walk back.

When you eavesdropped on me and Christofer I was so upset. I never wanted to see you again. And I stuck to that as hard as I could. You have no idea how bad you upset me John Ross.

Rebecca's words to me after my family left on my birthday. We had a short talk with poignant words exchanged.

Then I saw you with Maria... and I don't know. Something changed. I don't want to say it was jealousy, but maybe it was.

I went over our discussion in my head for months. I never expected someone like Rebecca to be jealous of anything, especially not jealous of a woman with whom I spent time.

Then finally I saw you kissing her on New Years Eve and then you took her back to your bunk for gods knows what.

Nothing happened, we just cuddled, I said.

It doesn't matter. It isn't my business. But that's when I knew I had to tell you this.

Everyday I honed my sword blade, or I sanded my wooden training sword to keep it strong and smooth, or tighten my bow strings. Doing these manual labor tasks gave me time to think and reflect on Rebecca's words.

I want to be friends again. Maybe I want to be more than that. I feel something for you that feels deeper than what I felt for Christofer. The stories we've shared with each other about our lives. We've only scratched the surface of what could be. I don't know what it could be. If nothing else I want to at least have you as a regular part of my life outside of training.

I always smile at this point. I smile in the memory and in my reflection of this memory.

I don't want you to feel like you have to give up Maria as a friend. I know how much she means to you. I just want to be included in your circle of friends.

It's more of a triangle right now, I said jokingly. *You can make it a square of friends.*

Rebecca laughed with me.

I heard something, a popping sound, and then another pop. I didn't recognize the sound. I put my sword down and stepped out of my bunk room. The sun shone directly into the doorway so at first it was hard to see. I heard screaming.

I shielded my eyes from the sun and saw two black clad men holding shotguns.

Firearms grew largely out of vogue since regular ammunition did not pierce Dragon scales and Dragon's Bane melted at combustible temperature. That isn't to say firearms became extinct unfortunately.

I watched in shock. People ran from the gunmen. The blonde gunman lowered his shotgun and pulled out a handgun. He took aim and fired twice and two people fell. The black haired gunman continued firing at whoever was close enough. He stopped and reloaded.

I had to do something. There was no way I could rush them, they would take me down with their guns. I slunk back into my bunk and grabbed my bow and quiver of arrows. I crouched down and ran towards them making sure to keep cover around me. I pulled an arrow and nocked it. I peeked over one of the barriers we used for shooting targets or throwing spears. I saw the gunmen as they moved from one bunk to the next. They fired at the doors and never bothered to open them. I needed to be closer for accuracy on such small targets. I crouched back down and moved to another closer barrier. I looked again. Still out of range. The gunmen continued their assault.

Frustrated, I crouched again and ran towards them, this time the barrier was much smaller. When I reached it, I thought they might have caught a glimpse of me because they turned and started to where I crouched.

"I think someone's there," one gunman said to the other.

"We'll fix that bastard."

I rolled out from behind the barrier to my right, their left, and took aim. My first arrow missed, but I kept running around them firing one arrow after another at them until I ducked behind a larger barrier.

"You hurt?" one gunman asked the other.

"Just a graze."

"He's behind that board."

"Blast his ass."

I crouched again as the shot blew a hole in the wood right where my head had been. I held my breath and stepped out in a crouch. I aimed and fired hitting the blonde gunman in the chest.

The black haired gunman fired, but I rolled back behind the barrier. He fired twice more close to the ground blowing two holes in the wood where I would have been breaths earlier.

"Harry?" the remaining gunman said.

No response.

I heard him reload the shotgun. I only had one arrow remaining in my quiver. The shotgun blasted another hole in the bottom of the barrier next to the two it already blasted in pursuit of me. The barrier creaked and then fell down on top of me. The oak wood weight was crushing, but I tried to wriggle out from beneath it. I was able to get my head out, but the black haired gunman waved his shotgun barrel in front of my eyes.

"You killed Harry, you son of a bitch."

My trapped hands couldn't push the barrier off of my chest. I couldn't move.

"I ought to open your head like a can of beans."

The gunman cocked his shotgun. He brought the barrel to

rest right in between my eyes. I could feel the warm metal as it rested on my forehead. I didn't close my eyes.

"You killed Harry," he said.

"How many people have you killed? And for what?"

"I welcome our new Dragon overlords, you should too."

"I'll never do that. So you may as well kill me."

"Gladly–"

I heard a wet sound. I didn't comprehend at first, and neither did the black haired gunman. As the shotgun moved from my forehead my eyes could focus, and they saw the javelin sticking halfway through his body.

The black haired gunman crumpled down to his knees then onto his left side. The javelin went so far through his body it almost poked my eye out. I could see the slow drip of blood coming from the tip.

I tried to push the barrier off of me, but I couldn't budge it. I felt exhausted, not physically so much as emotionally. Getting shot at takes its toll on a person.

The javelin drew back from the gunman's body. I looked up and saw Kingsley standing and holding the javelin carefully.

A couple of the other sergeants rushed to me and lifted the barrier off of me. I still didn't feel I could move. I didn't want to move. The sergeants called for a stretcher. They removed my quiver from my back and loaded me onto the stretcher. They carried me to the infirmary and carefully laid me on an uncomfortable mattress. They covered me with a cotton blanket and a bearskin throw blanket. Anguished cries came from the others in the infirmary, but I didn't make a sound. I wasn't hurt, not really.

I want to be friends again. Maybe I want to be more than that. I feel something for you.... We've only scratched the surface of what could be. ... I want to at least have you as ... part of my life....

I smiled, remembering my conversation with Rebecca, as I passed out in exhaustion.

I regained consciousness a couple hours later. The rest of the infirmary lay unconscious now, they must have been sedated. I wiggled my toes to make sure they were still alive. My fingers worked like normal. My legs. My arms. I breathed like normal.

I was sore, but alive.

Slowly, I sat up in the bed. I swung my legs off of the side and moved my neck. The nurse saw me rising and said in his deep voice, "Hey, be careful. You have just been through a traumatizing experience."

"I'm fine. Where is everyone?"

"Everyone who is hurt is here. A wagon just left for Bellato with the more serious cases."

"What do you mean more serious cases?"

22 — Aftermath

Harry Erickson. Kyle Diebold. Dragon Sympathizers. They mounted an attack on Fort Kingsley. They killed twelve recruits and one sergeant. They injured twenty five recruits and officers. I didn't know any of the recruits or the sergeant they killed. But they shot Maria in the arm.

Maria lay in the infirmary unconscious and I sat next to her. The bullet passed cleanly through her arm and the bleeding stopped. Walt and Rebecca occasionally came by to check on us. They brought food when meal times came and I ate, but I didn't want to leave Maria's side. I felt responsible for her injury. Maybe if I had been quicker and gotten to the gunmen faster I could have stopped them from hurting her. I didn't share this concern with anyone else. I just held Maria's hand as she breathed in and out.

Maria regained consciousness at dusk. Her eyes opened slowly and she smiled when she saw me. "Hi JR."

"Hey sweetheart. How are you feeling?"

Her brows furrowed. "Not good. What happened? I remember the guys with guns."

I reassured her. "They are gone now. It's over."

"Good. Glad to see you're okay."

"Do you want anything?"

"Hamburger. Painkillers."

I smiled. "I'll see what I can do."

I leaned over her and kissed her forehead. "You rest and I'll go see about getting you something to eat."

"Thank you. Love you JR."

"I love you too Maria."

I walked first to the nurse's station and informed her of Maria's wakefulness and request for painkillers. Then I made my way to the mess hall. I peeked into the training area, but saw no one there. All the recruits congregated in the mess hall. I saw Walt, Rebecca and Chen sitting together. Recruits talked in hushed tones. This was not a normal day.

I smiled at Walt and Rebecca, but I didn't stop. I continued to the kitchen window and asked about getting a hamburger for Maria. I received a confirmation. The cook told me to come back in five minutes. I walked back to Walt and Rebecca. I sat down next to Chen. I felt eyes on me from across the mess hall. I looked around and everyone stared at me.

I turned my head back to my friends and said, "Why… is everyone staring?"

Walt said, "Well, you're kind of a hero buddy."

"Me? I just did what anyone else would have done."

"But no one did," Walt said. "I heard talk of giving you a medal of valor."

"Wow, I hope not. I just took out a Symp. It's not a big deal."

Rebecca spoke, "It really is Gerstung. When everyone else cowered, you stepped up and fought."

I didn't feel like a hero. I felt sore. My ribs ached and my back hurt. My forehead could still feel the press of the warm shotgun.

"Maybe if I'd been faster or a better aim, no one would have gotten killed."

Walt replied, "No one could have known it was going to happen. They took out the two door guards before they could sound the alarm. From there it was just their whims. They had this planned out. Someone told them that the recruits would be in the yard, but not ready to fight back. Someone had the intel and passed it on to them. Everyone has suspicions, you know mine."

I knew Walt was trying to distract me. He hadn't let up on thinking about Lance as a Dragon Sympathizer. I kept it to myself, but I was beginning to come around. Lance and I never had any animosity, but it did seem convenient that Lance wasn't hurt and that he didn't try to stop them, considering that he was supposedly the top recruit in the fort.

The cook poked his head out of the kitchen window at me with the hamburger prepared. I stood. "You guys take care of yourselves. I'm going to sit with Maria. Feel free to spend time with us, but no talk of the attack around her. I'm not sure of her state right now."

My friends nodded. The cook packed the hamburger in a paper bag and thanked me as I took the bag. I walked back out of the mess hall feeling the eyes of every recruit on me.

I walked the dark fort. Only the torches in the training yard illuminated anything. I have always had decent night vision. I made my way back to Maria. I saw her sitting up and talking to someone. Lance Robbins.

I walked closer inconspicuously.

I said, "What are you doing here Lance?"

He replied, "Hey Gerstung. I'm just visiting here with Ms Ward. She looked lonely."

I stepped closer. "I was getting her something to eat. I'll take it from here, thanks."

"Whoa, Gerstung. What's the matter?"

I growled. "You. You told the Symps what they needed to know to come in and attack the fort. Didn't you?"

Lance's face curled into a frown. "I don't know what you're talking about. You're obviously traumatized."

"Yeah, maybe I am, but you don't seem to have a problem at all with what happened."

"Gerstung, look, I'm trying to keep a brave face here. No one feels this attack harder than me. I've already asked Kingsley if I can take a group of recruits to the Symp camp and destroy them."

"So you know where the Symp camp is huh? And just how do you know that? The Symps are secretive. Only someone in cahoots with the Symps would know."

Lance paused. "Gerstung, you've got me all wrong. So I'm going to go until you cool off. I'm sorry Maria."

Maria said nothing as Lance walked away.

I sat next to Maria and put the hamburger next to her. She looked at me. "Why did you have to be so rude to Lance? He was just here offering me some support."

"Don't you think it's fishy that he was gone during the one day the supply caravan was attacked. The same supply caravan that you risked your life trying to find. Then this attack happens and he is nowhere to be seen until the smoke clears."

"Well not everyone can be a hero like you JR. Don't hold that against him. They had guns."

"Shit, Maria. I'm not a hero. I'm just... shit."

Maria touched my hand. "Don't worry about it. You're probably just stressed. What did you bring me?"

"Hamburger."

Maria smiled. "Thank you."

Maria ate in silence.

Later Walt, Rebecca and Chen joined us. They sat around Maria with me. Occasionally we spoke, but not about anything important.

The fort doctor came to check on Maria. She checked Maria's injured left arm. She asked Maria to move it. Maria was unable to move her arm below the shoulder. She couldn't flex her bicep or tricep.

The doctor marked this on her clipboard and told Maria that after she had regained some of her strength she would try again. It could just be shock related immobility.

Small tears made their way down Maria's cheeks. "What if I can't move my arm? What will happen to me?"

I looked at Walt. He looked back at me. Rebecca had the most knowledge of fort procedures. "Maria, if your arm doesn't regain its function, you'll probably have to leave the army. The Human Army cannot allow someone to fight Dragons when they aren't as close to 100% as possible."

Maria closed her eyes. She didn't sob, but tears continued falling down her cheeks. I squeezed her right hand and she squeezed my hand back. She said, "I don't want to leave the fort. You all are like family to me. Except you Chen, I don't really know you. No offense."

Chen replied, "No offense."

Maria said, "I didn't even make it through a year. How

pathetic."

We consoled her. I had to find a way to make sense of this tragedy. Thirteen people killed, 25 people injured including Maria. I just knew Lance was responsible. He seemed too smooth. No one else could be that smooth after this attack, not even the officers. I understood what Walt thought when it came to Lance.

Just before midnight Walt, Rebecca and Chen left to return to their bunks. Workers tried to patch up the doors and walls of the bunks, but they were exhausted. So breathed an exhausted sigh, but I didn't want to leave Maria.

She opened her eyes briefly. "Go to bed JR. I'll be fine I promise. Bring me some eggs in the morning."

I smiled. "Yes ma'am I will."

I stood and stretched as Maria drifted back off to sleep and headed out of the infirmary. I was met with Kingsley's unhappy face. We stood staring into one another's eyes for more than a minute without words.

Finally, he said, "You need to come to my office. We have to talk."

23 — Suspicion

Kingsley led me to his office. He closed the door behind me, though at just after midnight I doubted we would see anyone skulking about. He sat and instructed me to do the same.

"Gerstung, I know these past two days have been difficult for you. Was that the first time you killed a man?"

"Yes sir."

"Compound that with Recruit Ward getting hurt, you probably are feeling pretty low lately."

"Yes sir."

"Tomorrow you go on your seven day leave. I will allow you to take an extra few days off to help you recuperate from whatever shock you might be feeling."

"Sir?"

"I figure you're planning to go back to Meton. Don't rush back right away. The trip isn't short."

"Are you trying to get rid of me sir?"

"No, Recruit, of course not. I want you to be at top physical and mental form when you return. You're going to be a Hell Bringer, son. You have to figure out how to shed whatever guilt or pain you might be feeling from killing that man. He was a misguided fool, but he was still a Human and it can't be easy."

"No sir."

Kingsley pulled out a calendar book. He opened it and flipped a few pages. "So instead of coming back April 30th, I want you back May 5th. That will give you five extra days to think over what has happened. I don't know if that will be enough time, but I think you'll be able to come around faster than most."

I sighed. I didn't know if I could ever get over killing someone.

Kingsley stood and I did as well. He approached me and put a hand on each of my shoulders.

I really hope you do move past it kid. We're going to need you.

I shook my head.

"What's wrong Gerstung?"

"Nothing, sir."

I turned and reached for the door. I stopped and turned back. "Permission to speak freely sir?"

"Go ahead."

"I think Lance Robbins is a Dragon Sympathizer."

"Excuse me?"

"Recruit Lance Robbins. I don't know what it is about him, but something rubs me the wrong way. He's a nice guy, but I feel like there is something sinister beneath that."

How did he get onto Robbins so quickly?

"Recruit Gerstung, Robbins has been training here as a Hell Bringer. I don't make mistakes like this about people I choose to be Hell Bringers. I chose you didn't I?"

"Yes sir, but..."

"No buts Gerstung. Robbins is solid."

"Yes sir." I turned to leave.

"Gerstung, wait."

I stopped, but I didn't turn. "Yes sir."

"The doctor told me that Recruit Ward will be unlikely to recover right away. She posits there may be some nerve damage to Ward's arm. You are tasked with escorting Recruit Ward to her home in Bellato when you leave tomorrow."

"Yes sir."

"Dismissed."

"Thank you, sir."

I exited and closed the door behind me.

I walked through the dark, chilly spring morning. I

reached my bunk and looked around. Only the moon shone overhead illuminating the growing grass inside the fort training area, the recruits long since extinguished the torches. I thought I heard foot steps. I turned and put the door at my back.

I only felt the first punch in my left temple.

I stumbled to my right and turned my head. There was no one there.

I said, "This is going to turn out badly for you... whoever you are."

I turned my head to the right, but held up my left forearm to block the attack from that direction. I shot out a right and left punch and hit torso with both punches. I threw a left kick at my attacker, but whoever it was dodged. I only saw a shadow. A stocking mask covered the face. I threw a right punch at the shadow, but it dodged.

The shadow tried to kick me, but I caught its foot with my right hand. I pulled the shadow close to me and I grabbed it with a bear hug. I delivered a head butt to the shadow and hit something that felt like a chin. I heard a groan. I tried another head butt, but the shadow jabbed fingers in my eyes. I cried out in pain and had to release the bear hug.

I fell to one knee swatting outwardly at wherever I thought I heard the shadow. I heard a bunk door open.

"JR! What happened?"

"Walt?"

"Yeah man, it's me."

"Someone attacked me. He was wearing a mask, I didn't see his face, he jabbed me in the eyes while we fought."

"Dirty fighter."

I rubbed at my eyes.

"Do you want me to take you to the infirmary?"

"No, no. It wasn't that deep. Just guide me to my bunk."

Walt did so. I climbed up into the bunk and groaned.

Walt asked, "Who do you think it was?"

I said, "I have no idea honestly. Of course I have a suspicion, but no confirmation."

"Robbins?"

"Yeah. Lance Robbins."

"Do you need anything?"

"An ice pack."

"I'll get you one."

I heard the door open and close. Minutes later Walt returned. He handed me an ice pack and I put it over my eyes. The cool compress was soothing. I hoped it would keep down the swelling. I fell asleep quickly.

I awoke a few hours later and my injured eyes no longer hurt. I remarked to myself that Walt gave me some magic ice or something, but he already left the bunk so I couldn't share this insight with him.

I exited the bunk and stretched. The sun warmed up the ground and air to a comfortable temperature. Recruits trained, but no sergeants instructed them. I needed to find Lance Robbins' bunk.

This posed a problem. Fort Kingsley is composed of four walls each a mile across. An average of 50 recruits is enlisted to Fort Kingsley every month. These recruits stay for a total of 24 months. Fort Kingsley is equipped to house these recruits for their stay. This means there are about 1200 recruits at Fort Kingsley. This means there are 600 bunks to explore along the sides of the fort with 300 10 feet wide bunks per side. While these bunks are numbered, the names of the cadets are not branded on them. I didn't know which bunk belonged to Lance Robbins.

I looked at the vast number of bunk doors on my side and across the fort. The East Gate stood open in exactly in the middle of the mile wide side. Guards stood watch with bows and arrows. The lesser used West Gate was only opened in cases of evacuation. It stood parallel to the East Gate and provided the division between the mess hall on the Northwest corner and the infirmary on the Southwest corner. Officer living quarters were on the North wall, sergeant offices were against the South Wall.

I remembered the gunmen fired at the doors of the bunks without opening them. They started along the North Wall, but they didn't get to the South Wall before Kingsley and I killed them. If I found any bunk doors that didn't have holes in them, I could be looking at Lance Robbins' bunk. Either that or he has a bunk on the South Wall.

I began my search at 300N, the bunk on the furthest

Northeast corner. Holes. 299N. Holes. I continued down the line. Holes, holes, holes. One door being repaired. No holes in 201N. I stopped. I knocked. No one answered. I opened the door and peered inside. The room was empty. I closed the door and continued down the line. The holes stopped completely at 175N. This is about where I started shooting arrows at them.

"Gerstung! What are you doing?"

Lance Robbins approached me. He didn't look happy.

"I was, uh, looking for you. But I realized I didn't know where your bunk was."

"I was in the mess hall. I just had a breakfast. What can I do for you?"

"I uh, just wanted to apologize for what I said yesterday. I was upset and I just took it out on the closest person to me. I'm sorry it was you."

Lance's face softened. "It's fine. I understand. Times have been stressful as of late."

Lance walked by me and opened door 176N which was full of holes. He turned. "Was there anything else?"

"No, not at all Lance. Are we okay?"

"Yeah, sure Gerstung. See you around."

I turned and walked to the mess hall. I was hungry. I was also confused. Lack of holes certainly didn't mean he wasn't the spy. He could have just planned to be out of the bunk when the attack came.

I reached the mess hall and sat with Walt, Rebecca and Chen. They finished up their breakfast and just sat and talk. They seemed to be in better spirits. I grabbed some food from the line and sat with them.

Walt reached over and patted me on the shoulder. I said, "Walt, I'm not sure if Lance really is the spy."

"Man, don't try to tell me that."

"I just saw him go into one of the bunks that was shot full of holes by the gunmen."

"That doesn't prove anything."

"Not conclusively no, but we should consider other options too."

Rebecca stood shaking her head. "You guys are not the world's greatest detectives. You should give it up. Let the authorities handle it."

"We're going to have to be the authorities eventually," I said. "If we can figure it out then we can remove weakness from the fort."

Rebecca opened her mouth to respond. I saw Maria poke her head into the mess hall. Her left arm was in a sling. She walked carefully towards us.

I stood and smiled. She smiled back. "You forgot my eggs."

24 — A Beautiful Walk

April 23, 1999

The End of April First Year recruits planned to set out early in the morning. Most of them would be due back April 30th. I had gotten an extra amount of leave because of my special circumstances. Maria started a few months after us, but she wasn't coming back. She still didn't have movement in her left arm. She shed tears when she realized she would have to go home, but she appreciated having the opportunity to serve.

I stuffed my clothes in my duffel bag. I sheathed my sword. Arrows filled my quiver. My bow fit easily over my shoulder. Walt waited for me by the East Gate. Most of the other recruits exited their bunks the same time I did. I looked down the row to Maria's bunk, but I did not see her come out. I walked along the bunks to hers.

I knocked. No one answered, but I heard grunting.

I knocked again. Still no answer, but still grunting.

I knocked again. Maria sighed in response.

I opened the door and she stood with her back to me, barely dressed, trying to stuff her clothes into her duffel bag. Her left arm being basically useless and stuck in a sling hindered her.

I entered and closed the door. "Don't you have a roommate who could have helped you?"

"She had to get to her training. She's been in trouble a lot lately. She didn't want to get yelled at again."

"Do you want me to help you?"

"Could you?" she asked plaintively.

I put my stuff on the floor of the bunk and walked towards her. She turned to face me. She couldn't get her single piece brassiere on properly so her breasts rested, one in, and one out of the supports. I caught myself staring, and then looked up into Maria's eyes embarrassed. "I... uh...."

She smiled. "It's okay. I understand. Help me out here."

"I'll warn you, I've never done this before."

"It is fine. I'll tell you what to do."

She guided me as I lifted her bra off of her and eased her left arm through the opening. I guided the head hole over her head and pulled the bra down over her again.

"Thank you JR. Will you help me with my pants?"

Maria managed to put on her cotton panties herself, but it appeared the leather laces of her pants needed tightening and tying. I crouched down and grabbed the trousers at her ankles and pulled them up her perfectly toned legs and rear. I felt a bit of a tingle, but I quashed those feelings. I pulled the brim of the pants around her waist tight and carefully tightened the laces from the bottom up so they would fit her snugly, but not too tight.

Maria was determined to wear her button up green recruit shirt as she left. She wanted to leave the fort with pride. I helped her slide her left arm into the left arm of the shirt and I buttoned the cuff. I started at the bottom of the shirt, buttoning each button quickly.

I said, "I always imagined the first time I'd be with a girl like this, I would be the one who had taken the clothes off of her."

Maria replied, "Well, if you show the same skill taking clothes off as you do putting them on, the first girl you take them off of will be a lucky one."

I smiled, but said nothing. I finished buttoning her shirt and helped her tuck it into her pants. She smiled half heartedly. I hugged her softly. "It's going to be okay Maria. When your arm gets better maybe you can come back."

"I don't think so. Even if my arm gets better I am not cut out for the army, not really. I'm more of a cook, or an entertainer, or something. I am better behind the scenes offering support for those who fight."

I didn't reply. It was true she didn't have great fighting

skill, but she had heart.

We packed up her belongings. We searched through the bunk to find all of her stuff intermingled with her roommate's stuff. Finally we collected everything of Maria's. She said, "I'll send for the rest if I remember anything I've forgotten."

We put her left arm into the sling and secured it. Maria reached for her duffel bag, but she couldn't get it up and over her shoulder. I offered to help her, but she declined. She said, "Just grab your own stuff. I'll get mine. I got it in here. I'll get it out."

"Don't hurt yourself, Maria," I said. "You got it in here with two working arms."

"Shut up, JR."

I grabbed my duffel bag and weapons and stepped out of the bunk. I held the door for her. Maria breathed deeply. She carefully stuck her head under the duffel bag strap. She steadied the bag with her right hand. She lifted with her legs and the bag fit properly on her back.

"See?" She smiled.

"That I do. I guess all those calisthenics paid off huh?"

Maria smirked and walked past me toward the East Gate. The training recruits stopped. Everyone clapped and whistled. Maria waved to them and blew them kisses as she walked through the training areas. Numerous friendly hugs and kisses from people I didn't even know she knew showered her. It was a beautiful walk.

At last we reached the East Gate. Most of the other recruits had left, but Walt and Rebecca waited for us. Chen wasn't going to Bellato. He lived north of Fort Kingsley so he walked with a different group.

We kept pace with Maria. She walked slower not at full strength, but we didn't mind the extended walk. I didn't walk fast anyway. Luckily it didn't take long to walk the mile from Fort Kingsley to Bellato.

We reached Bellato and the guards greeted us suspiciously. We showed them our dog tags and they waved us in.

Walt went home to see his father. Maria's younger brother lived in Bellato. After I made sure Maria was alright, my eventual destination was Meton. Rebecca basically lived in Fort

Kingsley. She just needed a break every year or so.

When asked what she planned to do, she replied, "Oh, I'll probably get a room at the hotel and sleep for a week."

I offered, "Do you want to come to Meton with me?"

Rebecca smiled, but declined.

Walt and I embraced before he scampered off after his three milkmaids. Rebecca kissed my cheek before she disappeared in the crowd.

Maria and I stood alone. She threaded her right arm through my left. She led me to her home in a one room building. The Artist's Cove Tavern and Apartments stood nearby. She said she knew the owner, Sonny Oldman, and would probably get a job there, maybe even finagle him into contributing to the daily army effort.

We stopped at the door to her house. Maria pulled my face down to hers and kissed my lips and cheeks. "I love you JR. Don't forget that, no matter what, I love you."

I smiled as I kissed her back. "I love you too Maria."

I watched as she opened the door to her house. I caught a glimpse of the little scamp, Nicky, who stole my shuriken pouch the day before I started in the army.

I continued to my Uncles' homes. They were happy to see me. I didn't plan to stay the night. I wanted to get on the road and get as far as I could to Meton before dark. I did have a meal with them and we talked about life at the fort. My aunts brought up Rebecca. My uncles brought up Maria because they had heard what happened. My younger cousins wanted to feel my muscles.

Ajax stayed busy training in the field while I visited, except for the meal. He stayed quiet and no one probed him to talk. My uncles told me Ajax stopped talking after he heard the Dragon Sympathizers killed so many people at Fort Kingsley. He made no release condition of his silence.

Later I tried to talk to Ajax, but he just trained. I told him if he wanted to talk to me, I wouldn't tell anyone he spoke and he could keep his vow of silence. He didn't speak. I told him I would see him when I got back to the fort May 5th. I said my goodbyes to my family and headed to the East Gate.

As I left the fort I noticed something new. It was a giant

wooden sign above the gate, supported by other beams of wood. Black and white lettering painted a wood backboard.

HONOR YOUR FELLOW HUMANS
HELP WHERE YOU CAN WHEN YOU CAN
GIVE FREELY AND RECORD NO DEBTS

25 — The Three Guidelines

April 23, 1999

The bustle of Bellato slowly drained from my ears as I walked to my childhood home. After a while I only heard the occasional dings of the town bell on the hour. Further down the road I even didn't hear that. The road looked clear. Not many travelers did so late in the day. The sunset reddened the horizon behind me. I didn't know how far I could get on my walk before I needed to stop to camp.

When I first visited my uncles a year earlier I dropped off my hammock. I used it to sleep in the trees when feral packs were reported. I hadn't seen any reports of ferals, but I figured sleeping in a tree was safer.

The sign above the gates of Bellato served as a reminder to all Humans of our solidarity. Differing religions still existed, but practitioners, even the most fervent worshippers all realized that the Dragons posed a bigger threat than someone else using a different holy book. Some Humans blamed religion for dividing Humanity in the first place. They said if we hadn't been so busy fighting over which religion was right and which was wrong we would have been able to defend ourselves against the Dragons more cohesively. Proponents of war commented that the fighting tempered Humans to the point where Dragons wouldn't be able to wipe us out so quickly. Everyone had good points. I suspected the truth existed somewhere in the middle of it all.

The Three Guidelines of Humanity came to be exactly a

year after the attack on Marcinelle. Old school Humans had a flair for the dramatic and the significant. The greatest leaders of Humanity at the time came up with The Three Guidelines. These core values intended for every Human to elevate themselves in what could be our last days.

My mother tried to teach me the meaning of The Three Guidelines. Meton was not a Sympathizer town as far as I could tell, but they certainly did not honor everyone. This made it hard to learn the guidelines as the people of the village didn't seem to follow them.

I learned and understood The Three Guidelines during my summers with my uncles. My uncles personified all of the guidelines in their every day lives. While never becoming leaders of the city; still, they were highly influential in Bellato. Many followed their example when it came to how to act.

Uncle Oli watched over a good portion of Bellato at first. He helped organize building the schools and reinforcing the walls of the city. He coordinated the tunnel expansion. He made it known that every building should have easy access to the tunnels in case of a Dragon attack. He went above and beyond the call of duty. Uncle Oli never asked for anything in return. He cited the Third Guideline: "Give Freely and Record No Debts."

Uncle Max wasn't as book smart as Oli, but he capable with tools. He could build anything. Even if he'd never seen what someone asked for, he asked them to describe it and once they did, he could recreate it. He shared this gift frequently. He didn't just build. He taught others how to build. Whether it was stone or wood, Uncle Max could teach the basics and aid the potential builder in improving their skills. With all of his activities, he never gave more than he was able. His family came first. His actions represented the Second Guideline: "Help Where You Can When You Can."

Uncle Zack had the hardest time after their father, my grandfather, was killed. Zack traveled the continent searching for meaning. He learned about religion and philosophy. He learned many different forms of artistic expression and combat. He soon realized that even arts meant for self defense or attack could be expression. "Everything is expression," he said to me often. Zack realized that his father wasn't killed by Humans, however, before the Dragons attacked many Humans killed each other. He took the First Guideline to heart, "Honor Your Fellow Humans" and made it his own creed.

Communities responsibility for their own defense. This included defense against Dragon attacks and Human crime. Police forces no longer existed. Vigilante justice flourished in Humanity. Everyone could defend themselves, or knew someone who could defend them. Communities devised their own ways of dealing with criminals. Some criminals suffered banishment and city guards memorized the faces of the criminals. People knew the guards weren't perfect and never expected them to be. The guards served the community, treated as equals, not superiors or subordinates. Capable members of the community served as guards at some point in their lives, but it was always voluntary.

Communities were voluntary in general. People contributed what they did well. Blacksmiths contributed swords and armor. Farmers contributed produce or livestock products. Creatives contributed art, music, or poetry. Medicine workers helped the sick.

The natural leaders specialized in planning and organizing, but there were no officials, and the leaders of the communities often made other contributions. There was no mayor of Bellato. If someone led a town, it meant other people of that town followed that person most of the time, but it was always voluntary. These people received no special treatment from their peers, at least in theory. The leaders simply worked in their most useful capacity to the community.

In general, no one gave more than they could and no one took more than they needed. If someone could sacrifice a little more to help someone else they would do it, but only on their own terms. Communities helped those in need. Communities built houses for the houseless. Communities fed those who were hungry. Those helped would in turn help others when they could.

Darkness fell and no one could hear me in Bellato if something attacked. I felt exhausted physically and emotionally so I needed to rest. I saw a strong tree where my hammock would not fall. I quickly climbed up and hung the hammock on two strong branches. I hung my bow and quiver of arrows on a nearby branch. My sword in its scabbard and strap hung on another branch. My duffel bag served as a pillow, but it didn't feel cold enough for a blanket.

I closed my eyes, and then reconsidered the blanket. I pulled it from the duffel bag and wrapped it around myself. More comfortable, I closed my eyes again. I soon slept.

I dreamt that night of being reunited with my mother. I saw Diana. White light enveloped everything. Beauty enveloped everything. Then red enveloped everything. The face of Gomez. The mob of Meton. They attacked me. I defended myself. We fought and fought and fought. Their corpses littered my feet. I stood covered in blood. Smoke enveloped everything. I spewed the flames.

April 24, 1999

I slept restlessly to say the least. I've always had nightmares. They quieted when I trained, or other situations I had some modicum of control over. Going back to Meton I didn't know what to expect. I knew would face trouble. I had no idea how bad the trouble would be. Would they chase me out of town? Would they attack my mother?

I continued walking and pondering exactly what I would say to anyone who asked. They told me to leave for good. I told them I would come back to visit my mother. They tried to banish me as a pervert for the situation with Diana even though she acted as a willing accomplice.

April 27, 1998

Diana knocked on my door later. She smiled as I answered the door. She held the poem I wrote for her crumpled, but folded and smoothed in her hand. She leaned in to my ear and whispered, "I loved this poem. I will cherish it forever. I'm sorry I couldn't say that in front of the boys. The girls and I are going to the hot springs to bathe. I want you to watch me."

I reacted tingly immediately. I pulled my head back from her whisper and said, "Are you serious? What if I'm found?"

"You won't be. No one else knows we are going. It's almost dark. No one will see you. The hot spring gets excellent moonlight so you'll be able to see me from the trees. You're going to have to be quiet. I can't know you're there. Thinking you're there would be... nice."

She kissed me quickly and left. I knew I shouldn't have gone. On the list of bad ideas, it ranked pretty close to top. But the opportunity to see the things I had never seen before.... My 16 year old brain said I shouldn't pass it up.

26 — Meton

The sun still shone in the sky as I caught sight of Meton. I could be in the city gates in less than an hour. I considered the last words said to me by representatives of the village, the Bollin Ballers, *Leave and never come back.* I didn't want to cause any more trouble for my mother if I could help it.

I approached the village cautiously. I ducked off of the road when I saw two men coming out of the village. I hid behind trees or bushes. I recognized their faces as they passed, but I didn't know their names. They seemed happy. One man tripped and fell. The other laughed and picked him up.

Whenever I fell, or someone knocked me down in Meton, they kicked me until I got back up. They ignored me in the best of times. The teachers. The people in the marketplace. Todd Bollin and his brothers paid me enough attention to go around. Also Diana. Diana's mother and father paid attention to me with shouts of anger when they banished me. Despite their treatment of me, the citizens of Meton seemed to treat each other with respect and good nature. They could even have been good people at heart.

The passersby walked out of sight. I climbed out of the bushes and continued down the road to Meton. I could almost see the Meton guards. I knew I had to hide until night. I climbed up a tree close by and waited.

I saw the guards from my perch. I also saw the

dilapidated walls. Meton existed in sharp contrast to Bellato. The walls of Bellato were fervently maintained. Even the smallest cracks in a plank or if a stone fell out of place engineers replaced it, many times within an hour.

An observer could see where the walls of Meton should have been. They stretched about a mile in a square, like most towns. The walls of Meton were all wood, where Bellato had stone reinforcements. The wood didn't look the most pristine. Slats of wood fell out of place. To be fair, few Sympathizer attacks happened on Meton. It was not a major city. The guards stood guard until dark, but then they closed the gates and went to bed. Only two gates stood for the village: the West Gate where I looked; and the East Gate near where my mother's hut stood. I could almost see her hut, except there stood a taller building in my way. I saw a clearing off to the south of the East Gate. I couldn't see the nearby hot springs from my vantage point due to the trees.

The fountain in the center of Meton acted as the marketplace focal point. Next to that stood city hall where adult meetings were held at night and the schoolhouse during the day for the children.

I scanned the horizon and I saw the castle of Jonathan the Tyrant. It was about three miles away from Meton to the east, but it stretched high enough into the sky that I could see it well from my tree. As far as I knew, only Jonathan lived there, but being a Dragon, the space felt warranted.

A group of women approached the Meton West Gate. They talked cheerfully with one another. I didn't recognize any of their voices. Their pleasantness with one another baffled me.

May 20, 1997

I accompanied my mother to the market. She wrapped a white bandana around her head. Her long black hair threaded out of the back of the bandana and bounced as she walked. She wore a one piece, leather dress that hugged her form without being tight. She moved easily as we made our way to the center of town.

We sheared the sheep and she made the wool into spools

to contribute to the community. The expectation to contribute was something set out by my grandfather, no matter how much shit people dumped on her, she wouldn't go against it. She brought me to the market despite my displeasure. I didn't want to subject myself to taunts.

She said, "You're going to have to learn how to get along in this village. You're going to have to deal with what I have dealt with eventually."

"Why don't we just leave?" I asked.

She stopped and turned to me. Her blue eyes were no longer icy. I remembered them from my younger days. They didn't flash anymore. They held the flatness of resignation. They were still beautiful.

"We can't. You know I can't," she said.

"You keep saying that, but you never tell me why."

"You won't understand."

I insisted, but my mother wouldn't relent. We continued walking and reached the center of town. There were no more spots near the fountain, not that any of the other townsfolk would have made it comfortable for us to sit there. We set up our awning quickly and the table beneath it with the spools of wool. We stood and watched. People approached the awning. They saw our faces. They smirked. Some people took a spool or two of wool. Some people laughed and continued on their way. The disdain in the air felt heavier than a boulder.

The villagers grabbed three fourths of the wool over the next hour. Mother sent me out to get food. I grabbed some of the bags we used to carry wool in and took them around to the different townsfolk. Most of the people treated me with indifference. Some of them looked outright angry that I took from their cart, basket or table. A few of them called me "Bastard child" or "Whoreson." No one said I couldn't take anything from them.

I filled the bags with medium quality vegetables and cured meats. It would last us a week or so. I walked back to our awning. Jorge Gomez and two lackeys stood in front of the awning.

"Why don't you get out of here whore?" one of the men said.

"We hereby declare you a menace to cleanliness," said the other.

Gomez laughed. "Seriously though Aurora, why do you persist? You know this town hates you. Why do you stay?"

"Maybe she's hoping for a repeat performance on how she got her son," the first man said.

I stepped calmly in front of the men. "You need to leave my mother alone."

"You scrawny little bastard, how dare you speak to me," Gomez said. He raised his hand to me.

I lightly set down the bags and prepared for him to strike. Hell Bringer or not, I was going to fight him this time. How *dare* they insinuate my mother wanted to be raped again?

I clenched my fists.

Gomez's hand came down fast. My mother suddenly blocked his strike and pushed him backwards. "You will not strike my son."

My mother's work bronzed skin glowed in the setting sun. For a moment I saw her eyes, no longer flat, shining with icy brilliance. "Deal with ferals before me, Gomez."

Gomez and his lackeys strode away from us as if nothing out of the ordinary happened. He wouldn't allow his posture to suffer at the hands of Aurora Gerstung.

"And to think, that bastard leads the rest of the mob of this village," I said. I moved the bags under the awning.

My mother said nothing. She said little of anything in general. One of the biggest lessons she taught me: Don't back down from a bully. Turning the other cheek only gets it slapped or worse. If a bully attacks you, fight back. Even if you lose, the bully will think twice about attacking you again. Bullies prey on the weak and the meek. Bullies don't stop until they are stopped.

She also taught me to defend the ones you love. You do what you can when you can to help the people you care about.

My mother said, "John Ross, let's pack up and go home."

We slowly repacked the wool into the remaining bags. We folded the table legs and carefully took down the awning.

The sun nearly disappeared from the horizon. Red enveloped the town.

April 24, 1999

The sun nearly disappeared from the horizon. Red enveloped the town.

The guards closed the West Gate. I climbed down the tree. There were plenty of holes and weak points in the village walls that it was going to be no problem for me to get into Meton at night. The villagers only mounted torches only along the main streets. I knew all of the short cuts. I would find my way in and find my way to my mother's hut by the light of the half moon.

27 — Returning Home

April 24, 1999

The darkness shrouded my entry through a hole in the south east corner of the Meton wall. I scratched myself on a nail. The blood shone black in the moonlight. I grimaced, but kept on. I would take care of it when I got to my mother's house.

I didn't notice anyone on the streets. Typically no night time guards patrolled the streets. The occasional teenagers scampered around after sneaking out of their homes, but I noticed none of these either.

I kept to the shadows created by the moon over the houses. I walked with a cross step against walls. I crossed brighter areas fast and noiselessly. Only the main avenue of Meton that ran from the West Gate to the East Gate had pavement so I avoided this way. The rest of the roads consisted of crumbled gravel and old broken cement so I could walk quietly.

I saw my mother's hut. I slinked towards it behind the houses on the gravel street. I avoided any fences denoting gardens. I reached the fenced off area for the sheep at the back of the hut. I hopped the fence and startled the sheep. I unsuccessfully tried to shush them.

I heard a rustling inside the house. I quickly ducked behind and below where the door opened. I tucked myself next to the steps. The door opened and I saw the small bare feet of my mother take one step down. I looked up at her. She held her knitting needles like daggers. She took another step down. She listened, but the sheep bleated too loudly.

Her musical, but tired, gravelly voice shushed the sheep and they obeyed. She took the third step down and then the fourth to the mushy grass. It recently rained and the sheep kept the ground soft.

I breathed softly up to this point. I just knew she hadn't heard me. Mother took a few more steps into the middle of the yard. She stopped. Without warning she turned and let her knitting needles fly in my direction. They stuck into the wall on either side of my head. Half a second later her face met mine nose to nose. "Who the hell... John Ross?"

"Hello Mother."

"I nearly killed you."

"Nearly."

"What are you doing here?"

"One year leave. I got a little extra time off since the shooting."

"Yes, I heard about that. Are you okay?"

"Mostly."

"Good." Mother paused. She grabbed her knitting needles and took a step back. "Come in John Ross."

Minutes later we sat in the front room. The fireplace contained a modest fire which heated up the small house.

There were four rooms in the house. The front room consisted of a sitting area and the kitchen area. If an observer looked at the fireplace, the door on the right led to my mother's room. Her room was about half the size of the front room. I hardly ever went in there, but I knew there was a simple mattress on a bed frame. Mother turned her mattress every other month to keep it from going flat. All of her personal effects were there.

The room leading to the back door was less of a room and more of a hallway to the back door and a storage area. Mother kept multiple blankets, pillows and sleeping mats for when guests (usually my Uncles and their families) visited. There was a door to this room from both my mother's room and my own.

The sheep had two outbuildings in the yard. One of the buildings had sheep care items. The sheep went to this building to escape inclement weather. The other building acted as a storage building which (in addition to other things) had additional bed frames when we had room to put up guests.

My room was to the left of the fireplace. My things stayed in the same place as I left them a year before. My window shone with moonlight right onto my bed. I looked down at my arm where it was bleeding earlier, but there was no sign of a cut. Curious. Unfortunately I knew I would have to close my blind, lest someone look in on me while I slept and alert the rest of the town. I had every intention for this to be a secret visit.

I set my stuff down in my room and joined my mother near the fireplace. She had her knitting close. She didn't work on it. She looked me over as I sat down. "John Ross, you have grown in the past year."

"I'm fed on the scent of Dragon's blood and pain, at least according to the sergeants."

Mother laughed. "Have you made friends?"

"Actually I have. There is one guy, Walt, we met the day before recruiting. He is a little girl crazy. He's chased every piece of tail... I mean... he's talked to every attractive girl he can see."

Mother smiled. "How about you? Do you have any special girls in your life?"

"Well, there are a couple girls I like. One of them, Maria, was injured in the shooting. Her left arm doesn't work right now. Doctors are hoping she'll get better eventually, but she had to resign from being a recruit and go back to Bellato."

"That poor girl," Mother said.

"Yeah. The other girl is the daughter of Plato Kingsley. Rebecca."

"Ooh, I remember Plato Kingsley. He was a handsome devil years ago. I was so jealous when I learned he was with Annie."

I asked, "Lieutenant Kingsley said he knew you."

Mother nodded. "Oh yes. We had a beautiful day and I thought he would come to call on me after that, but I didn't hear from him again for a while. I was not broken hearted per se, but I was disappointed."

"Lieutenant Kingsley asked about you. You should go see him. You never know what could happen."

Mother's mood immediately darkened. "I know exactly

what would happen."

"What do you mean?"

Mother hesitated.

"Tell me, please."

"The Tyrant. He has been attacking the village since you left. He made no formal proclamation, but he started killing the day after you left. He killed one in May, two in June, three in July. He keeps increasing his death toll every month you are gone. He has killed 10 so far this month, but the villagers are predicting two more before the end. They have tried to ask for aid, but no one has come. The reason I was so defensive earlier was because I thought it was another vandal coming to punish me for his actions as if they are my fault."

I said, "People always need a scapegoat. So far it has been us. Why should it stop now? Maybe the Tyrant just got tired of letting this town rot on its own and wanted to help bring it down." I didn't entirely believe that.

Mother said, quietly, "Yeah, maybe."

I mused, "But why would the killings start after I left?"

Mother did not answer, but I knew she knew something.

"Mother?"

My mother still did not answer. She grabbed her knitting. She walked to her room and closed the door.

I sighed. I walked into my room and closed my door as well. I pulled my curtains over my window blocking out the moon. I lay on my bed and looked at the ceiling. I knew what I would do in the morning. I would go out into the marketplace in disguise and wait to see if Jonathan the Tyrant attacked. If he attacked, I would stop him.

I looked over my shelves and saw a folder filled with papers. It was my poetry. I rose from the bed and grabbed the folder.

I sat next to the fireplace and opened the folder.

Oh Diana you drive me wild
Your skin so soft your touch so mild
Your lips so red and hair so fine
I wish that you would just be mine

You have a grace and flowing walk
But no one sees us when we talk
This secret love I have for you
Stopped by their disgraceful views
You can't acknowledge heart felt pines
Attempts we make are undermined
You must present shallow façade
Feigned allegiance to violent gods
I hope I can save you one day
From oppressed life and secrets' pain
Let our love be free to be
I know I'm worth your bravery

I sighed and put the poem down. Most of my work was written about Diana. I hadn't written at all since I left Meton. Maybe when I got back I would start writing more. I could obsess about Rebecca. That might be good for me.

There was a knock on my window. I snapped out of my trance. I crept silently towards the window. I moved the curtain slightly out of the way and saw her. Speak of the devil.

Diana.

28 — The Dragon

April 25, 1999

Just after midnight, Diana's face appeared in my window under my curtain. The air blew in softly, rustling the curtains. We didn't speak.

The half moon angled in such a way that I could see the light shining on her skin. Her hair looked longer, but she tied it in a pony tail. She wore a white cotton shirt and brown leather pants.

I opened my mouth. "Would you like to–"

"You killed my father."

I heard no anger or accusation in her matter of fact tone. She simply stated her truth.

"What are you–?"

"You killed my father. The day after you left, the Tyrant came to the village, swooped in and took him high in the sky. Moments later my father fell from the sky and into the fountain. His head hit the lip of the fountain. The fall broke his neck and shattered his skull. It took us months to get the fountain back to where it was drinkable. I still can't drink directly from the fountain."

"I'm sorry. I didn't know the Tyrant was attacking villagers until I got back tonight."

"You don't get news at the Fort?"

"No. Not from Meton. Occasionally we get news from Bellato, but with the amount of Dragon attacks that happen all over the country our eyes start to glaze over reading them. The sergeants like to keep us sequestered in the Fort as much as possible."

"That's sad."

"What is?"

"That you can't stay updated on news like this, especially in your own town."

"This isn't really my town. It's the place my mother won't leave. I would never come back here if she didn't live here."

"I'm tired of standing, can you help me in?"

I opened the window wider and helped Diana enter my room through the window. She stood just out of the moonlight. I suggested we sit next to the fireplace. The fire illuminated her face. It had a different effect than the moon.

Diana said, "You didn't wish me happy birthday."

My face scrunched. "That's today?"

"Yup. The big One Seven as of midnight."

"Do you feel any older or wiser?"

"Older, yes. Wiser, not so much."

"How are you and Todd doing?"

"We aren't together. After you left I told my dad I didn't want to be with Todd and if he tried to make me I would leave. He didn't have time to press the issue and mom has been a mess since then."

"I'm sorry about your dad. I wasn't his biggest fan, but I know how much he meant to you."

"Thanks. How have you been holding up? Are you enjoying the army?"

"It's alright. I'm getting stronger and learning a lot about life."

Diana smiled. "I miss you. I wish I had told everyone the truth about us. I wish you didn't leave."

I sighed. "I'm glad I'm not here anymore. I was getting tired of all the shit everyone put me through. In the army, I get yelled at, but it's because they want me to be a better warrior and a better person."

"That's really nice, JR."

I asked, "So, how did you know I'd be here?"

Diana smiled again. "I willed it. I told the universe I wanted YOU for my birthday. The universe had no choice, but to comply."

I laughed softly. "Well here I am. Now what are you going to do?"

"This." Diana leaned towards me. She threaded her left hand full of slender brown fingers into my hair and pulled me towards her. She pressed her full lips against mine. I felt her tongue probe my lips. I met her tongue with my own. My left hand moved through her soft, thick, brown hair. My right hand lightly caressed her full left breast.

Diana pulled back from the kiss. I drew my right hand from her. She smiled. "JR, you've gotten adventurous."

I smiled sheepishly. "I'm sorry. It just seemed like the right thing to do."

Diana said, "It was. But I have to go. I don't want my mom to find out I'm gone. She'll go feral. Can I see you tomorrow night?"

I replied, "I'll be here."

I helped Diana back out of the window. She kissed me again before she left. I closed the window and collapsed on my bed. It was going to be an interesting day.

I woke up a few hours later. The smell of eggs wafted through the house. I exited my room and sat at the kitchen table. Mother turned to me with a worried look. "So I heard Diana in the house last night. Was she trying to get you into trouble again?"

I apologized, "No, no. She just wanted to talk. Sorry if we disturbed you."

"No, you didn't. I understand how things go. I also know she left. If I had heard you doing anything else I would have burst right in."

I said, "Well I'm glad you didn't hear us making sweet passionate love."

Mother put a plate of eggs in front of me. "It must not have been that passionate if I didn't hear it."

I ate the eggs slowly, savoring them for my impending adventure.

Mother asked, "What are your plans for today?"

— **141** —

I swallowed the eggs in my mouth. "I planned to grab a hood disguise and head to the marketplace. I was going to try to get captured by Jonathan the Tyrant and see if I could beat some sense into him."

Mother's face turned deadly serious. "What?"

I laughed. "I'm just joking Mother. I was going to sneak out and meet Diana out in the forest to talk for a while. It's her birthday."

Mother shook her head. "Don't joke about that kind of thing. Jonathan the Tyrant is a very dangerous... creature."

A few minutes later, I donned a hooded cloak, slid my katana into its scabbard and slung my bow over my shoulder with the quiver. I pulled the hood over my head.

Mother asked, "Why are you taking weapons?"

I answered, "You never know what kinds of dangers lurk in the forest."

I poked my head out of the hut to scout for villagers. I saw no one so I exited fast and put some distance between me and the hut for my mother's sake. I reached the avenue through the center of the town. The marketplace had plenty of folk milling about, but it was too quiet.

I didn't have to wait long for people to start screaming. Overhead flew a giant Red Dragon. The Dragon seemed familiar to me. It looked like the Dragon that saved me from the ferals as a child. Everyone scattered and headed for the nearest doorway, except me. The Dragon's wingspan stretched wider than the avenue. I pulled my bow and arrows and fired the Dragon's Bane arrows at the Dragon to get his attention. I hit him twice in the back legs. The Dragon roared in pain and pulled the arrows out of his scales.

Stupid boy.

I shook my head and fired again aiming for the chest. The Dragon landed and avoided the shot. The Dragon breathed a fireball at me which I avoided. I shot another arrow at the Dragon which missed. The Dragon stood only 20 feet from me.

I slung the bow onto my back and drew the katana. I growled and ran at the Dragon. The Dragon spun around swiping his tail at me. I dove into a roll just under the tail. Once I reached the end of the roll, back to my feet, I jumped into the air with my katana in the air coming down onto the Dragon.

The Dragon used his enormous head to strike me and knock me into a house. My katana flew from my hand and clanged on the pavement. The Dragon stomped towards me and sniffed me as I lay on the ground.

Stupid boy.

The Dragon turned and started walking towards the East Gate.

"Oh, no you don't," I said under my breath. I quickly got up, grabbed my katana and ran towards the Dragon.

The Dragon's wings extended and it flapped once. As it flapped, I sheathed my katana and jumped up and towards the Dragon. I caught a hold of its back leg, the one I had shot the arrows into.

What in the Three Hells?

I held on tight as the Dragon flew higher. The Dragon tried to shake me off of his leg, but I wouldn't let go.

I yelled as we flew, "You won't get rid of me, Tyrant!"

This boy just doesn't know when to give up.

The Dragon continued to try to shake me off of his leg. The shakes didn't feel as strong as I thought they should have. There must have been some Dragon's Bane from the arrows lodged in his muscle.

The Dragon flew straight for the Tyrant's castle. Then suddenly the Dragon took a turn to the left and towards the lake. The Dragon dove into the chilly waters, but I clung tight. We resurfaced and he flew back towards the castle. We landed at the open castle door. The Dragon curled the leg I held under him and sat on me.

The sudden rush of air leaving my body caused me to let go of the Dragon. I lay winded as the Dragon walked into the castle door and slammed it behind him with his tail.

29 — Lessons

I rose slowly from my position on the broken concrete stones mortared together in front of the huge double doors. I looked all around. Chunks of concrete constructed the entire castle. The castle resembled pictures of medieval castles I saw in books as a child. The walkway I stood on led behind me to a drawbridge over an honest to goodness moat. I walked to the edge, looked over and saw no crocodiles, but the water looked about ten feet from the bridge. The castle stood close enough to Lake Erie that water actually found its way through the moat.

I turned back to the doors. I walked up to the middle of them and gave a hard shove. Nothing. I tried focusing all of my power on the left door and again I shoved. Nothing. I tried the same with the right door. Again, nothing.

You could try knocking.

I growled and shoved one more time. Still nothing. Exasperated, I raised my hand and knocked loudly three times.

The doors opened.

I scoffed and entered slowly drawing my katana. Red bathed the hall. Floor to ceiling banners with gold trim draped down the sides of the main hall. The stitched gold and silver insignia inside the banners resembled two intertwining Dragons. I continued down the hall until I reached another huge hall crossing the path. There were three ways to go and they all seemed endless.

I took the left hallway. I moved more quickly since I saw or heard no immediate danger. I stopped mid step and swung my sword behind me stopping half an inch away from the neck of a small Green Dragon. The Dragon's wings flapped slightly, but it didn't move.

"Who are you and what do you want?"

The little Dragon tilted its head blinked. It didn't seem at all threatening, but looks could be deceiving.

"I'm not here to hurt you. I'm here to find Jonathan the Tyrant. Can you take me there?" *I'm talking to a Dragon, what am I thinking. They can't understand Human speech....*

The Dragon turned and walked the other way down the hall and past the cross hallway. The Dragon turned and seemed to motion with its head for me to follow.

Come with me.

I walked carefully behind the little Green Dragon. It led me to another huge set of doors. These doors stood ajar. Red carpet led to a throne. A man in a red robe sat on the throne.

The man said in a deep, powerful, but not unpleasant voice, "Please come in John Ross. Nama, you are dismissed."

The small Green Dragon turned and scampered out of the room. Its little claws clicking on the cement ground.

I walked closer. "How do you know my name?"

"I know everything about you, John Ross. I know about your family in Bellato. I know your mother, Aurora. I even know about your grandfather, the man who had your name before you did."

"How do you know all of this?"

"You could say, I am a Gerstung enthusiast." The man laughed loud enough that it echoed through the room.

I walked closer. "Who are you?"

The man looked puzzled. "Don't you know?" He paused. "Of course you don't. She never would have told you."

"What are you talking about?"

The man stood and approached me as he spoke. "You see, I knew Aurora, intimately, about 18 years ago."

"What are you trying to say?"

Figure it out, stupid boy. You're my son. I am your father Jonathan the Dragon King.

I beat at my head.

"What's wrong with you?" The man asked with a devious smile.

You're my son. I am your father. I am the one they call Tyrant.

I groaned as my head twisted back and forth without me even willing it. "What the hell is this? Are you some kind of sorcerer?"

I have been called a sorcerer. I know no magic. I can shape shift. I shifted into this form you see now. I seduced your mother. She fell in love with me. We mated. You were born. You are my SON!

I fell to my knees. My katana dropped from my hands, clanging on the ground. "How are you doing this?"

The man stood three feet away from me. He crouched down and put his hands on the floor in front of him. He peered at me almost innocently as he tilted his head to the side. "What is my name?"

"J-J-Jonathan."

"Who am I to you?"

"I d-don't know."

What felt like a house of cards around me crumbled to falling. I remember my mother telling me, "Lying is not always wrong John Ross. It's only wrong when someone stands to get hurt."

The pain of uncertainty ripped through my heart and skull.

You are my SON! I am your FATHER!

I screamed and punched Jonathan in the face as hard as I could. He spun around and fell on the cement floor. I jumped up and kicked him in the ribs three times before he responded by kicking me in the back of the knee.

I groaned as my knee buckled. I fell onto him and started pummeling him in the face.

Jonathan punched me in the ribs and blocked one of my face punches. He grabbed my head and threw me off of him. I reached a standing position the same time he did. I threw off my cloak.

Jonathan wore his grey hair down the middle of his back. My brown hair hung about the same length. His robe half sleeves

— **146** —

showed off the bottom of well defined biceps and forearms that could have been steel bars. I flexed my biceps and forearms with the same definition. Jonathan's broad chest was defined rather than beefy. I could only see the valley between his pectoral muscles. They matched my own perfectly.

I took a step towards Jonathan and he towards me. At the moment, his eyes were dark blue. My eyes tended to change in the sun. They would get brighter if there was a surplus of light at hand. I didn't know what my eyes looked like at the moment.

"Dark blue," Jonathan said.

I shoved Jonathan away.

"How can this be? How could my mother have ever fallen in love with a monster like you? You kill people! Your kind has waged a war against Humanity for over 50 years." I flailed my arms madly swinging at invisible enemies as I ranted. "How could she have forgotten her family? Three Hells, you fought my grandfather! How could she betray our family like that?"

"You can't blame your mother for being in love."

"Shut up! You are *not* my father. I don't care if you and my mother did... I can't even say it."

"Mate. Make love. Have sex. Procreate."

"If you don't shut up I'm going to kill you."

"Try it, hatchling."

I looked at my katana on the ground. I looked back at Jonathan. He smiled.

I crouched down and grabbed my katana. I sprang back up and swung it at his head. He ducked and punched me in the stomach. I doubled over.

"You are no match for me, my son. As long as you think about your intentions, I will always be one step ahead of you. Dragons and their kin have a psychic link which gives them access to other Dragons' thoughts."

"I am not a Dragon," I said. I attacked Jonathan again with an overhead slash. He moved to the side and wrapped his right hand around my right wrist. I struggled against his grip.

"You are half Dragon. This means you are susceptible to this as well. The only way you can keep your thoughts shrouded is to act on instinct. Other Dragons will know you immediately for what you are. Humans may fear you or they may embrace you. You could be a weapon for their salvation or destruction."

He used his wrist hold to throw me to the ground. My katana clattered out of reach. "That was lesson one. This is lesson two."

Jonathan threw off his robe and turned away. There was not a hair on his body. His tan skin changed into reddish scales. I heard cracking and popping. His legs bulked up. His feet expanded in size. His arms grew larger. His ten fingers and ten toes became three claws on each foot and hand. He bent over and landed on all fours.

His neck extended. A tail extended from the bottom of his spine. A three inch spike trail grew along his spine from the back of his neck to the tip of his tail.

As Jonathan turned towards me his wings burst out of his shoulders with a span at least as long as his body. For a moment, his head still resembled a Human. He grinned devilishly as his face elongated and expanded.

Three horns grew from just above his eyebrow ridge. Two horns grew out from each side of his jaw. One horn grew down from his chin. His huge nostrils looked like scale caves full of mucus. His thick, inch long teeth held sword points. His two inch long eye teeth looked even sharper. Jonathan's breath smelled like rotten eggs.

Lesson two, shape shifting Dragons shift fast.

I looked into the eyes of my father. They changed from dark blue to fire red. The irises seemed to burn.

Lesson three.

Jonathan inhaled and blew a cone of fire at me. I closed my eyes and held my arms up to shield myself. I felt my clothes burning around me.

30 — Vrack

April 25, 1999

Finally, the fire subsided. I put my arms down. My clothes had been completely burned off of me. My lungs breathed smoke in great waves. At this point, I wasn't sure if it came from Jonathan's fire, or my own body. I looked around, but I didn't see Jonathan. I did see Nama, the little Green Dragon. It, she, approached. Her claws clicked on the cement. My tongue stuck to the roof of my mouth. Where I would normally be expecting to sweat, instead my skin tingled. She grabbed Jonathan's cloak in her mouth and brought it to me. She sat looking at me expectantly swishing her tail back and forth. My cloak hadn't survived the fire.

Confusion burned inside me. What made her think I would wear his clothes?

Because you are roughly the same size and you are naked.

Grumblingly, I took his cloak from her and wrapped myself in it. I looked at her quizzically. *What species of Dragon are you?*

I am a Fairy Dragon.

Is your kind typically smaller?

I'm the same size as you. Her green eyes blinked expectantly.

Okay I see your point. Sorry, dumb Human brain.

Yes, I am fully mature. I am 111 years old.

How long have you been with Jonathan?

Long enough to know you're a very lucky Vrack.

That didn't feel polite. *Any powers I should know about?*

Fairy Dragons are resistant to every form of Dragon attack. Also, I am learning to shape shift.

Jonathan is teaching you?

Do you know of any other shape shifting Dragons in the area?

I said aloud, "Looks like I'm getting the hang of this psychic link thing."

Your mother would be so proud.

"Thanks."

I grabbed my sword and tied it around my waist to keep the cloak closed. I slung my quiver of arrows across my back with my bow over that.

So that lesson, I'm fire proof?

The offspring of Dragons inherit resistance to their parent's veras.

Veras?

It is what Dragons call their ability, for example, to breathe fire is your father's veras.

Got it. Is there a special name for what I am?

You are a Vrack, the child of a male Dragon and female Human.

So that's what you meant before. Are there many like me?

There are more than you might think.

"Great."

I turned to leave the throne room.

Wait, son of the king.

I turned back to Nama. "Yes?"

He will kill you if you come back and are not strong enough. A king's hatchlings always come against their father to usurp them to take their power. If they are not strong enough they are killed.

I don't want his power. I just came to stop him from attacking the village.

He will not attack the village again. But he will expect another challenge.

"He'll get one." *But I don't want to rule anything.*

I made my way out of the castle. I saw no sign of anyone.

— **150** —

I crossed the bridge and my feet hit the road leading back to Meton. I stopped and sighed. The road ran three miles. My bare feet and knees hurt. I wished I could get there faster. My shoulder blades suddenly itched like crazy. I ran to a tree and rubbed my back against the bark until they stopped.

I breathed out a sigh of relief and resumed my walk down the path.

How could my mother lie to me like this? How could she betray the Human race? How could she let me live in this ignorance? Maybe if I had known I could have somehow made the villagers see that I wasn't such a bad kid after all. Maybe they could have accepted me.

As I walked, I rammed my fist into a number of trees to take out my frustration. Sure, it wasn't the trees' fault that my mother had done this, but I saw no other target for my anger at the moment.

"Strike!"

Just what the doctor ordered.

Minutes later I stood in the middle of four Bollin Brothers lying on the ground writhing in pain. I didn't seriously hurt any of them as much as I wanted to. I approached Todd and crouched down. He looked up at me, "What the hell, you Bastard."

"You know, Todd, I'm not such a bad guy. You might have known that if you had bothered to get to know me. Now it's too late. I can't even hate you at this point. You are so far below me. You don't matter in the slightest anymore. I have bigger enemies to fry."

Todd coughed. "Go to hells, Bastard."

"Seriously? When is this 'Bastard' stuff going to lose its steam? It isn't original, it's just ignorant. Goodbye Todd. If you or your brothers ever come after me again, I'll kill you and I won't even notice."

I made it about 20 yards down the path before I heard, "Bastard – Aaaah! Shit!"

The arrow landed an inch from Todd's face.

I quickly jogged back to grab the arrow. "Can't waste a good Dragon's Bane arrowhead, now can I?"

Todd said nothing more.

Beating the crap out of Todd and his brothers wasn't the

best use of my time, but it made me feel a little better. Not in the way of I liked to cause pain to others to mask my own. It was more like I needed the exercise to work out the frustration that was building.

The frustration returned when I saw the mob gathered at the Meton East Gate. At their head I saw Conchita Gomez, Diana's mother.

"There's that bastard! Let's get him!"

The mob started moving towards me. I growled and held up my hands. "You have no idea what I've been doing for you. I went to the castle to stop the Tyrant from attacking your families. I succeeded. You don't need to thank me. You just need to stay the hells out of my way."

As I walked through the crowd into the town, I heard murmurs. "Let's attack him. He's nothing, but a Dragon Sympathizer."

I drew my sword as I turned. "You want to attack me? I guarantee I'll cut half of you down before you can kill me. Dragon Sympathizer? Pfft. I can't even comment on that."

When no one stepped forward, I sheathed my katana and made my way to my mother's hut. I burst in the door.

Her eyelids were the color of cherries. "John Ross."

I held up a hand to her. "I have to change."

I took off my katana, my bow and quiver of arrows and put them next to the door. I shut my door. Diana was in the room.

I asked, "What in the Three Hells are you doing here?"

She said, "I just wanted you to know, I didn't tell them. They saw your face when you were taken by Jonathan."

"I wasn't going to accuse you. Now get out. I need to put clothes on."

"Why?"

"Jonathan burned off my clothes, but was nice enough to leave his cloak for me." I scoffed. "It smells like rotten eggs. Go."

Diana said, "I don't mind seeing you naked."

"Well I do. I'm not really in the mood for you at the moment. Who let you in anyway?"

"Your mother. She let me in the front door."

"Well, you need to go back out the front door. I want to be alone. I can't be alone with you here."

Diana approached me. She pulled my face down by my cloak. Her lips pressed against mine. I didn't kiss back, but I didn't stop her. She pulled away and walked out of my room shutting the door. I heard the front door open and close after a thank you to my mother.

I threw off the cloak and tossed it into the corner. I lay on my bed and covered myself with a blanket. I didn't want to deal with the inevitable. My mother lied to me. I fought one of the most powerful Dragons in the world and I lived to tell someone about it. That Dragon was my... I still couldn't say it.

I closed my eyes. I felt like all of the energy had been drawn out of my limbs. I couldn't move. I didn't want to move. I wanted to shrivel up and disappear. I slept.

There were no figures in my dream. The world around me spun shades of red: Fire; Roses; Blood; Fire; Jonathan's eyes; Cherries; Cheeks; Raw meat; Fire; Dragon scales; Rebecca's reddish brown hair; The veil over my eyes when I was angry or frustrated; The build up in my chest which accompanied that kind of anger; Fire; I wanted to explode; My throat felt like it was burning; Sweating; Fire; Fire; Fire.

I sat up as I woke up with a fiery belch. Night fell, but I didn't see the moon. I wasn't ready to be awake. I lay back down and closed my eyes again.

What was I going to do now? Would the officers at Fort Kingsley need to know about this? What would I tell Rebecca and Walt? My hands went to my head and I passed out again.

31 — The Truth

April 26, 1999

I don't cry, but I awoke with tears in my eyes. I lay in bed and looked out the window. I heard my mother making noise in the kitchen. I smelled a familiar smell of meat and potatoes cooking. I stretched, got out of bed and put on my clothes. I walked out of my room and sat stiffly at the table. Mother put down eggs, potatoes and ham in front of me. I grabbed a fork and started eating quietly.

She turned back to the stove and said, "I'm sorry I broke your trust. You deserve to know the truth about me and about your father."

"I'm not sure I want to hear this right now."

"Regardless, I need to tell you. I need to explain to you why I did what I did. Inevitably, I know you will say we should leave, now that you know the truth, but I need to explain to you why that can't happen either."

I took another bite of food and sighed. "Okay. Tell me."

January 18, 1982

Screams of labor pierced the frigid January morning. Aurora lay exhausted with her new baby sleeping silently swaddled in her arms. Oli, Max, and Zack built this hut for her months earlier. Aurora looked softly at her brothers and their wives.

Aurora's eyes closed and she thought back to the man – the creature – she loved who now threatened her existence and her family.

Jonathan.

July 24, 1981

Rain threatened the dark, cloudy, humid night. Jonathan stood at the door of Aurora's hut. He wore a smile and his most regal, red robes over the red sweater she knitted him a few months earlier. Jonathan intended to propose marriage to her. He'd scented her impending announcement. He knew Aurora called him to visit for a reason and he was certain he knew why.

"Jonathan," Aurora began. "I called you here for two reasons. Before I say these things though, I need you to know that you... are... an amazing creature. The words my father said about you did you no justice. You are nobler than he ever knew."

"Aurora," Jonathan interrupted, moving towards her cupping her cheek in his hand. He moved in to kiss her softly, but she put her left hand on his lips.

"No, Jonathan, let me finish please," Aurora said.

"Yes, My Sweet One," Jonathan replied.

"I'm pregnant, but..."

"Pregnant?! My love that is great! That is wonderful! That's exactly why I hoped you'd call me to you tonight. I wanted to..."

"... I cannot see you anymore."

Jonathan's enthusiasm shriveled like a worm in the sun. His heart sank in his chest. His hand left Aurora's face and he took a step back as if Aurora's Dragon's Bane dagger had been plunged into his chest.

"Aurora... w-why?" Jonathan stammered.

"My life... I cannot live it with you. I cannot live with you in your castle. I cannot betray my father like that, marrying the Dragon who betrayed his friendship. I simply cannot dishonor his memory like that."

"Aurora... you mean everything to me."

"I know. You mean everything to me as well, but something like this cannot persist."

"Why?! *Why* can't we have this? *Why* can't we be together and live like a family should?"

She loved Jonathan so much. She didn't care about her deceased father's approval or lack thereof.

No. The reason delved deeper.

"My child cannot be near you Jonathan. After the things you've done I can't have that kind of influence on him. I can't have him growing up in a world where Humans are treated the way that you treat them," Aurora's eyes stared straight into Jonathan's. She would not blink. Neither would he.

"Aurora, I'll change," Jonathan said.

"No Jonathan. I'm sorry. I've made up my mind. Please leave now."

Aurora turned away from him and walked towards her bedroom. She could barely hold her tears back.

Smoke rolled out of Jonathan's slightly open mouth. He couldn't believe what was happening. The woman he loved was leaving him because of his past.

He would get his revenge.

April 1, 1980

An 18-year-old Aurora smiled as she trotted off into the world. Bellato was her childhood home, but she was leaving to see the world. She had no idea where she would go, but she took up a pack of food and went. Oli, Max, and Zack had taught her how to defend herself from attacks, how to hunt, how to survive in the wilderness and especially how to avoid Dragons.

Earlier in her life, Aurora made her way east.

Before, she wanted to see the ruins of New York City and Washington D.C.

Before, she wanted to see where the Battle of Yorktown was fought.

Now, she wanted to feed her own need. She needed to find the beast who defeated her father, but spared his life. She needed to meet Jonathan the Tyrant.

September 4, 1980

Aurora had heard stories about Jonathan the Tyrant. The Tyrant controlled much of the land surrounding Bellato, but was never able to take over Bellato because of the efforts of Aurora's father and brothers.

Aurora remembered the bedtime stories her father had told her about the Tyrant.

June 17, 1966

"Aurora," John Ross said. "Jonathan the Tyrant is possibly the most powerful Dragon in existence. Even with a Dragon's Bane sword, there's little chance for any human, to kill him."

"Even you Daddy?" Aurora asked. "I thought you could kill any Dragon!"

Her father said shaking his head, "No, unfortunately, I had my chance and he nearly destroyed me."

"Oh no, Daddy! When was this?" Aurora asked.

"A long, long time ago, before you or your brothers were born."

September 4, 1980

Aurora stood in Meton. She saw the castle. She felt drawn to it, yet afraid of it.

One of the villagers tapped Aurora on the shoulder. "Miss, you look like you've never seen the castle of Jonathan the Tyrant before."

"I haven't," Aurora replied. "Is that really it?"

"Aye, it is," the young man said. "In that castle lives the evilest Dragon that Humanity has ever known."

"I bet he's not so bad," Aurora said softly.

"Not so bad!" the young man exclaimed. "Miss, this beast once destroyed an entire company of Human soldiers trying to defend this here town. Jonathan the Tyrant… he's a demon!"

Aurora looked at the man. His eyes snapped wide in near disgust at Aurora. In Aurora's mind there could be no better place than in Jonathan's grasp.

Aurora cleared her throat and said farewell to the man. Without thinking, she started walking towards the castle. The rocks marked the well worn path. The trees almost blotted out the sun as she drew closer to the castle. Sounds of the village faded into the distance. The castle steps rose only a few feet ahead and Aurora panicked. She considered turning around and going back to Meton.

Aurora's heart threatened to burst from her chest. She could smell the Dragon's scent. She couldn't back away now. She took her first tentative step onto the stairs leading to the front door. Her legs shook as she climbed the stairs. She felt more and more wary as she drew closer and closer to the huge oak door.

Aurora reached the door. It was open. She slowly poked her head into the door half expecting it to shut on her and decapitate her. When it didn't she eased herself into the door and looked around.

Aurora's heart pounded inside her chest. She could be killed at any moment and that thought somehow thrilled her. Any danger she encountered on her journeys felt minimal compared to the danger she found herself in now. Aurora drew one Dragon's Bane dagger from its sheath and held it ready. She sniffed at the air and followed the scent of what she thought would be Jonathan. Her eyes scanned the corridors as she silently stalked through.

Aurora's exploration brought her to a room with huge, closed, red doors. Aurora wasn't sure if she should continue on.

She whispered, "This must be the throne room."

Aurora took another step toward the throne room doors and peeked in what appeared to be a keyhole. She saw a huge, red throne, but no Dragon.

"AHEM!"

"AAAAH!"

Aurora jumped and landed on her bottom. Her dagger hit the cement floor with a clang.

"Who are you," the gruff voice of the man asked.

"Aurora," she replied small and scared. Her heart clawed at her ribcage to escape and run away.

"Don't you know this is trespassing?"

"Y-yes sir."

"The Dragon-Mage would simply not have a Human walk out of here alive after getting so far into his castle. You've walked into your death, young lady."

Aurora stood frozen in fear. She didn't know this man, but he seemed intent to kill her.

The man looked down at her. He pointed to the door and said, "Open it and go in."

Aurora still stood frozen in place.

"Now!"

Aurora grabbed her dagger quickly sheathing it, sprang up from the floor and pushed at the door unsuccessfully.

"Pull, My Sweet One."

Aurora cheeks reddened. She grabbed the huge iron ring on the door, pulling with all of her might. She could only move the door enough to get her body through. She slid into the room and turned to face the door.

The man's large fingers poked around the door. He easily pulled it open further and strode in. His mouth curled into a grin.

Aurora stood ready to fight. Her hand held her dagger. She knew it could kill a Human just as well as a Dragon.

The man walked towards her unafraid of her dagger. Aurora yelled, "Stop, I'll kill you I swear!"

The man did not stop.

Aurora lunged at the man dagger first.

The man slid to the side and grabbed her dagger hand and pulled it out and away from his chest. Aurora struck out with a punch to his face, but he blocked it and used his palm and pushed at her chest. Aurora nearly fell as she went backwards from the force of the push. Aurora touched the spot where he pushed her, right between her breasts. Her face exploded with anger.

"You son of a bitch! Don't ever touch me like that!"

The man laughed at her, "I'll touch you any way I want to. You are trespassing in MY castle, you are MY property."

"Your castle? I'm sure the Dragon-Mage would have an issue if he heard you say that."

"Who do you think I am, My Sweet One?"

Aurora looked at the man, clothed in red. His eyes briefly flashed red irises before returning to dark blue.

Aurora drew back her dagger hand and prepared to throw

— **159** —

her weapon at the Dragon-Mage. She spoke as calmly as she could, "My name is Aurora Gerstung. You fought against my father John Ross Gerstung during the Supremacy War. You spared him. I beg you to spare me."

The Dragon-Mage Jonathan said, "Why should I? You wandered into MY castle. I should just rape you and kill you right now for your insolence."

Aurora's heart jumped. She tried to remain calm as she replied, "Please, My Lord, my father told me that you were a noble creature who did not kill wantonly. The stories he told me, you were not the devil most Humans make you out to be. He told me…"

"Stop."

Aurora dropped the dagger and moved to him. Jonathan approached her and they pressed themselves against each other.

Aurora whispered, "I have dreamed of this moment for as long as I've had thoughts like this. You are what I've been searching for."

Jonathan smiled. "I'm glad you found me."

April 26, 1999

"Jonathan scooped me up and carried me to his bed chamber."

I interrupted. "Don't tell me that part."

Mother smiled sheepishly. "Sorry."

July 24, 1981

The rain spattered all around Jonathan as he stood out in the square of Meton. He yelled, "Vile Humans of Meton hear my calls!"

Aurora stood at the doorway of her hut. She dreaded what was coming and could do nothing to stop it.

Jonathan yelled again as heads poked out of huts.

"Humans, one of your own is a harlot," Jonathan pointed directly at Aurora.

"This woman has been my lover for over a year now without telling any of you! She is now carrying MY child and she will NOT marry me! She would rather have a bastard child than to be my wife. Discard her as she has discarded you in falsity and me in treachery!"

Jonathan's eyes flashed red in a lightning strike. His body grew in size and ripped his clothes as he took the form of a Dragon. He roared loudly, sending all of the Humans back into their huts. His wings flapped once, twice and he rose into the air, screeching all the way to his castle.

Aurora pulled her head back into her hut. She closed the door and leaned her back against the door. Tears stung her eyes. She slumped like a towel on the floor. She hugged herself tight because no one else would. She wouldn't cry. She wouldn't.

January 18, 1982

Knock. Knock.

Aurora held her baby in her arms as she awoke from her dream. Her brothers and their wives heads all were turned towards the door.

"Who could that be?" Max asked.

"Answer it," Oli said.

The three Hell Bringers stood at the ready.

Max walked toward the door and slowly opened it.

Cordially the Dragon-Mage said, "Greetings, is my son born yet?"

"It was a girl," Max said bitterly.

"You're a liar, just like your sister," Jonathan said. "Move aside boy."

Oli and Zack stood right behind him.

Max said sharply, "You will have to kill me to get to this child."

"That can be arranged," Jonathan spoke matter-of-factly.

Aurora shuffled into the front room holding the child. "Jonathan, don't do this. I already told you I don't want you anywhere near my son. Please respect me this much."

"Why should I? You hurt me deeper than any Dragon's Bane?"

"Because it's best for the child, don't you see? He can't know who you are. He can't know what kind of creature his

— **161** —

father is."

Jonathan turned to Max. "Do not cross me again boy. Your father was the lucky one. You won't be."

Jonathan's face scanned the room. His eyes at last focused on the child. He spoke to Aurora, but stared at the child. "If you leave this town, I will kill everyone you have ever known or loved. You all know I have that power."

Jonathan turned to the door. He stopped. "What is my son's name?"

Aurora breathed in deeply. She sighed his name.

John Ross.

32 — Mothers

I sat staring into my cold, half eaten, breakfast plate. I wasn't sure what to make of this story. I didn't know how to process it honestly.

I asked, "Why didn't you leave? Oli, Max and Zack could have protected you. They could have enlisted the entirety of the Human army to fight him."

My mother turned her head away and stared at her hands. "You don't realize how powerful Jonathan is. He would have destroyed all of them. He would have fought a war to keep me under his thumb. He is a Dragon King. He could amass an army so great it would darken the skies as it laid siege to Bellato, or wherever they took me. I'm not Helen of Troy. I couldn't be the cause of that. Humanity isn't ready for a full scale war."

"Do my uncles know why you chose not to come back with them?"

"Yes. And before you ask, I told them not to tell you, so don't hold this against them. Focus your blame on only me."

"I already do."

My mother's face rose to meet my eyes. I knew I had wounded her. I didn't hate her, but I was not happy with her at the moment.

I asked, "You loved him didn't you?"

"Yes."

"Why didn't you just marry him then? Life wouldn't have

been much different for us. The village would still hate us. They would just hate us because we were living comfortably in a castle instead of in this shack. I'm not sure how you felt about being verbally berated, but I certainly did not enjoy it, or the daily beatings I received from the other children."

Mother sighed. "I didn't want you to become cruel like him. I was the only one who saw the vulnerable side of him. I was the only one who saw his soul. But his actions spoke louder than any sweet words he spoke to me. I knew about his attacks on Human settlements at the beginning of the war. I couldn't have that kind of influence on you. I've had enough bad influence for the both of us."

"What do you mean?"

"I wasn't always the wise old crone I am now, John Ross. I was once a stupid girl making stupid mistakes."

"Well, obviously," I said, trying to make a joke.

My mother chuckled. "You remind me a lot of your grandfather. You're headstrong and honest, maybe a little too honest. He died near my 14th birthday. My brothers did a lot of my looking after. Our father, like our mothers, was not around much."

"Mothers?" This wasn't a story I had heard before.

Mother laughed. "I guess with all of the reputation surrounding your grandfather, his wives... er, lovers... er, consorts kind of get shuffled into the deck of history. But I remember them. They were an unlucky lot. From what they told me, my father was unbearable in a general sense."

"Tell me about them," I said.

Mother began:

"Our mamas were the first four women who trained to become Hell Bringers. Back then the Human Army was much less egalitarian than it is today. They had to fight their way to the top of the heap. Countless men fell by the wayside as they battled. They fought alongside your grandfather in the first battles against the Dragons, before Dragon's Bane was invented. They could have been sisters. Your grandfather definitely had a type when it came to looks. They were all about my height, all had black hair, except one, all had blue eyes, except another. You can see it in Oliver, Maxwell, Zachary and me.

"Oliver's mother was named Emily Sharp. That was the perfect name for a woman warrior. She and your grandfather met when he made his first trek to New York City before anyone knew anything was wrong. The story was Emily was crawling away from the city. Her arm was broken and your grandfather helped her to safety and to a doctor. Emily stayed with him after that. She followed him when he left New York to return home.

"Maxwell's mother was a girl from your grandfather's hometown named, Esther Stine. They had encountered each other again by chance when he had returned from New York City to find Cleveland mostly destroyed. She was niece to Tony Bellato, the man who was responsible for the first plans to resurrect the city. She was instrumental in getting Bellato and your grandfather together and forming the first of the Hell Bringer units. I remember her deer brown eyes.

"Zachary's mother was called Erin O'Neill. She met your grandfather after Cleveland had been destroyed. She came to help build the town of Bellato. She had a thick Irish accent, it was quite lovely. The only difference between her and the other three was her hair was fire red instead of black. She was largely an outsider. She was loud and an immigrant in a time when that was not embraced fully, but your grandfather did embrace her willingly as an ally.

"My mother…"

My mother stopped. This was probably the most about my relatives that I had ever heard. My mother wasn't usually such a fount of information about the family tree.

She began again:

"My mother was beautiful. All of our mothers were beautiful, but there was something about her that shone deep inside. She was an American Indian woman. Cherokee. She had a white father whom she had been living with off of the reservation for a long time. Apparently she made friends with your grandfather when she heard about the destruction of Cleveland and came to help, but this was different than Erin. She had heard your grandfather's story. All of his women loved him, and he loved them. But I think my mother was the only one he was in love with."

I asked, "What was her name?"

"Eve Fallingstar."

I smiled. My grandmother's name was Eve Fallingstar. It felt good to know that. "Why weren't they around much?"

My mother resumed:

"Your grandfather, as I said, was unbearable as a companion, even to my mother. One would think there would be jealousy pouring out of them looking upon one another as each of them bore a child from the same man, but the experience of dealing with the same eccentricities in your grandfather brought them closer together.

"The houses where your uncles now live are where their mothers lived once upon a time. My mother lived in a teepee outside of the city, she was a bit eccentric, but she and I came to the city every day so I could play with my brothers. For the first few years our mothers stayed and watched us together, but my father trained every day.

"Fort Pierce was a booming establishment at the time and many eager soldiers were there to learn to defend Humankind from the Dragons. My mothers wanted to stay in shape, but they knew someone had to be around to watch the children. They would take turns. One would watch the children while the other three went off to fight.

"When Dragon's Bane was developed in late 1970, that gave our mothers an even better reason to keep training. We were all older – nine, ten or eleven – and we could do most of our looking after ourselves. We were growing up fast, at least in body. The boys were learning to fight and they were teaching me. Each day we grew further apart from our parents and closer to each other. Eventually we stopped missing them during the day and barely noticed when they came home at night.

"The times apart grew longer and longer. It stretched to two days. Three days. Four days. Days stretched to a week. Two weeks. I know now that our parents were training to stay ready to fight the Dragons and keep the rest of the world safe, but while I didn't miss them anymore, I started to resent them. Why did I have to be the one to sacrifice my mother for the greater good when so many other mothers stayed home to love and cherish their children? I wouldn't doubt my brothers felt the same, but they never shared it.

"The Hell Bringer force was training for a campaign in the North. The Dragons were amassing near Detroit. They were probably planning to destroy the Dragon's Bane construction plant there. Our parents were planning to head up that way, of course, since we were the closest fort that could send warriors.

"It was about a month before my birthday. I lay in the teepee wrapped up in bearskin blankets. I wasn't asleep, but I was getting tired. Mother came home to tell me the news, but I already knew. She was leaving for Detroit. The grapevine traveled news well in those days.

"Mother slid herself up under the bearskin with me and wrapped her strong arms around me. She tried to wake me up with her voice like soft wind chimes saying my name, 'Aurora, Aurora, Aurora' over and over. I pretended to sleep because I was so mad at her: for having to leave; for being away so much; for any number of reasons a 13 year old girl is mad at her mother.

"Mother leaned over me. I think she knew I was awake, but she was respecting my silence. She whispered in my ear that she was sorry, but she had to go and she missed me and she loved me and she wanted me to know that she was done after this battle. She wanted me to know that she wanted to be there to help me grow into a woman. I felt a tear hit the side of my face, but I dare not wipe it away to reveal my ruse.

"Mother kissed my cheek again and lay back down to sleep."

My mother paused. She sighed. I think I saw a glint of a tear from her eye. "If I had known then what I knew now I would have turned around and hugged her and told her I loved her more than anything.

"The next morning, my mother was gone before I awoke. I never saw her again."

33 — Changes

May 1, 1999

I hugged my mother goodbye and kissed her on the cheek. I acted as a more attentive, good son for the rest of the time I spent with her. She had returned to her normal, non-talkative, self after telling me about her mother. I enjoyed the talkative mother, but the familiarity of her silence comforted me especially with all of the information I had to process now.

I was the son of a Dragon and a well intentioned liar. Grandson of a workaholic war hero and his physically, if not emotionally distant, consort. Confusion and discord flowed through my veins. I needed to work it out before I returned to Fort Kingsley.

I closed the door to my mother's home behind me and turned on my heels to go. In my way stood Conchita Gomez with Diana behind her. "Mother, stop it," Diana pleaded.

Conchita's raspy voice sounded as if she had been yelling, or crying, or both. "You will leave now. You will not come back. If you come back, we will kill you."

I looked down into Conchita's eyes. "I wish I could say I was sorry for your husband's death, but it was not my doing. Do not blame me for the problems your town has incurred. I am not your enemy. I went to the castle to fight the one who is. I didn't win, but I won't give up. From this point on, you will not threaten or harass my mother. I will hear about it, and when I do, I will come back and mete out the punishment to whomever deserves it. We are not your victims."

I turned to walk to the West Gate. Conchita didn't follow, but a group of villagers gathered and heard most of what I said to her. I heard the volcanic rise of the rabble. Without thinking about it I drew my sword, turned and cut through the air, and a stone, in one motion. Todd Bollin stood in front of the rest looking like he had just thrown it. I sheathed my sword and stomped towards him. He tried to escape through the crowd. They stood too stunned to move. I grabbed Todd by the back of his neck and pulled him towards me. I cocked my powerful right fist and slammed it into his chest knocking him into his brothers.

I screamed at them all. "LEAVE ME ALONE!"

As I screamed, heat rose in my chest. The heat traveled through my throat and into my mouth. I didn't believe it as I saw the fire shoot out of my mouth. The villagers ran away screaming, except Diana.

The fire ceased as quickly as it began and I doubled over coughing. Diana took a tentative step towards me. "Are you alright JR?"

Cough. "Yeah, I'll be alright." Cough.

She asked, "What was that?"

I replied, "Felt like fire to me."

"Looked like it too. How is that possible?"

"Must be a side effect of my condition."

"Your condition?"

"Being the son of Jonathan the Tyrant."

Diana didn't respond. I recovered from my coughing fit and stood. "You mean you didn't know?"

"There were rumors you were a Dragon Sympathizer, but no one ever said anything about you being his son."

I sighed. "I didn't even know about it until a few days ago when I went up to the castle to fight him."

Diana approached me and hugged me tightly. I hugged her back. "I'll miss you," she said.

"Will you look after my mother?" I asked. "She will need it. I don't know if she trusts you, but you're the only one in this village who I could trust even a little."

Diana said softly, "Yes, I will do that for you."

We didn't kiss. I turned and left the rickety walls of the

village behind me again.

Miles down the road stood Jonathan and Nama. I intended to just walk past them, but Jonathan stopped me with a hand on my chest. "Wait, my son."

I growled. "You might be my father, but I will never call myself your son."

"Fair enough, but regardless, I saw you breathe fire and I'm very proud. You will experience a lot of changes in your body from now on."

I scoffed. "As if puberty wasn't bad enough."

Jonathan said, "This is your awakening as a Dragonkin. Don't resist it. You will only cause yourself pain."

"Speaking of pain," I said. "Don't cause this village or my mother any more pain. She might not be willing to start a war to be free of you, but I am."

"It would be a war you would lose, my son."

"Regardless, I would be free of you."

"You would be willing to die to be free of me?"

"You've caused me so much pain without me even knowing who you are. The existence of your kind in this world has caused pain in innocent people for almost 50 years and probably longer for all I know. Yeah, I'm willing to die to be free of that."

Jonathan's hand dropped from my chest. He turned away from me. I met eyes with Nama. *Be well my little green friend.*

Unless you have a death wish, train hard. This isn't over.

I walked on.

May 3, 1999

I reached Bellato fairly quickly. I slept fitfully and intermittently during my walk. I felt all of my cells on fire. I itched all over especially between my shoulder blades, especially when I thought how much faster it would be if I could fly.

The gates of Bellato greeted me with the Three Guidelines. I clasped hands with the guards as I passed. I was a Gerstung. No, I was more than a Gerstung. I was a Human. Respected. No one had any idea about my parentage and it felt good that way.

I reached my uncles' houses without issue. I knocked. Jennifer let me into the house. We embraced. Soon my cousins and other aunts surrounded me and hugged me tightly. It felt good to be in a place of warmth and love.

My uncles were noticeably absent. I asked where they were.

Jennifer answered, "They are up at the fort helping with Ajax's transition."

I asked, "What is the problem?"

Jessica replied, "He still will not speak and no one can get him to explain why. He has come under scrutiny by the sergeants. He is in danger of being expelled for insubordination."

Jane said, "He has written his purpose finally. He wrote that he holds silent vigil for the victims of the massacre. He wrote he does not wish to speak until the Sympathizer tribe is brought to justice."

I sighed. "They cannot understand how deeply Ajax feels about this. First, Alana left...."

"—Alana was brainwashed into leaving. It isn't her fault," interrupted Jessica.

"I'm sorry Aunt Jessica." I disagreed in my head, but I didn't mean to harsh a tender topic. "But regardless, Ajax is experiencing a lot of change. He wants to fight it. I hope an arrangement can be made. He needs to be in the army."

Jane took the lead in changing the topic. "Dinner is on the table. John Ross, would you like to join us?"

I smiled. "I would love to."

We all dispersed to the yard where the tables sat in the cooling spring dusk. My aunts set a place for me. We all dug in. The food was delicious. We ate ham with stuffing and pasta. We ate salad and fruit. I ate voraciously. I hadn't packed enough food on my trip back to Bellato and ran out halfway to the gates. I noticed my appetite growing since discovering my true origin.

I also noticed my body burned hotter than I had ever remembered it, even with no sun around me. I turned to Max Junior sitting next to me and asked, "Do I seem any different to you?"

Max shook his head, "Naw. A little less pretty, but otherwise the same."

I scoffed. "Thanks. I love you too cousin."

After dinner, I hugged my aunts and told them I was going out to see a friend in town, but I would be back before long. I put my things in the guest house and walked through the slightly less busy streets.

Walt and Rebecca's orders called them back by April 30th. I knew I wouldn't see them in town. I hadn't really made a whole lot of close friends during my stay in the fort. Only one person occupied my mind at that moment.

Rain threatened. I could smell it in the air. Lightning cracked. Thunder boomed. I walked faster. Water fell from the sky and it felt like new. My hot skin seemed to steam as I trotted through the early parts of the rain. It felt almost refreshing. I felt as if all responsibility drained from me with the water.

I reached my destination. The Artist's Cove Tavern.

34 — Poetry

The Artist's Cove Tavern was so named because all of the most enlightened and creative Human minds visited to share their wealth of culture. Culture was important in an age that could have descended into self serving barbarism just to survive the Dragons.

Paintings by local and traveling artists hung on the walls. Many of them depicted familiar scenes of Dragon battles. Others showed beautiful scenes of trees and valleys untouched by Human or Dragon influence.

The smoke and noise filled the one room tavern. I caught parts of speeches as I walked through the crowd.

"– you see we need to forge peace with the Dragons –"

"– trolls have begun attacking bridges again –"

"– Crown Prince of Humanity, HA! Not on my watch –"

I looked around the room. She had to be here somewhere.

"– the strongest should be the ones breeding. It would only make sense in the –"

"– you know, and don't tell anyone this, but I'd be okay with a royal family, as long as they –"

I approached the bar and sat on a wooden stool. The bartender was a tall, gruff man in his early 50s. His thick torso was probably more muscle than fat. He stroked his full long, whiting beard.

The bartender grunted as he looked me over. "You old

enough to be in here boy?"

I grunted back. "I'm in here aren't I?"

The bartender nodded. "What'll you have?"

"A whiskey. And Maria."

"Maria? What are you to her?"

"I'm a friend from the Fort."

The bartender plopped a small glass on the bar in front of me. He filled it with a translucent brown liquid. "Blast you and the army. You went and hurt my girl."

"Are you Sonny Oldman?" The proprietor of the Artist Cove Tavern.

"Naw. Oldman is up at the stage. He's about to get the poetry ready." The bartender pointed at the bar. I took my drink, smelled it, and then drank it quickly. It tasted awful, but I had to look like I belonged. I turned my head and saw a black haired man about my height and who looked about my age. I looked back at the bartender and thanked him with a nod then stood and turned.

"JR?!" A female voice yelled from my right. I turned and saw Maria. She ran to me as well as one can run between a packed house. I stood in one place for ease of meeting. She raised her uninjured arm to wave and I waved back. A sling tied to her body held her left arm. She reached me and I embraced her warmly and tightly. She lightly kissed my lips then my cheek.

The room was loud so we had to speak directly into one another's ears as we stood. I found out that Maria was working as a waitress just like she had planned. Her left arm was growing stronger slowly. She could wiggle her fingers, but the rest of her arm was still useless. The doctor said it would take a long while to get all use of her arm back.

A thin man came up from behind Maria and threaded his skinny arms around her waist. Maria yelled, "Oh yeah. This is Kim Street. He is Bellato's top poet."

I extended a hand to Kim, he shook it. I yelled, "I'm John Ross Gerstung."

Kim nodded. He yelled back, "Maria has spoken of you. Are you here for the poetry night?"

I shook my head. "No. I'm just here for Maria."

Kim frowned. "She's with me now."

Maria turned her head. "That has not been decided. I'm with myself now. You just get the pleasure of my company while I decide what I'm doing. JR, you should do some poetry."

"I don't have anything with me."

"That's okay. This is in the moment poetry."

"People!" The man on the stage yelled.

"What?" yelled the response from the audience. Then silence permeated the room. I could hear the bartender pouring more whiskey and other drinks. People took quiet footsteps to their seats. Maria pulled my hand with her and Kim to their booth by the wall. An unnamed man sat at the table with us. He and I shared a side which was awkward since it seemed unlikely I would be given the opportunity to ask his name. Kim let Maria slide into the booth first, next to the wall and he sat on the edge.

"For the one or two of you who do not know, I am Sonny Oldman, purveyor of poets and accumulator of artists. Thank you for coming to The Artist's Cove Tavern for a night of poetry. As we have been discussing for many weeks, tonight is a night of competition. The Ancient Greeks used to include poetry and other art forms in their Olympic events, but since there are no Olympics, we are having our own Poetry Olympics. The winner will be decided by audience reaction. All poets please come to the stage."

Kim stood. The man next to the wall pushed at me so I slid out of the seat only to let him out, but the river of poets swept me away. I somehow made my way to the brown painted thick nailed wood of the stage. I saw the mortar between the slats, Oldman certainly did not want the stage to crumble which I feared it would when 50 or so men and women stood upon the stage.

"The first round is the rhyming round. I will say a line and the first poet will rhyme that line. Not only must they rhyme it, but the line must draw a reaction from the crowd. If no one reacts, the bartender, Warner, will ring a bell and the poet is eliminated. Audience, your reactions are necessary, groans, laughing, crying, angry cursing and more are all accepted, but if the lines do not incite you, remember to stay silent. If the poet draws a reaction or a bell ring, the next poet will riff off of that line with another rhyme and so on down the line. Poets, do you understand?"

The poets around me nodded and I stood dumbstruck.

Oldman cleared his throat. "Her skin was pale as milk."

"Her body was well built." Silence. Ding. The poet left the stage.

Kim said, "Her pussy was liquid silk." Reargh.

"My heart she did filch." Ding.

"Red and green colored her kilt." Ding.

I said, "Her skin differed from all her ilk." Ooooh.

The man from the booth, "Her eyes did not betray her bilk." Nice.

Warner, the bartender dinged more times than not. Eventually words were used over again, but by the end of the line three quarters of the poets were sitting.

Oldman looked pleased. "The second round is couplets. They do not necessarily have to rhyme, but they have to mean something. Again, the crowd will decide who stays and who goes. Audience, it is still your job to react or not to the words these poets speak."

Kim was first. He stared at Maria.

"I see your eyes, navy blue and gold. / I want to swim inside you until we fade into the black." Awwww.

I was next. I focused my gaze at Maria as well.

"It was my duty to keep you from harm. / I hope every day to heal your arm." Awwww.

The man from the booth did not stare at Maria. He had his eyes closed.

"Thousands collaborate in revelry. / But the free do not realize they are not free." Wooo.

After that a considerable number of dings rang out. Two more poets advanced, one male, one female.

"I am a traveling poet, riding town to town. / I'm loving out of a suitcase wishing you were around." Awwww.

"We are only cards in the playing deck. / Who is the next Dragon to collect our necks?" Damn. Hell yeah.

Oldman spoke, "Well done poets. Our final round will continue as long as it needs. This is the "Muse Round." Maria, please come to the stage."

Maria stood and approached.

Oldman resumed. "Maria, our muse, will inspire the poetry of these five finalists. Finalists, your job will be to focus on Maria and muse on her. Audience you will decide if the poetry is worthy of Maria with a resounding Yes or No. Warner's ears will be the judge."

Kim went first. "I will cherish you and give you everything I can. / Just decide on me and I will be your man. / I yearn for the day I can touch you free / and hope for the kiss you will bestow to me." Yes Yes no Yes Yes. Kim bowed.

I looked deep into Maria's eyes. "I'm returning to the fort in two days / and I need you to know. / Without you there, / my heart feels bare / and I don't want to go. / Maybe when your strength returns / and you can hold a pot, / you can come cook up at the fort, / but you'll never be forgot." Yes Yes no no Yes. I smiled and Maria smiled back.

The next three poets did not advance.

It was Kim's turn again. He put his left hand on Maria's right cheek. "Maria you know the way I feel / and there is no room for doubt. / I want to marry you my dear. / That's what this is all about." Kim pulled out a gold ring and took her left hand. Maria looked at him strangely. She curled her hand away from the ring. No No yes No yes.

Oldman coughed. "Well that was certainly unprecedented. Do you have a response poet?" He was looking at me.

I smiled as Kim stepped aside. My eyes locked with Maria's. "I had no plans to wed you / that was never my design. / But maybe someday if I'm lucky / I can call you mine. / I have to head back to the fort. / I have to earn my place. / Above all else, you must know / I simply miss your face."

The look on Maria's face resembled a wild cat. Sonny Oldman and Warner looked at the crowd who looked at each other.

35 — Return to the Fort

May 4, 1999

Just after midnight I strode out of the Artist's Cove Tavern arm in arm with Maria. I held in my hands the winning trophy of Dragon's Bane and gold. The winners of the poetry contests were asked to come back and defend the trophy, but I knew I would not have the time. I needed to be back to the fort the next day to resume my training. I planned to leave the trophy with Maria when we parted ways.

We walked together to Maria's apartment a few blocks away from the Artist's Cove. The wooden steps up to her apartment were surprisingly strong. We reached her door and she unlocked it and we entered. Maria lit her oil lamp in the middle of the room. The lamp illuminated most of the kitchen.

"Do you want something to drink, JR?" Maria asked.

"Just water if you would," I said. I wanted to keep a clear head after all that it had been muddled by over the past few days.

She brought me a cup with a jug. The water she poured was clear, I was surprised. Maria said, "Bellato just installed a new water filtration pump. Only a few lucky families and houses have indoor plumbing, but everyone has access to the covered fountain and can get clean water. Everyone is pretty excited. Omaha doesn't even have filtration yet."

I drank from the cup and the water was refreshing. I drank it all in one swig. I smiled at Maria.

"JR, I've missed you so much. I'm glad you're here."

"Thank you Maria, I have missed you too."

"Will you stay the night with me?"

I brought the cup to my lips and then remembered I had drunk it all and lowered the cup.

"What about Kim? He seemed pretty attached to you.

"Kim…," Maria started. "Kim is a conundrum. He has only known me a week. He has been going on and on about my beauty, but he doesn't know who I am. He looks at me like someone he has to protect because of my arm and only like someone he has to protect."

"He doesn't realize you probably could kick his ass."

"He has no idea."

"Do you like him?"

Maria paused and filled up my cup again. "I don't know. I don't dislike him. I'm just not sure I want to be with someone who doesn't get me. Do you know what I mean?"

"I know exactly what you mean." I take another drink of water, this time I do not drink it all. I set the cup on the counter.

Maria took my hand and led me into the next room. Her apartment was spartanly furnished. The kitchen had an ice box where she kept her water jug and other things that needed to be cold. It also served as the dining room with a table and two chairs. Counters lined the walls and above them were cupboards. The oil lamp partly illuminated the next room. The bedroom it seemed. The bed was covered in a cotton blanket. Maria pulled back the blanket to reveal a silk sheet. She pulled back the silk sheet to reveal a cotton sheet tucked around the mattress of unknown origin, but probably cotton stuffing.

Maria stood in front of me. Her right arm caressed my left cheek. "Will you undress me JR?"

I cleared my throat. "I would love to."

I reached around her neck and unfastened her sling. Her left arm gently extended lifeless next to her body. She pulled herself to me with her right arm and kissed me softly. I kissed her back with every nerve in my body tingling.

Her peasant blouse was tied at the top with a leather thong. I slid off her sling and untied the top of her blouse. I kissed my way down her chest as I pulled the blouse open as far as I could. I ran my hands down her body until my fingers

— **179** —

reached the skin of her hips. I slid my hands up her sides bringing her blouse with them and over her head taking care around her left arm. I reached around her and unfastened her brassiere. We pulled it off together. The glow of the lamp shone off of her breasts as they rested naturally tan with dark nipples angled slightly upward.

"Could you help me with my pants?" Maria asked. "I have figured out how to do it on my own, but it is so much easier with another set of hands."

The pants were also tied with a leather thong. I untied the knot holding them on and stretched the pants out and off of her hips. She wore white cotton panties.

"You really like cotton don't you?"

Maria grinned. "I just don't like the feel of leather that close to... well you know. I like to have a barrier."

Maria tugged off her panties by herself and slid into bed. She moved so fast I only caught a glimpse of her pubic pelt. She smiled. "Are you coming?"

I smiled. "Breathing heavy."

Maria laughed. "I'm okay with it if you aren't ready. You can still lay here with me and I won't try to tempt you."

I shook my head. "You tempt me every second I'm around you. But I don't want to dive into something I'm not ready to handle. I can't sleep here, even though every part of my body is screaming at me right now."

Maria smiled slyly. "My body is screaming at you too, just so you know."

I pulled the silk sheet over her bare breasts, then the cotton blanket over the silk sheet and tucked Maria in. I leaned down and kissed her. I probed my tongue to her lips and danced with her tongue for a moment. Then I pulled back. The bulge in my pants was strong enough to push my leather trousers out. Maria noticed and smiled as I pulled away.

"Lock the door as you leave," Maria instructed with a yawn and closed her eyes.

I turned off her oil lamp letting only the light from the moon shine in. I located the locking mechanism and affixed it to lock when I closed the door behind me. I stepped out and sighed as I closed the door.

Kim waited at the bottom of her steps. He did not look pleased.

"You bastard," he said. "You screwed my girl and just left like nothing."

I stared at Kim. "I have three things to say to you Kim. One, never EVER call me a bastard again. Two, I didn't screw Maria. Three, she will never be your girl if you keep treating her like a possession. She is a person perfectly capable of defending herself from everything in the world. The faster you get that through your head, the better off you will be. Maria wants someone who wants to know her not just for her beauty, but for her strength of character. You need to look deep beneath the surface to understand Maria, but I can guarantee if you take the time you will be richly rewarded. Maria is one of the best women I know."

Kim's lips were tight against his teeth. I could tell he wanted to say something. I didn't give him the opportunity. I walked tiredly away. The next day would be busy.

May 5, 1999

I spent the next day recovering and mentally preparing myself for the walk back to the fort. As long as I showed up sometime during the day I wouldn't be reprimanded. I wanted to make it sooner rather than later. I said my good byes to my family and began to walk. I took a circuitous route to the North Gate so I could wander by Maria's apartment, but I caught no glimpse of her. I waved to the guards as I left the city and walked to the fort.

I reached the fort not long after noon. I showed my credentials to the guards of the fort and they let me in, one of them took off running through the middle of the fort. I saw the recruits who were already training. The recruits who joined the same month as me had to be back a few days before I did because of my experience with the gunmen.

I didn't see anyone from my unit as I walked to my bunk. I looked for Ajax on the field, but didn't see him either. I figured I would drop off my things and report to Lieutenant Kingsley since it was he who told me I should take extra days off.

My bunk was empty except for Walt's stuff. I put my stuff on my bed and walked back out. I followed the wall back to the offices. I reached Kingsley's office and knocked with no answer. I tried to peer in through his window, but saw nothing. I turned the knob and it opened. I saw no one as I poked my head in.

I went to the fort secretary and inquired about Lieutenant Kingsley. He directed me to the West Gate. So I continued to the West Gate. The guards let me pass saying I would have to walk down the path until I heard the shouting.

So I did. I thought about how much easier it would be to find them if I could fly above the trees and see down. My shoulder blade started itching so badly I had to rub them against a nearby tree. Finally the itching subsided and I continued my walk.

Silence fell upon me. Not even the sounds of the birds could be heard. Something was different. Something.

I spun around and blocked Walt's punch as he came from behind me. Chen attacked at my left and I ducked. Lance threw a kick at my ducked face which I blocked and pushed him back. Rebecca ran at me with a jumping kick which I rolled under just as Walt swung his foot at my face. I reached my feet and two recruits I didn't know came at me from my back. I ducked again avoiding them both.

"Rules of engagement sir?" I asked out loud.

"Survive," said Kingsley's voice.

36 — Intensity

June 2, 1999

Walt, Rebecca, Chen and I sat laughing loudly at the mess hall table. Walt just said something humorous about Crush being slow and the rest of us thought it the best thing ever. The rest of the recruits in the mess hall watched us. They talked as normal, but there was always an accusatory eye on the Hell Bringer recruits. We didn't purposefully separate ourselves, but the rest of the recruits no longer came around us unless absolutely necessary. Ajax would sometimes join us. He already felt the ostracism of his chosen silence. I was the only person he knew, but even he kept his eyes on his plate as he ate. I tried numerous times to get him to talk to me at least, but Ajax would have none of it.

As Hell Bringer recruits we trained with one another. Our fighting helped to improve our agility and enhance our senses. Every day held a new challenge. The first fight when I reached the Fort after the week off was intense. It was Kingsley's intent to test me and make sure I hadn't gone soft in a week. I held my own.

Not every class of recruits forged Hell Bringers. In fact, in all the fort, only Walt, Rebecca, Chen, Lance, and the recruits Phyllis Green and Steve Jones trained with me. Lance had been a Hell Bringer recruit the longest. His graduation was set for the end of the month so he acted as our unofficial leader.

I trained with Lance. We practiced hand to hand combat.

These exercises were meant to improve our speed while we avoided Dragon attacks and found the right moment to strike with our Dragon's Bane.

I barely avoided Lance's fast punches. He threw fewer kicks, so I compensated with kicks of my own. He fought too smart for that and blocked or avoided most of my attacks.

Lance tried to be encouraging. It felt more like condescension. "Pretty good Gerstung. You're slow though. You need to be faster. Dragons are huge, but they are fast. They will swallow you whole before you can blink."

I growled and flexed. I felt the heat build inside me. I faked one direction and attacked at another direction. Lance didn't fall for it, but I almost hit him anyway. "That's better, Gerstung."

That night brought exhausted sleep. It also brought a penetrating noise that woke me from my exhausted sleep.

I quietly slid out of bed and slipped on pants. I peeked out of my bunk and eased myself out the door. Walt did not wake.

The moon illuminated the East wall and I saw two shadows creeping towards the guards. One shadow ducked into the door to the upper guards of the fort, the shadow on the ground attacked the guards inside the gate.

I raced towards the gate unarmed, but unexpected. I hoped to catch the assailants unaware. The gate opened slightly and the other two guards on the ground fell as they investigated. I reached the gate and saw three guards. They were not dead, just hurt. Phyllis was one of them. I called for help and the medics arrived and took the guards to the infirmary. I raced up the stairs to the upper guard post, but I only saw Lance and two other guards on the ground writhing in pain.

"Gerstung." Lance coughed. "They went over the wall."

June 3, 1999

Security increased after that. Two guards per side of the gate on the ground and two guards per corner above the gate became four at each corner and gate. The Sympathizers had gotten in deeper than they should have been able to. Buzz grew around the fort about a mole, someone on the inside who knew the lay of the fort and knew the weak points.

Lance didn't look much worse for wear when he came to practice that morning. He limped, but something felt off. Walt nudged me. I nodded. Walt hadn't given up his suspicions of Lance, though he kept quiet about them.

The seven of us stood in a line. Kingsley stood facing us not speaking. He considered all of us.

What am I going to do with this bunch. They aren't ready.

Thought speak doesn't have accents or sound. No thought speak can really be differentiated through how one receives it. Mostly, the thoughts just come across the Dragon lineage. I didn't see any Dragons around. I didn't want to look around, Kingsley would kick my ass. Then I realized. Kingsley. He was like me somehow.

Kingsley looked at me then looked away and began pacing back and forth.

"You seven are not ready to be Hell Bringers. Even you Lance. Somehow or another, I have failed to bring to you the importance of this training. Last night, Sympathizers got into our fort and hurt some of our good men and women. The Sympathizers are becoming better trained and stronger every day. We need to increase our own power and become more vigilant in our fight. In the past, I have not engaged my recruits because it wasn't fair. The recruits were not ready to fight someone like me. I hate to sound arrogant, but Dragons fear me for a reason. I am your best hope in this fight. You need to get on my level. The only way that is going to happen, is to fight me."

We seven looked at each other. Kingsley was the man who had never been beaten, let alone touched in combat. Kingsley took a simple combat stance. "Come."

We were unsure of ourselves as we took our own stances. Kingsley, faster than our eyes, attacked.

Jones fell first. His skilled punches missed Kingsley completely and Kingsley took him down with a kick to the stomach. Walt attacked with a kick of his own, but Kingsley blocked and shoved him hard. Walt flew backwards into Lance. Chen held a Snake Style stance and attacked where Kingsley's eyes would have been, but Kingsley dodged the attack curved his head around Chen's arm and head-butted him in the wrist.

Rebecca cried out as she flew at Kingsley with a punch, but he side stepped and roundhouse kicked her in the side of the head. Green received the same treatment after a missed flying knee.

The recruits moved fast, Kingsley moved faster. I held back. I studied Kingsley. I listened for his thoughts. I heard none. Jonathan told me about this, fighting without thinking. Instinct.

The recruits kept attacking. Kingsley put all of them back down. Walt landed at my feet and looked up, panting. "Why... aren't... you... fighting...."

Kingsley threw Rebecca at me. I caught her and set her down, but she crumpled to her ass on the ground, defeated. Lance, Jones, Green and Chen all sprawled out around Kingsley.

Kingsley spoke, "Well Gerstung. Are you here to fight or are you wasting my time?"

Before I could answer, Kingsley attacked. I knew I had to duck. I knew I had to dodge. I knew I had to block. But I did none of these things. Two punches and a kick battered me. I tripped over Lance behind me and I rolled backwards into a crouch position. Kingsley came at my head with a kick. I blocked and tried to punch him in the knee. Kingsley's leg already moved back before I formed the thought. I jumped and threw a spin kick, but Kingsley ducked and punched me three more times in the chest knocking me back.

I growled. Kingsley grinned. The fire grew inside me. Kingsley came at me again with a kick. I moved to the side. Kingsley had a punch ready to fire, but I pushed myself into the fist instead of away from it. I threw a left hand chop at Kingsley's head, but he threw his forehead into the chop. The rebuff stung, but I didn't react. I swung my right hand around to clutch Kingsley, but he spun quickly and grabbed my wrist instead. My left hand shook once to get the feeling back and swung a punch, but was blocked. Kingsley threw a knee into my midsection. I staggered back, until Kingsley pulled me to him by my right arm and clotheslined me, knocking me for a loop.

I lay winded. Kingsley stepped back. "Are you finished already?"

I coughed. "No." My muscles twinged with my movement. I slowly took my feet. I motioned for Kingsley to come at me.

He did.

It was as if things were in slow motion. Kingsley floated high into the air with a right jumping front kick. I caught his foot with my left hand. Kingsley landed and I had to bend backwards to absorb the force of his blow. My right foot went to his left foot. I straightened up, which took Kingsley off balance and swung a left kick into his left thigh. Kingsley spun in a barrel roll in the air at the same speed I spun around. I lashed my left foot out again in the same move and struck him in the ass. Kingsley spun around laterally, end to end. He landed with his head at my feet. I smiled and fell backwards with my head near Rebecca's ass. Worst timing ever.

I expected Kingsley to pummel me now. But it didn't happen. I heard Kingsley take his feet and stumble a little. He spoke, "Recruits, don't be afraid to kick your instructor in the ass from time to time. You're going to need to do it if you ever expect to survive the Dragons."

The other recruits picked me up and patted me on the back as Kingsley left us. Walt and Rebecca helped me back to the bunk. Rebecca kissed me on the cheek and smiled, but said nothing. Walt helped me onto the bunk and said he'd be back after he had some chow.

I sighed and lay with my eyes closed.

I heard breathing. Then a voice I had not heard for a long time, "Lance is a Sympathizer."

37 — Steve Jones

June 30, 1999

We silently encouraged Lance Robbins as he began his testing to become a Hell Bringer. Three Hell Bringer recruiters stood in front of us.

Sergeant Razor's head was shorn bald and the tattoo on his bulging left bicep read "Razor" in black ink over brown skin. He wore a flat evergreen ripped sleeveless shirt obviously to show off his arms. His matching slacks were dirty.

I noticed Walt, the womanizer, had an eye on Sergeant Raven. Her features were slender except in the obvious places where they were fuller than what might be expected for her build, but she walked with ease and a bounce that attracted even the attention of Chen, Jones and I. The bob of her black ponytail matched her movements. She buttoned her shirt halfway up emphasizing her assets and her sleeves were intact ending in pale fingers. Her slacks were immaculate and form fitting.

Rebecca punched me in the arm for staring at Raven. Her green eyes flashed.

Lieutenant Hawk's bronze and red skin glinted in the sunlight. His braided long black, brown hair hung down to his lower back. His shirt similar to Razor and Raven, but his sleeves were rolled up and he had more accolades. He wore no slacks. Instead he had brown tanned leather chaps with a loin cloth covering his sensitive bits.

I caught Rebecca staring at Hawk and I punched her in the arm. She stuck her tongue out at me.

A series of tests awaited Lance. His endurance test consisted of running a mile non stop in a certain amount of time. His combat test meant fighting Razor, Raven and Hawk. Fighting a Dragon would test his commitment.

Kingsley sent the rest of us away. Only Hell Bringers were allowed to attend to the tests.

The rest of us sparred in the main training area of the fort in our free time. Rebecca and I partnered up and went at it fairly hard. Gender served as no barrier in the policy of combat. Rebecca would have been pissed if I held back. Rebecca moved fast. I missed more often than I actually struck her. I had the benefit of a tougher body, so when she struck me, I could take it. At the end of our sparring, the skin on both of us tingled and our hearts beat heavily.

The six of us relaxed in the mess hall. Rebecca sat across from me. Chen sat next to her, Walt sat next to me. Jones and Green sat across from each other and on the other side of us. I felt my foot accidentally touch Rebecca's. She didn't pull away, only smiled secretly to me.

Lance stumbled into the mess hall. Black blood and scratches covered his skin. He looked like he may have been crying. We looked at him bewildered. He sputtered. "I made it. I'm a Hell Bringer."

September 17, 1999

Steve Jones personified the everyman. He wore short brown hair and brown eyes. He stood about five feet ten inches and was average weight. Of the Hell Bringer recruits he had the most contact with those outside of that circle. No one could pick Jones out of a line-up. That was to his advantage and his disadvantage. He could have been perfect for infiltration of a Sympathizer camp, but he was often left out of activities which he may have enjoyed. Jones never intruded. When he wasn't invited he didn't attend.

Things changed when Jones fought.

Put a weapon in Steve Jones' hand and you asked for trouble. Standing toe to toe, hand to hand with Jones was not much wiser. He possessed unmatched intelligence when it came to fighting. He could work joint locks, pressure points and choke holds as well as he threw punches and kicks. Jones fought with passion and precision.

This was his birthday, and unfortunately, no one was celebrating with him. I noticed him sitting alone in the mess hall when the other Hell Bringer recruits and I walked in. I immediately motioned for the rest of us to join him. I sat in front of him. Green sat next to him and smiled a crooked smile. I didn't know Jones that well, but from what I could tell he had a crush on Phyllis. Green started three months ahead of him and so he admired her by default. At least that was my impression.

Green knew and she worked Jones with smiles and tossing her short cropped blonde hair. She was thin, but muscled and about Jones' height.

Other than my striking of Kingsley in June, none of us had been able to touch him. I became a fort wide celebrity, but the other non-Hell Bringer recruits still kept their distance from us as a whole. In reality though, Jones got closest to Kingsley consistently. Kingsley even looked worried on occasion when fighting Jones one on one.

But today was Jones' birthday. No talk of fighting.

I said, "Congratulations on another lap around the sun. What would you like to do with your day?"

Jones smiled. In an unremarkable tenor he said, "I think I'd just like the company of my friends."

"Your friends," Green said in a light sing song voice. "Would we be considered your friends?"

"Well, of course," Jones said. "You guys are acting like you don't know me or something."

"We don't really," Walt said.

Jones nodded. "Well, you've all fought me on numerous occasions. You know me better than anyone else. I'm nothing when I'm not doing what I love. And I love fighting. It fills me with..., it fills me with light. When I'm about to fight, my fingertips crackle with electricity and my legs become springs.

"My father said, 'you have to do what you love or you'll never be happy.' I'm not here to kill Dragons necessarily, but if that is what I'm good at doing while I'm doing what I love, then I'll kill me some Dragons."

Walt spoke, "Jones, I think that is probably the most I've ever heard you say in one clip."

We all laughed.

Chen, who rarely spoke, said, "You saying, you want to fight us for birthday?"

Jones nodded. "If you wouldn't mind."

I said, "Isn't there some kind of prohibition on training on your birthday."

"Not that I know of," Jones replied quickly. "The tradition is you do what you want to do."

So we did. Jones led the way out of the West Gate. The fighting didn't feel physically strenuous, but nevertheless intense. Jones showed us some of his early training with tai chi. The energy Jones channeled felt incredible.

When we finished we all felt the energy Jones described. My hands tingled.

We headed back to the Fort. The guards let us in. It was nearly dark, but not late. Jones turned to us all. "Well, I think it's time I hit the sack."

Jones looked at Green. He grabbed her hand and she smiled. They walked to the North wall where his bunk awaited.

Walt looked at the rest of us. "You know, I haven't gotten laid since we started training as Hell Bringers."

"There's always Maria's old roommate," I suggested.

Walt perked up. "By the gods you're right!" Walt was gone a second later.

Chen slinked off without a word. He did that a lot. He didn't stare angrily at me as much lately.

Rebecca looked at me. Her green eyes shone in the torch light. She said, "I suppose you want to get laid too huh?"

I blushed. Hopefully it was too dark to tell. "I, uh, nev –"

Rebecca laughed. "I'm just messing with you Gerstung. I'd kick your ass if you tried anything."

Rebecca grabbed my hand and we walked to my bunk. I felt the power in her grip. I opened my door and she pulled me into the bunk. She slammed the door and kissed me hard. It was not unpleasant. My heart jumped into my throat as her fingertips roughly stroked the skin of my back under my black tank top shirt. She lifted it off and over my head.

"Which bunk is yours?" she asked.

"Top," I said.

She smiled and peeled off her tanned leather halter and then her cotton brassiere. The light from the outside torch leaked in through the ventilation cracks in the door. The skin of her cleavage was two toned with a natural tan on top emphasizing a few freckles and pale where it was usually covered. Her nipples hardened as she moved my hands to hold her breasts.

"Do you want me Gerstung?" Rebecca asked, but it was more of a command.

"You wouldn't believe." I responded.

Rebecca fondled the bulge in my trousers. "Oh I believe it."

I jumped in surprise and pleasure. "But I don't think I'm ready."

"Mmmm." Rebecca moaned. "That is too bad."

"I don't even know how to describe these feelings I'm having."

"It's called an erection."

"Yes, I know that. I mean my heart. I don't want to be one of those guys lead around by my dick. I respect you too much for that." My hands fell from Rebecca's finely formed breasts reluctantly.

Rebecca nodded. "I can respect that."

She kissed me deeply. I felt her wet tongue probe my mouth and I wrapped my arms around her waist meeting her tongue with mine. Kissing, I was good at.

Rebecca's bare chest pressed against mine and her nipples teased mine. I inhaled softly. Rebecca responded by kissing down my chest and over the bulge in my pants. She looked up at me as she grabbed her clothes from the floor. "When you are ready, if you want me, let me know."

She stood up straight again and kissed me softly on the lips. She quickly put her halter back on and exited. Seconds later she poked her head back into the bunk. "You know, you might want to take care of that." She was gesturing to my pants. "I've heard guys have a rough time of it when they don't." She closed the door again.

Take care of it I did. Twice.

38 — Birthday Present

January 18, 2000

My birthday came fast. I didn't even remember the date until I woke up with Walt hammering on my bed and leading a chorus of reluctant recruits from outside the bunk in singing the traditional birthday song:

It's another lap around the sun
You've made it and you are some one
Happy birthday from your best of friends
And we'll be with you 'til the end
Now you enjoy your special day
There simply is no other way
Your happiness is a joy to see
Hurrah Hurrah for Humanity!

Everyone clapped and smiled and wished me another lap in good health. As they dispersed, I groaned at Walt. "You know, not to be ungrateful, but I would enjoy my day a little more if I'd gotten to sleep in. Also, I hate that song."

Walt feigned hurt, "Well, I'm sorry Mister Grumpy Ass. Go back to sleep then." He bashed me with a pillow and stomped the two steps out of the bunk. His bellowing laughter reached my ears as he slammed the door.

I smiled and rolled over burying my face into my own pillow. I heard the bunk door open again and I turned, hoping for Rebecca, instead Ajax stood there.

Ajax spoke only to me as far as I could tell. His words

were few, but he was obsessed with training and with the Sympathizers. When Lance graduated as a Hell Bringer, Ajax warned me to be careful since Lance could choose to serve anywhere. If he chose to serve at Fort Kingsley there was a chance for trouble.

Lance chose Detroit. It was not far from Fort Kingsley. Detroit manufactured half of the Dragon's Bane weapons the Human Army used. If Lance truly were a Symp, then there could be trouble. The best of the best Hell Bringers stationed in Detroit since they had to be on guard constantly for Dragon attacks.

July 1, 1999

The yelling and cheering fan fare saw Lance Robbins ride off to the north towards Detroit.

Ajax's barely audible whisper said, "Lance chose Detroit to sabotage the efforts of the factory."

"How are you so certain of his guilt?"

"I saw him when he attacked the post guards. His partner attacked the gate guards. Think about it. There were only two post guards scheduled that night, but there were three people laying injured when you went up to check. Where did that third person, Lance, come from?"

I countered. "He might have just been trying to help."

Ajax sighed. "His bunk is too far away from the East Gate. He would never have heard the guards being attacked."

I shook my head. "I'm still skeptical, cuz."

Ajax nodded. "Good, be skeptical, but be ready."

January 18, 2000

"Lance has gone AWOL," Ajax said.

I asked, "How do you know?"

"I just heard from the Sergeant of my unit as he spoke with the Lieutenant."

"What can we do about it? Lance is in Detroit. We are stuck here."

"Your friends can be on the look out and be ready. The Sympathizers are coming."

Consider that a birthday ruined. I spent the rest of the day worrying about my safety and the safety of the rest of the fort. No attack came.

Neither did any of my relatives.

I sent letters to my family. They all replied saying they regretfully couldn't make it.

Maria responded to my letter saying she would try, but things grew more serious between her and Kim. Apparently Kim started treating her like a person instead of an object. I didn't expect her to show.

I spent the majority of the day in the mess hall. I didn't want to feel entirely like a lump, also the day was fairly cold and the blankets didn't do as well as the heat in the mess hall. I wrote letters to my family, my mother especially. I dated the letters. In general, I spent the day alone.

I didn't feel any different being 18 than I had as 17. I thought that the moment I reached "adulthood" I would feel stronger or surer of myself. In fact, it felt almost the opposite. I would be expected to act a certain way. I didn't know if I was capable of acting that way. I acted as an adult since I was 16 really, but now it hit me, others would expect me to act that way.

I decided to forego the post office and take a walk to Bellato to deliver my letters by hand. I bundled up and slung a bag across my shoulders to hold the letters.

The guard let me out and I started the mile walk to Bellato. My shoulders really itched. The worst they had ever itched. I stopped, rubbed them against a tree, and then was overtaken by a searing pain in my shoulders. I crumpled to my hands and knees. The fabric of my coat tugged at the front of my body. I felt and heard a rip. The skin of my shoulder burst. I heard wet sounds of blood splashing the ground on either side of me.

I turned my head first to the left, then to the right and saw them.

Huge, red, bloody, scaled wings.

The wings themselves weren't bleeding. The blood came from my shoulders bursting. The wings looked blood red beneath my blackish blood. They appeared darker than my father's wings, which surprised me. My wings hung limp against my body. I felt the cartilage inside them not yet strengthened to bone. I shrugged my shoulders and they flopped.

Someone approached. I grunted as I got back to my feet and dashed off into the forest. Hopefully whoever passed wouldn't notice the blood.

My wings extended and contracted as blood filled them. My heart beat heavily both from the act of pumping my wings full and my nervousness of potentially being discovered.

I peered around the tree and saw the person walking down the path. It was Lance! He wasn't taking many precautions. Someone having gone AWOL might be more careful strolling down the main road between a big city and a busy fort. Lance saw the fort and smiled then dashed off the opposite side of the path where I stood. He crashed through the forest.

I shrugged my shoulders again. My wings were less floppy, but not strong. They continued to extend and contract on their own. I walked after Lance, hoping to avoid making noise. I tried to step every time he stepped, but I stayed far enough back that if I didn't have wings he wouldn't have seen me.

Lance headed to a clearing. I didn't want to risk going across until my wings had made their mind up. He disappeared into the other side.

My wings still pumped, but I had to try something. I tried to tell them to flap. They moved, but with no force. I flexed my shoulders and the wings responded. I felt the connection of the wing humeri to my shoulder blades. I concentrated on moving the joints. The joints moved, but they felt weak.

My wings stretched and contracted. I felt the blood pumping. The wings reached their full length and breadth. I stepped cautiously into the clearing and flapped my wings generating a pitiful amount of wind. I flapped again with a different angle. More wind. I experimented with different angles until I felt a slight lift. I continued at this angle with faster flaps. I lifted off then my feet would touch the ground over and over. Sweat dripped down my face as I flapped. The little hops grew higher and farther as I flapped.

One flap became two flaps became three flaps. I grew tired. Flying promised to be exhausting so I'd better train for it.

Lance could wait.

I had to go back to the fort, but I couldn't do so with my new wings out. I had to figure out a way to hide them somehow. The muscles inside my shoulders flexed in a different manner. I shrugged them and the wings started to withdraw back into my body. It didn't hurt nearly as much as when they came out. I concentrated on the feeling. I felt the hard cartilage settle itself inside my back fitting neatly inside my body.

I concentrated on the feeling again and pushed the wings back out of me. I felt the cartilage and tendons slide out of me little by little as it caressed my muscles and skin. My wings felt and sounded like wet snakes sliding in and out of my body through my shoulders. After the third time I drew the wings back into my body I felt around my shoulders. I felt a three inch wide, scaled slit barely in reach of my fingers. If I lifted the scales, my finger felt wetness and the tips of my wings.

Talk about a birthday present.

39 — Attack

March 21, 2000

Suddenly, the electric lights extinguished at the fort. Someone cut the power. First year recruits acted most nervous. Admittedly, I was too. Second year recruits had their weapons at hand. We, the Hell Bringer recruits, readied our weapons as well. Kingsley instructed us to keep moving inside the fort. The Sympathizers outside the walls would not necessarily come through the gates. They had equipment which could put them over the walls where there were fewer guards.

"Oooooooooooooooooooooooo!" The sound we heard on the other side of the walls. Sympathizer tribes adopted this singular call to taunt those they attacked. Enough Symps making this call could be deafening. Survivors of Symp attacks reported shell shock and any time they heard a similar sound sent them back to the night they were accosted.

Ajax caught up with me. "I told you," he whispered as he walked with me. His sword held firmly in hand, despite being a first year. "I told you." He repeated. "Lance Robbins is leading this attack."

"We don't know that." I replied.

"You told me you saw him on your birthday walking nonchalantly in a clearing near where the Sympathizers are thought to be living."

"Yes, I did. But that doesn't mean –" I didn't know if I believed the words coming out of my mouth.

When fire arrows flew over the walls it didn't matter what I believed. A few recruits were hit, but mostly the arrows struck equipment we couldn't move easily. I struck down three arrows as they flew at me. Ajax moved equally successfully. Recruits panicked and moved away from the middle of the fort.

The first volley of arrows ended and the "Ooooooooo" began again. Hundreds of grappling hooks grabbed the North and South walls. The stone wouldn't burn, but it would provide good purchase for metal hooks.

Jones and Rebecca headed towards the West Gate stairs to get to the tops of the walls. Chen and Walt ran to the East Gate stairs to do the same. I growled and tore off my coat and shirt.

The sliver of the crescent moon was covered by the clouds so no one would see. I pushed my wings out and flew to the wall and slipped them back in. Hopefully no one noticed. I hadn't gotten around to telling anyone about the wings, even Ajax.

January 18, 2000

I waited until nightfall to head back to the fort. I cleaned my shoulder blades as best I could, but I discarded my shirt and coat because they were just too bloody to explain even at night. When I arrived bare-chested the guards questioned me, but I just told them I had a wild night in Bellato and I acted really cold so they would let me in.

I wasn't that cold. My Dragon lineage kept me pretty toasty, but I had to keep up appearances.

Walt woke as I entered the bunk, "Ah, I see you met with Maria after all."

"Yeah, that was it. I had a good birthday present."

"My man." He smiled and dozed back off.

I didn't feel good about lying to my friends, but I was more worried about them discovering my secret.

February 2, 2000

I practiced with my wings nightly. I took the stairs to the tops of the walls. I brought the guards something special from the kitchen so they ignored my visits. When I walked far enough away from them into the middle of the wall I took off my shirt and coat and then dropped over the side. I spread my wings and landed safely. For a couple hours a night, I worked on my flight, mostly training myself to get enough lift through flapping. My shoulder muscles received a real workout, but it was a workout they were ready for.

When I finished I came back to my spot on the wall and made one last flight back up to the ledge. The first night I tried this I failed so many times I almost gave up and went back to the East Gate and begged myself back in, but after the fear of being discovered or accused of any number of things I flapped back up to the wall.

Rebecca was one of the guards when I returned. "So JR, what do you get yourself into out on the wall?"

"Oh, um, nothing really I just like the solitude."

"Really? Because I walked out there to talk to you. I made it almost all the way to the other corner and you were nowhere to be seen."

I shrugged. "It's a big wall."

"Yeah, whatever, Gerstung." Rebecca was annoyed, but I didn't feel ready to divulge this secret.

March 21, 2000

I slashed my sword down on Sympathizer ropes attached to the grappling hooks. Various surprised screams arose as I did. Whenever I chopped a rope I dislodged the grappling hook and threw it hard down into the darkness and hoped I heard a scream of pain. Sometimes I did.

I went through the hooks on one side of where I flew. When I turned I noticed more hooks took their places. Sympathizers climbed higher on the wall. On places I did not cut the grappling hooks, hands of Sympathizers reached the top. I growled and rushed towards them. The Sympathizers all had iron swords.

Dragon's Bane is lighter than iron and easier to wield. However, it is a softer alloy than iron and clashing Dragon's Bane against iron will mean certain destruction for the Dragon's Bane.

I cut two grappling hooks from the walls, but instead of

listening to the satisfying crack of heads hitting the ground I sheathed my katana and grabbed the iron grappling hooks. They felt heavier than my sword, but I could defend myself.

The Symps moved clumsily. They swung heavy handed strikes that I defended against easily. I blocked with my left hook, then struck them with the right hook and knocked the first off outside the wall. The next I reversed and knocked off inside the fort. As I slid through the Symps I met Jones on the other side. He smiled.

"My Dragon's Bane broke, so I had to fight them barehanded." Jones smiled.

BOOM!

We were close to the West Gate when it exploded, but the people on the ground suffered. Wooden spear shrapnel flew out of the explosion, injuring recruits and sergeants on the ground with them many of whom had been beating out the arrow fires.

"Shit! We have to get down there!" I yelled over the chaos.

Jones agreed. I jumped and my wings spread. I landed and my wings retracted. I looked back and motioned for Jones to join me. He looked dumbfounded. He looked down the 40 feet to the ground, but thought better of jumping and ran to the closest stairs.

I realized what I had done. I shook my head. I couldn't worry about that right now.

Sympathizers mobbed through the door. I wielded my grappling hooks bashing and kicking as many Sympathizers as I could. Whether they had weapons or not, First Year recruits rushed at the Symps.

Even a marginally trained recruit is more than a match for the average Sympathizer. Sympathizers train more zeal than combat, which is why we usually rout them when they try to invade.

"Heaven Bringers!" A familiar voice yelled.

I saw Lance Robbins and next to him stood Phyllis Green. Green had graduated the day before New Year's and asked to stay on as a trainer for recruits in Fort Kingsley.

"Send these bastards to Heaven!" Green chimed in.

Lance held a heavy iron sword. Green held a smaller, but

equally dangerous looking sword. Muscled men with leather vests with white painted on them stood around Lance and Green.

I saw Jones fighting through the mob of Sympathizers. He and Green had grew close. His graduation was scheduled at the end of the month. He planned to stay at Fort Kingsley as well. From what I could tell he wanted to ask Green to marry him. Poor guy.

I continued to bash my way through to Lance. He saw me, but I saw no note of recognition in his eyes.

"Lance! Stop this!" I yelled.

Lance turned towards me and attacked. He moved just as fast as ever. He swung his heavy sword. I blocked and struck him in the stomach. He doubled over and grunted.

Ajax tore through a group of Sympathizers. He carried an iron sword. His Dragon's Bane rested in its sheath. "Cousin! I told you!"

"Shut up Ajax! Let me handle this."

I wrapped one of the hooks around the huge sword and disarmed Lance. I took Lance down to the ground and threatened him with the other hook. He didn't flinch and pushed me off of him. He stood and charged me. I nailed him with a front kick to the head which sent him backwards. He didn't move.

"Phyl, no!" Jones yelled as Phyllis Green came at me with an overhead chop. I rolled towards her using my body to take her down at the legs. I rolled up her body and grabbed her sword hand. I tore the sword out of her hand and rolled once more. Green stood at the same time I did and grabbed a sword from an unmoving Symp on the ground.

Jones held the sword towards her. "I loved you, Phyl."

Green smirked at Jones. "Sorry about your luck."

Green attacked. Jones was a better swordsman, but Green was faster. I moved back to Lance.

He moaned something, "Sk-sk-a-ja-sk-a-ja."

"What are you saying? Lance, why would you do this?"

"Where am I? This isn't Detroit."

"No, Lance, this is Fort Kingsley. You were attacking the fort."

"No! Why?"

"You tell me."

"I don't know." Lance groaned again. "Help me."

I sighed. "Okay. Let's go, I'll get you to the infirmary."

"Cousin! No!" Ajax yelled. "Kill him. He's dangerous!"

"He's a Hell Bringer!" I yelled back.

"Not anymore." Ajax approached with his sword. His huge muscles pushed me out of the way and stabbed down into Lance's chest.

Blood bubbled up into Lance's mouth, but I thought I heard, "Sk-a-ja" from his lips once more before he crumpled into death.

Ajax drew his sword out of Lance's chest.

Jones had Green on the ground. She was disarmed and defeated. One by one the other Sympathizers either ran, died or were apprehended.

40 — The Hell Bringer Recruiters

April 23, 2000

A month later, engineers almost completed the West Gate reconstruction. They repaired the fire damage. The dead and wounded received necessary attention. Anyone who lay dying after the attack rested. Anyone who still lived stayed alive. Most of them were on their feet.

Reports said at least a thousand Sympathizers who attacked that night. Phyllis Green wasn't their leader, but she turned out to be the daughter of the infamous Phillip Green, a Sympathizer who attacked Fort Kingsley in 1979. Born a few months after, Phyllis never knew her father and blamed the Human army for that. She spent her life training and infiltrated the fort to take her revenge.

The Heaven Bringers consisted of a fringe group of exemplary Sympathizer fighters who changed their allegiances after graduating as Hell Bringers. These Hell Bringer defectors also trained new Heaven Bringers.

This was a new day. This was the day we were to be tested as Hell Bringers.

Razor, Raven and Hawk returned for our test. They stood in a line, shoulder to shoulder facing us, Walt, Rebecca, me and Chen. Kingsley stood at a 90 degree angle from Walt on his right. Walt stared at Raven with intent. Rebecca took a long eye full of Hawk. Chen's chin quivered nervously. My heart beat hard in my chest, but I kept outwardly calm. Lieutenant Kingsley looked proud.

Lieutenant Hawk stepped forward. His black hair still hung braided down his back. His skin shone bronze and cheekbones high. He was muscular, but his strength did not seem to come from his body. He spoke with a clear, deep voice. "You four are an anomaly. Rarely is a Human fighter worthy to be called Hell Bringer. Yet, you, from the same month of recruitment have been trained to this level. We will see if you are worthy to take the mantle."

Sergeant Raven stepped forward as Hawk stepped back. She wore black hair cropped short on the sides, but longer on top. She moved like a jungle cat, not an ounce of fat on her body with well defined muscles. Her voice was audio velvet. She strode right up to Walt's face. He stopped staring at her and stared straight ahead. She took two steps back and said, "You will face three challenges. These challenges will require you to work individually because a Hell Bringer is a self sufficient fighter. The tide of battle can change at any moment so while you will fight as a troop in your assignments, you could be stuck alone somewhere with only yourself as backup."

Sergeant Razor stepped forward as Raven took her place in line. His dark brown skin beaded with sweat. He wore a bald head, but sported a handlebar mustache which bled into thick sideburns. His voice sounded gruff and gravelly. His biceps rippled. "Lieutenant Kingsley has helped us plot a course. On this course you will encounter four dangers.... Us. Your goal is to get through the course in a set amount of time. Stealth and quickness are your best options. You have twenty minutes to prepare as we distribute ourselves along the route. You will see the orange markers along your route. When we leave you will choose who goes first and then each of you will follow at five minute intervals. You will have an hour to make it through the course."

The recruiters and Kingsley went off along the trail. Soon they moved out of sight.

Walt spoke. "I think the fastest of us should go first. They stand more of a chance to get through and not get bogged down."

Rebecca replied, "If the slowest of us goes first, they

could feasibly make the path easier for the rest of us by occupying the first obstacle."

Chen spoke. "I think best fighter should go first. Could knock out Hell Bringers. The rest be easy."

The three looked at me. "I, uh, have no preference. I'm the slowest of us, so I'd either go first or last. I won't comment about the other suggestion."

Walt scoffed. "Man, you know you're the best fighter of us. I'll carry you across the finish line if it'll get you there fast enough."

I would have blushed, probably if I had the time. "Okay, I'll go first. You guys will probably pass me up though."

Twenty minutes passed as I stretched in preparation. We heard Kingsley bellow for us to start.

I trotted on my way down the path towards the first orange marker. I figured Kingsley would be first since he called. I kept an eye out for him. I didn't want to sprint because I wanted to save that burst to outrun him.

Why don't you just fly?

"Shit," I said in my head as I saw Kingsley coming at me from the left. I dodged his first attack and sprinted as hard as I could. My knee pained me. Kingsley kicked my leg out from under me. I crashed to the dirt and rolled onto my back as Kingsley mounted me. I immediately bucked him off and scrambled back to my feet. He got to his feet first and threw a kick at me which I blocked. I pushed him hard in the chest, drawing my arm back fast enough he couldn't grab it as he fell. I sprinted as fast as I could towards the next orange marker as Walt passed me running hard, but looking glad he didn't have to tangle with Kingsley. Walt soon ran out of sight and I ran out of breath. I walked as fast as I could, but my knee ached. However, when I reached the next attack area, I saw that Walt battling Raven for the rest of us. They fought, but it looked more like another kind of passion.

Chen passed me next. He looked a little worse for wear, but he probably passed Kingsley without much trouble, and Raven probably still battled Walt. I came upon Chen and Razor fighting. Chen was faster, but Razor was much stronger. Razor had Chen in a headlock. I rushed at them. I grabbed Razor around the waist and lifted him. He dropped Chen at that point and focused on me. I delivered a Gerstung Slam to Razor on his shoulders which winded him. Chen and I dashed off, but Chen moved much faster and left me in the dust.

Rebecca passed me next. She looked sufficiently bruised. We came upon Chen fighting Hawk. Rebecca and I came at Hawk as a team and hammered him down. The three of us took off, but again they left me in the dust. Walt caught up to me. I saw his face was covered in sucker bites and bruises. He obviously had to tangle with Razor and Hawk on his own. But even he passed me.

My knee throbbed and I made it only just over half way through the course. By my calculations the half the allotted hour had passed. At last I couldn't run anymore. I needed to walk again. The only way I could make it through the course would be to fly. With my practice, I could keep myself in the air well and move at a decent clip.

I took off my shirt and pushed out my wings. I flapped twice to get into the air and then flapped harder and faster to get moving down the path. I didn't want to go too fast. I still hadn't told my fellow recruits about my lineage and, to his credit, I don't think Steve Jones told anyone either.

I didn't fly far before I saw my friends as they ran the course full force. I landed far enough behind them they didn't notice and ran again. I had to keep up somehow.

At long last, with my lungs burning, but not with fire I crossed the finish line behind my friends. I had made it, barely. I wondered if it had been cheating to use my wings. I would worry about that later.

The recruiters joined us minutes later. Raven spoke. "Okay kids, get to your feet and prepare. Your next test is a fight for your life. You four get to fight against us three. Usually we make the recruit fight one of us at a time, but we figure you four can handle it. Usually where you fight just one Hell Bringer in Kingsley, you now have three who are his equal."

I laughed. "With all due respect, you three are nowhere near his equal, sirs and ma'am."

Kingsley grinned at my comment despite himself. Hawk, Razor and Raven looked offended.

Walt smacked me in the back of the head and pulled me in close. We met our foreheads in a circle. It was a meeting of the minds so to speak. We whispered.

Walt: Man what are you thinking? Are you trying to piss them off.

Me: Don't worry about it. They are just trying to worry us and psyche us out. We've got this.

Rebecca: How can you be so sure?

Me: Because I know us. We are strong.

Chen: Let's do this.

We stood and faced our test. Sweat beaded down my face. We took our fighting stances as the recruiters approached us. I sprang into action before they were ready. My left foot hit Hawk in the chest. He staggered back. Raven came at me with a kick. I blocked and chopped down onto her thigh. Razor swung a punch at my head. I dodged to the side and caught his arm throwing him to the ground.

Rebecca, Chen and Walt entered the fray. Chen was able to tag all three of the Hell Bringers with his quick punches and kicks. Rebecca's skill confounded the three as they tried to outmaneuver her. Walt's power cut each of the three down. He didn't even hold back against Raven.

At last, the three Hell Bringer recruiters were defeated. Each of them smiled at us. Kingsley patted us on the back as we calmed down.

After they had composed themselves, the recruiters came back and Hawk spoke to us. "You three did well, we commend you. Your final test will be unlike anything you have ever faced before."

Just then in the distance I heard four distinct screeches. Four minds clamoring at cages.

Dragons.

41 — Moment of Truth

April 23, 2000

Four huge emerald Green Dragons stood raging against their cages. The glint of sunlight that struck their scales made them sparkle. They were not happy to be contained in the cages. I also noticed reddened crisscrossing lines covering their scales.

Damned Roges! When I get out I will rip them limb from limb.

I am not even going to waste that much time. I am just going to eat them in eight quick bites.

I am going to let my poison drip through one of them they will be begging for death.

Grrrrrrrrrrrr.

I could not pinpoint which Dragon thought what. I only knew they wanted to kill us. Amidst the thought curses the Dragons also grimaced in pain. The Dragon's Bane bars burned them when the Dragons brushed up against them. I could almost feel the pain of the Dragons when they accidentally hit the bars. I even winced a couple times myself.

The recruiters stared in disdain at the Dragons in the cage. Hawk's hair flew in the breeze that picked up.

After a long moment of all of us staring at the Dragons, the recruiters turned back to us. Bruises littered their faces, even Razor's skin showed up darker than it had previously.

Only Hawk spoke. "Before you four stands your future. As a Hell Bringer, you will be entrusted with the task of defending the Human race through mounting offensives against the Dragon menace. It requires between 10 and 100 of the average Human soldier to take down the average individual Dragon, even a Fairy Dragon is difficult for the average Human soldier to kill. This is not a reflection on these soldiers' incompetence, rather the difficulty in killing a Dragon. I have personally seen the finest men and women warriors killed by Dragons because they simply were not ready for the fight.

"A Hell Bringer on the other hand can go toe to claw with a Dragon. It takes more than skill to fight a Dragon. They are larger, and stronger, and chances are they are faster than you. They can also fly. So how can a Human warrior, no matter how well they fight defeat and kill a Dragon? Two reasons and neither of them are Dragon's Bane, although that it is certainly helpful.

"Reason One: Adaptability. Humans are the most adaptable creatures on the planet. Hit us with a problem one day and the next day we have overcome it. The larger the problem, the longer it takes to solve it, but we always solve it. Before Dragon's Bane was developed, Humans were killing Dragons in defense with arrows through the eyes and some brave Humans were going right up to the mouths of the beasts and spearing them through the bones to the brains. Before we could fight them, we developed intricate ways to disguise ourselves from them. There is nothing we can't do when we focus.

"Reason Two: Unconquerable Nature. Humans have an indomitable spirit. When we put our will to a task we will complete it. This goes beyond our skills or know-how. The day after the Dragons razed New York City there were plans being made for defense and counterstrike. When we realized we could not hurt them with our weapons we set plans forth to find something we could hurt them with. It took us 20 years, but we developed Dragon's Bane and we started fighting back.

"While all Humans have these capabilities, Hell Bringers are able to apply them beyond the limits of known Human capability. A Hell Bringer can make will into instantly usable power. Where Humanity is an unstoppable iceberg over a terrain of Dragons, a Hell Bringer is an icicle stabbing through an individual skull. Without Humanity, the Hell Bringers would not exist, but without the Hell Bringers, Humanity would have been eradicated years ago."

Hawk stopped speaking. Razor spoke. "You recruits have been chosen by a Hell Bringer to help usher Humanity into safety. Only a Hell Bringer can see these qualities in a Human warrior. You four are lucky to have had the best of the best as your instructor." Razor turned to Kingsley. "What is your record for Dragons? Three at a time?"

Kingsley spoke softly. "Four."

Razor said, "As far as I know that's a record of simultaneous Dragon kills."

Kingsley said, "Braggs had five once, but he almost got chomped by the fifth before I javelined it."

Razor said, "That was before the eye laser right?"

Kingsley nodded.

Razor continued. "To become a Hell Bringer you must be able to kill a Dragon in a one on one battle. We just happen to have four Dragons for you to fight. These Dragons were captured with Dragon's Bane plated steel nets. We had our translator..." Razor paused to look at Kingsley "...inform them they can win their freedom if they kill you.

"If you did not notice by their scales, these are Green Dragons. Their weapons are their poison claws. Their poison will kill you if they scratch you. Their jaws will kill you if they bite you. Their tails will probably kill you if they hit you with it. They are permitted to fly to the tops of the surrounding trees, any higher and they will be captured again with the Dragon's Bane nets. They know we are good shots. They also know we will release them if they kill you.

"This is the moment of truth, recruits. Are you ready to free these Dragons one way or another?"

We looked at one another and nodded. Raven asked, "Who is going first?"

Chen raised his hand first. Raven nodded and said, "Prepare yourself. The rest of you step back with Hawk, Razor and Kingsley."

Raven walked to the cages and picked one of the Dragons. She pulled her sword and pointed it at the Dragon. The Dragon backed off and waited.

I am going to tear this rogah a new stomach.

Raven unlocked the cage and pulled the door open. The Dragon stalked out of the cage and went towards her. It reached a claw for her and she swiped down and cut off the digit attached to the claw. Black blood spurted from the cut. The Dragon screeched in pain. The noise was deafening.

Raven pointed at Chen and the Dragon turned, limping, toward its, her, fate. Even wounded, the Dragon moved quickly. She rose up into the air and came at Chen hard. Chen rolled and took his feet. His sword plunged into the Dragon's stomach as she passed over him. Her momentum extended the slash wound and her internal organs left her as she skidded dead on the ground behind Chen.

Chen sheathed his sword and put one fist into the other and took a traditional Chinese bow to the Dragon. He took his place next to us. Razor motioned for Chen to stand next to him, which Chen did.

Raven released the next Dragon for Rebecca to battle. My heart pumped harder as I watched her engage the Dragon. The Dragon took the note from his counterpart and did not try to snap at Raven. The Dragon lashed his tail at Rebecca like a club. Rebecca jumped over the first swipe of his tail and swung her sword down. She cut into his tail, but did not cut it off. The Dragon screeched and snapped his jaws at her. She ducked the snap and swung her sword up into the right side of the Dragon's neck. The Dragon jerked back and clapped his clawed right hand to his neck. As the Dragon walked on three legs, Rebecca ducked under a swinging right wing and cut him down at his right leg. The Dragon toppled onto his right side as Rebecca escaped his massive body.

Grrrrrr. Just finish me rogah.

Rebecca did.

Rebecca took her place next to the Hell Bringers. Walt stepped forward brandishing his huge broadsword. Raven smiled coquettishly at him. He softened for a moment and waved at her, then retook his focused posture.

Raven released the bulkiest of the Dragons. The Dragon stepped around his two fallen comrades. He sniffed the two dead Dragons and growled.

You're going to die rogoh.

Rogoh. Rogah. I wondered what that meant. The Dragon stared straight at me.

You are one of us?

I unsuccessfully tried to clear my mind. The Dragon turned his head and looked at the remaining Dragon.

This rogoh is one of us. Kill the rogon.

Yes, I know and I will.

Great, the Dragons are conspiring.

The Dragon turned away from Walt and stalked back towards the other Dragon. The bulky Dragon growled and spun faster than I would have expected him to. He slammed his tail into the Dragon's Bane cage. I heard the sizzle of the cage as the scales of the Dragon struck it. The cage rocked and the bars cracked, but didn't break. Raven came at the Dragon quickly with her sword, but he rose into the air and slammed his tail down onto the top of the cage. This strike cracked it further and the corner of the cage broke.

The Dragon inside the cage pushed at the cage with his nose as the bulky Dragon smashed into the other side of the cage with his tail. The front of the cage crashed to the ground.

The Dragon exited the cage. His nose still sizzled.

Dragons! We still have enough nets to catch you both and it will hurt more than breaking apart the cage did if we catch you.

Kingsley stared right at the Dragons.

Ha! Foolish rogon! You think we want to escape from this? We are just going to kill you for the greater good.

I stepped out of line to join Walt. I held my katana. Walt smiled at me and we moved forward. The bulky Dragon flew low at Walt, snapping his jaws. Walt dodged the snap and took a huge swing at the Dragon's mouth, but missed.

My Dragon was sleeker and moved quicker. He landed and pulled back his wings. The Dragon cocked his tail over his back like a scorpion. He twisted quickly and his huge tail lashed out at me. I rushed forward and jumped onto the back of the Dragon. I chopped down with the katana onto the Dragon's back. The smell of sizzling Dragon flesh reminded me of rust.

I noticed Walt's huge broad sword glinting red in the dying sunset. My attention was drawn back to the Dragon below me as I drove my katana further into the flesh. My Dragon screeched and extended his wings knocking me off of his back. I landed on my back and the Dragon roared as it brought his huge clawed hand down over me. I rolled out of the way, but I felt the tear of claw on my back. The pain of the Dragon's poison curled through my body instantly.

I regained my feet just as the Dragon snapped at me again. My insides boiled in anger and with the effects of the poison. I swung my katana and cut into the Dragon's neck. His scales felt like butter beneath my Dragon's Bane. The Dragon took three steps back, staggering. My heart beat faster, pushing the poison through my veins. It itched.

What kind of Human are you?

I am not exactly Human. The Tyrant King is my father.

That explains a lot.

The Dragon rushed at me. Without thought, my wings pushed out and I rose into the air over the Dragon. I breathed a cone of fire down onto my foe. The Dragon screeched. I came back down behind the Dragon's head and chopped clean through his neck with my katana.

The Dragon's body lay in a heap severed from his head. Walt took the last swings at his dying Dragon. I smiled to the recruiters who seemed unfazed. Rebecca and Chen looked skeptically at me. Kingsley had a knowing look. I stepped around the head and walked towards the Hell Bringers. Walt turned and saw my wings. They drooped as the poison moved through them.

I smiled at my friend, my brother in arms. My wings retracted and I fell to one knee, stabbing my katana into the ground for support. I lost consciousness before my face hit the dirt.

42 — Fort Indiana

April 24, 2000

The infirmary looked fuzzy. My eyes opened to four blobs looking over me. As my eyes focused, the blobs began to take shape. Walt, Chen, Rebecca and Ajax stood over me. My mouth smiled without me.

My friends smiled down at me.

Ajax touched my shoulder. "Cousin, good to see you are still alive."

My voice croaked. "Good to hear you speak above a whisper."

Ajax smiled. "Justice was had."

Chen spoke. "You gonna be okay?"

I replied, "Probably. My limbs feel a bit tingly."

Chen nodded. "Good. We fight later."

I sighed.

Walt patted me on the forehead. "We've got some talking to do when you're on your feet."

"Great," I said. "Remind me to never stand again."

Rebecca's hands wrapped around mine. "You have to stand again. You are a Hell Bringer now."

I smiled and my eyes closed. "Something to look forward to, like being poisoned or having fire breathed at me or worse."

Footfalls entered the room.

Are you okay, Gerstung?

Hrm. Lieutenant?

Yes.

I'll be fine I think.

"Gerstung needs his rest. You three get your gear packed. Gelh, you take care of Gerstung's gear. Other Gerstung, don't you have some training to get to?"

I heard a simultaneous "Yes, Sir" from four voices, then four sets of feet leaving the room and then the door closing.

I heard the sound of a chair scraping across the floor and settling on my right side, then the sound of a body settling into the chair.

"So, a Vrack huh?" Kingsley's voice.

I opened my eyes. "Yeah, that's what my fa – Jonathan the Tyrant called it."

"I have met a few of your kind in my years. You tend to live short, furious lives."

"Well, I have been told I'm a fiery individual."

"I can see that."

I pondered and then spoke. "So we know what I am. What are you?"

"I am what is called a Drackne. My father fell in love with a female Dragon shapeshifter. If you can believe it, I actually came out of an egg, a small one, but an egg nonetheless."

"Interesting."

"Your friends love you, but they distrust you for not telling them."

"Yeah, I kind of got that feeling from Walt."

"My daughter loves you."

"I didn't exactly get that feeling from her."

"She hasn't said it, but she does."

"How can you tell?"

"She's my daughter, I can't help but notice."

I pondered that.

Kingsley spoke again. "I see that you four have chosen Sunset Red as your post. Since I cannot go with you, I hope you will look after her. She is special."

"I agree she is special, but she doesn't need me to look after her."

"Maybe not, but still, I'm a father and I worry about my daughter."

"I'll do my best, sir."

"Thank you. You'd better get up if you can and get ready to go. You're due in Indianapolis in three days and the stage coach is ready."

April 28, 2000

I awoke from a stiff sleep in the stage coach just as we pulled in to Fort Indiana. Rebecca slept next to me. Walt and Chen took up the other side. With us rode the two drivers who switched off running the horses ragged, stopping for a few hours at a clip. You never knew who you could trust when traveling, so you trusted no one except the people at the forts. Our routes were plotted and our stage coach drivers knew the routes like the backs of their hands, having driven them for years transporting soldiers and civilians all over what used to be the United States.

Jason and Tammy were a husband and wife team armed with both 'Dragon killin' an Human killin' weppons' as they called them. They spoke in such a way that most people couldn't understand. I could hear the typos as they spoke, but once you get the hang of listening their words were easily translatable.

Jason did most of the talking. "Arr chillen up an lef us when they's old 'nuff. Its good tho. We taut 'em tuh be sef suffishint. One's a doc now in Omaha. One's a feral killer in Alaska. Good munny up thur."

Tammy spoke softly, "Arr daughter's a tavern maid in Flor'da. We ain't herd a her in yers. Nex time we get down 'ere we'll drop in awn 'er."

I shook the Jason's hand and kissed the Tammy's politely and joined my friends.

Our contact in Fort Indiana was Lieutenant Jones. Fort Indiana was about the same size as Fort Kingsley. We saw recruits pushing huge rounded boulders through the center of the training area. I thought that was rather strange.

Lieutenant Jones informed us that we would help train recruits and share with them, some of our Hell Bringer expertise. We saw fewer recruits in Fort Indiana than Fort Kingsley, so we each could take a quarter of the recruits without being overwhelmed by students.

— 217 —

My group worked in unison. When I sat them down to listen to what I had to say, they were all obedient. I wasn't sure I cared for that part.

I spoke loud enough so they could hear me. "What I want to tell you is… to be a powerful Dragon fighter, you have to be able to adapt. Each Dragon is different. No one method will kill all Dragons."

One of the recruits raised their hand, I pointed at him. "Our instructors have been teaching us Dragon kata. It is based on the formula of Hell Bringer kills. We use it on Dragons, young, old and eggs."

"You fight Dragons at this fort?"

"Frequently."

"But you are just recruits."

"The Dragons don't care how old a Human is they kill them just the same."

I sighed, "Ain't that the truth."

I don't remember the rest of what I said. I invited the recruits to spar with one another and take turns sparring with me. In general they were good fighters, but I can't say I approved of their method of Dragon disposal. Killing the Dragons as eggs is much easier than killing them as full grown beasts, but it seemed wrong in a way.

Later, I approached Lieutenant Jones. "Excuse me sir, I wanted to ask, why you teach your recruits to seek nests and destroy them."

"We kill the Dragons when they are easiest to kill."

"That's what I thought. What gave you this idea?"

"My family was killed. The Dragons didn't care that my wife and my children could not defend themselves. I stopped caring whether a Dragon could defend itself or not. Hell, even a baby Dragon can do some damage, so it is not like they are totally helpless. Like my daughter, my beautiful newborn daughter."

Jones turned away. "I will destroy every nest I find, Hell Bringer. Forever."

I walked away and rejoined my friends. We had orders to bunk in separate quarters. Luckily, Fort Indiana had plenty of empty bunks. We chose four bunks next to each other on the second level. Rebecca was on one side of me, Walt was on the other, Chen was on the other side of Walt. We said goodnight and entered the bunks.

I lay on my back on the bottom bunk. My eyes closed and I breathed deeply. I tried to get my imagination away from swords cutting through scaled Dragon eggs. The yellow covered Dragon embryos sizzled in my mind.

I heard a knock on the bunk door. I sat up quickly and banged my head on the top bunk. "Ow shit!"

Rebecca's voice asked, "Are you alright?"

I answered the door, rubbing my head. "Yeah, I just tried to give myself a concussion. What's up?"

"I am. I can't sleep."

"Yeah, me neither."

"Can I come in?"

"Sure." I moved aside and Rebecca entered the bunk. I sat back down on the bed and she sat next to me.

"What's keeping you awake?" she asked.

"The recruits told me that they hunt Dragon nests and kill all the young and the eggs. Lieutenant Jones told me how the Dragons slaughtered his family and how he wasn't able to stop them."

"Sounds like he's gone permanently maverick."

"My uncles always called a 'maverick' someone who took time off from rational thought to feed their emotional need to try to get themselves killed in honor of someone they had lost."

"Yeah, that sounds about right."

We didn't speak for a while. I felt the heat of her body on my left side. Without thinking I said, "I've been thinking through these months, over you hating me, then not hating me, then us training together, and then kissing, then–" I trailed off.

Rebecca picked up the trail. "I don't understand why you wouldn't tell any of us about what – who you are. You are a good person. Being a half-Dragon is not a bad thing, especially not in the Human army. We can use all the help we can get."

I chuckled. "Thanks. Good to know I'm of use."

Rebecca laughed softly. "I like you. I more than like you. It took me a while, but–"

Her hand went to my face and turned it toward her. She pressed her soft lips against mine. My hands caressed her breasts lightly as she probed her tongue into my mouth. My tongue met hers and pushed back with ferocity. Rebecca moaned into the kiss and tugged up my shirt. I curved my back to let her strip it off of me. I took her shirt off over her head as well. Her leather halter came off next. Her handful breasts felt soft, but firm as I held them. Rebecca moved her hands to my trousers. She moved in front of me, on her knees on the floor of the bunk and pulled the trousers down.

The moonlight shone through the cracks in the bunk. I could see her wrap her hands around my erection. Even in the darkness I could see her green eyes flashing as she took me in her mouth.

I reclined on the bed in a pleasure I had never experienced before. Just as the pleasure mounted to nearly a peak it ceased. I looked up at Rebecca who was now standing and taking down her own trousers. She coaxed me onto the bed and joined me, sliding one leg over my lap.

Breathily I said, "I've never done this before."

I could hear the smile in her voice. "I'll be gentle."

"Not too gentle."

43 — Fort Madison

May 2, 2000

It rained as we pulled into Fort Madison. All four of us crowded into the stage coach with the windows closed most of the way to keep the water out. Jason and Tammy trooped through and kept us moving under ponchos. Typically two of us would ride on top of the coach, just for a change of pace, especially when the sun wouldn't give us sunburns. It gave us opportunity to stretch our legs.

It also gave us opportunity to have conversations which we didn't want the world to hear.

April 29, 2000

Walt and Chen sat on top of the stage coach. This left Rebecca and me on our own inside. The stage coach moved along at a steady pace and the wooden wheels rumbled over the rubble of former highways. The noise provided some privacy for our conversation.

Rebecca curled up against me. "I wanted to talk to you about last night."

"Oh?" I wasn't sure how to take that.

"I want you to know, I thought it was great... being with you."

"I'm glad. I enjoyed being with you as well."

"But I wanted to let you know, we cannot do that again."

I was perplexed. "What?"

"Well, that's not exactly what I mean. What I mean is we have to use protection next time."

"My sword is always in arms reach."

Rebecca laughed. "No, dummy, I mean condoms. I can't really afford to get pregnant and neither of us can afford to get sick."

"Sick?"

"Venereal diseases, like syphilis, gonorrhea and the like."

"Oh." I felt like a kid again. I had no idea what she was even talking about. They didn't exactly have that kind of class in my one room school house in Meton.

We spent the next two hours or so talking at length about the dangers of sex without condoms. Well mostly it consisted of me asking her questions about the dangers. She answered them happily, telling me how she and her father had numerous awkward conversations about sexual health. Schools didn't teach this too frequently, so it fell to the parents to instruct their children on these matters. I wondered what else my mother hadn't told me.

Rebecca she had gotten a quick check up with the doctor at Fort Indiana before we left. He gave her what she called a 'morning after' pill just in case. She also suggested that we both get check ups in Omaha since they had the finest medical facilities on the continent. We were fairly sure I didn't have any venereal disease since that was my first time having sex, but Rebecca had been active since she was 17 so she got a check up once a year.

We ended the conversation with Rebecca telling me how she acquired a package of latex condoms at Fort Indiana and couldn't wait to jump my bones at Fort Madison.

May 2, 2000

The rain beat down hard upon the stage coach.

Fort Madison sat just over the Mississippi River. The river itself looked bloated. The locals expected it to crest any minute now. The rain moved across the area for the past three days. The ground squished under our boots as we walked to the bunks to drop off our things. We took up bunking arrangement at Fort Madison. This time was slightly different with Chen bunking next to me and Walt on the other side of him.

We each put on our rain gear and went out to join the recruits as we expected on our journey. More recruits trained here than at Fort Indiana. These recruits primarily dealt with the Water Dragons which patrolled the big river and its tributaries.

I had the least contact with Water Dragons. They seemed to avoid Lake Erie for some reason, probably the pollution.

Our guide, Punk, showed us the Dragon's Bane ballistae at the corners of the fort angled at the river. Occasionally, a Dragon tried to sneak by and they would be taken down. The ballista guards were highly trained Hell Bringers and hit 9 out of 10 targets. If the ballista guard missed they had to go down and retrieve the 200 pound arrow. This made it imperative they hit on their first shot. The arrows flew just as far in the air in case of aerial attacks.

The beefy Hell Bringer ballista guards could manhandle the arrows. I thought they would be a prime target for Dragons with all that meat.

I grabbed one of the arrows and tugged up. It was not light, but I was able to lift it up to my waist. A red haired ballista guard, named Nathan, smiled with approval as he grabbed another arrow with one hand and put it up over his head.

Each of the arrows had 1,000 feet of industrial strength rope coiled and attached to the wall of the fort. Two hundred pounds of Dragon's Bane was not easily replaced so the fort couldn't afford to lose arrows with fly-away Dragons. Dragons died tugging at the barbed arrows catching around their bones. I didn't envy the recruits who had to unhook the arrows from the Dragons killed.

When the Supremacy War intensified and more Dragons died in battle, the Dragon Disposal Corps (DDC) formed as a liaison to the Dragons. The DDC dragged the corpses away from battlefields to places Dragons could find them and tend to them in their own ways.

In the early days of the DDC, some disreputable Humans tried to cook Dragon meat and serve it as a delicacy. It would have worked except Dragon meat is inedible regardless of the number of Dragon's Bane cuts it receives. Dragons don't eat their kind for a reason.

Few Humans have witnessed Dragon burial rites. From the records, it seems to indicate that Dragons bury their dead. Some observations show increased plant growth in areas where Dragons bury their dead, but no one knows why. The dead are no longer part of a community, thus Dragons do not typically use markers and the community moves on. They remember their fallen family, but do not commemorate them with any identifiable service apart from the community digging the grave and filling it in on top of the deceased.

There is a myth that says when the blood of a Dragon in love is shed where the blood lands will grow a Blood Rose. A Blood Rose can be made into a cure for any disease or disorder. Unfortunately, Dragons rarely fall in love, or at least this myth is extremely hard to prove since no Blood Rose plants have been discovered since the Supremacy War started.

The scientists of Fort Madison sent out the occasional search party to find Blood Roses, but after many years they were still unable to be located. Many diseases existed for medical researchers to combat.

The sexually transmitted disease, Dragon-Related Immune Deficiency Syndrome, or DRIDS, increased. While researchers said it did not derive from Dragons, it was given a Draconic name to give it more emphasis as it compromised the immune system in Humans. The disease proved to be just as deadly as Dragons. A war raged between the medical establishment against DRIDS just as ferocious as the war Humanity fought with the Dragons.

Walt, Rebecca, Chen and I received a tour of the medical facility at Fort Madison. Patients afflicted with DRIDS lived there. DRIDS could not be transmitted other than through contact with blood or sexual fluids. I felt sorry for the people afflicted, but in my eyes they were heroes. They wanted to help however they could with eradicating the disease.

After hearing of my half-Dragon origin, the researchers asked if they could have five vials of my blood for testing. Inspired by the contribution the DRIDS patients made, I happily donated. As my blood drained out of me into the tubes I noticed the black and thick consistency. I asked if this was normal, but the technician drawing my blood had no previous experience with half-Dragons and couldn't give me an answer.

Before I could ask someone who knew, Rebecca appeared to tell me to come with her. Training had higher priority than curiosity.

Fort Madison invited Walt, Chen, Rebecca and I to join the daily rumble involving recruits and officers. The winner did not have to do daily chores. Their work was divided among the rest of the fort. I appreciated the community that encouraged their members with a contest like this. The rules were simple: combatants either winded or pinned for a three count, were eliminated.

The current champion was the red haired Hell Bringer ballista guard, Nathan. He was off shift and so eager for a chance for some exercise and not doing any chores. Hundreds of Human army recruits, two dozen sergeants and lieutenants, and six Hell Bringer ballista guards joined me and my three companions in the center of the fort training yard. Everyone stretched and flexed.

A whistle blew and chaos erupted. I caught a glimpse of Nathan as he wrecking balled through five recruits at a time.

Three recruits ganged up on Walt. He threw them off, then three more accosted him. It took five or six recruits on each limb to hold Rebecca down for a three count. Chen moved quick enough to duck and dodge through the crowd. One of the beefy ballista guards came at him. Chen dodged the huge swinging arms and tagged the ballista guard, knocking him cold.

More than one recruit would pin another, then be pinned as they lay on the ground, unable to get up because the pinned recruit would hold them down while another jumped on top. Piles like this stacked five or six high at some points.

I held my own. No one could get a good hold on me. I threw any recruit or officer off of me that tried, but I didn't really go for any pins or the knock outs. I had more fun tearing through the crowd. A few of the throws I delivered left the recipient winded for a three count.

Hundreds of combatants dwindled down to 10 or so after only a few minutes. Only one of the recruits was left. It was our guide, Punk. Punk was a wiry, tenacious youth who shaved her head every week or so. The officers intended for her to become a

Hell Bringer, so it figured. Punk screamed at Nathan and ran at him. She jumped from 10 feet away with a double kick to the chest. Nathan ran at her and swatted her down probably a little harder than he should have, but when she hit the ground she bounced up and kicked him in the back of the leg. Nathan groaned and swatted at her again.

I missed the rest of the fight because Walt and Chen came at me out of the blue. One each grabbed my arms, but as they did I rolled backward and threw them off of me. The five officers left tried to gang up on us as we wrestled and sparred against each other. I threw one officer down only to be crashed into by another.

Chen knocked out two of the remaining officers. Walt handled one. The one I slammed stayed slammed, and the other officer soon met the same fate.

Nathan stood over Punk with one foot on her chest laughing. She grimaced up at him, but could not fight back.

Walt and Chen came at me again. Chen tried a flurry of punches, most of which I was able to block. I pushed Chen backwards and jump kicked Walt in the chest. I saw something in his eyes. He seemed angry at me. I blocked Chen's next punch and turned the block into a throw harder than I had thrown most of the recruits and officers.

Walt growled and ran at me. He grabbed my shoulders and tried to throw me, but I reversed the grab and threw him instead. I went down with him, holding his arms with mine. "Are you alright?" I asked.

"Peachy." He coughed. "That was three, get off of me."

"I mean, are we alright? You seem angry."

"Yeah, I'm angry, now get offa me you lug."

I released Walt and stood, just as Nathan came at me. I ducked and barrel rolled into Nathan's legs. Nathan flew over me and crumbled into the ground. I yelled to Walt, "Hey! I'm sorry. For whatever it is, I'm sorry."

Walt yelled back, "Pay attention will you, he's coming at you."

Mud covered everyone's skin. The rain had not let up at all.

Nathan wiped the mud off of his face and roared at me.

He stomped at me in his approach. His arms swung faster than I expected from such a large man, but I still moved faster. I avoided his strikes until I wrapped one arm between his legs and another around his waist.

Gerstung Slam!

Nathan lay in the mud with the rain pouring down upon him. I silently counted three as my eyes focused on him. Everyone looked amazed and I received a rousing round of applause. I looked around for Walt, but didn't see him.

44 — Omaha

The sun shone high as we rode towards Omaha. From 10 miles away we could see the force field over the city. Omaha's 27 Mage, Doug Ingle, erected the force field. He called it an 'iron butterfly'. Anyone with good intentions could pass through a force field. For anyone with ill intentions came pain and an impenetrable wall. At least that's what the scientists said. City leaders asked citizens and visitors to dedicate 10 minutes per day on contemplation to donate energy to the perpetuation of the force field. Humanity learned the hard way with Los Angeles what happened when citizens didn't contribute.

I rode on the top of the stage coach with Walt. He watched the road. His gaze never strayed to me. I, on the other hand, stared at him. I had no chance to talk to him at Fort Madison. We passers-through were asked to help out there and I had a night time meeting with Rebecca.

Sick of the silence, I said, "Walt, what's going on between us?"

"I don't know what you're talking about Gerstung." His voice was hard. This was not the Walt I knew.

"You have been standoffish to me since we graduated. I hate it."

"Well, I have nothing to tell you."

"That's bullshit. This is about me not telling you about my parentage, isn't it?"

Walt looked at me. His eyes narrowed and his eyebrows resembled lightning bolts striking his third eye. "We were supposed to be friends. Friends tell each other that kind of thing. I told you about the painful stuff in my past, as a friend. I would only imagine you would do the same when you learned something painful."

"We are friends. I just didn't know how to handle it myself. I especially didn't know how anyone else would handle knowing that kind of thing. This isn't an easy subject for me, even now."

"But if we were friends, you should have trusted me enough to give me a heads up."

"What would it have mattered if I had told you? What would you have done differently? Would you accept me for who I am or would you accuse me of being a Dragon Sympathizer like my village?"

"I am not some close minded hick from Meton, Gerstung. I am, was, your friend. Being half Dragon is an asset in this war. You have really cool powers and you can fly. Why would I hate you for that?"

"Why does anyone hate anyone for anything? There is no rhyme or reason. I wanted to be okay with this myself before I brought anyone else on the ride with me. I was trying to save my friends from any stigma that might arise from being my friend. I wanted to be able to handle it."

Walt shook his head. "That's what you don't get. Friends are there for each other, no matter what. Friends stick together. Also, you don't need to save me or protect me from anything. I am a big boy. Rebecca is a big girl, well, a finely shaped woman. Chen is a not-as-big boy who can handle himself. We can all handle ourselves. We do not need a Gerstung umbrella above us to shield us from the rain."

I put my head in my hands. My cheeks blazed. The water welling up in my tear ducts stung me. "I'm sorry Walt. I hope someday you can forgive me and we can be friends again."

We said nothing else. I thought about his words and my shame associated with not only being the child of a Dragon, but not trusting the people who had deserved my trust.

About an hour later, my eyes were crusted with the dirt of

the ride mixed with old tears. A soldier stopped our coach in front of the road leading into the Omaha force field. It was Steve Jones.

Steve nodded in recognition to us, but he remained professional. "Okay, everybody out of the coach. Now you will walk in one at a time. Remember, as you walk in, you must dedicate energy to the force field. Concentrate hard. You will feel a tingle as you pass through, but you will move through without much trouble. Do not stop in the force field, the tingle will start to burn."

Jason drove the coach through without much trouble. The horses were probably used to the feeling. Tammy walked through next. Chen closed his eyes and followed them. Walt did the same, followed by Rebecca. I shook Steve's hand before I went through, silently thanking him for keeping my secret.

Omaha bustled. Buildings stood as far as I could see. Almost every building had solar panels on the roofs. Omaha lead many cities in the development of solar powered electricity. I heard rumors that the city stored enough power to run in darkness for 100 years. With Dragons constantly on watch, getting this information to other cities proved difficult. Just like getting water filtration from Bellato to Omaha.

If Humans declared a capital on this continent, it would be Omaha. Many of the greatest Human minds lived there formulating and designing methods and plans to keep Humans safe and to eradicate Dragons and other threats.

Through the grapevine I heard the major Human cities, Bellato, Seattle, Memphis and others were planning to declare Omaha the capital of the Human Resistance on the continent. I didn't know if I liked the idea of a centralized government, especially in times where cities could be destroyed in a single day. But maybe that's why I wasn't a politician.

We saw signs everywhere:

CHRISTOFER OSBORNE for MAYOR
VOTE CLEAN WATER, VOTE OSBORNE
HUMANITY FIRST, OSBORNE

I knew Omaha was progressive, but I was not aware they were bringing back elections. I immediately mistrusted this idea. Bellato worked fine without a stated leader.

I caught up with Rebecca and put a hand on her left hip. "Weird, huh?"

"Too weird," she agreed.

We headed towards Joslyn Castle. The huge Scottish Baronial style building constructed near the turn of the 20th century withstood a number of weather events and Dragon attacks before the force field came up.

Joslyn Castle held many of the administrative functions of the city. Teachers met once a month to discuss new learning tactics they would take back to their neighborhood schools. City guards met here once a week for new orders or reaffirming of their old orders.

We looked for the leader of the Omaha city guard to offer our services for the two days we planned to be here. Instead, we ran into Christofer himself.

"Rebecca!" He exclaimed as he rushed towards us. He grabbed Rebecca up and spun her around. Rebecca looked fairly uncomfortable.

"Uh, hi, Christofer," she said awkwardly.

"What are you doing here my pet?"

"I'm a Hell Bringer now, Gerstung, Gelh, Chen and I are headed to Fort Angel. We are just passing through to get fresh horses and offer our help to the City Guard if we are needed."

"Certainly. Once you've found Lieutenant Perez come find me and we will go to dinner and discuss things."

We four left Christofer to his doings as a candidate for Mayor and found Lieutenant Perez. Perez was a rat faced man squat of build with a thick chest. His voice curled with Latin flavor. "You Hell Bringers?"

"Yes, sir." We answered simultaneously.

"You here to help the City Guard?"

"Yes, sir."

"Good. Make patrols for eight hours per day. You choose. You can go together or separately. Just try to cover the city in your time here."

"Yes, sir."

"Dismissed."

The red sun set as we left Joslyn Castle. Christofer walked with us. He led the way to a building lit by candles surrounded by electric street lights.

"Omaha Steaks is the best restaurant in the city. As you know, Omaha is the steak capital of Humanity. This restaurant has steaks of all kinds for any tastes."

My medium well steak tasted exquisite. It did not melt in my mouth, but the chewing filled me with pleasure in itself.

I caught sidelong glances at Walt, but he seemed more interested in the women walking by. Chen kept his eyes on his plate.

I probed. "Chen, one thing I've noticed about you is I never see you looking at any woman, no matter how attractive she might be."

Chen looked at me. He spoke slowly, "My boyfriend would not like it."

"Oh." I stopped.

"He wait for me in Detroit. I look for permanent home. He comes to me and we live happily."

"Wow, that's cool." I had never considered Chen might be attracted to men.

"Family does not like it. But I cannot live for them."

I purposely did not horn in on the conversations between Rebecca and Christofer. No bad feelings exchanged between the two. Jealousy welled in my chest, but he wasn't being particularly untoward or rude, so I couldn't attack him for being too personal. Our earlier transgressions seemed forgotten, or at least pushed to the back burner.

"Hey Gerstung, how is the family?" This did not seem accusatory or to be inferring anything.

"They are okay. I saw my mom during the year leave. I had a little extra leave since I was directly involved with the massacre."

"Oh yeah, I heard about that."

"My friend Maria was injured. She lost the use of her arm."

"That is too sad. Where is she?"

"She's in Bellato working as a waitress. She convinced the owner of the pub to donate to Fort Kingsley."

"Good to know that she's still contributing."

"Yeah."

We finished our meals and left Omaha Steaks. Walt patted Chen on the back and said something about chasing one of the waitresses who just left the restaurant. Chen left to start a patrol. He preferred patrolling at night anyway.

Rebecca threaded her left fingers through my right hand and said, "Hey, do you mind if I catch up with Christofer for a bit? I'll meet you back at the living quarters."

"Sure," I said. "I'm going to take a look around the city, maybe start my patrol as well."

"Great." Rebecca kissed me quickly on the lips.

Christofer waved at me and they walked off together, she hooked her arm around his. The jealousy in my chest threatened to push the freshly eaten steaks right out of my stomach, but I breathed deeply to hold that down.

I felt lost. It was ten o'clock at night and there were still hundreds if not thousands of people on the streets. I scanned the populace and I did not know what I wanted to do.

I saw my wayward cousin Alana. She walked alone and stuck to the shadows, but walked quickly.

I said aloud to no one, "Well, I guess I know what I'm doing tonight."

45 — Agarue

May 7, 2000

I casually followed Alana. I kept an eye on things as I trailed her. I reasoned with myself that this was one of my eight hour patrols. Her consort, the man with long black hair, was bad news so I felt this was a proper use of my time.

Alana stopped. She spoke with a skinny man with thinning hair. Even after midnight the city still moved.

The skinny man smiled at her and she smiled at him. She took him by the hand and pulled him along with her. The man seemed enthralled with her. Most men would be. Her muscled frame had enticing curves. Her lips met his cheek and he shied away bashfully. Alana giggled and pulled him along.

Fewer people inhabited the streets where they walked. I had to better conceal myself. I was also more watchful for the man with long black hair. I hadn't seen him, but it made sense for him to be close.

The thin man was a target. I just didn't know why.

The thin man immediately turned around and I ducked behind a building. I listened intently. I heard steps coming towards me. I panicked and rushed as fast as I could around the next corner of the building. I pushed out my wings, jumped up and flapped twice to get to the top of the building. I pulled my wings back in and peered over the edge.

I saw the thin man looking where I just stood. Alana smiled and pulled him behind the building and kissed him hard.

The thin man did not resist. His eyes closed as Alana kissed him. I saw her right hand pulling a dagger while her left hand ran through his thinning hair. The dagger moved towards his neck.

I jumped down. "Alana!"

The thin man fell down in fright.

Alana growled. "What the hell are you doing here?"

"I'm stopping you from hurting this man," I said.

The thin man saw the dagger for the first time. He quivered.

"Go," I said to him.

The thin man scrambled out of the alley and was gone.

Alana sheathed her dagger. "Why the hell did you do that? Seriously, JR. I was hunting. That guy was a telepath. I was doing really well. I was keeping him distracted. I almost had his power."

"You have to kill them to take their power?"

"No, it just requires a lot of blood to get the power from them."

"So you were going to bleed him and leave him to die."

"No! Jeez JR. I was going to drink his blood and put a bandage on him and guide him stumbling to the hospital."

"Still not an excuse."

"Yeah, well, this isn't your life. This is how I live mine. I'm growing as a being. I don't need you meddling."

Alana sighed. "What are you doing in Omaha anyway?"

"I graduated as a Hell Bringer. I'm passing through to Fort Angel."

"Well, congratulations, cuz. Now keep passing."

"You know you're in deep trouble if you are ever captured by the Human army."

"Are you planning to turn me in?"

It was my turn to sigh. "No Alana. You're family. I can't do that to you, even though I should. I mean, look at you. Drinking blood?"

"This is who I am now. I am following my biological evolution. I am a hemathrope, not a Human. I follow a slightly different set of rules."

I didn't know what to say. I leaned exasperated against the wall.

Alana asked, "What's wrong?"

"This whole, not being a Human thing is frustrating."

"Oh…. You found out then?"

"About whom my father is? Yeah, I found out."

"That's tough, cuz. I wanted to tell you, but our parents swore us kids old enough to know to secrecy. They never told the younger ones because they would have blabbed the secret to you too soon."

"Too soon? I could have handled something like this better if I had known sooner. It probably wouldn't even faze me now. I just… everything is just going wrong. My best friend doesn't like me. The girl I love is spending the evening with her old boyfriend doing gods know what."

Alana asked, "Have you told her you love her?"

"No, not in so many words."

"Maybe if she knew, she could reassure you somehow. It's Kingsley's daughter right?"

"Yeah. How did you know?"

"I eavesdropped on you two talking one day when you were telling her about stuff from Meton. Also, I knew the Ward girl wasn't much of a fighter, there would be no way she would make Hell Bringer."

"Yeah. Maria is nice, but Rebecca feels deeper to me."

"You slept with her?"

"What?"

"Most guys sleep with a girl for the first time and they take it as a trophy, but you are not most guys. You have your first time with a girl and you feel connected more deeply than others might."

"I don't know if that's a good thing or a bad thing."

Alana smiled. "It's whatever you want it to be. But you can't let the jealousy you have over her spending time with her ex come between your feelings for her. If she has the same feelings for you then you will get through it. Who knows? It could be an innocent hang out."

"Not likely. Her ex is Christofer Osborne."

"Oooh, that politician asshole? I'll kill him for you if you want."

"Tempting, but no. Why would you do that?"

"He's putting in the new water filtration system."

"Why is that bad?"

"Because, dear cousin, hemathropes do not eat food to survive. We survive on the minerals in water. If the filtration system happens most of the minerals will be filtered out of the water and it will not sustain us. We will have to venture out and find water elsewhere. The more times someone goes in and out of the force field, the more times they are noticed. That is not what we need right now. That's why we left Bellato, because they were putting in the water filtration system."

"I had no idea. You know, you could have told someone."

"Yeah, I didn't want it to be a messy departure. I just wanted to be done with the army."

"Uncle Oli and Aunt Jess are worried. Write them a letter or something. They just want to know you are okay."

"Yeah, I'll think about it."

Silence between us. The road out of the alley was quiet. It seemed that Omaha really did sleep on occasion.

Alana spoke, "Look, I have to get going. Agarue will want me soon."

"Agarue?"

"The guy. THE guy."

"The one with long black hair?"

"Yeah. We are still together."

"How is that going for you?"

"It's scary and exciting. He is quite possibly the most violent being I have ever met, but when he touches me I feel so safe and surrounded. I've seen him rip off a man's head, but his touch is like a flower petal. He says it is because he knows if he ever struck me I would kill him in his sleep. He's right. I love him, but I would never put up with that kind of shit."

"I would expect nothing less from you, Alana."

Alana laughed. "Yeah. Hey, you take care okay? I hope you figure out what to do with your girl."

"Yeah. Try not to drink anyone's blood while I'm in town eh?"

"I can't promise that."

"I didn't figure. I love you, cuz."

"I love you too."

I watched as Alana walked quickly back to the street and vanished. I followed a few minutes later, giving her time to get away. I didn't want to see which way she went.

I walked around the city for the next few hours patrolling. There were no disturbances. Everyone was asleep. I passed a few regular street guards and we nodded. They must have been notified that I would be joining them.

As I walked, I saw a light on in the second floor room of a huge house. There were no curtains. Part of me felt improper as I looked up into the window, but the rest of me would not look away.

Shadows moved in the window. I moved to get a better angle on the window and I saw Rebecca's face and bare breasts. She bent over, out of the window sight, and then returned with her brassiere in hand. She pulled on her brassiere. Over it she pulled on a shirt. Christofer joined her in the window view and kissed her. She kissed him back.

My feet grew roots where they stood. My churning stomach bubbled. I breathed deep to hold it down. The kiss lasted impossibly long. I coiled my arms around my chest and shivered. The jealousy that I felt towards Christofer before paled in comparison to the disgust I felt now. My head felt like it was going to explode, but I couldn't look away.

Finally the kiss broke. Christofer put his hand on her lower back like he was guiding her out, but she stopped him and kissed him quickly on the lips and went out of window sight.

My feet ripped from the roots they had grown and I dashed away down the street. I had to sleep or do something else to get my mind off of this. No one was on the street so I pushed my wings out and flapped into the air. I flew fast to Joslyn Castle and landed in front of the steps much to the surprise of the guards. Their hands held their weapons, but when they saw who I was, they relaxed. Having a reputation can be useful.

I entered the castle and headed to the quarters we were assigned by Lieutenant Perez. I stripped down to my loin cloth and slid into the surprisingly comfortable bed. I pulled the cotton sheets over me and closed my eyes.

All I could see under my eyelids was Rebecca and Christofer kissing. My imagination put them in bed together locked in passion. My skin crawled. My stomach continued to churn. I opened my eyes again and growled. I leaned over onto my right side and stared at the wall next to me. I pushed my head into the pillow to muffle my scream. Without thinking about it, I punched the wall with my right fist, leaving a hole in the brick.

Now my hand hurt, but not as much as my heart.

Tears did not come out of my eyes. I wouldn't allow it.

I breathed deeply trying to bring myself to a calm place. I tried to put out of my mind what I saw and what I felt. Minute after minute my heart felt like it would pound through my chest.

Footsteps. The door to the room opened. I closed my eyes. Shuffling. Kicking off boots. Taking off of clothes. The cotton blanket lifted and Rebecca's warm flesh pressed against my back. She threaded her leg through mine. Her arm wrapped around my abdomen. Her breasts pressed tight against me. Her kiss was light against the back of my neck.

46 — White Eyes

May 19, 2000

I didn't bring it up.

I tried my best to deny I saw it. No, I tried my best to remember that I didn't own her. I loved her. If you love someone you have to let them be free to be who they are. In the world before the Dragons, the Powers That Be tried to force everyone into boxes whether the person wanted to be there or not. I could not do that to Rebecca.

Rebecca carried on like nothing had happened. Sort of. She acted especially cuddly during the ride to Garden City and from Garden City to Fort Albuquerque. I imagined Christofer touching her and my skin crawled.

I made excuses not to touch her. I offered to ride up on top of the stage coach whenever the opportunity presented itself. It was not as fun as it seemed at the beginning especially in drier climates.

May 10, 2000

I kept my balance fairly well on top of the stage coach. Walt sat there with me.

His standoffish posture softened, which was a good sign. I couldn't talk to anyone else about the situation, so I had to turn to him.

"I'm sorry," I blurted out.

"For what?" Walt replied less than cordial.

"I'm sorry for keeping from you something you should have been the first person I told. I didn't realize the repercussions. I should have been braver. You deserve more than that from me."

At first, Walt didn't speak. The stage coach hit a few bumps which jostled us, but once we recovered the smoother ride he spoke. "Okay. I accept your apology. But for gods' sakes, don't do that again. You have no idea how much it hurts to be left out from a secret like that. I could have helped you, or been there for you, something. That's what best friends do."

"Actually," I began. "I think I really do get it now."

"What do you mean?"

I told Walt everything about Rebecca. I told him how I saw her with Christofer and how she climbed back into bed with me like nothing happened. I told him how I'd been avoiding touching her when I could and tolerating it when I couldn't. I told him that despite all this, I still loved her and wanted to touch her and be with her. I didn't know if I could process this whole situation.

Walt pondered for a moment.

"Well, this is a slippery slope here. You can't exactly come out and tell her that you know. She will accuse you of spying on her and you'll be back in the dog house."

"I wasn't really spying."

"I know, but that will be her gut reaction. You know how Rebecca is with her gut reactions to things. Especially with your history as it relates to Christofer."

"Yes, so what do I do?"

"Try your best to move past it. You don't own her. Until you declare yourself and tell her you want some kind of commitment, you cannot expect her to wait for you... despite the fact that she was your first."

My stomach churned in anxiety. "It's really hard to even consider moving past this. Half of me would like to just get over it. My fist hurts when I let it affect me for too long. Half of me would like to cling to it, calling it betrayal, calling it stupid to trust anyone."

"It isn't stupid to trust her. Think about it this way, has

she ever tried to hurt you, physically, mentally, emotionally, spiritually? Even when she was mad at you, she didn't go out of her way to harm you, she was just indifferent."

I admitted this was so.

Walt continued, "She is not your enemy. She was being the person you love. You have to accept all of her."

May 13, 2000

The citizens of Garden City didn't have the fortified walls of forts or weapons. Garden City turned out to be more than just a name. Trees grew taller than the tallest buildings and concealed the city from the air. I flew up above the city to check it out and the city was concealed. I also detected a prominent scent to the city. It dulled my nostrils to anything else.

The denizens of Garden City told us the scent masked their Human scent from any Dragons that might fly overhead. The combination of the right flowers and plants put together produced a scent which shrouded the settlement below from Dragons.

Jason and Tammy tended to the horses. The four of us took the opportunity to look around. A blonde man and his blonde sister stopped Walt and Chen in front of a store that sold floral shirts. All four looked pleasantly attracted.

Rebecca and I continued on our way. Rebecca slid her fingers between mine and occasionally leaned her head on my shoulder. I imagined her body arching up to meet mine, and then Christofer's body superimposed over mine. I couldn't pull away suddenly, but I occasionally let my eyes carry my body away from her to look at something "interesting".

Rebecca joined me again after each separation. She took my hand again and looked at what I looked at. I didn't look her in the eyes.

After a few hours of browsing, we reconvened with Jason and Tammy. They said they were ready to go. None of us needed a rest so we decided to head out right away.

"I'll ride on top," I offered.

"Actually, I think Chen and I should ride on top," Walt said. "We have much to discuss having to do with blondes and their siblings."

Rebecca and I sat in the stage coach alone. I felt vastly more uncomfortable than she seemed.

She snuggled up to me. "Did you have fun today, Dear Heart?"

She had taken to calling me Dear Heart. I wasn't sure why, but it wasn't unpleasant.

"N-Yes I had a good time, My Darling."

My Darling was my nickname for her.

"Good."

I didn't bring it up then either.

May 19, 2000

Fort Albuquerque was a different kind of fort. The construction looked similar to other forts we visited. However, all around the fort had no houses as we knew them. Instead there were *hoohgan* dwellings. People milled around cutting meat, tanning hides, tending sheep and more.

Hoohgan dwellings were the traditional Dinè (Navajo) homes. They consisted of wooden poles curved and lashed together, then covered with thick packed earth. Seeing them reminded me of my mother describing the tepee she slept in with her mother.

The Lieutenant Joseph Eagle met us at the gate of Fort Albuquerque. His bronze skin seemed almost reflective as the red sun illuminated it. "Welcome Hell Bringers! I am glad you have come. But before you enter, you must be cleansed."

We four looked at each other confused.

Lieutenant Eagle pointed behind us. "Seek White Eyes. White Eyes is our healer. White Eyes will cleanse you."

Walt spoke. "Permission to speak, sir."

Lieutenant Eagle said, "Granted."

Walt asked, "Why is this necessary?"

Lieutenant Eagle smiled. "You'll find out. Now go. Dismissed."

Jason and Tammy had long since continued into the fort. I imagined they had already been cleansed.

We asked locals where to find White Eyes. Our search

led us to two *hoohgans* standing side by side. A tall, shirtless man stood in front of one. A thin woman with a long flowing dress stood in front of the other. They did not speak to each other.

As we approached, they spoke in one voice from two voice boxes. "You seek White Eyes."

We nodded.

The voice again, "Men take off your pants, but leave your undergarments on. Woman, wear this dress."

Walt said, "I-I'm not wearing any undergarments."

The voice sighed and the man threw a loin cloth at Walt.

The woman handed Rebecca a flowing dress much like her own.

Walt, Chen and I took down our pants and laid our stuff at the front wall of the *hoohgan*. Rebecca did the same on the other side.

The woman took Rebecca's hand. "White Eyes is here."

The woman led Rebecca into the *hoohgan* and closed the door behind them.

The man opened the other door. "White Eyes is here."

He motioned for us to enter the *hoohgan*. It was pitch dark inside the dwelling and the sizzle of steam rose through. There a small hole releases steam through the top of the dwelling.

"Sit," said the man. We sat.

A raspy voice from the deepest darkness of the dwelling said, "I have been waiting for you."

"What is this place?" Walt asked.

The man spoke, "This is a sweat lodge. You are here to be cleansed."

"I don't feel particularly dirty," Walt replied.

The voice from the darkness said, "You are not the dirtiest, but you have much to cleanse."

"Go with it," Chen said softly.

There was another sizzle of steam. Moisture clung to my skin. I inhaled deeply. I exhaled deeply.

White Eyes began his/her/their repetitive singing.

47 — Grand Canyon

May 24, 2000

We arrived at the Grand Canyon. The different colors of the vista shimmered in the sun. We unfortunately couldn't stay. We just stopped stretch our legs and rest. A small village with provisions posted near the canyon. Jason and Tammy took care of the provisions while Walt, Chen, Rebecca and I stood at the edge of the canyon and looked into it.

We all still reeled from the experience with White Eyes at the sweat lodge. I felt lighter. I didn't feel as jealous or as put off about the situation between Rebecca and Christofer as before. This made me glad. I still hadn't brought up seeing them, but it mattered less and less as the days went by.

We four looked out into the canyon and marveled. The heat reflected up hypnotically. I felt myself caught in the sway of the heat waves and I lost myself.

May 19, 2000

White Eyes sang repetitiously. His/her/their low singing rumbled my soul, but a higher tone stung me like a needle. The singing overwhelmed, but never deafened me. My mind felt lost to me. I had access to my heart only. My heart felt full of doubt and strife.

Through the singing I felt a message. *Dragon child, you are connected deeper than most to the tragedy befalling us all.*

You have access to something most of us do not. You can know the enemy. But you first have to know yourself. You have to be willing to divorce yourself from negative emotions with regards to the ones you love. Love is your greatest strength. You will be tested with so many hateful sources, it will seem like nothing else matters. Love is what will get you through everything. Love will keep you connected. Love will help you connect others to one another, to reunite a community.

I awoke, or it felt like I awoke from a deep sleep. No one sang in the sweat lodge. The door stood open to the warm night and aired out the lodge, letting in the Albuquerque air. Walt and Chen already stood outside.

The male aspect of White Eyes pointed to a dark pool about 200 feet away. I stumbled towards it trying to catch my bearings. I reached the pool and cool water covered my feet. I closed my eyes as I walked further. The water covered my knees. Followed by my hips, then my stomach, then my arms and chest then I dunked my head in the cool water. I let the air escape my chest. I felt bubbles tickle up my face from my mouth and nose. I felt my hair floating all around my face.

My feet touched something on the floor of the pool. I opened my eyes and saw Rebecca staring at me. I reached for her hands. Her hands reached for mine. Even in the cool water I felt the electricity between us. A yellow light shined above us. We looked up. The water refracted the light of the lantern hanging over us.

My lungs suddenly cried out for air. My heart beat out of my chest. I looked at Rebecca again and we walked together to the shore.

May 24, 2000

"JR! Earth to John Ross Gerstung!" Walt nudged me and I almost lost my balance.

"Huh?"

"We have to get going, man."

"Oh, okay. Thanks."

"This is such a beautiful place. It's a shame more people don't come here."

"Why don't they?" I asked before I realized I already knew.

"There was a supposed midair collision over the Grand Canyon just over a month before Marcinelle. 128 people were killed. I thought you knew that."

"I do, I just was off somewhere else. My mind hadn't returned to thinking yet."

"Yeah, you were just standing in one place chanting softly while Rebecca, Chen and I were in the village."

"I was remembering the sweat lodge."

Walt chuckled. "Yeah, good times."

"Do Jason and Tammy need help loading?"

"Yes. Let's get to it."

The provisions would be enough to get us through the last five days to Fort Angel. They weren't heavy, but once we finished I felt exhausted. I climbed into the stage coach. Rebecca climbed in next to me. It looked like rain so Walt and Chen covered the top of the stage coach with a canvas tarp. Jason and Tammy affixed their shelter on the front to keep them out of the weather.

"All abord!" Jason yelled good-naturedly.

Walt and Chen climbed back into the coach and reclined as much as they could. I felt unusually cold. I curled up with myself and closed my eyes. I must have shivered because I felt Rebecca's warm hands touch me. I relaxed a bit before I dozed off.

My dream showed a bunch of image blots. Nothing moved. I saw a man wearing black leather pants, but no shirt. His hair looked scraggly. He walked through the desert with his hands wide and his palms up. He had his back to me. He stood in front of a vast city that seemed to be growing with each blot. He turned to me. I heard his crooning voice, "This is a door that only opens to those who are open to it." The man's form became transparent. I could only see the borders of his form. He suddenly expanded and covered over the vast city which continued to expand. The force field barred attacks from Dragons. His form was still visible, but it was enormous around the vast, growing city. People moved in and out of the field offering a piece of their energy to it. Over time, people offered less and less to the field. Dragons broke through the force field and razed the city. They built their own settlement in the wake of rubble with a huge concrete nest rising into the sky. A Black Dragon with red eyes stood at the opening of the nest. It roared.

My eyes opened slowly. Everyone else slept in the stage coach. The coach continued on. The rain stopped, but the area still glinted with moisture. My body still felt weak and exhausted, but I didn't feel as cold as before. I wanted to get out. I wanted to stretch my legs, but I realized we were on a tight schedule. I lay my head back and closed my eyes again. I could wait.

May 25, 2000

Dawn came and we stopped at an outpost. My legs felt wobbly as I left the coach, but I stretched and felt the power returning to my body. Walt, Chen and Rebecca stretched outside the coach.

There were three wooden buildings at the outpost. The two on the sides had signs, "No Admittance." I entered the middle building and saw a plethora of supplies and artwork. The man standing behind the counter reminded me of the male aspect of White Eyes.

Behind the man behind the counter hung a painting of the man I saw in my dream. I pointed. "Who is that man in the paining?"

"That is Jim Morrison the 27 Mage of Los Angeles."

"Wait, if Los Angeles had a 27 Mage, then how were they destroyed?"

"People stopped contributing to the upkeep of the barrier. The barrier of a 27 Mage is impenetrable by any being or mode of entry which means harm to those inside, but if the 27 Mage does not have the sense of community necessary to sustain the barrier it will be broken. The barriers thrive on positivity."

My dream…. I thanked the man behind the counter and exited the building. My friends and our drivers ate breakfast. We ate fried bacon and eggs with milk and oatmeal. The food filled me up and I felt the energy renewing my body. This mission we accepted started taking shape in my heart.

When we finished eating we reentered the coach and left down the rocky road towards Fort Angel.

I spoke to my friends, "Have you guys heard about Jim Morrison, the 27 Mage of Los Angeles?"

Walt answered, "Yes, he supposedly hangs around Fort Angel haunting people there. Why do you ask?"

"I had a dream about him last night. It was a bit disconcerting. But I think I understand it now."

"What was the dream about?" Rebecca asked.

I told them all about the dream. When I finished, I added, "I think we are supposed to fix things at Fort Angel. I think we are supposed to bring back the 27 Mage over that area to protect it from Dragons."

Walt asked, "Why do you think that?"

I said, "I was given that dream. I was shown what happened before I even knew something happened. I lived it, inasmuch as someone can live something like that without being there. I think Morrison was trying to tell me he needs my help to resurrect the barrier."

Rebecca smiled. "I guess we have to light a fire under some people there."

Walt nodded. "People are strange though. They might not go for it."

Chen chimed in. "Strange days have found us."

I closed my eyes and reclined as much as I could in the seat. Rebecca curled into me. I loved her madly.

48 — Fort Angel

May 29, 2000

Fort Angel looked huge from a mile away. We approached from the east and looked north. We stopped on a hill and admired the expanse of land around the fort.

The fort was mostly stone. It looked at least twice as wide and long as Fort Kingsley. The walls looked at least ten feet thick, wide enough for guards to pass one another as they went by on their patrols. Each side of the fort included four entrances. This was a true military fort. Soldiers milled around outside and inside of the fort. I saw two ballista guards on every corner watching the sky and the ground. A Center Tower which overlooked the entire fort.

The makings of a bustling city surrounded the fort. On all sides stood wooden and stone buildings and occasionally guard towers with ballista guards watching the skies. The entire set up looked impressive. I had limited experience with Human settlements, Meton was so small it hid itself fairly well and a lot of Bellato was underground. Fort Kingsley was prominent, but not like this.

Fort Angel was bold. There were trees strewn all over the landscape, but not for concealment. It felt like they existed for shade or as decoration. I saw no obvious flamboyant colors. Instead there I saw a steady wave of green, brown and black, but Fort Angel didn't hide.

"That's beautiful," Walt said at last.

"What is?" Chen asked.

"Fort Angel. It is showing the Dragons that Humanity cannot be conquered. Los Angeles was destroyed and Fort Angel rose in its ashes," Walt said.

"Where is Sunset Red?" I asked.

"Turn around," Rebecca said. She faced the opposite way as we boys.

We all turned and looked south. Our eyes met the rubble and devastation of the former city of Los Angeles. The streets sat covered with crumbled buildings. Some areas looked cleared and the rubble circled around it. We couldn't see what was inside the rubble circles, but we guessed they were nests. We scanned the area. More and more nests extended west. The ocean coast seemed to be the cutoff, though the ocean made it harder to see.

We scanned east and the nests seemed endless. They sprawled across the landscape further south than we could see. At last, we saw the largest nest of all.

The behemoth of concrete and stone rose into the air far above any nest near it. The clear sky framed the dark stone making it easily visible. It reminded me of Jonathan's castle near Meton how it rose into the air. Jonathan's castle's grey stone blended into the often grey skies of Meton. This nest offended the blue sky of the former city.

"How do they even stack stone that high without it falling?" I asked.

"Very carefully I imagine," Walt replied.

"They stack both sides of wall. They go up as they can. Takes much time, dedication," Chen said.

"Probably had some kind of adhesive as well," Rebecca said.

"I've heard dead Humans make good building materials," Walt said.

We all looked at him like he was insane. Walt chuckled, but said nothing else.

Jason and Tammy stood with us, but had been silent until Jason said helpfully, "Ya kids don be sad. Wanna see summit great?"

We turned to him only slightly comprehending.

Jason waved us on. "Foller me."

We followed Jason as he took us down the hill. We saw what looked like backwards letters about 50 feet high. They were white wood on the back and braced. We carefully made our way down the hill and around the letters. We walked down until we could see all of the letters.

They read:

FORTANGEL

We all marveled for a moment. At last, Jason spoke, "Da Hollywood sign was here. Goin' ta shit when da Dragnz atakd. Dragnz d'stroyd Los angeles, firs thing dey did was fix da sign. Make up a new un." Jason cleared his throat, "Fort Angel. Iss purdy ya?"

"It's beautiful," Rebecca said.

After a few more minutes of marveling at the indomitable nature of the Human spirit, we decided we needed to get to the Fort before sundown. We rode the stage coach down through the dirty concrete roads to one of the South Gates. We disembarked the stage coach. The guards admitted us one at a time after they checked our identification. The guards were thorough, but uninterested in our arrival. They told us to visit the Center Tower to check in and get our bunk assignments. We had orders to see Lieutenant Nelson.

Jason and Tammy only intended to stay the night. Four Hell Bringers needed transport to Seattle.

Before we parted ways, Tammy hugged all of us and gave us all loud smooches on the cheeks. She said, "I luv yu kids. Yu gon do gud!"

Jason shook hands with Walt, Chen and me. He kissed Rebecca on the cheek. He said goodbye and smiled as he turned away.

As we walked away, I said, "I hope they get to see their kids soon."

My friends agreed.

We reached the Center Tower with little trouble and entered the south entrance. There was a huge desk and behind it stood a thin man wearing a green beret. Walt stood first in line, he checked in and received his assignment. Then Chen received his assignment.   Rebecca approached.   The man behind the counter, Lieutenant Nelson, ogled her a little too hard, especially after reading her name.

"So, uh, Miss Kingsley, are you free this evening?" Nelson said.

Rebecca replied, "Nope. I've got a lot to do, I have to organize my bunk and sharpen my sword."

Nelson said, "Maybe after you sharpen your sword you can polish mine."

Rebecca said, "I don't really like using pocket knives. Thank you though. Am I registered, sir?"

Nelson grumbled yes and she stepped out of line. I stood in front of him and gave him my information.

"Gerstung, John Ross. You are pretty young to be a Hell Bringer."

"Yes, sir."

"Related to the Gerstung Brothers?"   His tone sounded ambiguous.

"My uncles, sir."

"I met them. Didn't like them."

"Sorry to hear that, sir."

"Don't like you either."

"Sorry to hear that as well, sir."

"You being a smart ass?"

"No, sir. I am genuinely disappointed that you do not like me upon first meeting me without getting to know me."

"That sounds like smart ass talk."

"No, sir."

"You talking back to me, boy? I will have your ass thrown in the clink faster than you can say 'Cowardly Gerstung brothers'."

Heat rose into my eyes. My brain overrode what my voice wanted to say, "Am I registered, sir?"

"No! You aren't registered! You are one step from being Dragon food you little bastard. You want me to come over this counter and kick your ass."

"If you must, sir."

Lieutenant Nelson jumped the counter and pushed me. I threw my stuff to the side and backed up. Nelson threw a right hook at my head. I dodged and threaded my right arm around his, placing my right hand on the back of his head. He tried to kick me backwards, but I stomped on his right ankle causing him to cry out in pain. I pushed Lieutenant Nelson in the middle of the back with my left hand hard enough that he fell to the ground and smacked his face on the stone floor. His green beret skittered across the floor.

Lieutenant Nelson bounced back up red faced. He readied himself to attack again when a booming voice echoed the hall. "NELSON! GET BACK TO YOUR POST!"

A man at least a full head taller than me approached. He stood taller than even Walt. His body was wider than Crush's. His muscles looked like angular granite. Even under the flat green button up shirt I could tell see his highly defined abdominal muscles. His broad chest and pectorals led to a valley leading up from his cut abdominals. His bald head was dark skinned and in place of one of his eyes was a glowing red glass with grey metal around the eye socket.

Nelson grabbed his beret from the floor and slowly walked back to his post behind the counter. As an after thought he said, "Yes, General."

Walt, Chen, Rebecca and I immediately snapped to attention. This was General Braggs.

Braggs spoke without malice, but in a baritone that rumbled my chest. "You four are from Fort Kingsley, yes?"

"Yes, sir." We answered simultaneously.

"At ease."

We relaxed.

"How is Lieutenant Kingsley, these days?"

Rebecca spoke, "My fath – I mean Lieutenant Kingsley was doing well when we left the fort. He was excited to see us go off to this fort to fight with you."

Braggs smiled. "I'm glad you four are here. We have some big things happening in the fort and we need all the power we can get to make them happen. You find your bunks and get them set up. Tomorrow you all start your patrols. As you progress you will be given different assignments, but everyone starts with patrols.

"Don't mind Nelson. He's a hot head, a misogynist and the worst fighter I've ever seen. But I guess those who cannot do, teach. Those who cannot fight, strategize. He's won some battles for me over the years. But don't let him push you around. Just because he's a higher rank doesn't give him a right to be an asshole to you. There are too many other dangers for you to have to worry about out here."

"Thank you sir," we said in unison.

"Dismissed."

Braggs turned and walked out into the milling fort. My friends had their papers, but I had to get back in line. Luckily, the line was short. We soon made our way to our bunk assignments. Thankfully our bunks were in the same block. The bunks had their own separate buildings off of the walls. Every bunk was constructed with stone and housed two personnel. Walt and I bunked together again. Having a name close to your best friend is more of a blessing than many realized. Chen's bunk was close to us with someone named Jackson Chance. Rebecca's bunk was with a woman named Raven Jenkins not far from us.

"Raven?" Walt asked.

"Yeah," Rebecca said. "Do you think it could be her?"

We walked to Rebecca's bunk after dropping off our things and saw it was none other than one of our Hell Bringer recruiters, Raven.

Her black hair now cropped short, but the top bounced as much as her body did as she stalked towards Walt. Her familiar velvety voice said, "I thought you'd never get here." She smashed her body into Walt's and he seemed like he wanted to devour her as well.

Raven broke the kiss and grabbed Walt by the back of his head. She threw him into her bunk and slammed the door behind her.

I cautiously approached the door, "Do you want me to bring your stuff and leave it outside the door?"

Walt's breathless voice: Yes!

Raven's breathless voice: No! Someone will steal it. Bring it by in an hour. Now go away!

And we did.

49 — Day One

May 29, 2000

Rebecca, Chen and I went back to our bunks. We met Chen's bunkmate, Jackson Chance, a tall, wiry, young man, age about 18. His hair hung long and blonde, tied back in a pony tail. He carried an epee and a bow and arrow strapped to his back. His voice sounded high and musical.

"Hey there!" Jackson said. "You all must be new. I'm Jackson and I just arrived myself. Though to be honest I grew up in the city around Fort Angel. I know where just about everything is, so if you ever need directions, just come find me."

We all greeted Jackson with smiles and handshakes. When he shook hands with Rebecca he exclaimed, "Oh my god, your eyes are so beautiful!"

Rebecca smiled and blushed a little. Jackson turned to me and said, "You better hold onto this one. With eyes like hers she's gotta be a tigress, if you know what I mean." Jackson kissed Rebecca on the cheek.

He looked at Chen and smiled. "We are going to have the best time as bunkmates. Come. Let's get you settled in." Jackson grabbed Chen's hand and practically dragged him to their bunk.

Out of ear shot, Rebecca spoke, "He was cute. Strange, but cute."

"Chen is going to have a hard time keeping his commitment to his boyfriend," I said.

"Agreed."

Hours later, Rebecca and I lay in my bunk side by side naked and sweaty. My left arm rested under her head and she curled against my side. Her left leg wrapped around both of mine and her left arm hugged my chest. She dozed and I didn't feel like moving. I examined the lamp illuminated room.

There two dressers with four drawers each stood inside. The bunks were similar to the ones in Fort Kingsley, one on top of the other. The difference here, the bunks had some semblance of comfortable. I felt actual cushioning.

There weren't any windows in the bunks, but the stone was breathable. When the wind blew we felt it. I noticed a wooden door on the ground between the dressers. It had a metal handle sticking up and hinges on the opposite side.

I carefully slid my arm out from under Rebecca's head. She woke up almost instantly. "Where you going?" she asked sleepily.

"I want to check out this door."

Rebecca seemed unconcerned. "Oh. Okay."

I went down on my knees and lifted the door. It squeaked, but was light to lift. I looked down and saw a square, stone hole. Inside the hole, I saw a bar fastened into the stone. The hole was mostly dark, but I saw a glimmer of light as I poked my head down further.

"I think this is a tunnel," I said.

"Yes it is," Rebecca replied.

"You know about this?"

"Yes. Fort Angel has tunnels from every building on the ground floor. They all lead to a central tunnel that branches off out of the Center Tower. There are exits to the west, east and north."

"No south exit?"

"There used to be, but it was compromised and the exit from the Center Tower crumbled. No one tried to fix it. People say Abdul the Butcher lives there."

"Who?"

Rebecca sat up and rubbed her eyes. "Abdul the Butcher is a legend, or a myth, or… something. He was said to be insane killing Dragons and Humans alike if they came too near him."

"Has anyone ever seen him?"

"No one I know, but then again I don't know many people out here. I'm sure if you asked around you could find out more."

I pondered this for a moment. Changing the subject, I said, "Do you want to go have a look around? Our duty doesn't start until tomorrow."

Rebecca smiled. "I think I would rather stay in bed." She added with a sultry tone, "Wouldn't you?"

I closed the door to the tunnel and joined her, happily.

June 25, 2000

Hell Bringers everywhere!

Fort Angle acted as a military-operations grade fort. This meant that this fort attacked Dragon settlements en masse. This also meant the fort could withstand onslaughts from Dragons with minimal, if any, casualties. Fort Angel had the best ballista guards in the Human army. If necessary, many of the guards could fire two arrows in a minute which was basically unheard of considering the size of the arrows. Teams of arrow retrievers stood ready in case of an attack. They followed the chain to the fallen Dragon, draw the arrow out and carry it back to the guard as fast as possible. Each guard had a team of assistants which pulled the arrows back up the side of the fort to the waiting guard. Each ballista guard had ten arrows each. Each team of assistants possessed deadly accuracy with bow and arrows.

For every seven males there were about three females. The women didn't just cook and clean. They patrolled and sparred with the men.

Personnel patrolled or worked otherwise for 12 hours, then off for 12 hours, free to do whatever they wanted in that time, including sleep. There was always activity at Fort Angel. No one had the exact same schedule as anyone else.

As Braggs had said, we all started out patrolling the fort and the surrounding city. From there our strengths and weaknesses would be determined and we would be assigned new areas.

Walt was assigned to train to be a ballista guard. When I first heard this I wasn't sure if he could handle the arrows as well as the some of the others. Later in the day, I caught a glimpse of him handling an arrow fairly easily.

Rebecca's orders were to join the strategic division. Lieutenant Nelson was her superior officer. I grimaced in sympathy for her as she trudged off to her post.

Chen and I received patrol assignments. Chen was part of a defensive patrol. This meant he had orders to patrol the city around the fort as in our first few weeks, but his job also meant to serve as a police force to resolve issues in the city.

My orders placed me as part of tactical strike and reconnaissance patrol. The strategic division sent down orders of where we should explore to determine a threat of the Dragons and then report back. If there was a threat our orders became to eliminate it.

July 15, 2000

For the first few weeks I only did reconnaissance. My commanding officer, Lieutenant Musil, lead our group of 10 around the outskirts of Sunset Red. We wanted to gain information about the big nest in the eastern part of the area. No one had ever infiltrated the nest and lived to tell about it.

Musil was a short, stocky man. He wore dark tinted glasses, even at night. He had no apparent hair and his skin was bright white so he often covered up or painted his skin with green and brown paint. Musil did not speak unless he needed to. When he spoke we listened.

We crouched low over the hills outside of Sunset Red. We reached a ledge as close as we could get to the huge nest without falling down the hill.

Oh, no. Roges.

I turned my head and about 100 yards behind us I saw a baby Green Dragon. I tapped Musil and pointed. He signaled for me to capture the baby and keep it quiet.

I crawled closer to the baby, he saw me approach.

Oh, no. Mommy!

I quickly thought, *Quiet down, I'm not going to hurt you. We are here to scope out the land that's it. If you stay quiet, you'll be safe.*

Liar! Liar! You killed my mommy. You killed her!

As I got closer to the baby I saw there was the head of a Green Dragon behind him. I didn't see the body.

Wait! Wait little one. We did not do that. I don't know who did it, but we did not.

Liar! I'll kill you!

The baby Dragon galloped towards me snapping. I rose from my crouch and swatted it down to the ground. He slashed his claws at me and caught them before they could wound me. I twisted the baby down to the ground and driving his claws into the ground. I held his mouth closed.

Quiet now little one. I'll let you go as soon as we're done okay?

The baby struggled against my grip.

At last the reconnaissance finished. My patrol quickly and carefully departed from the area and headed back to the fort. Musil stopped near me.

"The mother's dead? You may as well kill this one. It's got no chance."

"Yes, sir," I said obediently.

Okay, we're going to leave. I'm going to hit you in the back of the head. This will knock you out, but you will live. You need to get back to your kind. They are just over the hill. Good luck little one.

I struck the baby in the back of the head and he collapsed unconscious.

We reached the Fort to report back to the strategic division. The walls of the nest stretched too high. We weren't able to get close enough to the nest to discern anything about it. We would need a better plan.

No one had any ideas about how to get information. Planes were too noisy and would be destroyed almost instantly. Ground approach would be similarly perilous with all of the nests.

At last, I suggested, "I could always fly over it."

50 — Lunar Eclipse

July 16, 2000

I wore flat black paint and Dragon pheromone to disguise me in flight. My katana held snug in my black scabbard. Hopefully I wouldn't need it. My orders: fly over the large nest; look down; get as much information as possible. Simple. I needed to discover the nature of the nest as a roosting ground or a hatching area. If discovered, I was supposed to evade, bug out as fast as possible and not get killed in the process.

Astronomers talked about the full lunar eclipse happening this night. I looked up as darkness fell and saw the red moon. It seemed fortuitous almost. Red wings. Red moon.

Rebecca stood with me at the middle East Gate. Nelson stood back scowling at me. Rebecca rebuffed any comments he made to "polish his sword". Watching her kiss me annoyed him. Braggs acted proud that a soldier had the courage to make a flight like this into virtually unknown territory. Musil shared some of that pride, since I was part of his unit.

The creaking wood and metal hinges of the East Gate opened. Light from inside the fort illuminated the night outside.

A small figure silhouetted, then revealed. The baby Green Dragon sitting with his mother's head next to him.

I looked around nervously. Musil now scowled as harshly as Nelson. "I thought you killed that thing."

I said, "I thought I did too. I guess the little guy was tougher than I thought."

The baby Green Dragon stood on all fours and walked towards us.

Wait!

The baby Dragon stopped. *You saved me. I have nowhere else to go.*

I took a step towards the Dragon. *These guys are going to kill you.*

The baby Dragon crouched down and laid with his forelegs and back legs splayed out. His wings were not fully formed. They looked too small to sustain flight. He splayed them out as far as he could. His tail extended behind him and his head on the ground. *I miss my mommy.*

I walked to the baby Dragon and crouched down to him. *Why don't you go and find your family in Sunset Red?*

My family isn't in Sunset Red. We were traveling south then we were attacked. It was me, mommy, daddy, brudder and sissy.

Don't you think you could find help in Sunset Red?

Mommy and Daddy said to stay away. The drakoh in Sunset Red is causing too much trouble for our kind. His skakoh follow blindly and they are going to get us all killed.

I reached my left hand out to the baby. The baby raised his head worriedly. My left hand touched his snout softly. *I'm sorry. I don't think I can keep you here. You wouldn't be safe.*

I'm not safe anywhere. I'm really hungry. The baby Dragon laid his head back down on the ground. *Kill me if you want. I'll die anyway.*

I stood and looked at Braggs. "He's an orphan. His family was traveling south. They are not part of the Sunset Red clutch. Someone killed his family. The head of the Dragon he was carrying is his mother."

Nelson spoke, "We cannot board a Dragon inside our walls! He could be a spy!"

I said, "He's too young to be a spy. Also he tells me his family was avoiding Sunset Red because their King is leading his followers blindly to the death of all Dragons."

Nelson practically screeched. "General, you cannot abide this!"

General Braggs turned to Nelson. "Don't tell me what I

should or should not do with my fort." He turned to me. "But Nelson is right. This is too dangerous of a situation. We cannot put up the Dragon inside the fort."

I asked, "Is there a building in the town that is vacant where he could be kept for the time being?"

Nelson said, more calmly, "There is a waiting list of people, Humans, who want to move to the town. We never have vacant structures and if we did, we would have someone ready to move in almost immediately. There is no room for Dragons."

I asked, "Is there any course I can take then?"

Nelson said, "You need to get on course and get on your recon of the nest. The longer you wait the less likely you'll get anywhere you can see the nest."

Rebecca added, "Nelson is right. Look. I'll look after the baby until you get back, but you need to go."

I crouched back down to the baby Dragon. *Do you understand when Humans speak?*

The baby looked up. *A little.*

I pointed to Rebecca. *She is going to look after you while I go do what I'm about to do. You mind what she says and I'll be back soon.*

Okay.

Do you have a name?

Human mouths cannot say my name.

We'll call you Peace.

I said aloud, "Peace."

I like that name.

I turned to Rebecca, "His name is Peace."

"Casimir," Musil said. "It means Peace in Polish."

I looked down at the baby Dragon and said, "Casimir."

That's a good name.

I kissed Rebecca again and patted Casimir on the snout. "I'll be back before you know it."

Casimir rose to all fours and rubbed his head against Rebecca's leg. Even as a baby, Casimir weighed as much as Rebecca. She adjusted her stance to accommodate his friendly gesture.

I pushed out my blood red wings. It no longer hurt. I practiced with them daily on my off hours. No one acted shocked

— **263** —

anymore that I had wings or could fly. It felt freeing to be rid of the newness associated with this strange mutation.

I looked back at my compatriots, my lover, and apparently my new baby Dragon. I shook my head, turned to the east and flapped my wings to take off.

I rose into the night sky. The Dragon pheromone overpowered my sense of smell even with the wind blowing harder as I rose higher into the air.

The lunar eclipse provided enough light that I could be seen, but did not shimmer off of me making me more apparent to the Dragons. At least, I hoped so.

I caught an isotherm and glided through the short trip towards Sunset Red. I saw no Dragons in the sky. I saw groups of Dragons huddled in their nests around the huge nest. There were no hatchlings apparent in the nests outside of the huge nest.

I glided over the huge nest and looked down. It was harder to see than I imagined it would be. I could tell from my vantage point this was a layered nest. There was a circular ledge near the top. Then about 20 feet below was another ledge, smaller and further in. I could see one more ledge about 20 feet below that, but nothing further. Since the nest was far taller than 60 feet, I could only imagine the nest stretched further in smaller circles until the bottom.

On each level, Dragons slumbered in stone nests lined with wood and leaves, probably uprooted trees. There appeared to be hatchlings in each of the smaller nests.

"Wow," I said softly. "That's a lot of Dragons."

Vrack!

A Red Dragon flew fast towards me. Its, her, mouth opened wide full of fire. I stopped flapping my wings and lost altitude to avoid her flame. I rose back up as she passed over me.

Can we talk about this?

The Red Dragon swung back around and blew fire at me again. I flapped up and out of her reach. I came back down on her back. I drew my katana and drove it down through her back into her heart. The Red Dragon screamed as the Dragon's Bane burned like acid into her body. I withdrew my katana as she fell into the nest. I heard the crumbling of rocks and the angry screeching of Dragons from inside the nest.

"Shit."

I sheathed my katana and flew to the west. I heard the flapping of wings as Dragons were no doubt rising out of the huge nest to follow me. I felt the angry personalities of the Dragons as they chased me. I flew over the water and dove down into it. I heard no Dragons dive in after me.

I turned to look up towards where the Dragons hovered watching me. The red moon lightened. The full moon light shone deeper into the water. The angry personalities turned into something almost jocular. I turned towards the darkness of the ocean.

Got you now rogoh!

I barely escaped the snapping jaws of a Blue Dragon. I pulled my katana, but it would be moving more slowly since the water would be resisting. The Blue Dragon turned fast and came back at me with his jaws wide. I dodged the snapping again.

My lungs held knives. I used my wings to swim up to the surface to breathe. My head popped up to the water. To the left of my head, the molten rock of a Black Dragon attack splashed. The water sizzled next to me.

"Shit!" I dove back down, barely avoiding the Blue Dragon's jaws again.

The Blue Dragon turned in the water and came back at me jaws wide. I moved to the left and held my katana out to the right. I felt the blade cut into the Dragon's jaw with little resistance from the scales. The dead Blue Dragon's right foreleg smashed into me.

I shrugged off the Dragon as he sank into the deep. I looked up one more time to see the night sky fully illuminated with full moon light and the Dragons still waiting for my demise.

I dove down as far as I could go and swam north along the coast for as long as I could with the air remaining in my lungs. My wings pushed me along at a decent speed, but my heart pounded out of my chest and my lung knives now felt like molten steel. My eyes blurred. I finally swam back up to the surface and to the shore. I ran as fast as I could into some underbrush and collapsed breathless. I pulled my wings back into my body and turned on my back.

The full moon shone bright as I faded to dark.

51 — The Plan

July 20, 2000

The strategic division agreed with my deduction. The nest probably stepped down getting smaller as it went lower with Dragons on all ledges. The Dragon Heart likely made his home in the nest as opposed to outside of the nest.

A regiment from Seattle just arrived along with regiments from other surrounding cities over the last few days to take part in this attack. The plan was to catch the Dragons while they slept and catch as many of them as possible before they took to the air. Once they took to the air, archers would take them down with arrows. Mobile ballistae would fire from the cliff overlooking Sunset Red.

Grappling hooks were prepared to fire up and into the huge nest to help Hell Bringers climb up and into the nest. This would be the most precarious part since the warriors climbing would be at a disadvantage until they got over the edge. The contingent of archers would be responsible for keeping Dragons off of the climbing Hell Bringers.

Casimir found me after the reconnaissance mission. I collapsed, tired, after the fight with the Blue Dragon and didn't make it back to the fort right away. Casimir insisted upon accompanying the search party of Rebecca, Walt, Chen, Raven and Jackson. Casimir smelled me out right away and found me passed out in the tall grass near the ocean. I received no injuries, I was just exhausted.

After that, Casimir became part of the group. We built him a shed to sleep in outside of my bunk. We realized this would not last long since he was growing every day. Nelson had a problem with a Dragon living inside the fort, but Braggs okayed it after Casimir found me.

We sat together in the mess hall. I sat across from Rebecca. Walt was to my left with Raven across from him. Chen was to my right with Jackson across from him. Casimir lay on the floor on the end closer to Walt. Walt rubbed Casimir's head with his booted foot. Casimir's mental moans of pleasure were a bit annoying, but tolerable.

Our little group became more cohesive since we arrived at the fort. Walt and Raven, of course, paired off. Raven worked as part of the tactical group. She and Rebecca became friendly. Jackson guided to reconnaissance groups since he knew the area from an early age. He and Chen also hung out around on their off hours.

Chen told me how he really liked Jackson. He didn't know what he wanted to do about it since he still had a boyfriend. I suggested writing a letter to the boyfriend letting him know of the situation. This wasn't a conversation I wanted to have. I wasn't exactly the best person to go to for relationship advice.

Rebecca and I spent as much time together as possible, but since we worked on different units and different time schedules, we typically only got to see one another at night or during meals. This worked out well for us. It meant we had plenty to talk about. We also had plenty of pent up frustration to take out on one another at night.

Walt immensely enjoyed his ballista training. He got good enough to fire two ballistae every three minutes, phenomenal for a new recruit. We sparred once or twice a week. I felt his strength increasing. His punches hit harder than before.

Usually, my off hours happened when Walt was on duty. It felt too bright to sleep so I visited my friend. I walked up to his post. He scanned the blue skies for anything threatening. I only saw clouds.

"Hey Walt! How's it going?"

Ever vigilant, Walt didn't turn to look at me. His voice sounded bright. "I'm pretty great buddy. What can I do you for?"

"I just came up to see what it is you do here."

"Well, I'm keeping my eyes peeled for Dragons. I'm literally not allowed to look away from my piece of horizon. Since I'm new I get the north east corner. There are less likely to be Dragon attacks on this corner, so if I'm less than competent it's okay. As I get more experience, they'll put me on one of the west corners. Only the salty veterans get to watch the south east corner since that is where Sunset Red is."

We stood in silence for a while. Walt suddenly blurted out, "I think I love Raven. Really, really love her. Love her enough to give up other girls."

"Wow," I said. "That's a big step for you. Is it the sex?"

"Well, the sex is life changing, but it is the moments before sex and the moments after sex that... make everything else worth it. The way she casually touches me fills my heart with a need to live. She doesn't complete me, but she makes my self-completion that much better."

"That's awesome." I didn't know what else to say.

"How have you and Rebecca been doing? Are you over the thing with Christofer?"

"Yeah, I haven't even thought about it in months. She is with me. I haven't said the words 'I want to commit to each other', but I think for now that's better."

"Yeah, don't put a label on it until you are ready. You are still young. Enjoy the freedom of the love you have right now because right now is all we really have."

I stood next to my best friend and clapped him on the back. He didn't budge.

"Wow, I used to be able to get you to move with a clap like that."

"Yeah, when you move 200 pound arrows constantly you get strong. Try to lift one."

I walked to the huge, neatly stacked arrows. They were about as long as I was tall. There were no handles on the arrows to cut down on wind resistance. I wrapped my hands around one and lifted it. It was not easy.

"Try to put it over your head," Walt suggested. "Be careful not to mess up the cord. My commanding officer will

— **268** —

have a shit fit."

I struggled, but I was able to get it over my head. I felt accomplished.

"Nice dude – Oh shit! Dragon!" Walt immediately moved behind his ballista observing.

I dropped the arrow back to the stack and turned to the horizon. I asked, "Should I call someone?"

"No," Walt said. "This one is still too far away to hit anyway. If they keep their distance we do not sound the alarm."

An alarm shrilled from behind us. Walt did not turn, but I did and saw the blue southern sky filling with Dragons of all colors.

From the west was another contingent of Dragons. In the east rose yet another group. I looked back in Walt's north and saw the Dragons approaching there too.

The Dragons thought primarily the same thing, *Kill all the Roges.*

"I'll catch you later buddy," I said as I hopped off of the corner to the ground making way for Walt's archers to back him up.

I found Lieutenant Musil and my patrol. "Orders, sir?"

Musil said, "Get ready."

I felt a scaled head nudge me. *I am scared.*

Go hide in your shed, we will handle this. Stay out of sight of Humans and Dragons you do not want to be caught in the crossfire.

Okay. Casimir galloped off to his shed.

I took my bow off my back and nocked an arrow. The Dragons flew in figure eight patterns around the sky on all sides of us. They screeched louder than the shrilling alarm.

I scanned the minds of Black Dragons for the Dragon Heart. I never met this Dragon personally so I didn't know which one it could be. One Black Dragon kept repeating *Wait for my orders, wait for my orders.*

I took aim and said, "That Black, right there, might be the Dragon Heart. He is telling everyone to wait for his orders."

"Do not fire unless Braggs gives the order, or they attack," Musil said.

"Yes, sir."

Lightning ripped the blue sky to shreds. Five cracks of lightning struck each of the corners of the fort and the center tower. Many soldiers were struck with fire, molten rock, boiling water and shards of ice raining down.

The Yellow Lightning Dragons screeched and opened their mouths again to lay another lightning strike. I moved my aim from the Dragon Heart and into the chest of the closest Yellow. My arrow struck. I pushed my wings out and flapped into the air. I, then, fired arrows at the closest Dragons.

Arrows blackened the sky as archers and ballista guards fired upon the diving Dragons. A couple arrows almost struck me before I landed at the southern wall and put my wings away. I continued to aim fire until I depleted my arrows. I tossed down my bow and quiver and drew my sword.

Thankfully Dragons do not have an unlimited supply of their attack. They deplete usually after one or two volleys. The Dragons needed to attack us at our level. This gave us an advantage when they got close enough.

A Yellow tried to swoop down to snatch me. I jumped into him and slashed him through the neck. We crashed down outside of the fort. I pushed my wings back out and flew into the air grabbing a Green from behind and slashing through the top of her head.

I found the Dragon calling himself the Dragon Heart and blew a volley of fire at him. He screeched and blew smoke with molten rocks at me. I dodged the larger rocks, but I one still hit me in the chest. I pulled it out, burning my fingers. The Dragon Heart reached me. His left front claws clutched my body. My free right arm chopped down onto his left foreleg. The Dragon screeched and dropped me. I flapped my wings and flew back up. I hacked at his midsection hearing the sizzle and the screech that followed.

The Dragon fell to the ground. I dove down and thrust my sword into his chest. *I have killed you Dragon Heart.*

Fool. You have not slain the Dragon Heart.

The Dragon died.

The Dragons dispersed as quickly as they arrived.

Ten Dragon corpses lay inside the Fort and 20 outside of it. We dragged the corpses outside of the fort for the DDC to handle.

The last Dragon corpse was a Red. Walt and I headed towards it to help Chen and a few other soldiers with the removal. The Yellow Dragons almost obliterated his post so he joined the clean up crew.

Twenty feet away from the Dragon and his eyes opened. The Dragon rose to his feet and blew a column of fire directly at my best friend. I moved too slow to block the column of fire. The fire cut off fast with a slash of Chen's sword.

Walt had no time to scream. The fire instantly engulfed him. I tackled him and put out the flames with my body and wings. Other soldiers gathered around.

I leaned back into a crouching position and pulled in my wings.

Walt didn't move.

His skin – charred black.

His eyes – froze open.

52 — The Sticky Feeling

July 25, 2000

"One hundred and thirty-three people died five days ago," General Braggs said to us all. "Fifty-one of these people were Hell Bringers. Some were my subordinate soldiers whom I did not have time to get to know by face and name. Some were my friends whom I would have laid down my life to protect."

General Braggs paused. He stood on a podium that made him seem taller. He wore his most ornate green uniform. His polished boots gleamed. It looked like someone shined up his eye socket. His dark bald head shone in the noon sun. I saw no clouds in the sky.

Fifty-one airtight caskets lay in a row around the center tower only leaving room for people to go in and out of the doors. Some stage coach drivers arrived to take some of the bodies back to their homes with their belongings to the families of the fallen soldiers.

I sat as close as I could to Walt's casket. An unfamiliar feeling built in my chest. It felt similar to the feeling I got in Meton whenever people would call me 'bastard', but this feeling felt stickier and made me feel like vomiting. I read his name carved into the side of the casket

Hell Bringer Walter Gelh.

Next to him.

Lieutenant Hell Bringer David Nelson.

Apparently a White Dragon ice shard killed Nelson as he warned someone else about a Black Dragon volley.

Raven sat on my left on the aisle. She didn't wail like some of the Hell Bringers in the crowd. Tears trickled down her cheeks, but she held firm. I reached over with my left hand to grab one of hers. She turned to look at me harshly, then smiled apologetically and brushed me away.

Rebecca sat on my right. She clutched my hand tightly squeezing occasionally. She laid her head on my shoulder in intervals with rubbing my right leg. She didn't cry.

To Rebecca's right sat Chen. Chen's mask of sad stoicism kept tears from his quivering eyes.

Jackson sat to his right holding Chen's right hand. Jackson cried profusely. He was one of the wailers. I felt worse for him than I felt for myself at that moment.

Casimir rubbed his head against my right leg.

I am sorry you lost your friend. Casimir thought this all morning. I told over and over to stop apologizing. It wasn't his fault, but he must not have been able to get a proper handle on his telepathic link so he continued thinking it.

Every member of the audience held a rose. Casimir held one in his mouth.

"We cannot forget our friends. We cannot forget why we are here. Our friends and compatriots would want us to continue on in their name and keep doing the job they came here to do with us. Please, bring your roses up and lay them on our brave soldiers' caskets."

Row by row everyone in attendance laid their roses on one casket or another for whomever they felt most connected. After I laid my rose on Walt's casket I whispered, "Thank you for everything my brother."

Hours later I stood on the south west corner of the fort. The sticky feeling in my chest grew. I felt like I needed to cough, but only a dry heave came out. The four corners of the fort were still pretty obliterated after the Yellow Dragons' lightning strikes, but ballista guards stood on the remnants of the platforms.

I saw a group of about 50 DDC Humans with ropes pulling the last two corpses of the Dragons south along the grass. I followed their movement as they dragged the bodies out of my sight and towards Sunset Red. My katana clanged as I jumped over to the outside of the fort.

I walked towards the coastline. As I reached the sand, I removed my boots and socks. I reached the beach about the time the sun reached the water. The reddening sun caressed the landscape. To my surprise, Raven was already there also barefoot with her boots next to her.

"You following me now, Gerstung?" she asked.

"No, I came out here to get away from everything, same as you," I said. "I don't see a weapon. You know that's not safe."

"I'm always armed, Gerstung." Raven drew a knife from her coat. "There are more of these for any suicidal Dragon who wants to mess with me right now."

We watched the ocean and didn't speak for a while. The warm water lapped at our feet. "Gods damn that man. Why did he have to go and do that?"

I asked, "What do you mean? Die?"

"No! That's not his fault. Something else."

"What? Tell me."

Raven paused. "Why did he have to go and love me like that? Why did he have to make me feel like everything was going to be alright? Why did he say that we were going to be together and be happy in this messed up world?"

"That's just the kind of guy Walt was."

"No he wasn't! He was a dog among dogs and I was fine with that. I was fine with him wanting me and wanting other girls and everything being fun and sex and that's it. Then he told me he was falling in love with me. He told me he wanted to be with me. He told me he hadn't even looked at another girl since he got to the fort. He was telling the truth too. He was so focused on his job and on me. I believed him when he said we would be together. I believed him."

Raven dove into my arms, sobbing. I clutched Raven close. She had never shown me any kind of emotion outside of fierce focus. This was new and I didn't know how to handle it.

— 274 —

My own emotional processes were going haywire. It felt good to have someone feeling just as messed up as me about Walt's death.

Raven sobbed for a few more minutes as we stood in the light of the sunset. Her sobs subsided. She pulled away from our embrace. "That asshole got me pregnant."

"What?!"

"Yeah, you heard me. He knocked me up about three weeks ago. I told him the night before... you know."

"That explains why he was so happy when I came to talk to him at his post. He didn't tell me what was up, but he was practically bursting with happiness."

I wondered why he didn't tell me when we talked. I figured he probably wanted to keep the news to himself for a while, to revel in it. I can't begrudge him that. The sticky feeling hardened inside me. My chest felt constricted, hard to breathe. I stayed blank.

"Really?" Raven asked. "He was happy? He seemed more shocked when I told him."

"Well, shock would be the normal Human reaction. But I came to talk to him, just before... and he kept his eye on work, but I could hear it in his voice."

"I have been thinking about giving it up."

"The baby?"

"Yes."

"Why?"

"I have no support system. My parents are gone. There is no one to help us."

"Walt's father is still alive. I'm sure he could help you if you needed."

"Bellato is a long way from here."

"You've got eight months. Maybe you can ride back with whoever comes to take Walt back to his father. I'm sure Kingsley could use another officer at the fort until you get too big to move. You've got a support system. You just have to ask for it."

Raven didn't respond.

I said finally, "It is your body, you are free to do with it what you want, but I know if you have the child they would receive all the love in the world."

Raven smiled at me. She pulled my face down to hers and kissed me softly, platonically on the lips. "Walt said you were a good friend. The best he ever had. If I have the baby and it's a boy, I'll call him Walter John."

I smiled. "That's cute."

Raven grabbed her boots and walked back to the fort.

The sun now only showed a sliver above the water. I turned to the south east, towards Sunset Red. I pushed out my wings, ripping my green uniform. My wings flapped once, twice, thrice to get into the air. The ground became further from me as I rose into the air. I propelled myself towards the clutch.

Walt's face floated through my mind. My lungs and heart felt hard as steel and dangerous as Dragon's Bane. "You were going to be a father you crazy bastard. How does that strike you?"

After a few miles I reached the first of the nests outside of the huge nest. I landed softly on the edge. One large Red Dragon slumbered inside.

I drew my katana and dove in, slicing his, its head off.

53 — The Dragon Heart

July 30, 2000

Days passed as they tend to. On duty hours I attended my responsibilities with the fort. I spent my off hours striking Sunset Red. I started small. I attacked the multitude outlying nests and killed the Dragons inside. My sword cut cleanly and the Dragons did not wake.

I was trying to draw out the Dragon Heart. An assault on the huge nest would have been suicide, but if I could piss off the leader of Sunset Red enough to come out and try to stop me itself I would have a shot at killing it.

Rebecca found me just after I went off duty. "Hey stranger, I haven't seen you in a few days."

"Yeah, I've just been busy. Working through a few things," I said.

"The south gate guards tell me you've been going out every night since Walt died."

"Yes."

"You want to tell me what's going on?"

"Not really."

Rebecca's green eyes flashed in anger. "JR, come on. This is me. You don't have to hide from me."

"I'm not hiding from you."

"I'm worried about you."

"You shouldn't. Everything is okay. I'm just working through things."

"And your sword comes back smelling like Dragon blood. I know what you're doing. You're going out and killing Dragons."

"Isn't that what we are here to do? Kill Dragons?"

"Not like this. Not recklessly. We are supposed to work as a team to take down the Dragons together. Mavericks get killed, JR. Mavericks go crazy with blood lust and die in stupid ways. They are not heroes or avenging angels. They just die. I don't want to lose you. I love you."

A tear rolled down Rebecca's cheek.

"I love you too... but this is something I have to do... for Walt."

"You have to die so you can go be buddies in Hell? Is that it? Gods damn JR! And not only are there Dragons, but there are reports of a huge pack of ferals in the area. You know what a danger they can be."

I had no response.

At last, Rebecca huffed and grabbed my face with her hands. "I can't stop you from doing this, but I swear to gods, if you die I will never forgive you."

Rebecca kissed me forcefully, passionately, sliding her tongue into my mouth, cradling my head with her hands. I placed my left hand over her heavy beating heart.

When the kiss broke, Rebecca said, "Raven is leaving in an hour with Walt's casket. You should say goodbye."

I intended to leave the fort before Raven left with Walt, but now I couldn't. I had to say a final goodbye to my brother and the woman carrying his child.

Jason and Tammy returned to Fort Angel to make the trip back to Fort Kingsley, then Bellato to drop Walt and Raven off with Walt's father. Word went ahead to Thom Gelh the day before the funeral so he knew what to expect.

Caskets were all vacuum sealed to stop decomposition before the box was put under the ground. This would be helpful on the long ride back to Bellato.

I helped Chen and Jackson load Walt's casket on the top of the stage coach. Other stage coaches traveled with them in a caravan for safety and because other stops needed to be made along the way.

I shook hands with Jason and Tammy laid a smooch on my cheek. They offered a few barely decipherable and inconsequential condolences.

Raven and Rebecca embraced. They grew to be friends in the time they spent working together. Rebecca made promises of visiting next leave to see the new baby.

I hugged Raven softly. She whispered in my ear, "Thank you for being there for me. I don't let people get that close to me usually. You will always have a friend in me."

I kissed her on the cheek. "Thank you. That means a lot."

Raven shook hands cordially with Chen and Jackson, then she got into the stage coach and it began on its way.

I turned to head to the southern gates. Chen placed his hand on my left shoulder. "You should not go. There are many danger. You have people to care."

I turned to Chen. "I have things to do. Don't try to stop me."

Chen said, "I stop you."

I growled.

Chen said, "Rebecca means much to me. I fight you to stop you."

"This isn't a fight you want to have, Chen."

"Not want. Will."

I didn't want to fight Chen, but I was prepared to. I squared myself towards him. "You've got one chance."

I waited. Chen did not attack.

I turned and walked towards the southern gates. I felt a push from behind. I turned and Chen was in my face. I shot a right punch to his abdomen. He batted my hand away. My left hand punched Chen in the jaw. Simultaneously my right knee rose to crack Chen in the head. Chen fell backwards to the ground.

Rebecca rushed in with a punch. I grabbed her arm with my left hand and my right palm struck her chest combined with a foot trip sending her to the ground.

I didn't follow up on either attack.

I turned back to the southern gates without anymore trouble.

August 8, 2000

    This was the anniversary of the first Dragon attack in Sunset Red. My days and nights progressed much the same as they had with some differences. Rebecca slept in her own bunk house. Chen avoided me. In fact, most of the Hell Bringers avoided me. Any time any one of them tried to talk to me, I met them with a blank or angry stare. I followed orders from my commanding officers, but they never told me I couldn't go outside of the fort when I was off duty.

    Even Casimir stayed away from me for the most part. He, it smelled the Dragon blood on my sword first. Casimir alerted Rebecca who also smelled the faint blood on my blade. Casimir might not have been a fan of the Dragons of Sunset Red, but they were still kin.

    I attended the vigil for those fallen in the Supremacy War. I burned a candle that night, but I left early to pursue my nightly obsession.

    Three Dragons in for the night I realized something felt different. I heard mental whispering.

    He is close. I can feel him thinking.

    I quieted my mind and listened.

    Where did he go?

    I hid in the nest of the White Dragon I just killed.

    I whispered mentally, *Over here.*

    Four huge claws came from above me. I barely dodged the claws as I flew up and out of the nest. My katana slashed at the beast, but I missed. In the moonlight I saw a Red and a White on the ground to my right rear. A Black Dragon clung to the edge of the nest I hid inside.

    So you are the rogon who has been killing my family at night. Who do you think you are?

    Who do you think you are? Let me guess, the Dragon Heart?

    Yes as a matter of fact I am.

    Ha! I killed one who told me the same thing. I am beginning to think the Dragon Heart is just a poorly constructed fairy story.

    Oh, I am the real Dragon Heart. I am the same Dragon

who fought your father and won.   I could have killed him, but I felt pity and spared him.   It seems I should not have since he went on to make a rogon like you.

'Rogon' was becoming more annoying than bastard ever was.

Your insults will not make your death come any quicker.   I am already not a fan of my father.

Few of our kind are. The Dragon Heart attacked me with its huge mouth.

I swiped at it with my katana. The Dragon Heart dodged my attack and clobbered me with its tail.

I flew off of the nest and crashed into another.   The commotion roused other Dragons in Sunset Red.   The Red Dragon came down with its teeth bared. I rolled out of the way and onto my feet. In the same motion, I slashed down and sliced the top of the Dragon's head off.

The Dragon Heart blew a volley of smoke and molten rock at me. I barely avoided three big chunks of rock. The White Dragon breathed ice shards at me. I blasted a cone of fire at the White Dragon, melting the shards before they could reach me. I flapped up into the air at the Dragon Heart with my katana drawn.

I missed my slash at the Dragon Heart who swatted at me with its tail again. I swiped at its tail and heard a sizzle, then a screech.

My tail! Rogon!

Dragons stirred and rose from their slumber.   Some watched us fight. Other Dragons stretched their wings to attack me.

The Dragon Heart swooped down and breathed another volley of smoke at me. This time a molten rock hit me in the chest. My resistance to fire only partially protected me from this attack. It still hurt.

I crashed to the ground. The White Dragon stood over me. Its teeth bared, ready to chomp.

"Allah Fire!"

A fire blast engulfed the White Dragon and blew it off of me. The dead Dragon crashed into a nearby nest wall. A dark tan skinned man wearing a red *keffiyeh* and a black *agal* rushed onto the scene. He grabbed my arm and easily lifted me over his shoulders. Just as quickly as he arrived, we vanished from the nests.

54 — Abdul the Butcher

August 9, 2000

I sit in the sweat lodge. The hot rocks illuminate White Eyes in the corner. White Eyes sings:

> *Coyote knows if there's no death*
> *That soon there will be no room left*
> *The world will swell – we'll lose space*
> *We'll lose sight of our spirit's face*
> *So smear with ash – do not be marred*
> *So our dead friends will reach the stars*
> *Do not cry – our friends must go*
> *The animal hide has sunk you know*

The door to the sweat lodge opens and light fills the lodge. Suddenly I am walking through a desert. The sun is bright, but I am not hot. Smoky wafts rise from the ground hindering my vision. I see someone walking through the smoke. It's a man. He's tall.

I yell, "Walt!"

The man wears no shirt. His pale skin is not reddened by the sun. He wears black leather pants with tousled curly hair on his head.

Each rising column of smoke becomes a person. We are walking through them.

I lose sight of the man. Suddenly he is in my face. His blue-grey eyes swim into my soul.

"I can't do nothing, man. But I can't do anything either."

"What can I do?"

"Bring them together, as many of them as you can find. They have to want to be protected."

"The barrier? You want to resurrect the barrier."

"It's child's play, man. If they want to help, they'll help. They know how, if they want to do it, then I guess they'll do it."

"How do I bring everyone together?"

"Love, man."

My eyes snapped open to a fire burning. I felt the warm stone walls. Across the fire sat the dark tan man who saved me from the Dragons. His blood stained red *keffiyeh* and black *agal* lay on the ground. His beard grew long and grey, but his hair was cut short. A scimitar lay on the ground next to him. I stirred and tried to sit up.

"You were hurt. The Dragon was about to eat you." His voice did not sound gruff like I expected. It sounded light, like a young man singing. I heard a purr in his voice.

I mustered up the strength to get myself to a sitting position. "Thank –."

He interrupted. "Do not thank me. I did not save you to be thanked. You have power. You will help me kill the Dragon Heart."

I groaned. "Not that I'm opposed to killing the Dragon Heart, but why should I?"

"You owe me a life debt and I will collect with your life or mine."

"Is this something you do a lot, collect life debts?"

"No." He paused for a long time. He stared into my eyes. "Mostly I just kill people who get too close."

"Such is why they call you 'The Butcher'?"

"My name is Abdulwaheed Hassan Oudief, son of Abdulazeez, son of Abdullah. Brother to Ahmad, Arjun, Amrinder and Analilia. I am sworn to vengeance against the Dragon Heart and the miserable Dragon scum. I am close to reaching my goal, Allah willing."

"When did your family die?"

"They were killed when the Dragons attacked Los Angeles."

"Wow, you've been fighting for almost thirty years? That's impressive."

"Impressive? My family cries out for the vengeance of their deaths and you call that impressive?"

Abdul did not rise from his seat, he did not rant and rave and threaten, but his stare deepened. It felt like he wanted to kill me from the inside out.

I said, "That's not what I meant. I meant you have a lot of experience. The Human army could use someone like you who has fought for a long time and could teach their soldiers something new."

"Nothing I know, can I teach."

"Why?"

"Because it was Allah who taught me and only me. This is not something others can know."

I didn't know how to respond, but it didn't look like Abdul needed me to.

August 28, 1975

Abdul followed the tradition of his father and grandfather before him. Abdullah married Indrani in Yemen forty years before Abdul was born. They emigrated from Yemen when Indrani was pregnant with Abdulazeez. They wanted their son to be born in America, where he could hopefully prosper and build a grand life for himself.

Abdulazeez was born in 1918. He did as well as he could growing up. He achieved more than his father ever dreamed. He married Sunayana and they had Abdulwaheed in 1944, the first of their five children.

Abdul experienced the presence of Dragons since age 12. He would have considered himself used to the presence of the beasts if a person can be so.

Abdul and Analilia ran errands beneath the apparent safety of the force field. Something felt different today. They saw purple and blue waves fluctuating in the field. They offered their daily prayers to Allah and their daily concentration to the field, but they questioned the commitment of everyone else.

Ahmad returned home on leave. He trained at Fort

Albuquerque, but this was his Year One leave. Being 28, he got a late start, but he was a promising warrior. Their other brothers Arjun and Amrinder also trained in the army helping to defend Humanity.

Abdul sought no combat. He thought he best served his Human brothers and sisters by providing food for them. He served fast, faster than anyone else. Patrons came to him and left quickly with smiles on their face and bags full of essentials.

Analilia helped him at the market. Her beautiful black hair and dark features were the envy of the other women of Los Angeles. She chose not to wear the *hijab*. Thus, she gained attention from many suitors, followers of Islam and not. Abdul adored his sister and personally screened her dates, much to Analilia's chagrin.

Being the oldest of his siblings, Abdul took it upon himself to protect them inasmuch as he could. He realized he could not fight the Dragons for his brothers. He could not fight off the inevitable marriage of his sister. He could however keep the circle of Humanity going by providing his wares for everyone who needed. This protection would find its way to his brothers and sister.

The first attack from the Dragons bounced off the force field like usual. The next swooping Dragon broke through the force field. An otherworldly scream rang out through the city of Los Angeles as Dragon after Dragon laid volleys of attacks over the city. His father, mother and grandparents were killed.

Abdul ushered his sister away. They made their way into the hills. Ahmad would not join them, he took up his weapons and tried to fight, but was killed by a Red Dragon.

The city was completely leveled in a day. Concrete fell upon Analilia. Abdul lifted the concrete off of her broken legs and carried her to safety.

September 7, 1975

Hot days were spent with little shade. Abdul did his best to splint Analilia's legs, but he was not a doctor. He tried to find someone who could help her, or who would be willing, but no one could or would help.

Infection ravaged Analilia's body and her eyes closed finally with the setting sun.

January 12, 1976

Abdul took up arms against the Dragons. Slowly his legend grew as he slew more and more Dragons.

Fort Albuquerque sent a contingent of soldiers and Hell Bringers to establish a new fort. Among those who arrived were Amrinder and Arjun. They heard from the local Humans about Abdul the Butcher, the saving grace of Humanity. He struck fear into the hearts of the Dragons of Los Angeles, or Sunset Red as it was being called. Abdul did not call himself a hero. He only sought justice for the deaths of innocents of Los Angeles and for the loss of his sister and brother.

When Amrinder and Arjun tracked him down, Abdul rejoiced. The three brothers bonded and Abdul thought to lay down his arms at last because at least part of his family still lived.

The Dragons had other plans.

Fort Angel was only about halfway finished. The Dragons attacked the unprepared Human soldiers. The soldiers defended the structure valiantly and drove the Dragons away, but Amrinder and Arjun were killed in the collapse of the southern tunnel exit as they tried to get every noncombatant out of the fort.

Abdul made his new home in the southern tunnel. This acted less as a home, and more of a dungeon where he punished himself for not protecting his brothers and sisters. Abdul resumed his quest to destroy the Dragons, but when he came across other Humans they would rarely be saved from his wrath as well.

His reputation grew into something dark, cold and fast like the wind.

August 9, 2000

Abdul stopped speaking and closed his eyes. I didn't know if I wanted to know what went on in his head. Grief caught this man deep. The Dragons took his family not once, but twice.

"It is Allah that has given me the power of death to give to others. I give it freely."

55 — Suicide Mission

August 11, 2000

"I have needed someone like you for years to distract the Dragons from their leader, so that I may slay it. It is difficult to get to. It is usually in the large nest. It has its vile minions bring it food when it requires. It only comes out for important battles. Consider yourself honored that it came to kill you itself," Abdul said. I heard a tinge of sarcasm I didn't think possible in the man.

Maybe my sarcasm rubbed off on him. "I feel enchanted that I warranted a visit from the leader of Sunset Red. At least I know I'm a threat."

"It seems more likely that it just wants revenge for the lives you have taken in the past few weeks."

"Revenge is a common theme in this theatre of war."

"Revenge is the only thing keeping me alive."

At least Abdul was honest with himself.

I asked, "So after we kill the Dragon Heart, will you kill yourself?"

Abdul pondered this for a moment. He stopped pondering and continued drawing on the ground our plans for attack. "You will fly to the nest and draw out the Dragons. You will draw them all out while I make my way up into the nest to battle the Dragon Heart. You must keep them distracted. The death of the Dragon Heart will be quick, it cannot escape me."

"So my job is to be bait while you catch the fish."

"Your metaphor is crude, but accurate."

"Once I have killed the Dragon Heart, I do not care what happens. You can save me, or leave me to die, your choice."

I thought for a moment. "Why don't I see if the fort has any bombs they could fire at the nest to cave it in around the Dragons? We could coordinate the attack that way. Any Dragons that make it out of the rubble, we cut them down."

"I do not need their help. It is bad enough I live beneath their fort in this tunnel."

"If you don't like it, why don't you go up and join the city?"

Abdul stared at me. "Why would I do that?"

I sighed. "I don't know, to be a part of civilization: to live life instead of being stuck in this circle of vengeance; to have a reason not to offer yourself as a sacrifice after killing one Dragon."

"I have not killed just one Dragon."

"That isn't the point. The point is there are people who could love you up there. You don't know them yet and they'll never replace your family, but they can help make it easier."

I stopped speaking and turned away. I realized that is what Rebecca and Chen wanted to do. They tried to make things easier for me by stopping me from going out. Getting blood on my sword and my conscience was not justice for Walt it was vengeance for my loss.

Now here I stood in front of a man who lost everything. Twice. This man had as much reason as anyone to try to live again, but his prison of vengeance held so tight he might never want to come out. He might never survive if he did come out.

I turned back to him. "Abdul, I will help you. I owe you this for saving my life. But I hope you strongly consider asking for help from the soldiers at Fort Angel. This is a suicide mission and I know your brothers and sister would not want you to kill yourself on their account."

"My brothers and sister are with Allah now. They are not concerned about me."

I sighed again. "Again, not the point. Look. I'm going up to the fort. If I'm going to go on this suicide mission with you, I'm going to say goodbye to my friends. If you want to come check out the fort with me, feel free. I know it'll be hard at first, but you might find you like it."

Abdul did not speak. He showed no sense of confirmation or denial.

A few hours later, I awoke from a nap. It wasn't a long walk to the fort from the exit of the south tunnel, but I wanted to be rested. I looked at Abdul, but said nothing. It seemed he never slept. He stared at me over the glowing coals of his fire.

I walked to the end of the tunnel and exited. It was almost dusk. I pushed my wings out and flapped twice into the air. I kept low over the landscape to avoid detection by Dragons. I landed at the path which began at the city surrounding Fort Angel. People milled around, but the southern part of the city was not as busy at the other sides.

I walked briskly, but not hurriedly to the southern gates. The guards recognized me and let me pass. I found Lieutenant Musil almost immediately.

Musil fumed. "Gerstung! Where the hell have you been?!"

I never heard him raise his voice before, let alone be this angry. A crowd gathered around us. "Uh, sir. I was out making a patrol and I was injured. I had to find shelter."

"He was with me." Abdul's voice.

Everyone jumped back when they saw Abdul the Butcher standing behind me. Seeing his scimitar hooked to his belt, some reached for their weapons.

Musil held his hands out to steady everyone. "I'll deal with you later, Gerstung." Musil turned to Abdul. "Are you who I think you are?"

"I am Abdulwaheed Hassan Oudief." He cleared his throat. "I have been told I have been called 'The Butcher'."

Musil said, "Why are you here?"

Abdul pointed at me. "This one told me that we might be able to work together to slay the Dragon Heart."

"This one? Really?" I said.

"Quiet Gerstung," Musil ordered. "Please continue."

Abdul replied, "That is all I had to say. Is this true what he said?"

Musil nodded. "It could very well be. Would you like to meet our General?"

Abdul nodded in return. "Yes, take me to him."

Lieutenant Musil led Abdul to the Center Tower. The bewildered crowd followed. I hadn't paid attention before, but the Center tower received damaged in the attack in July. Funny how I would have missed that.

I watched them walk away. I walked to my bunk. I looked inside and saw no one. The shed outside my bunk was empty. I pushed my thoughts out to find Casimir. I found it, him in Rebecca's bunk.

I knocked.

The door opened. Rebecca's hair hung disheveled. She looked like she had been crying. Casimir sat behind her. He was larger than when I had last seen him.

Rebecca rubbed at her eyes. "What do you want?"

"I'm here to apologize. I should never have fought you and Chen. I know you lost a friend too. It was selfish of me to think this was just my pain to bear."

"You're an asshole," Rebecca said.

"I am the worst kind of asshole, but I hope you will forgive me."

"I'll need time."

"Take as much as you need."

"You better believe I will."

"May I apologize to Casimir?"

Casimir, upon hearing his name lifted his head to look at me. He rose and walked to the door, pushing past Rebecca's legs. I backed up to let him out of the door. His head reached my chest. His body was almost too wide to fit in the bunk door.

I am sorry my friend. You did not deserve the insults I paid you. Can you forgive me?

Casimir tilted his head. *You were mean. It made me sad. If you are really sorry I forgive you.*

I am really sorry.

Good! Casimir licked my face with his rancid smelling tongue.

What have you been eating?

Fish, lots of fish. Casimir pulled back his scaled lips to reveal his teeth in a close approximation of a Human smile.

Someone needs to brush your teeth. I smiled back.

Rebecca said, "You should go."

"I understand. I'll give you time." I turned to go.

"Wait."

I turned back.

"Tell me you love me."

"I love you more than anyone else in the world."

Rebecca grabbed me by the shirt and pulled me to her. She kissed me hard thrusting her tongue into my mouth. My heart started racing as I kissed her back wrapping my arms around her waist.

The kiss broke. Rebecca smiled. "You really need to brush your teeth."

"It's been a few days so, yes, I suppose I do."

I turned to go. Casimir followed me. We reached my bunk. At my door stood Abdul.

He looked at me, then at the Green Dragon following me. "You!"

Casimir looked up at Abdul and growled. *This is the Human who killed my family!*

Abdul pulled his scimitar. "You are consorting with Dragons in this fort? I cannot be here. These are the enemy!"

Casimir growled behind me. *I am going to kill this man.*

I yelled, "Stop it, the both of you."

Abdul stared at me trying to explode my head from the inside. "I knew this was a mistake. You cannot be trusted."

"Abdul, wait!"

He vanished.

56 — Without Thought

August 11, 2000

General Braggs stopped me from leaving the fort to follow Abdul.

He said, "You were gone a long time, soldier. We thought you had deserted. We were about to send out a hunting party to bring you back and put you in lock up."

"Sir," I started. "I would never leave the fort like that. I would not go against my pledge to serve the Human Army against the Dragons. Abdul is a Human just like the rest of us and I don't want him to be killed if I can help to save him."

"That Abdul came up with a sound plan. Everyone distracts the Dragons while he goes in to battle the Dragon Heart. That beast is so powerful I'm not sure who among us could win in a fight."

Braggs continued, "Regardless, you may have to be punished for going AWOL."

I responded, "But I came back. It's obvious I didn't go AWOL, not really. I was hurt and Abdul was taking care of me. We weren't even that far from the fort, we were in the southern tunnel."

Braggs sighed. "You're missing the point."

"With respect, sir, I think you are missing the point. A man could die and I think I'm the only one who can stop him."

"Three Hells, Gerstung. Kingsley told me you'd be a handful. Go, we'll deal with this later."

"Thank you sir!" I turned, pushed out my wings and flapped up and out of the fort going south.

I reached the southern tunnel and entered. Abdul stood by the fire. He wrapped himself in black cloth, probably for a night strike.

"Abdul, I'm glad I caught you."

"Get away traitor."

"Stop! I'm not a traitor. Casimir is not a threat to anyone."

"You cannot domesticate a beast like that. It will turn on you."

"No, I saved Casimir from being killed. I saved him after you killed his family."

"I do not remember killing that one's family."

"Well you did. You killed his mother, father, brother and sister. You left him alone. How do you quantify that in your vengeance?"

"I was left without family too if you remember."

"So it's right for you to leave others without a family?"

"Isn't that what we both do, killing Dragons, leaving them without families. You are not so much better than me. You cannot take the high moral road."

"No, maybe not. But we don't have to be like this. Peace has to start somewhere. And if not peace, at least not... killing yourself like this."

"How else should I die? I would rather die in the quest for vengeance of my family."

"I've already told you. You can make a new family, not to replace the old, but to bring you some kind of balance."

"Why would I trust you? You consort with Dragons."

"Abdul, I am HALF Dragon myself. Where do you think my wings come from?" I pushed out my wings. The fire illuminated the blood red scales. I saw a shimmer I hadn't noticed before.

I continued, "My mother consorted with one of the most powerful Dragons in the New World, Jonathan the Tyrant. Should I shun her now because she loved a 'beast' as you call them? I cannot. And I can't shun a baby Dragon just for being a Dragon. Everyone deserves a chance to show the world who they

— 294 —

are before they are judged for being something they are not. I thought that is what the Supremacy War was supposed to have taught Humanity about our flaws in judging one another."

The fire in my eyes burned. His black irises enhanced his cold black stare.

He blinked.

"Okay," he said finally.

"Okay what?" I asked.

"Okay, I will try to not kill the baby Dragon when I see it next."

"Does that mean you're coming back?"

Abdul sighed. "Yes. I will try to come back."

I sighed with relief. "Good."

"We should go," I said. "It's getting dark."

"I move faster in the dark."

"Regardless, the Dragon Heart is probably out there and wants to kill us. We need a plan of attack."

I thought I almost caught a glimpse of Abdul smiling before he extinguished the fire in his tunnel.

We made our way out of the tunnel. I sensed something wrong as did Abdul.

I whispered, "What do you sense?"

"The Dragon Heart."

Ferals howled over the windy dusk sky.

Jonathan told me of your existence.

"He's here," I whispered to Abdul.

The voice of the Dragon Heart entered my head, *Jonathan said he had sired a child with the rogan of his rogoh enemy.*

My grandfather was not a rogoh. He was the first Human to kill any of you. My mother was not a rogan. She is stronger than anyone I know.

Your thoughts betray you.

I will send you to the Three Hells, Dragon Heart. My father might not have been able to defeat you, but I will.

The Dragon Heart seemed so sure of himself. *It does not matter who your father is. It does not matter who you are. You will die like the rest. Then I will go and kill the roges there. Then I will lead my skakes onward. We will destroy every group of roges we find. Skakes from all over the world will join me. No little vrack from a rogon drakoh will stop me.*

As I heard the Dragon Heart's next thought I looked where Abdul had been, he was gone. I heard a screech and rolling in the grass. A couple trees crashed to my left. I ran as fast as I could towards the noise. The Dragon Heart stood with his tail up in the air crouched with his head moving back and forth listening for Abdul.

I could not see Abdul.

I pulled my bow from my back and nocked an arrow. I drew and aimed. I felt a hand on my left shoulder. I saw Abdul in my peripheral vision.

The Dragon Heart's head pointed directly at me. He breathed a volley of smoke at me. I fired my arrow into the volley and rolled to the right to avoid any molten rock. I heard a Dragon scream.

As the smoke cleared, the Dragon Heart made a clunky sound similar to a chuckle. *You will never learn. You will always be defeated because you cannot stop your mind. Dragons fight from instinct alone.*

I remembered the countless sparring sessions with Kingsley. He always fought one step ahead of me. Except when I hit him.

I remembered fighting Jonathan, my father. He deflected every attack I could offer.

I remembered the Red Dragon who killed Walt. I didn't hear the thought of the volley of fire before it took my friend.

I needed to clear my mind. I needed to fight from a more primal place.

"Allah Fire!" The light and heat burst forth followed immediately by the pained screech from the Dragon Heart. I saw the moonlight glint off of the Dragon's Bane scimitar Abdul wielded, but I did not see him in his black clothes.

The Dragon Heart snapped, but missed Abdul. A slash caught one of his wings. The Dragon Heart turned and swiped at Abdul with his tail, but Abdul already moved.

My body turned and my hands fired another arrow at the Dragon Heart, striking in one of his forelegs. He screeched again.

I thought to the Dragon Heart, *How did you like that one? No thought involved with that.*

I am going to bite you in half.

Dragons do not eat their own kind.

I might make an exception in your case.

It is almost over for you Dragon Heart. I do not know where Abdul is, but I know he is about to kill you.

I closed my eyes and listened for the Dragon Heart's next thought. Nothing. He listened for Abdul.

I opened my eyes and turned. He pulled the arrow out of his foreleg and my hands shot another into the side of his neck. He screeched in pain and Abdul came down out of a tree with his scimitar slicing through the air. My hands fired another arrow at the Dragon Heart aiming for his back leg.

My arrow struck at the same moment the Dragon Heart opened his mouth and closed it over Abdul's body. Abdul didn't have time to scream. His scimitar fell from his hands and clanged on the ground.

The Dragon Heart chomped twice and swallowed Abdul.

"Shit," I said out loud to myself.

Fire filled my chest. I remembered Walt. Another life lost at my hands. I growled and smoke rolled out of my mouth. I dropped my bow.

My body turned and fire flew from my mouth towards the Dragon Heart. My wings pushed out and flew me low towards the Black Dragon King. The Dragon Heart stepped back from the fire on his scales. My hands grabbed Abdul's scimitar and swung it towards the Dragon Heart.

I felt some resistance to the scimitar as it slashed up into his chest. It was not a vital hit, but I heard the Dragon Heart's satisfying scream.

My wings took me up into the air. The Dragon Heart jumped up and snapped at my legs. I barely avoided the snap and then swung the scimitar back down. The Dragon Heart moved out of the way.

A ballista arrow crashed through the trees towards the Dragon Heart. The arrow barely missed the Dragon as he cursed and flew away towards his nest.

This is not over!

57 — The Barrier

August 13, 2000

I walked. I existed somewhere between awake and asleep.

It was different than a dream. I felt my naked body moving through sand. Sun beat down upon me. I felt like I was cooking in my skin. Thermal waves rose from the sand marring my vision.

I walked. My bare feet sank into the sand. I saw the vibrating vision of the 27 Mage Jim Morrison standing next to a cactus.

"Hey man. Is everybody in?"

"I have to tell them about it. They aren't going to believe me."

"They'll believe you, man. They've seen it before. I'll be there next to you. Tell them to focus on you at first and I'll take it from there. Remember, man, this is about the love for Humanity, not hate for Dragons. This is about a community, not a mutual enemy. That's why the barrier didn't last before. Everyone was in it for themselves, instead of for everyone."

"I understand."

Jim smiled at me and White Eyes appeared next to him.

White Eyes simply said, "You are free."

My eyes opened to Rebecca curling my hair around her fingers. The lamp in the bunk illuminated the windowless room. My hair had grown longer since the last time I paid attention to it. It extended past my shoulders now. It always knotted up in the morning when I woke up and didn't tie it up the night before.

Just after dawn. I heard soldiers stirring. Seattle contingents, Soldiers from Fort Albuquerque and a number of smaller groups of men and women arrived over the last few days ready to fight.

I whispered out loud, "We are going to need every man, woman and child to bring this barrier back up."

Rebecca's eyes opened slowly. She smiled at me.

I looked into her sleepy eyes. "I love you, my darling."

"I love you, dear heart."

We kissed tenderly and caressed each other's bodies. The light shone off of her perfect skin. Even in the western sun she kept her skin healthy. Her soft curves pleasantly contrasted her musculature. My member hardened as I touched her softly.

I growled softly and rolled us over onto her back. My fingers probed her wetness. I stoked her passion with alternating light and hard touches inside her and outside her.

Rebecca whispered, "Now."

I found necessary protection then lowered myself onto her, into her. Her liquid silk enveloped me, clinging to me with every movement.

I put my left hand over her heart. I moved in and out of her with the same rhythm of her heart. As her heart beat faster and harder, so did my movements.

We moaned softly in unison. She clutched my buttocks, digging her nails into me as I felt her tighten around me. I continued moving deeper into her until I finally released.

We basked contentedly next to one another. Rebecca trailed her fingers on my chest. I heard a knock on the bunk door.

Lieutenant Musil's voice said, "Gerstung, get out to the Central Tower. You're needed. Bring Kingsley with you."

We dressed quickly and headed to the Central Tower. Casimir followed closely.

The bulk of the soldiers gathered around the tower. Musil saw us approach and waved us up into the tower. Besides me and Rebecca, only the lieutenants were here. We passed Chen on our way in, but he stayed with his unit.

Lieutenant Musil said, "Reports are coming in the Dragons are amassing a huge force in Sunset Red. We believe they are going to attack and if they have as many as we think they do, it will destroy us. We need options."

"We have to resurrect the barrier," I said.

Everyone looked at me like I was crazy. I may have been.

"Look, the 27 Mage Jim Morrison has been coming to me in my dreams. Man, this sounds insane. He told me we have to resurrect the barrier."

General Braggs stepped forward. "You must have flipped your lid, Gerstung. The barrier and the mage are gone for good. We are in this alone."

"Sir, please, I know how this sounds. I have no proof of his visiting me, but when we were in the sweat lodge in Fort Albuquerque –"

Braggs bellowed, "A sweat lodge? Give me a freaking break, Gerstung!"

"It's true, General." The voice belonged to Lieutenant Joseph Eagle from Fort Albuquerque. "He was in a sweat lodge. And while I cannot vouch for his sanity, our healer, White Eyes has kept us safe for 50 years. If White Eyes has guided this soldier, I am behind him one hundred percent."

Braggs lost part of his indignation. He obviously respected Lieutenant Eagle's opinion and judgment. "Does anyone else want to weigh in?"

Lieutenant Musil said, "A barrier is the only way we are going to repel that many Dragons. We are ready to fight we have been training our lives for battle, if this can give us an edge, I think we should try it."

Rebecca worked hard in the stead of the fallen Lieutenant Nelson. She basically ran the strategic division. She recently received a promotion to Sergeant. "General Braggs, my personal feelings aside from Gerstung, I think this is a good plan. If we can defend against the Dragons' initial assault we can mount a counter offensive through the southern tunnel. A team just unblocked the tunnel yesterday and it is ready to be used for an attack."

Braggs sighed. "Okay. How do we do this Gerstung?"

Everyone stood outside of the Central Tower. I felt the vibrations of the morning sun rising from the concrete. I saw a flash which could have been the 27 Mage.

I yelled as loud as I could:

"Everyone! We have to resurrect this barrier. If we do not, our brothers and sisters, our family will be killed. Love is the focus of the barrier. We are here because we love our family. We love Humanity. We are not fighting a common enemy with this barrier. We are protecting the people we love."

I looked to my left and saw the 27 Mage Jim Morrison standing beside me. I continued:

"Focus your energy on me. Project your love for Humanity, your desire to protect the people around you, your hope for the future."

The backs of my hands met at the middle of my chest. My eyes looked out amongst the people watching me. One by one they closed their eyes. I closed my eyes and bowed my head.

At first, I felt a tingle. I felt pins and needles in the palms of my hands as if they were receiving new blood.

You're doing good, man. I am feeling it.

The tingle grew into warm shivers running from my perineum, to just above my member, to my navel, to my chest, to my throat, to between my eyebrows and to the crown of my head.

You're on fire, man. Keep going.

Another wave of energy started at my feet and ran quickly through my body. The backs of my hands stayed together as they rose up above my head. My body rocked and swayed back and forth.

We're almost there, man!

Fire rose in my chest. My wings extended as far as they could stretch. The energy crackled audibly around my body. My hands separated, extending outward, as a scream of exhilaration flew out of my mouth.

My eyes opened to see me floating twenty feet in the air covered in crawling red energy. Another exhilarated scream burst forth from me as the crawling red energy expanded outward from me. The energy expanded past the gates of the fort. The energy expanded to the hills in the south and no doubt the same distance north, east and west.

An audible voice from the sky:

"Thank you all. Remember, I can protect you as long as you are committed to protecting each other."

The transformed red energy from around me became a light tinge in the sky around Fort Angel and the surrounding city. The sun shone just as brightly through it as ever.

I lay crumpled on the ground in front of the Central Tower.

Casimir clicked his ever growing claws on the ground as he galloped up to me. He sniffed at me and nudged me. *Are you okay?*

Yeah, I am fine.

Rebecca lifted my head and kissed me gently. "Thank you."

Braggs crouched next to me. His baritone still rumbled my chest. "Look at what you have done. I never thought I would see this happen in person. This is amazing Gerstung. Thank you."

Braggs lifted me easily with his huge muscled body.

Swarms of Dragons dove at the barrier. The barrier repelled each Dragon. Every Dragon repelled made a musical sound reminding me of an organ. I smiled as I watched and listened to the symphonic barrier barring the Dragons from their attack again and again.

I said, "It wasn't just me, sir. It was all of us. We all did this. It is up to everyone to protect Humanity. Whether it is through barriers or through battles, it is our responsibility."

"This one is for you Abdul," I said to myself.

Your move, Dragon Heart.

58 — The Battle of Sunset Red

August 16, 2000

The howls of ferals echoed over the dawn landscape. The wild dogs were reported closing in on Fort Angel. Experience taught us that they would be repelled by the barrier since they could not project the right kind of energy to enter. We all felt relief. We already had enough creatures trying to eat us. Even if they found the tunnels into the city, the barrier would stop them there too. It didn't just stop when it hit the ground. The barrier protected us on all sides.

More soldiers arrived over the past three days. Hell Bringers came from as far as Omaha. One group even arrived from Toronto. There were 5,000 soldiers, Hell Bringers and citizens beneath the barrier. With each new person contributing energy the barrier grew just a little bit.

Rebecca was always giddy before a fight. I was privately happy her role was to stay back with the strategic division. I knew Rebecca could take care of herself in a battle, but I didn't even know the scale of this battle. I knew I would never have to watch her back for her, but I felt safer knowing she was staying under the barrier.

A buzz alit from the northern gates.

Murmurs of, "He's here" echoed through Fort Angel.

Chen, Jackson and I talked and sparred. I profusely apologized for the grief I caused them, mostly Chen, and let him have a couple free shots while we sparred. He seemed sated with that small bit of payback.

Rebecca pounced me. "He's here!" She took off again towards the northern gates.

I looked at Chen who shrugged. We made our way through the crowd. Braggs pushed his way through to the front. Being almost a head taller and a chest wider than everyone else made others give him a wide berth.

At last I saw him.

"Plato Kingsley, you son of a bitch!" Braggs clapped him hard on the back while they embraced.

"You didn't think I would miss this fight did you?" Kingsley's eyes shone bright. "I lost some good friends in Los Angeles."

Kingsley hadn't changed much. If anything he looked stronger than when I'd last seen him. His hair still cropped short and grey. His muscles still defined, but not bulky. His javelin held strapped across his back and his sword fit easily in the scabbard on his belt.

Rebecca pounced her father. They embraced. She kissed him on the cheek.

I pushed my way through with Chen right behind me. I smiled broadly as we shook hands. Kingsley pulled me in for a man-hug. Chen bowed respectfully.

"Who's watching the fort?" I asked.

Kingsley said, "I have Raven taking care of that. She received a promotion to Lieutenant upon taking up the position at the fort. By the way, I was sorry to hear about Walt. He was my favorite of you four."

I said, "Yeah, it was hard, but I think he would approve of how I am living now."

Rebecca added, "But the weeks previous to that were sketchy."

I said, "True enough."

Lieutenant Kingsley looked at me, "I heard about those too."

I looked at the ground sheepishly.

Kingsley said, "Don't sweat it, when we lose someone we tend to go a little mad. I know you and Walt were close."

Braggs said, "Okay that's enough. We have to fill

Kingsley in on the plan."

The plan was simple. No, that isn't the right word. The plan was straightforward.

One hundred ground breaking missiles were stockpiled at the fort then moved to the exit of the eastern tunnel. The eastern tunnel team would be moving them up to the hill overlooking Sunset Red. When dark fell the missiles would be launched into the sides of the huge nest crumbling the nest inward on itself.

Simultaneously, a team on the ground would lay siege to the nests around the huge nest, killing every Dragon they could find. The Dragons would eventually catch on and retaliate, but this is where a third team would rise from the southern tunnel and take the Dragons by surprise. The eastern team after firing off the missiles would enter combat with the Dragons that could make it out of the rubble of the nest.

In the history of the Supremacy War, never had so many Hell Bringers been assembled in one place. This promised to be the biggest battle to this date.

Chen and I were part of the ground force set to attack when the first missiles fired at the huge nest. I took the head of the force because I could move the fastest and I could report Dragon activity and warn the others.

Kingsley joined the southern tunnel group. They would be our much needed back up.

Jackson guided the eastern tunnel group to the best places to fire their missiles from.

Dark fell. The moon shone bright. The stars illuminated the sky. We could see like it was almost daylight.

The huge nest crumbled beneath the fury of the first missiles fired. I heard no Dragon screams beneath the nest. I heard no Dragon thought speak calling out from their home nests.

I pushed out my wings and flew in front of the ground force. I reached the closest nest and landed on the edge. I looked down and saw no Dragon inside. Same with each nest I hopped.

The missiles succeeded in crumbling the huge nest, but the ground force found no Dragons in Sunset Red.

Screams of surprise and terror rose from the east. The sky lit up with the fire of Dragons attacking the eastern force.

I yelled to the ground force, "Head to the east, but watch

your back, there could be a group waiting for us when we turn around. I growled and took wing towards the battle. My comrades would have to run the distance, about two miles, to get to the battle.

Two miles could mean the eastern force was dead.

I flew faster.

The eastern force consisted of mostly ballista guards. The ballista guards were strong enough to move the missiles quickly. They were not fast, but they were still Hell Bringers.

I flew over the "F O R T A N G E L" sign and saw the Hell Bringers engaged with the Dragons. It was not the massacre I was expecting, but it was not looking good for the eastern force.

Behind me I saw another group of Dragons attacking the ground force. "Shit," I growled. I was closer now to the eastern force than I was to my own ground force.

The ground force had more hardened fighters than the eastern force. I wasn't sure which way to go.

Hahaha. Poor little rogon confused as always. Do not worry, we will kill all of your friends.

The Dragon Heart.

I thought, *Where are you? Come and fight me coward.*

You cannot taunt me. I will kill you when I am ready. For now, you can watch your roges die.

That will not happen!

I pulled my sword and dove into the battle the eastern force waged. My sword took off the top of the head of a Red about to blow a volley of fire.

A cone of fire blew from my lips at a White. My wings propelled me forward with my sword slashing through the midsection. My sword quickly sheathed and my bow drew from my back. My arrow fired and connected with one, two, three Green Dragons in a row.

My bow returned to my back and my sword drew. My wings turned me and I slashed down through the head of a Black that I hoped to be the Dragon Heart.

Still there? I thought.

Yes.

"Dammit."

A small contingent of the beefiest ballista guards dove

down into their tunnel.

My body continued to fight without me. My mind acted as a spectator feeling every movement every cut, every dodge.

The ballista contingent emerged with their Dragon's Bane ballista. Arrows flew and connected with the Dragons. Struck Dragon scales sizzled with the contact.

Another small group of ballista guards went down and grabbed their ballista. When they returned and fired, the Dragons finally flew off to the south to attack the ground force.

I growled and flew south after them. The Dragons there still battled, but I felt the fight leaving them.

Kingsley brought the southern tunnel force up and flanked the Dragons as well as could be done to flying creatures. Kingsley impaled Dragon after Dragon with his javelin, ran to the corpse, pulled his javelin and impaled another.

I caught a Red with my katana, cutting through the top of the Dragon's head.

The new infusion of Dragons did not improve their battle morale. Within minutes the Dragons flew west over the water where we could not reach them. Eventually the Dragons flew out of sight.

I landed and shrugged my wings back into my body. The Hell Bringers around me cheered, but I felt something off.

"Look out!" Chen said pointing behind me.

I saw and felt the dark claws of the Dragon Heart dig into my shoulders and carry me off faster than anyone, even Kingsley could react.

59 — Food

The claws dug deep into my shoulders. My black blood spurted intermittently from my wounds. I could touch my katana, but I could not draw it well enough to slash at the Dragon Heart's legs. Not that it would be too smart to do 200 feet off of the ground.

You are mine now rogon. You cannot escape.

We flew over a desert with sharp outcroppings of rocks everywhere.

The Dragon Heart dropped me.

I fell too fast to unleash my wings before I slammed into the ground, thankfully missing any of the rocks. I rolled with the momentum of flight and falling. I stopped rolling as I crashed into the side of a large rock.

Howls and barks of dogs sounded close. I lay a pile of pain with my right arm under my body. Not a good position to be in if swarmed by ferals. I grunted and shifted myself up and freed my right arm. My right hand went to the handle of my sword, but I did not draw.

I groaned and pushed myself up to a sitting position. I checked my wounds. They were bleeding, but less so than before. I healed fast, maybe not fast enough. "Thanks Jonathan."

I heard steps approaching. Human steps.

"Jonathan is the worst of all traitors," a voice that felt familiar said.

I groaned and turned towards the voice. A man about my height and build walked towards me. His hair had a shocking streak of red through black. His skin looked sun tanned. He wore no clothes.

"What the hell?" I grunted.

"What? You don't recognize me?" The man reached down and grabbed me by my shirt and lifted me up. He dug his thumbs into my shoulder wounds, reopening them to bleeding. "Remember me now?"

"AAAAAH!"

The Dragon Heart threw me into a large rocky outcropping. The back of my head struck the rock, dizzying me as I slid down to the ground.

"At last, I get to make you suffer the way I have suffered for what your family has done."

I groaned. "What has my family done to you? The Gerstungs are Dragon killers, but I'd like to know specifics, just so when I die I can go out smiling."

The Dragon Heart rushed towards me and kicked me in the chest with the top of his foot. I toppled over into a convulsive coughing fit. The Dragon Heart leaned down to me, "Not the Gerstungs, though they have been a thorn in the side of Dragonity for many years. No, rogon, I speak of your father."

I looked up from my position on the ground. "Who hasn't he offended in some way, really?"

The Dragon Heart stomped on my head. "He has done more than offend me. Jonathan the Traitor killed my brother."

Jonathan the Traitor. Funny. I said, "And what was your brother's name? The Dragon Liver? The Dragon Stomach? Oh, I know, the Chicken Heart."

"You bastard!" The Dragon Heart grabbed me and lifted me by my throat.

September 18, 1987

I ran through the forest around Meton with my favorite stick in the whole world or at least for that day. I diligently tapped the stick on every tree. I thought it was a fun game. Diana was busy with Todd and his brothers so I was on my own.

I liked it better alone, no one called me bastard.

I ran through a field and closed my eyes enjoying the almost fall sun. I was five years old and didn't have a care in the world at that moment.

Slam!

My tiny body ran smack into what felt like a tree. I shot backwards five feet. My stick left my hands. My surprised eyes opened as I hit the ground. I looked through my feet at the scaled leg that rose from the grass. My eyes followed the leg further up to the chest then to the neck and head. I saw the giant head of a Red Dragon.

The Red Dragon growled softly at me and leaned its face down to me. I felt its nostrils inhale softly around me. The red scaled lips of the Dragon pulled back revealing teeth in a menacing smile.

I whimpered. Tears dropped one by one down my face.

Calm down hatchling. I will not hurt you.

I didn't know it at the time, but this was the first time I had heard thoughts in my head that weren't my own.

A roar came from overhead. I turned my head as the Red Dragon looked up. The shadow of a Black Dragon crossed over the both of us. The Red stepped over and in front of me. Smoke rained down as well as red rocks. I heard the Red react when the rocks struck it, but no rocks struck me. The Red reached back with its head and grabbed me by the shirt with its mouth. The Red dropped me behind a tree.

Stay here hatchling. Stay out of sight.

I had no idea what was going on.

The Black Dragon landed and roared at the Red Dragon. The Red roared back with equal ferocity. I screamed in fright. The Black looked towards the tree I hid behind. It took a step towards the tree.

Your food?

No, not my food. That is my son.

Hahaha! Your son is a rogoh, just like his rogon father.

Regardless, you will not harm him.

You will not stop me.

The Black attacked the Red with its claws. The Red retaliated with a tail smash followed by a bite to the flanks. The

Black swatted at the Red with its tail. The Red caught the tail and dug its claws into it. The Red moved its bite to the back of the Black Dragon's neck.

I heard the bones crunching. I saw the Red shake his head back and forth accompanied by more bones crunching. The Black stopped moving.

The Red Dragon dropped its opponent.

I cried and thought it would first eat the Black Dragon, then eat me.

Dragons do not eat their own kind hatchling.

The Red Dragon grabbed me by my shirt again and carried me to the outskirts of Meton. It dropped me, growled softly nudging me with its nose and turning away.

Mother was upset after that episode, but she was mostly glad I was okay. She put me into bed and I slept almost immediately forgetting the day for a long time.

August 16, 2000

Being choked by the Dragon Heart somehow triggered my memory of this fight. I witnessed the death of the Dragon Heart's brother.

The Dragon Heart dropped me. I fell back to the ground. The Dragon Heart asked, "You saw him die?"

"Yeah," I coughed. "But I was only five. I didn't realize until now that's who it was."

"Did he fight bravely?"

"I think he wanted to eat me. I am sure he was driven by hunger and disdain for Jonathan."

"Fair enough."

The Dragon Heart stepped away from me.

I groaned as I pressed my feet against the ground and my back against the rock to reach a standing position. I saw no weapon on my opponent.

The Dragon Heart said, "You are really bad at the instinctive thing aren't you?"

"Just taking a mental inventory. I can't help it if you are nosy."

"You're going to have to do better than that if you want to

kill me. I could have killed you three times already, tonight."

"Why are you giving me so many chances?"

"Because I want Jonathan to see your body bruised and bloodied on his door step when I overthrow him."

The Dragon Heart turned and dashed towards me.

My right hand went to my katana and drew. The blade cut his chest as I side stepped. I didn't cut deep, but I heard the sizzle of his Dragon flesh beneath the blade.

The Dragon Heart clutched his chest. I swiped at his back, but the Dragon Heart moved and I only grazed him. Still, he grunted in pain.

My body jumped forward and my legs kicked the Dragon Heart hard into the rocks. I pressed my blade against his back. I heard the sickeningly loud sizzle of Dragon's Bane to Dragon flesh.

The Dragon Heart did not scream, but the thoughts in his head felt ferocious and vulgar. He knew if he moved the blade would go deeper into his flesh without my even pushing.

"Kill me if you are going to do it! If you do not kill me, you will regret it. I will kill everyone you know, everyone you love."

I sighed. "I'll be honest. I'm tired of death. I don't really want to kill you. But I know you're not lying. You'll try to kill my family and my friends. The good thing about that is though, most of my family and friends are Hell Bringers and you're going to have a helluva time killing any of them. I think they are safe."

My hands pulled back my sword and cracked the Dragon Heart in the back of the head. He fell hard to the sand, unconscious.

Growls of ferals rose from behind me.

I turned slowly. There were at least 50, probably closer to 100 dogs staring at me hungrily.

"Shit." I had one maybe two volleys of fire I could blast out, but that wouldn't be enough to dissuade them all to leave me alone. Also the Dragon Heart lay unconscious next to me. I wouldn't feel right about leaving him there, but I wasn't sure if I could fly with the weight of the both of us.

I pushed out my wings and flapped them roaring at the ferals. The dogs did not back down. I crouched and grabbed one of the Dragon Heart's hands with my left hand. I sheathed my sword.

My fire lit out from my mouth at the closest ferals. A few of the dogs ran away on fire. Some of the dogs stepped back. The hungrier ferals stepped forward.

I flapped once, then twice, then three times and got off of the ground with the Dragon Heart's body in tow. Some of the ferals ran at us and snapped at me. Others went for the Dragon Heart's body.

"Oh no you don't!" The Dragon Heart, now conscious, swung his other hand to one of my legs grabbing hard and distracting me enough to cause me to fall right into the middle of the feral pack.

I growled. My right hand drew my sword and chopped off one of the Dragon Heart's hands. I blew another volley of fire at the dogs and took off again fast.

Some of the ferals jumped and snapped at me, but most of them swarmed the fallen and bleeding Dragon Heart. They had a stomach ache in store for them, but I could do nothing now.

The Dragon Heart called out in pain, but I sensed no terror in his thoughts.

Maybe he felt peace at last.

60 — Another Lap

I hadn't realized how far the Dragon Heart took me away from Fort Angel. I didn't arrive at the barrier until well after midnight. The barrier guard, a soldier I didn't know, rushed to grab me as I collapsed ten feet away. I slid my wings back into my body and passed out.

I awoke in my bunk. Without windows, I had no idea the time of day. I heard Rebecca slumbering above me. I heard Casimir's sleeping thoughts outside of the bunk.

I sent thoughts down to my feet they wiggled. My fingers twitched and flexed. My knees bent: the left more painful than the right. My arms flexed and my hips raised my legs. I turned my head side to side cracking the bones as much as possible. My lungs inhaled deeply and exhaled too deeply causing me to cough.

Rebecca jumped down from the top bunk. "Are you okay?"

A small strand of smoke left my lips. "Yeah, I'm fine. What time is it?"

"About noon. I'm off duty right now so I thought I would crash here until you came to."

I smiled. "Thank you my darling."

"You're welcome, dear heart." After a moment, "Oh yeah, Braggs said he wanted to see you when you were awake."

"Damn."

I spent the better part of an hour 'waking up' with

Rebecca.

I begrudgingly headed to the Central Tower. I didn't have to go up to General Braggs' office, because he waited for me in the main lobby.

"Gerstung!"

"Yes, sir."

"Come with me."

"Yes, sir."

We walked out of the tower and made rounds through the fort. We didn't talk much, but we walked a long way. All of the soldiers stared at me as I walked with the general. I saw Lieutenant Musil. He, Lieutenant Eagle and Lieutenant Kingsley argued about something combat related. Soldiers and Hell Bringers sparred. Soldiers pulled a cart full of supplies into the mess hall. It was an excruciating wait. I thought I was in trouble.

At last Braggs said something, "Do you know why I asked you to come with me on my rounds?"

"No, sir."

"I wanted you to look around at this fort and the people in it. From the most highly trained tacticians, to the best swordspersons, to the citizens who help keep us fed, you saved all of us."

"I didn't do it alone, sir."

We left the fort and stopped near the outskirts of the barrier, not near an outpost.

"If it hadn't been for you, Gerstung, we would have died. You shared with us your commitment to the protection of the Human race. You channeled the energy of the 27 Mage and you created this barrier for us."

Braggs touched the barrier and it made a light organ sound.

Braggs continued, "When you went maverick after Gelh's death, no one blamed you. Your friends only wanted to save you from yourself. That is your cross to bear, your amends to make. As far as I'm concerned you did nothing wrong by Humanity as a whole. You were AWOL, but you were injured. I cannot fault you for that. I'm sure Abdul was thankful for your company for those few days."

"I'd hate to say it, sir, but it might have been my influence that killed him."

"No, Gerstung, death happens every day, especially when there are Dragons. You cannot blame yourself for the deaths of anyone in this war. But again, that's amends you have to make with yourself. I can't tell you how to live, but I know there are a lot of people who want to see you live well."

"Thank you, sir."

We continued walking, back towards the fort.

Braggs added, "I wanted to let you know, you're going to be promoted. A lot of soldiers are moving up in rank and you're one of them."

"Sergeant?" I asked.

"That's right. You'll get more responsibility, but more prestige. We know how your family likes prestige." Braggs smiled wide.

"Well –" I started.

"I'm just teasing you a bit Gerstung. I knew your uncles. They never wanted to be anything more than sergeants."

"They will be pleased regardless of my rank."

"Certainly."

Later that day held the ceremony for all of the soldiers and Hell Bringers who received promotions. Rebecca and her father beamed proudly at me for my promotion. Chen and about 200 other warriors who fought bravely and intelligently in the battle received the promotion to sergeant.

We also mourned the death of almost 50 soldiers and Hell Bringers. There was no one I was particularly close with, but they were my people.

I looked into the distance at the red sunset. I thought of the Dragon Heart and Abdul, two entities propelled by hate and pain and revenge. I hoped they found peace. I thought of Walt, a man driven by love and a lust for life.

I turned my thoughts to the living. I met so many on my journey to this moment. Rebecca, Chen, Lieutenant Kingsley, Crush, Maria, Agarue, Christofer, Steve Jones, Jason and Tammy, Lieutenant Eagle, Jackson Chance, White Eyes and Casimir. I believed in so many reasons to live and fight.

I held Rebecca close to me that night and thanked which ever gods allowed these moments.

September 17, 2000

Exactly a month later, I won the Fort Angel poetry contest. In our reconnaisance missions we saw absolutely no Dragons in Sunset Red or anywhere in the vicinity. Whenever I flew around I listened for Dragon thoughts, but heard nothing.

We didn't dial back our defenses, obviously the regiments from Fort Albuquerque and Seattle left. Groups from the outskirts also left. Lieutenant Kingsley led his band back to Bellato, much to the teary eyes of his daughter.

But with the low activity, I could focus a bit on my poetry. I won the contest with this:

Life, though wide in measure is fleeting,
taking advantage of such a gift can lead to bleeding.
Whether the sky grows dark, or is a dangerous clear blue,
remember to hold those you love close around you.
No matter the dangerous trials and tribulations
your friends will keep your trains in the station.
When you seek to take your final trip
your friends will show you it's a journey to skip.
Though we cannot choose the day we die,
the ones we love will make our lives worthwhile.

I didn't get a trophy, but I got to take a day off of duty. Of course, I spent it sleeping and writing more poetry.

October 31, 2000

People used to call this day Halloween. No one really dressed up anymore since we didn't need to invent monsters to scare us.

Chen chose this day to write to his boyfriend in Detroit that he wanted to break up. Cole Chen and Jackson Chance grew close in their time as bunkmates. From what Chen told me, his boyfriend hadn't even told his family about Chen, whereas Jackson's family loved Chen to death.

I don't remember if Chen got a letter back.

January 1, 2001

"Congratulations to everyone on another lap around the sun!"

Most of us drank more alcohol than we should have. I tried to get drunk, but the chemicals just ran right through me. I wasn't disappointed. I enjoyed watching everyone else imbibe.

January 18, 2001

"Congratulations on another lap around the sun, Gerstung!"

The coast gave me a gloriously cool day. Five months passed since anyone saw a Dragon in the vicinity. I heard talk from Omaha about dialing down some of the military strength from Fort Angel and sending warriors to other forts which didn't have barriers.

Rebecca felt homesick and asked for a transfer to Fort Kingsley. I felt like I could be a big help in the training department so I also asked to be transferred there. Chen decided he wanted to stay at Fort Angel with Jackson for now.

April 30, 2001

Chen, Rebecca and I joined the Human Army three years ago to this day. These two people I felt closest to, though with Jackson and Chen getting closer, Chen was moving further away. I made piece with this. It was time for Chen to move on anyway.

We met our three heads, like we used to do including Walt.

Chen: We will be friends forever.

Me: Agreed. If you ever are back in Bellato, look us up.

Chen: I will.

Rebecca: I'm going to miss you.

Chen: Me too.

We broke formation and turned away to our new lives.

Jason and Tammy waited for Rebecca and me to get into the stage coach. She and I held hands as we walked slowly out of the fort gates.

Tammy said, "Y'all make a gud cuppa."

Jason added, "Like me 'n Tam back in duh day."

Casimir bound out of the fort after us. *Wait!*

I turned and almost instinctively crouched. I realized I didn't need to. Casimir stood taller than me.

You are really leaving?

Yes, Casimir, we are.

But what about me?

What do you mean?

If you leave, I have no family.

You have Jackson and Chen and everyone in the fort who love you, or at least tolerate you.

But they are not you. You saved me.

I reached up and stroked Casimir's snout.

Rebecca asked, "What is it?"

"Casimir wants to come with us."

Rebecca looked up at Casimir, "It's going to be cold sometimes where we are going."

Casimir butted her softly with his nose.

She is not lying. It will be cold.

I do not care. I am a Dragon. I can handle it.

That is another problem. Many people might try to harm you just because you are a Dragon.

I can stay away from those Humans if you tell me.

Dragons will want to hurt you for being around Humans.

I can stay away from those Dragons on my own.

I sighed and turned to Jason and Rebecca. "Do you guys mind if Casimir follows us?"

Jason smiled, "Long as he don't draw no drag'n trubba."

I turned back to Casimir. *Can you keep a low profile?*

I do not know what that means, but yes.

I laughed. *Okay, you can come, but you need to listen if I tell you to hide. People will not understand, and trust me, you do not want to get an angry mob after you.*

I understand.

I patted Casimir on the snout. *Okay follow us.*

Rebecca and I entered the stage coach. Jason closed the door behind us and soon we set out for Bellato.

Rebecca snuggled into me as we rode. She said, "I wonder what's in store for us back home."

I smiled as I leaned back. "I dunno. Do you want to meet my mother?"

Sneak Preview

Dragon's Bane

Book 2

Rust & Blood

61 — The Reporter

September 1, 2000

Aurora ignored the knock at the door. *It is probably just those damn kids again,* she thought as she bustled nervously through the house. Correspondence just reached her from Fort Kingsley that Lieutenant Plato Kingsley left to join the fight at Fort Angel on the west coast. They headed out to fight the Dragons of Sunset Red. This was the fort her son John Ross was stationed. If things were under control out west, they wouldn't need to send Plato Kingsley, the greatest Human warrior of the Human Army. Would they?

The correspondence gave no other information about the "whys" and "hows," in fact, the information she did glean wasn't really intended for her in the first place. She overheard it in the market place. The other villagers, at best, paid her no mind unless she interacted with them and, at worst, threw rocks at her or called her a whore.

She endured almost 19 years of poor treatment from the villagers supposed to be "defending Humanity," but Aurora couldn't leave. There were too many other people in the equation to think about.

Another knock. A young woman's voice, "Miss Gerstung? Miss Aurora Gerstung? Are you home? I'm a reporter from the Bellato Chronicle. I wanted to interview you about your son, John Ross Gerstung."

That is a new one, Aurora thought. It wasn't uncommon

for the kids of Meton to provide a false story to get Aurora to open the door and get a bucket of water in the face followed by bird seed which stuck surprisingly well when wet. *Okay, so that only happened once,* Aurora recounted. The next time she heard a knock she was ready with a broom. She chased the hooligans 100 feet whacking them with each step. *I am the daughter of the first man to kill a Dragon and sister to three Hell Bringers,* she thought proudly. *Deal with ferals before you mess with me.*

Another knock. "Miss Gerstung? If you're there, please open up, my editor won't let me come back to the paper without a story." It wasn't Diana's, John Ross' childhood crush, voice either.

"Gods dammit," Aurora said. Her voice was smooth, aged like wine, with the bitterness of years of torment by the villagers.

Hurricane Aurora ripped open the door and glared at the young woman standing before her. She held a notebook with pencil in hand which she dropped, partially from the wind movement of the door opening and partially from the fright of seeing Aurora with broom in hand ready to strike.

"Oh dear!" The young woman quickly stooped to grab her fallen notebook and straighten her thick black rimmed glasses. Her sun lightened brown hair was tied back in a leather thong. Her face dotted with summer freckles. Her white cotton buttoned shirt and flowing black skirt clung to her unbelievably thin frame. Bones could be easily identified in her wrists, ankles and legs. The reporter kicked her walk worn shoes together, straightened her skirt and shirt and then offered her right hand in greeting.

"Good afternoon Miss Gerstung! I'm here to interview you about your son. He's a hero for the Human race doncha know?"

Aurora was puzzled. The last thing she heard about Fort Angel or her son was about Kingsley going to Sunset Red to help. Aurora's calloused hands clasped the soft hands of the reporter and shook it once. "Won't you come in?"

Aurora offered the reporter a seat at the kitchen table and Aurora started boiling water for tea. The fireplace needed stoked so she bent down to add sticks and a log to it. She moved to the kettle and filled it with water from the storage tank and placed the kettle on the metal grate over the rising fire.

"You move with such grace, Miss Gerstung," the reporter said. "I bet you are the reason John Ross is such an amazing fighter."

Aurora chuckled lightly. "That might actually have more to do with his uncles. They are trained Hell Bringers. They taught him most of what he knew before the army."

"Yes, they are on my list for interview as well," the reporter said. "But my editor thought it wise to approach you first."

"Why?"

"You are the mother of one of the greatest Human warriors in history. John Ross Gerstung killed the Dragon Heart, one of the most powerful Dragons of the Supremacy War. I'm surprised you haven't been bombarded with interview requests by other city newspapers."

"Well, there aren't a lot of newspapers close by other than the Chronicle."

"True, but this is a huge story. John Ross was instrumental in turning the tide out west. Everyone is buzzing about him. We have an informant out west who rode back as fast as he could to get us this information. He nearly killed three horses in the process by running them so hard."

"That's sad." Aurora smiled. "I mean for the horses."

The reporter giggled.

The kettle whistled just as Aurora finished piecing out the tea leaves into each cup. She grabbed the kettle and poured the hot water. She said, "I realize it is fairly warm out, but this tea is only good hot."

The reporter said, "I don't mind. I can't drink cold tea anyway. It's too bitter."

Aurora placed a sugar bowl with spoons on the table next to the cups. "Help yourself."

The reporter dished in two spoons of sugar and stirred the tea. She took a tentative sip and smiled. "What kind of tea is this?"

"Ginseng tea. It gives the drinker more energy. I make my brothers bring it with them when they come to visit me every month or so."

"Your brothers? That would be Oliver, Maxwell and Zachary Gerstung?"

Aurora nodded. "That would be them. All trained by Lieutenant Plato Kingsley."

The reporter scribbled in her notebook. "Kingsley is actually on my list of interviews. I am more interested to talk to your brothers."

Aurora smiled. "They have good stories to tell. You will be enthralled. I've heard their stories numerous times and I still enjoy every word."

The reporter looked up. "But first, I am here with you. I'll be honest. I've only interviewed one person before you. It was a girl who survived the April 20 massacre, but her arm is disabled. She was actually how I learned of John Ross to begin with. It seems your son is pretty heroic. Has he always been so brave?"

Aurora sipped her tea. "My son is amazing. I'm not just saying that because I'm his mother. He has been through so many awful things. Some of which I unfortunately put him through. I've never seen him act out of malice or with ill intentions. I know he isn't perfect. I know for sure he has a temper, considering his father after all. But –"

The reporter stopped her. "Who is his father?"

Aurora moved her contemplative gaze to the reporter. "Are you sure you want to know? It might sully your image of John Ross."

The reporter cleared her throat. "This world is full of chaos. I am honestly not sure even the smallest baby doesn't have an unsullied view of it. Day one for all of us is full of screaming, blood, liquid, crying, sometimes spanking and breathing the cold air of death. Our lungs fill with death every time we breathe. Sure, the Dragons have put a stop to the industrial revolution so our air quality is getting better, but the death they deal is just as bad for us spiritually. Humans are really no better. We are killing them at the same rate, if not faster. Like every other problem Humanity faces, we find a way to declare war on it and kill it before it kills us."

Aurora put down her cup in surprise. "Wow. I never

thought a reporter would be so opinionated."

The reporter sipped her tea. "Just because I can't report on my opinions, doesn't mean I can't have them."

A long, comfortable pause ensued between the two women. They stared at each other feeling out the energies that existed between them.

Finally the reporter said, "So, do you want to tell me who John Ross' father is?"

Aurora said, "Well there are two options, I can tell you the short version, or I can tell you the long version."

The reporter nodded. "Okay, tell me the short version first and if I'm intrigued, you can tell me the long version."

Aurora said, "John Ross' father is Jonathan." She gestured towards his castle easily visible from her window.

"Okay." The reporter scribbled in her notebook. "Wait, what?"

"Yep. Jonathan the Tyrant, as most people call him."

"Okay. I am sufficiently intrigued. You are going to have to tell me the long version, the longer the better."

Aurora sipped her tea. "You're going to need more paper."

Dragon Dictionary

Drakoh/Drakah – King/Queen Dragon.
> **Drakon/Drakan** – Offspring of King/Queen Dragon.
> **Drakeh** – Egg/Hatchling/Pre-gender Identification.
> **Drakes** – Plural of Drakoh/Drakah gender irrelevant

Drackne – Offspring of a Male Human and a Female Dragon.

Rogoh/Rogah – Male/Female Human, translated to Weakling or
  Waste of Flesh.
> **Rogon/Rogan** – Translated to Traitor. Offspring of a
> Waste of Flesh.
> **Rogeh** – Pre-gender Identification.
> **Roges** – Plural of Rogoh/Rogah gender irrelevant.

Skakoh/Skakah – Male/Female Dragon Low Born Adult.
> **Skakon/Skakan** – Offspring of Low Born Dragon.
> **Skakeh** – Egg/Hatchling/Pre-gender Identification
> **Skakes** – Plural of Skakoh/Skakah gender irrelevant

Vrack – Offspring of a Male Dragon and a Female Human.

Veras – It is what Dragons call their ability, for example, to
  breathe fire

Azriel Johnson is an inkspatter analyst by day and a serial writer by night.

He enjoys everything about the written word, even the things that annoy him like text speak.

He relishes imperfection, so if any of his readers finds a typo in any of his books he will sign their copy and write them a short letter of philosophy and thanks.

He is cautiously optimistic about the future of the Human race, Dragons or no. He believes in prophecy and the Dragon's Bane Series comes straight from a part of himself he believes probably exists... somewhere....

In his spare time (what's that?), Azriel plays fantasy games, practices yoga, blogs (sometimes), listens to music, meditates and practices shamanism. You can also find him asking interesting questions on his Facebook Fan Page.

Other Full Length Books by Writing Knights Press

The Squire: Page-A-Day Anthology 2015
Nothing, but Skin — Quartez Harris
In the Beginning and the End (2nd Edition) — Siddartha Beth Pierce
The Squire: National Poetry Month Anthology 2013
Graffiti Wisdom — Skylark Bruce

Find More Releases at WritingKnightsPress.blogspot.com